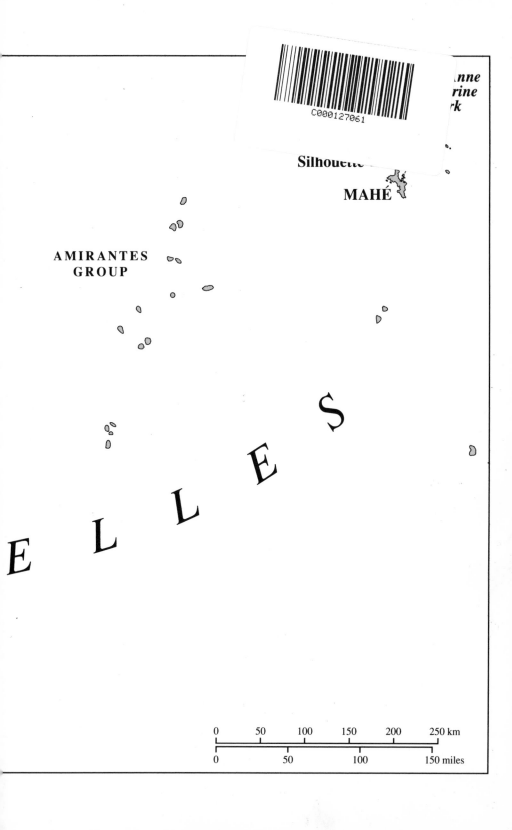

**anne
rine
rk**

Silhouette

MAHÉ

**AMIRANTES
GROUP**

E L L E S

0	50	100	150	200	250 km

0	50	100	150 miles

VOICES IN THE WIND

ALSO BY DANIELLE THOMAS
Children of Darkness

DANIELLE THOMAS

Voices
in
The Wind

LONDON NEW YORK SYDNEY TORONTO

This edition published 1993 by
BCA
by arrangement with Pan Macmillan Ltd

CN 5802

Typeset by Cambridge Composing (UK) Limited, Cambridge
Printed and bound in Great Britain by
Mackays of Chatham PLC, Chatham, Kent

For the two most important men in my life
my husband, Wilbur Smith,
and
my son, Dieter Schmidt,
with all my love

Contents

Acknowledgements

The author wishes to make grateful acknowledgement to Doreen Valiente's *ABC of Witchcraft Past and Present* and to Janet and Stewart Farrar's *Eight Sabbats for Witches*, both published by Robert Hale Ltd. The Farrars' book provided the background for the wiccaning ceremony described in this novel.

Lines quoted from *Eight Sabbats for Witches* by Janet and Stewart Farrar are reprinted by kind permission of Robert Hale Ltd.

CHAPTER ONE

London and Sussex
1960

 I

The Sussex Weald is old, immeasurably old, and the ancient soils of this English forest are now barren and sour. For over seventy million years, cataclysmic forces convulsed the Earth. The cretaceous seas advanced and retreated. Storms and gales scoured away the chalk dome cupped between the hills of the Downs, leaving a heathland of clays and greensands. The woods pockmarking this place conceal the remains of dinosaurs beneath their roots and hold memories of great hunts and pagan rites in their dark branches.

The moon was no longer full. The forest pines were needled in silver and the shadows were blackened to soot.

Two figures slipped quietly into the woods, their passage marked by the chittering of birds disturbed in sleep and by a soft susurration in the gorse and heather as creatures of the night moved deeper into thickets.

The couple walked quickly and confidently, keeping to the shadows. Only glimpses of their swirling cloaks and pale faces were caught in the moonlight.

'It's a good night for a wiccaning, Emma,' Giles Killick whispered, pressing the bundle in his arms closer to his body. 'The witches will welcome this baby.'

Emma glanced up at her husband. The light frosted his beard and swept-back mane of hair. His close-set eyes were dark in his powerfully sculpted face.

'A pity the moon is waning,' she answered. 'The ceremony

is always best when the goddess Diana shows her full beauty. Her brightness strengthens our powers.'

'That would have been possible, had my sister kept to the original date for her trip to London,' Giles muttered.

'Change is natural to Virginia. Her birth sign is Aquarius, ruled by the planet Uranus. She'll never conform.' Emma skipped a few steps, trying to keep up with her husband's long strides. 'And we have Laura,' she added. 'I was so afraid that Virginia would change her mind again and take her with them.'

'London,' Giles snorted, 'taking a baby only a few months old to the noise and pollution of the city.' His strong fingers moved rhythmically across the bundle. 'At least Ashley showed more sense than his wife. He realized it would be better for Laura to remain at Lyewood with us. If only I could persuade my sister not to return to the Seychelles. She should be at Lyewood where we were born. After all, it's her inheritance and she should be showing some interest in the running of the farm.'

Emma stroked the flower spikes of vervain which she was carrying. She let his rancour wash over her, unheeded. 'Virginia and Ashley may return to their tropical paradise,' she said, 'but tonight Laura will be ours.' She lifted her face to the moon and her eyes widened as she stared up at the silver orb. 'All ours,' she whispered.

The intensity of her voice and the glitter in her eyes worried Giles. He thought that, with her forty-fifth birthday behind her, she had accepted being childless. But since Virginia's return to Lyewood to have her baby, Emma's battle to possess the child had been subtle and relentless.

Suddenly Giles stiffened and his fingers dug into the blanket. A fallow deer broke cover and bounded across the path. The white spots on its coat shone like newly minted coins in the moonlight.

Emma smiled. 'Another one of Diana's creatures out to honour the moon goddess tonight.'

Giles looked down at his wife. The hood had fallen away from her face and her raven-black hair, straight at the roots then tightly crinkled, swung across her elfin features. She was a beautiful witch. Giles tilted her face up in the chalky light and ran his broad thumb lightly across her heart-shaped mouth. His hand lingered on her throat and he felt the beat of her pulse throb beneath his fingertips.

Emma stared up at him without emotion, her green eyes as dark as the shadows beneath the pines. He slid his hand through the opening in her cloak and felt her body, naked and warm.

A thin wail pierced the silence. Giles started then gently rocked the bundle in the crook of his arm. 'Come,' he said, 'the others will be waiting.'

They hurried on through the Weald, the dry bracken crunching beneath their feet.

The smell of wood-smoke laced with incense hung lightly in the air and pale tongues of flame flickered behind the thick oak and quickset hedge. Giles quickened his pace and forced his way through a gap in the enclosure, bending low to avoid the entwined holly branches. Emma followed, pausing to untangle the brambles from her cloak.

The sacred pagan site was old. Since the earliest memories of man, those who practised the ancient Craft of the Wise had joyfully worshipped their lusty horned god, Pan, and Diana, Queen of Witches, in this secret place.

Giles breathed in the crisp night air, and the thrill of the coming ceremony prickled the hair on his forearms.

A solitary hawthorn twisted its branches over a flat slab of sandstone. The slab formed a natural altar and lay in the middle of a ring of ancient oak and beech trees. A fire had been built to one side of the enclosure, and the firelight caught and held the silver disc that was placed in the centre of the cloth covering the stone. The symbols engraved on the silver pentacle shimmered and moved as if alive.

'Ah,' breathed Emma, lifting her gaze from the magical seal and scanning the heavens, 'this will be a good Esbat. I know it, Giles.'

She searched for the stars, bleached by the moonlight. She believed, as had generations of witches before her, that stars were composed of the fifth element, the invisible Quintessence. She knew demons used this essence to make their simulated

3

bodies and this gave great power to the pentacle. She glanced back at the sparkling disc on the altar cloth and her eyes glistened as they roamed over the preparations for the ceremony.

The coven had woven garlands of holly and oak leaves starred with slender spires of mauve and white vervain to mark the circle in front of the stone altar. A cauldron, set in the middle, overflowed with fruit, daffodils, early bluebells and the bright yellow flowers of rue.

'Good,' she said, placing her bunch of vervain in the cauldron. 'Rue and vervain will please the goddess. They are her flowers.'

Giles and Emma swung the cloaks off their shoulders and as they stood, sky-clad, the night air pimpled their naked bodies. The coven of witches turned to them, moving away from the crackling bonfire, eager to greet their Priest and High Priestess and to see the baby for whom this wiccaning had been prepared. The moonlight and fireglow painted their bodies as they moved; both young and old were made beautiful.

'Blessed be,' greeted one of the young witches, taking the tightly swaddled baby from Giles.

'Blessed be,' he answered, with a smile, as he recognized her.

She blushed and dropped her head. She was not ready to look into those dark eyes. At the last full moon she had been initiated into the third degree of Wicca, the Craft of the Wise. Giles had been in his ritual attire of animal skins. Behind Pan's horned mask his black eyes had studied her naked body as she lay beneath him. She was ready to give herself to the god Pan, eager to participate in a religious event which dated back to neolithic times; to experience the great rite which had been part of the Eleusinian Mysteries. He had stared down at her, unblinking as he began the first slow movements of intercourse, conferring sanctity upon her. She accepted the hard phallus into herself and writhed beneath the symbolic thrusts of the God of All. His eyes, dark as secrets, had examined her. Drugged by the scent of incense and the hypnotic wailing of pipes, she opened her legs wide and cried out her joy and acceptance of

4

Pan, the 'All-Devourer', the 'All-Begetter'. Later she would be able to look at her High Priest, but not yet.

'Come, my pretty one,' she crooned to the bundle. 'Come with me, until they're ready for you.' Keeping her head bent, she carried the child to the witches clustered round Emma.

Emma folded down the blanket so they could see the baby. Then, setting a silver circlet adorned with the crescent moon on to her thick hair, she left them hovering round Laura and walked to the stone altar to the north of the circle.

A sword gleamed on the altar and Emma ran her fingers lightly over the steel blade. Instinctively she straightened the witches' individual athames, leaving the black-handled knives inscribed with mystic sigils in a neat row. The scourge of cords and the wand lay near the bowls of salt and water. Emma smiled, a small cold smile, and ran her tongue down the gap between her front teeth.

She struck a match and lit the north candle that stood tall behind the pentacle. The flare of light brightened her eyes, widely spaced and mysterious. She then moved the flame to the two red altar candles. The plaintive and haunting strains of the seven-reeded Pan pipes drifted across the pagan site. Emma turned from the altar.

Giles lit the candles placed in old hurricane lamps at the watchtowers: the east, west and south points of the circumference of the circle. The members of the coven were now seated inside the ring of greenery close to the cauldron, facing Emma. She looked up at Giles. He placed the gold band on his head. As the sun symbol rested high on his forehead, he became for her the embodiment of the great horned god, Pan. Words ancient and half-forgotten whispered in her mind.

> *In caverns deep the Old Gods sleep*
> *But the trees still know their Lord . . .*
>
> *The leaves they dance to the goat god's tune*
> *And they whisper his name to the wind*
>
> *And the oak tree dreams of a god with horns*
> *And knows no other king.*

He was the masculine power of life, the goat-footed deity of Nature, both wonderful and terrifying. He was her consort and she was the naked spirit of that powerful mother of light and darkness, Diana, the triple goddess who ruled the heavens, earth and the mysterious underworld.

Together they turned and knelt at the altar. As smoke from the incense burner curled in the still air, the magic of the old religion gripped her and her hand shook as she plunged her athame into the bowl of water standing on the pentacle.

'I exorcize thee, O creature of water.' Her voice wavered as she spoke. 'That thou cast out from thee all the impurities and uncleanliness . . .'

Her breathing was shallow as she put down her athame, and her hands trembled as she lifted the bowl of water. She watched Giles plunge his black-handled knife into the bowl of salt which replaced the water on the silver disc.

'Blessings be upon this creature of salt . . .'

She listened to his deep voice intone the words of the opening ritual and it calmed her. Her hands were steady as she held up the bowl of water and watched him pour the salt into it. She spoke clearly and forcefully as she lifted the sword. 'I conjure thee, O Circle of Power,' she chanted as she walked clockwise round the coven, slowly drawing the ring of magic. '. . . A boundary between the world of men and the realms of the Mighty Ones, a rampart and a protection that shall preserve and contain the power that we shall raise within thee.'

The sword was heavy in her hands and, as she tightened her grip on its haft, she visualized a beam of strong golden light flowing down the steel blade and forming the circle.

She smiled, replaced the sword on the altar and watched intently as three witches strengthened the circle. Walking deosil as had their High Priestess, they sprinkled the male and female witches and the perimeter with the consecrated water, then smoked the circle with the incense-burner, and finally carried an altar candle from north to north.

Laura wailed thinly and the initiate chosen as maiden for the night put her finger into the little mouth, unwilling to have a baby's cries disturb the ritual. Laura snuffled and sucked and pulled on the warm fingertip. Emma was oblivious to the baby's cries. Giles stood tall and still at her side.

Emma faced east and slowly drew the invoking pentagram of the earth in front of her, calling on the Lords of the Air to witness the Rites and guard the Circle. She was respectful in her summons to the powerful lords of the four watchtowers who control the elements. Facing south, she summoned the Lords of Fire. Turning to the west, she called up the Lords of Water, Death and Initiation.

Finding no warm milk on the finger, Laura cried again. The maiden joggled her in her lap, trying to quieten her, as she watched the High Priest 'draw down the moon' on the High Priestess.

Emma faced the coven. Her arms were crossed over her breast and she held the wand and the scourge tightly in her hands. Pale as starlight, she rigidly held the position of Osiris, Egyptian god of the underworld, and stared, unseeing, over the heads of the coven.

Giles knelt on the sand in front of her and, as he bent low to kiss her feet, his hair swung forward and dusted her toes. 'Blessed be thy feet, that have brought thee in these ways.' He raised his head slowly and ran his powerful fingers through his hair, smoothing it beneath his sun crown. 'Blessed be thy knees,' he intoned, 'that shall kneel at the sacred altar.' And he ran his lips lightly over her knees.

Emma trembled as his beard tickled the inside of her thighs. As his mouth touched the delicate skin above her black pubic hair, she opened her arms to the blessing position.

A shiver ran through the maiden as she listened to his resonant words. 'Blessed be thy womb, without which we would not be.' The maiden jiggled Laura excitedly as Giles rose and kissed Emma's full breasts and heavy lower lip. She stared, entranced, at the Priest and High Priestess while he invoked the Mother Goddess, touching Emma half a dozen times on her breasts and womb with his right forefinger.

Looking deeply into Emma's eyes the priest's voice cracked. 'I invoke thee to descend upon the body of this thy servant and Priestess.' He knelt down and kissed her foot.

7

The young maiden held her breath as she saw a silvery blue aura lick at the sky-clad body of the High Priestess. Emma seemed to grow and fill the magic circle as her consciousness expanded and the strong delta rhythm usually found in deep sleep made her one with the universe.

> *'Of the Mother darksome and divine.*
> *Mine the scourge, and mine the kiss.'*

Her voice was powerful and throbbed in the witches' ears. They stared mesmerized at their earthly goddess. Their invocation had not brought down the goddess of the moon, but it had raised their Priestess spiritually and she was able to work magic. She was now attuned to the divine flicker deep within herself.

Her wand traced the Earth's pentagrams in the air in front of the High Priest and the hairs rose on Giles's forearms as she spoke the final words for the drawing down of the goddess.

> *'The five-point star of love and bliss –*
> *Here I charge you in this sign.'*

Emma became the mysterious principle of life itself, the naked goddess of fertility, man's first object of worship. She held and knew the power of darkness and of light.

In the depths of their minds the male witches returned to matriarchal times when women were the wise ones, the listeners to voices in the wind and the workers of magic. Women held and gave birth to life, they were mysterious and powerful and they ruled man.

Emma placed the wand and scourge on the stone altar and turned to recite the Great Mother Charge to her coven.

'Whenever ye have need of anything . . .' The silence was deep, broken only by the snap of logs in the fire. Her words floated on the mystical wails of Pan pipes and the witches were held spellbound.

'. . . Then shall ye assemble in some secret place and adore the spirit of me, who am Queen of all witches . . . ye who are fain to learn all sorcery, to these will I teach things that are yet unknown.' Emma's heavy breasts were washed with gold in the light of the fire and their nipples were hard in the cool night air.

'. . . ye shall be naked in your rites; and ye shall dance, sing, feast, make music and love, all in my praise.'

The maiden stared up at Emma, her eyes wide in awe and adoration. She whispered some of the words softly.

'If that which thou seekest thou findest not within thee thou will never find it without thee . . .'

As she mouthed the age-old words, she was warmed by the knowledge that the rite she had undergone with Giles proved the truth of the Charge Emma was reciting.

Giles had heard Emma recite the Charge hundreds of times, but the power and beauty of the words still thrilled him; he tightened his buttocks as excitement flooded his loins.

'For behold, I have been with thee from the beginning; and I am that which is attained at the end of desire.'

Emma's words hung and trembled between them. They faced the altar and folded their thumbs and forefingers into the palms of their hands and gave the 'Horned God salute'.

'Great god Pan, return to earth again. Come at my call and show thyself to men.'

Giles, his voice deep and strong, called upon the Shepherd of Goats. Lowering their arms from the salute, they solemnly consecrated the wine, the culmination of the invocation of their god and goddess. Giles knelt at Emma's feet, his strong hands cradling the heavy chalice. As she plunged her athame into the wine, he bowed his head before the strength of the goddess. He accepted the power of the goddess and the duality of the divine, both male and female.

He placed the chalice, untasted, on the altar. Tonight they would not dance. They would not enjoy the wild excitement of weaving and twisting and chanting age-old runes. The hypnotic mood and change in consciousness created by magical dancing could frighten the child.

9

The clear skies and bright sun, which had warmed London for most of the week and had coaxed open the daffodils, had been supplanted by grey clouds and a nipping westerly wind. The lawns in Regent's Park were littered with petals torn from the spring flowers.

A couple, tall and striking, strolled through Queen Mary's Gardens, oblivious of the wind tugging at their clothes.

'Oh, look, Ashley.' Virginia Challoner took her hand from her husband's arm and pointed to a pair of ducks sheltering in the lee of a bush. The birds were veiled with petals blown from a flowering cherry tree. 'They look like a bridal pair covered in confetti.'

'An indignant couple,' he teased as the ducks quacked and fluffed out their feathers. 'I think they know you're laughing at them.'

Virginia slipped her hand into the pocket of his tweed overcoat and twined her fingers through his. She pressed close to his side, and he squeezed her hand gently.

The roses in the gardens were still tightly budded, hiding their glorious colours from the visitors. Virginia and Ashley walked quickly past the drab beds and cut across to the tree-lined Broad Walk. Ashley listened to Virginia breathing heavily and slowed his pace, pretending to study the tall trees. He waited until she had recovered before he spoke.

'Happy?'

Quickly, she pushed aside all thoughts of the forthcoming visit to the neurologist, a meeting which was nagging at her like toothache.

'It's been a magical week,' she answered. 'I've enjoyed every moment.' She paused to flick away a strand of hair which had blown across her mouth. 'When we're in the Seychelles or at Lyewood I forget how much I love life in London.'

'And I forget that my island wife is really a city-slicker. In seven short days I must have seen every play in the West End,

10

visited every major and minor art gallery in the city, had my bank balance severely depleted, and enlarged my liver on British cuisine.' Virginia laughed and Ashley grinned to see her so happy. It was a welcome echo from healthier times before Laura's birth.

'If your liver is swelling, blame your Cambridge pals and the red wine you old boys guzzle in your stuffy clubs.'

'Old boys, guzzle, stuffy indeed!'

Virginia was as tall as her husband. Her skin, pale as fine porcelain, showed hairline cracks at the corners of her grey eyes. Her lips were soft and gentle as she looked at him.

Ashley tucked his wife's thick, ash-blonde hair behind her ears. It no longer swung out at the level of her chin like a sheet of burnished metal; her illness had dulled the sheen and now it hung limply. He swallowed and forced himself to smile as he held her to him, noting again how tightly her translucent skin was stretched across her facial bones. He kissed her gently on her forehead. 'I love you, Virginia Challoner,' he said.

Her eyes darkened and she was suddenly serious. 'I love you,' she whispered, 'and will, for—'

She stopped in mid-sentence and blinked back the tears which threatened to spill over on to her cheeks. Then, with one of her mercurial changes of mood which after almost thirteen years of marriage still stunned and sometimes alarmed him, she whirled away from him, singing a tune from the musical they had seen earlier in the week.

He watched her cashmere wrap enclose her like a poppy's crimson petals as she twirled. Her red leather pumps flicked up a spray of fine gravel and her legs were as long and shapely as those of a young girl beneath her flying white skirt. Let the neurologist have good news for us today, he thought.

'Come here, you dilly wench.' He walked quickly to her and put his arm round her waist, afraid that the dancing would cause her to lose her balance and fall. She leaned against him.

Arm in arm they walked to the entrance of the zoo. They stood firm as a group of Japanese tourists engulfed them, chattering and clicking their cameras.

11

'Do you know that this is where I fell in love with you?' said Virginia, still a little breathless as they walked towards the monkey cages. 'Right here, on Monkey Hill in the zoo.'

'On our very first date.'

'Hardly a date. It was VE Day.'

'The eighth of May 1945,' said Ashley. 'We spent all night singing and dancing in the streets with thousands of others.'

'Do you remember, at sunrise we were sitting on one of the bronze lions in Trafalgar Square and drinking luke-warm champagne from a bottle when we suddenly decided we wanted to see the monkeys in Regent's Park?' she continued.

Ashley ran his fingers through her hair as they walked. 'It was the best possible way to celebrate the end of a war,' he said.

'It all started here, didn't it, Ashley?'

'Yes, our life together started here,' he answered, watching a green monkey walk towards them, its long tail arched high at the tip. It pressed a black face against the wire and white whiskers quivered as it studied their empty hands.

'No, I meant my illness,' she said quietly. 'That pain behind my eye started here. I thought it was only a champagne hangover.' She stared at the yellowish-green monkey holding out its hand, as piteous as a subway tramp.

'I was blind in that eye for three days. That must have been the beginning of whatever this illness is.' Ashley hugged his beautiful and impulsive wife. 'That was fifteen years ago,' she continued. 'It seems impossible that symptoms can stay hidden for such long periods and then reappear.'

'And in another fifteen years we'll visit these green fellows again,' he promised, 'and you'll be well.' One of the monkeys skittered across the floor and snatched up a nut its mother had dropped. Retribution was swift. Screaming in pain, the monkey clambered up the dried tree and huddled on a thin branch.

'I don't think that I'll be here,' Virginia said softly.

A tremor prickled the thick hairs on Ashley's arms. Over the years he had learnt to trust Virginia's intuition. She lived in the future and what she predicted usually came true. 'It's a firm date. One I expect you to keep, my lady,' he replied.

12

Virginia stood away from him with her head cocked to one side as if listening to sounds only she could hear. This habit had earned her the nickname 'Fody', from the tiny cardinal bird found in the Seychelles. She studied Ashley intently. Though slim, he was physically powerful. Sometimes she felt scorched by his vitality and had to distance herself from him. His dark-brown hair, bleached into streaks by the fierce tropical sun, shone with health and his skin was tanned to a burnt amber.

Her bracelets jingled and sparkled in the cold grey light as she wrapped her arms round his neck and looked into his eyes. She stared into his irises, flecked and starred like rich blue sapphires, and she knew that they could see into her soul. With a small sob she pressed herself against him and kissed him.

For a second Ashley was stunned. Virginia seldom demonstrated affection publicly. He held her close and, oblivious of the nannies and small children chortling over the antics of the monkeys, he lost himself in the joy of hugging this usually aloof woman, his wife.

'Thank you,' said Virginia as she pulled away. 'Let's have a quick look at the chimps.'

Her sombre mood vanished as she watched one young chimpanzee teasing a mother chimp who was nursing her baby. The mother had covered her head with a torn cardboard box and pulled the flap over her face.

'Oh, he's wicked,' said Virginia as the youngster snatched the box off the mother's head.

The ape's arm shot out, quick as the flick of a snake's tongue, and she made a grab for the box. The flap was ripped off in the tussle and Ashley hiccuped with laughter as she tried to replace the torn carton on her head while fending off further forays by the young chimp.

'If that was a human mother, the youngster would have a very sore bottom,' said Virginia.

'He's probably one of her children,' answered Ashley.

'I'm lucky that Laura was born good,' Virginia laughed as the female chimp swatted at the youngster.

'Ah-ha, here comes trouble,' said Ashley as they turned

13

away from the enclosure. 'Big brother has arrived to claim the young one's piece of cardboard.'

Virginia hung back, watching the chimps lope after each other, supporting the weight of their forequarters on their knuckles.

'Come,' called Ashley, glancing at his watch. 'We must leave now if you want another look at the Nash houses in the Crescent, before your appointment with the doctor.'

She tucked her hand into the crook of his arm and together they hurried towards the southern end of the Park and Harley Street.

━━━●|◉|◈|◉| III |◉|◈|◉|●━━━

The suffocating silence in the neurologist's consulting room was broken by his low voice as he murmured into the telephone. He swung his chair away from the handsome French ormolu desk and Virginia could see only the top of his polished head. Her breathing became quick and shallow. She sensed the presence of previous patients. She felt pain, anger and resignation lodged in the room like record files. She dropped her gaze from the neurologist's scalp and concentrated on an onyx bowl, filled with ivory and crystal eggs, which he had pushed to the corner of his desk. She longed to pick up one of the polished shapes and hold its coldness against her hot cheek. She fought hard to control her breathing and keep her face expressionless.

Ashley crossed his legs and relaxed back into his chair, happy that Virginia seemed so calm and composed.

'Sorry about that,' said the doctor. He put down the phone and swung his chair around to face them. 'Just some results I needed urgently.'

The Challoners smiled at him and waited.

He shuffled a pile of papers on his desk and, as he bent forward, his rimless glasses slipped to the end of his snub nose and his chin disappeared into the folds of his neck. He pulled out a sheet of green paper then looked at Virginia over the top

14

of his glasses. 'Mrs Challoner,' he began, 'on your last visit to my rooms in Queen Square I told you that I felt something might be wrong with your neurological system.'

'Yes,' said Virginia quietly, 'and you sent me to have a myelogram.'

'Correct,' he answered. 'You do realize that I ordered the lumbar puncture so that we could run X-ray contrast material up and down your spine in order to exclude any structural lesions?'

'Structural lesions?' Ashley queried.

'Tumours or damaged discs, Mr Challoner,' replied the neurologist. He took one of the ivory eggs from the bowl and rolled it on the leather desktop. 'The myelogram was clear.' He raised a finger as Virginia started to smile. 'I have, however, now made a diagnosis based on clinical observations.'

He paused. Tapping the egg lightly with a fingernail, he swivelled his chair to face Virginia.

'I'm sorry that it was necessary for you to visit Queen Square so often, Mrs Challoner, but this diagnosis has to be made with the utmost caution. So many things – spinal cord and cerebellar tumours, and the Guillain-Barré syndrome – can all masquerade as it.'

'As what?' Virginia broke in. 'What do I have? What's wrong with me?'

The neurologist stopped tapping the ivory egg and began to stroke the silky surface with his thumb. 'There is no easy way to tell you this. You have multiple sclerosis, Mrs Challoner. It's a chronic but painless disease involving both sensory and motor systems.'

'I . . . I don't understand,' whispered Virginia, pleating her scarlet cape nervously.

'It's a disease of the central nervous system, the brain and spinal cord,' the specialist explained. 'The myelin sheath, which insulates the nerve-fibres and helps to conduct impulses travelling down the nerve, becomes scarred.'

Virginia felt his words cutting away her life and she sat upright, pale and tense.

'The scarring or sclerosis causes some of the nerve-fibres to

15

fail,' he continued. 'They don't transmit the impulses which are necessary for muscle movement, such as sensitivity to light, and pain. You can lose your balance. The senses of smell, vision and hearing can also be affected.'

'How bad does it get?' Ashley asked soberly.

'It's a crippling disease, Mr Challoner. I wish I could be more reassuring, but Mrs Challoner's disabilities may vary from impaired vision and speech to incontinence or even to severe paralysis, leaving her bedridden.'

'No,' said Virginia, threading her fingers. 'No.'

Ashley walked across to his wife and sat on the arm of her chair. He unlocked her fingers and held her hands tightly.

'Mrs Challoner,' the neurologist went on, leaning across his desk, 'MS is a disease which has attacks and remissions. You had your first symptom at about the age of twenty-eight with unilateral blindness. You did not go to a doctor because the symptoms vanished within a few days. It was thirteen years before you experienced vomiting and dizziness and that feeling of your skin being too tight? Those symptoms appeared just before your pregnancy.' He smiled reassuringly. 'You enjoyed thirteen years of good health, did you not?'

'These symptoms I have now, the imbalance in walking and the need to keep running to the toilet, will they go away?' Virginia asked.

'They certainly *could*, but remember, just as the vision in your right eye has never been as good as it was . . .'

Virginia nodded soberly. She knew that she would always see colours in pastel shades. '. . . so with the other symptoms. You'll recover after they go, but never fully.'

'Is there no cure, doctor?' Ashley pleaded, stroking Virginia's arm. 'No hope?'

'It's a terrifying and depressing disease, and also inexplicable, Mr Challoner. It can burn itself out and just vanish, or the symptoms can exacerbate. In this case they have become worse. It is usual after childbirth.'

'Laura,' Virginia whispered, 'my baby.' She pushed back her chair. 'Excuse me,' she said and lurched to the door. Ashley jumped up. 'No,' Virginia said. 'I'll be back in a few minutes.'

16

She gave him a small, sad smile. 'One of my symptoms is calling.' She closed the door quickly behind her.

'I'm sorry, Mr Challoner,' the neurologist said quietly. 'You'll have to be prepared for your wife to undergo bouts of depression, anger and possibly humiliation over this debilitating disease.' Ashley nodded and was silent. 'In the later stages she may even exhibit mild dementia, become forgetful and absent-minded or inappropriately euphoric.' The doctor rolled the ivory egg under his fingertips. 'Mrs Challoner seems to be an independent and intelligent woman and I have a feeling that she will react sensibly to this change in her physical health.'

'Will her attitude affect her chances of long remissions?' Ashley asked, glancing at the door.

'I believe that her attitude – and taking proper care of herself – can reduce the relapses,' the neurologist answered. 'Only forty per cent of all diagnosed MS cases will progress to the severe form.'

'*Only* forty per cent, doctor? I find that unacceptably high,' Ashley retorted.

The door squeaked open and he stood up to help Virginia to her chair.

'Doctor,' she said, 'my baby, will she have inherited this disease from me?' Ashley felt slightly queasy. He had not considered the possibility of his only child having MS.

'We may not know very much about the disease, Mrs Challoner, but we *do* know that it is not hereditary, contagious or infectious. Your baby is safe.' He pulled a leather-bound notepad across the desk and uncapped a gold fountain pen. 'Now that we know what we're up against,' he said, 'I'd like to start you on a course of steroids. A short, sharp course of cortisone tablets for ten days and then we'll reduce the dosage quickly.' His pen scratched across the paper and he continued to explain as he filled the page with cramped black letters. 'It won't influence the outcome of the attack at all, but it will reduce the length of time for improvement.' The neurologist smiled at Virginia. 'You have three things in your favour, Mrs Challoner. One, you don't smoke. MS patients are advised not to flirt with tobacco. Two, you are slim. I advise patients to

17

reduce their fat intake. Three, you have the broad shoulders and the body of a sportswoman. Do you exercise?'

'I spend a lot of time swimming and diving in the Seychelles,' Virginia said.

'Excellent.' The neurologist beamed. 'Swimming in tepid water helps to strengthen the muscles and keep them supple. That of course will help your balance. But,' he warned, 'be careful not to overdo it. Avoid heating up your body. No lying in the sun or taking very hot baths.'

Virginia nodded.

'Yoga,' he added.

Virginia looked bemused. 'Yoga?' she echoed.

'Yes, tremendous for relaxation and muscle control.'

Virginia watched him roll the polished ivory between his palms. 'I used to do yoga,' she said, 'during the war. Long before it became popular. Our ATS captain believed that it calmed the spirit. She said it would help us accept the terror of air raids.' She sat quietly for a moment. 'She was right then. Perhaps yoga will help again.'

'Emma has a friend in West Hoathly who runs a yoga class,' said Ashley. 'You could join that.'

'Good,' said the neurologist. 'I realize that this has been a shock, Mrs Challoner. I'd like to see you in my rooms at Queen Square a week from today. Followed by regular visits for the next six to eight months.'

'Next week,' echoed Virginia in dismay. 'I have to be back at Lyewood. Laura—'

The neurologist looked at Ashley. 'I'm afraid that regular visits are necessary, Mr Challoner.'

Ashley loosened the folds of cashmere from between Virginia's fingers and held her hand cupped in both of his.

'Don't worry, Fody, Giles and Emma will be thrilled to have Laura to themselves for another week. She's in very safe hands.'

Virginia sighed. 'Your work. The Society has just granted you extra funds. You can't leave your research for six months. We can't stay here until autumn. It's impossible.'

The neurologist studied Virginia as intently as a linesman at Wimbledon. He evaluated every nuance and expression, seeking

18

clues to help him counsel and guide this beautiful and independent woman.

Precise as a computer, Ashley did a quick mental scan of the six months ahead. He was eager to start research on the terrestrial ecology of Aldabra, one of the far-flung coral islands lying almost eight hundred miles west of the main island of Mahé. But that could wait. He would have to find someone from Cambridge to study the harvesting of the green and loggerhead turtles in July and August. The student would be based at Cosmoledo, one of the islands in the Aldabra group and the centre of the harvesting. The youngster could easily sail to Aldabra and check on the breeding turtles for him. It would be difficult to arrange everything within a few weeks, but he exuded confidence as he turned to Virginia.

'Those atolls have been there for almost seventy-five million years, Virginia. Six months more won't make much difference. Your health and well-being are far more important than coral-capped islands.'

The neurologist had very little interest in a sprinkling of islands in the equatorial part of the Indian Ocean, but he wanted to defuse the situation. 'Seventy-five million years!' he exclaimed.

Virginia looked at him, distracted for a moment.

'The granite islands in the group are far older. They've been dated to about six hundred and fifty million years,' said Ashley, welcoming the diversion. 'It's the old Continental Drift theory. When the mega-continent, Gondwanaland, cracked, Madagascar and India drifted away from Africa, and the Seychelles are the fragments which were left trailing behind near the equator.' Ashley chided himself silently for describing one hundred and ten islands, which cover an area four-fifths the size of France, as fragments.

'Interesting,' murmured the doctor, watching Virginia closely.

She was looking more relaxed after his interruption, and the neurologist allowed himself a small congratulatory smile.

Ashley turned his attention back to his wife. 'We'll spend the summer in Sussex. It'll give me time to do plenty of reading research here. I want to spend a few weeks up at Cambridge in the geographical department, where they're conducting some very interesting studies on Indian Ocean coral reefs. I'll be able to discuss Aldabra with them. It's an opportunity I should not miss.' Ashley squeezed her hand gently. 'It'll also give me time to try and wring some money or help from the Royal Society.' Virginia ran a polished fingernail across her lips. A soothing gesture, one she often used when unhappy or deep in thought. 'By the end of the summer we'll know much more about this multiple sclerosis. Your treatment will be over and you'll be strong and well,' he urged.

Virginia squared her shoulders and sat up straight in the delicate Louis Quatorze chair. 'I'll keep my appointments with you, doctor, and we'll pray for another long remission.' She looked up at Ashley. 'But I don't want Giles and Emma to know why we're extending our stay. I'll tell them later.'

The neurologist and Ashley glanced at each other over the top of Virginia's head.

'With your positive attitude I'm certain that we'll have many remissions, Mrs Challoner.'

The neurologist closed the door quietly behind them and walked across to the window. He dropped the ivory egg from one hand into the other as he watched a squat black taxi draw up to the kerb in response to Ashley's raised umbrella.

He remained unmoving long after Virginia had swirled her scarlet wrap round her body and climbed into the cab. The picture of her blonde head dropping disconsolately on to her husband's shoulder and his lips brushing her hair lightly, stayed with him long after his next patient had been ushered into the room.

Giles and Emma turned from the altar and faced the coven. The young witch shivered. Now came the wiccaning of the baby. It would be placed under divine protection. 'We are met in this Circle to ask the blessing of the mighty God and the gentle Goddess on Laura, the daughter of Virginia and Ashley Challoner, so that she may grow in beauty and strength, in joy and wisdom . . .' said Giles.

'. . . when at last she is truly grown, she shall know without doubt or fear which path is hers and shall tread it gladly.'

The maiden gasped as suddenly Giles broke with tradition. 'We are to be godparents to Laura and tonight stand here in place of her parents.' Was this baby to be wiccaned in the witches' way, without the consent and knowledge of its parents? The young witch dismissed the thought quickly. Their Priest and High Priestess would never do such a thing. The child's parents must have given them permission to bring the baby.

Giles looked at Emma and her green eyes sparkled in triumph. She smiled at him, a small, tight smile, urging him to continue with the wiccaning.

The silence lengthened and the witches moved uneasily. Emma squeezed Giles's hand and slowly he nodded. 'Now bring her forward that she may be blessed,' he said.

The maiden scrambled to her feet and took her position beside Emma. Laura whimpered.

'Has your child also a hidden name?' Giles queried.

Emma answered, 'Her hidden name is Tanith.'

He took the baby from the maid and dipped his finger into the bowl of oil that Emma was holding.

'I anoint thee, Laura, with oil and give thee the hidden name of Tanith,' he said as he marked the pentagram on her forehead.

Laura's whimpers strengthened into determined wails, drowning the music. Giles then anointed her with wine in the name of the god Pan, and with water in the name of the goddess of fertility, Diana.

A thin trickle of water and wine fanned across Laura's nose

21

and she screamed her indignation. Her tiny face was red and crumpled and her clenched fists flailed the air. Giles handed her to his High Priestess. Emma pressed the little face against her warm breast and wiped away the oil and water with her thumb.

'Eho, Eho, Azarak,
Eko, Eko, Zomelak,
Eko, Eko, Pan . . .'

She sang an old witches' rune and patted Laura gently. Giles joined her and they walked to the watchtower of the east to present the baby.

'Ye lords of the watchtower of the east, we do bring before you Laura, whose hidden name is Tanith and who has been duly anointed within the Wiccan Circle.' Laura continued to squall unremittingly and only fragments of his words were heard by the coven.

Emma looked down at the baby and, lifting one of her full breasts, she ran the pink nipple round Laura's mouth. The baby's tightly closed eyes opened and her fists snuggled up under her chin as she found and sucked at the empty teat. Emma smiled as Laura snuffled and hiccuped. The strong tugs on her breast sent warm shivers down to her barren womb and she felt Laura was her baby.

'My little witch,' she breathed, 'you'll always be mine.'

They presented Laura to each of the watchtowers in turn and the baby made soft, wet, sucking noises as she was placed under the protection of Pan and Diana.

In front of the altar Emma gently pulled her nipple away and handed Laura to the maiden. Laura opened her mouth to protest, then chortled as the sparkling silver moon on Emma's crown attracted her attention. Her dark-blue eyes crossed and she concentrated on trying to touch the circlet.

Emma breathed a sigh of relief. Virginia's baby had been christened in the wicca religion and she would make certain that one day Laura would be a witch. She and Giles lifted their arms, calling in turn on their god and goddess to bestow on Laura the gifts of strength, beauty, wisdom and love. Then, as godparents they turned to face each other, and the young maid moved quickly so that Laura could still see Emma's crown.

'Do you, Emma Killick, promise to be a friend to Laura throughout her childhood, to aid and guide her as she shall need, to watch over her and love her as if she were of your own blood?' asked Giles.

'I, Emma, do so promise,' she replied.

Giles made his promises then closed the wiccaning.

> *'The god and goddess have blessed her,*
> *the lords of the watchtowers have acknowledged her,*
> *we her friends have welcomed her,*
> *Therefore, O Circle of Stars, shine in peace on Laura,*
> *whose hidden name is Tanith,*
> *so mote it be.'*

The coven answered with one voice, 'So mote it be.'

'Let us all be seated within the circle,' said Giles. The coven sat on the ground, and he and Emma passed around the chalice of consecrated wine and the crescent-shaped cakes. Emma collected the gifts the coven had brought for Laura and set out the party food and drink. Soon the circle was filled with talk and laughter.

'Tell me,' said one of the male witches, swallowing a mouthful of red wine, 'where are the parents? They are supposed to present their baby to our goddess. Why are they not here?'

The young maiden took the chalice from him, sipped a little wine and gazed at Giles over the rim. It was easy to look at him now.

'In London,' answered Giles.

'Ill,' said Emma.

Seeing the man frown, Giles hastened to explain. 'The mother had a very difficult pregnancy. She was ill for months before Tanith's birth and is still weak.'

'She's already forty and it's her first child,' Emma added.

'They want to return soon to the Seychelles, where they live, so we had to have the wiccaning now,' said Giles.

23

'The parents are in London consulting doctors,' said Emma. 'We don't know when they'll be back.' She looked down at Laura who lay quietly in her lap, playing with the buckles on the leather garter that was strapped tightly round her thigh.

'One day you'll be a witch Queen and wear a garter like mine,' she whispered. 'You too will give birth to new covens.'

Laura yawned and her eyelids drooped. Her head fell sideways, the fluffy blonde curls crushed against Emma's stomach. Emma carefully lifted the tiny fingers away from her garter and kissed each pearl-tipped nail before tucking the hand under the blanket. Giles looked at Emma and the baby, and his heart ached for her. She should have had children of her own.

'Giles,' said the young witch, satisfied with the answer he had given. 'Tell us more about your book, about the Craft of the Wise.' She smiled at her High Priest across the circle. 'What part are you writing now?'

'Yes,' echoed the male witch, his disquiet about Laura forgotten. 'Tell us.' The chattering died down as the coven gathered to sit cross-legged in front of Giles.

'Aradia,' he said, 'I'm writing about Aradia. Not only is she the daughter of Diana, but she's also the younger version of the goddess herself.' He stroked his beard and marshalled his thoughts.

'According to the Old Religion of witchcraft, the ancient cult of the moon goddess, Diana, was created first. She was darkness. Lucifer, her brother and son, was the light.' The young maiden hugged her arms over her breasts, rocking slowly as she listened to Giles. 'Diana used the very first act of witchcraft on Lucifer. She persuaded the cat who slept on his bed to change forms with her. She became her brother's cat. While he slept, she resumed her own shape and made love to him in his sleep. She was impregnated by her brother and gave birth to her daughter, Aradia.'

Emma smiled a sleepy, languorous smile. 'So darkness conquered light,' she said.

'And still does,' said Giles, studying his wife's delicate features.

24

'That's why cats love witches and have always been considered to be mystical,' nodded one of the older women.

'Go on,' pleaded the young maiden. 'What did Lucifer do when he found out?'

'He was very angry, but Diana sang to him and calmed him. Her singing wove a powerful spell of magic round him.'

'Yes,' breathed Emma. 'Diana spins the wheel of life, she controls the lives of all men. Lucifer merely turns the wheel.'

'Aradia,' one of the men broke in. 'What of Aradia?'

'Ah,' said Giles. 'Diana was sickened by the misery of the poor people on Earth, so she taught her daughter the secrets of witchcraft. She then sent Aradia to Earth to start the secret society of witches.'

'So that's how our craft started,' said the maiden excitedly.

'Yes,' Giles answered, with a smile. 'Man has always been fascinated by mysteries. Our worship of the power and magic of Nature is much older than Christianity and other religions. We worship life itself. Our semi-magical and religious practices started with the beginning of man.'

The witches nodded.

'When Aradia's work was completed, she left the world and returned to Diana,' said Emma, continuing the story. 'But before she left, she told our people to meet every month at full moon and worship the spirit of Diana. She said we should sing, dance, make music and then make love in the dark, for Diana is darkness.' Emma lowered her eyes as she said this for she did not want the coven to read her desire.

'Aradia said we should perform our rites naked to show that we are truly free,' Giles said. The witches smiled. 'Diana was so delighted with the work Aradia had done on Earth that she allowed her to give powers to the witches who invoke her. The two great powers are the power to bless and the power to curse.' Giles coughed and studied the coven solemnly. 'We must beware of the power to curse. The spirits envoked are dangerous, and our magic can become black and perilous. Remember, magic can be both dark and light, like the two faces of the moon goddess we worship.'

Dangerous, yes, thought Emma, her eyes still lowered and her head bowed over Laura. But I need power. The blackness of Hecate frightens you but it excites me. I'm not afraid to use it to make Tanith mine. Her grip tightened and Laura grunted softly in her sleep. Mine, my little witch, she promised silently. She traced the outline of the baby's ear with her tapered fingers. Diana has blessed you and we'll teach you all the dark and beautiful secrets of the moon goddess.

'Teechah, teechah!' The strident call alerted the witches.

'The chaffinch's alarm-call,' whispered one of the men. 'Something has awakened and frightened the bird.' They sat in silence, their ears straining to hear footsteps and their eyes probing the darkness.

'Is it someone spying on us?' the maid asked, chewing the inside of her lip.

'Pikeys?' another whispered. 'They say the little forest dwellers still move by night and sense when strangers are near.'

Giles motioned to her to be silent, and for long minutes they sat as unmoving and solid as stones in a druid's circle.

'It's late,' said Giles at last, 'and the goddess has almost left the sky. Let's prepare for the banishing ritual.'

Emma placed her folded cloak in the fireglow near the altar and cuddled the sleeping baby into it. The coven collected their athames and took up their positions facing east behind the Priest and High Priestess. '. . . Ye Lords of Air, we do thank you for attending our rites,' Emma intoned, solemnly drawing the banishing pentacle in the air, 'and, ere ye depart to your pleasant and lovely realms, we bid you hail and farewell.'

'Hail and farewell,' echoed the coven.

Her lips flattened on the steel blade as she held the knife to her mouth. She then pressed it to her breast and the maiden blew out the candle in the lantern. The members of the coven imitated her gestures faithfully. When they reached north, the maiden blew out all the candles, leaving the circle lit by the dying fire. Within minutes the sacred enclosure was cleared and the fire doused. The hooded figures slipped away into the night, silent as black bats.

'Go safely,' Giles whispered, 'those of us who are able to will and to know, and can dare be silent. Go safely.'

The red wine soaked into the dry ground beneath the twisted thorn tree, the wet patches melting quickly into the dark shadows. Emma crumbled a cake and sprinkled the pieces over the wine. Through the fretwork of tangled thorn branches she watched Giles burying the dead fire.

As he kicked sand over the wet, black embers, dust veiled him and he sneezed loudly. Emma glanced at Laura, but she slept on, undisturbed.

Shaking the dust from the folds of his cloak, Giles walked to the stone altar. 'Emma,' he called softly. 'Emma, where are you?'

She smiled and stroked the trunk of the old tree with long lingering caresses, and her tongue kept her lips moist as she waited for him, deep in the shadows of the ancient thorn. 'Aradia commanded us to dance, sing, make music, and then love in the darkness,' she answered.

As Giles bent to walk under the branches of the thorn tree, he untied his cloak and spread it on the ground. Kneeling on the soft, dark wool, he held out his arms to Emma.

'This is a wapping thorn and we must honour it by making love in its shadow,' she said throatily as she stood in front of him, smoothing his thick hair.

'We'll wap beneath its branches,' he said. 'Tonight has been a special occasion and the tree will be respected.'

His strong hands pressed her legs apart. As she looked down at him, she felt his strength and urgency. She knew that tonight he would be brutal and she trembled with excitement. She gasped as his fingers dug into her buttocks and she stood astride, thrusting her pelvis forward, eager for his questing tongue.

He kept his face buried in her. His hands were a vice, pressing her hard to his mouth and, as her soft moans gave way to cries and entreaties, he tightened his grasp. He was oblivious to her hands thudding down on his shoulders and to her nails raking his back again and again as she shuddered against him.

27

Eventually he released her and stretched out on the cloak.
'Come,' he said and pulled her limp body down on his.

The stars were pin-pricks in the heavens when Giles reached down and twined his fingers in Emma's hair. He lifted her head from his loins and swung her around to lie beside him. Nestling her head in the crook of his arm, he kissed her swollen mouth. 'You've done well, my witch. Diana will smile on you,' he said.

She stretched up her arms to the latticed branches of the thorn tree and ran her fingers along the thorns. Pressing the sharp points lightly into her fingertips, she enjoyed the hint of pain. She could feel the tree's vitality seep into her.

Giles leaned over her and looked deep into her eyes. She dropped her arm across his shoulder and he found her hand and kissed her palm, rubbing the soft skin over his beard. 'Let's leave. Soon it'll be light and Laura will wake,' he said.

He stood up and pulled her to her feet. He pressed her naked body quickly to his, then picked up the sleeping baby.

Emma watched as he tenderly tucked the blankets round Laura and prepared to leave the sacred enclosure.

'Yes, you're right, Diana will be pleased,' she whispered, 'but it's black Hecate and her minions that I'll have to use to keep the child.' She wrapped her cloak round her body and hurried after Giles. 'I'll do anything I have to. Tanith is mine.'

Giles paused. 'What's that?' he asked.

Emma started, quickly thinking of something to say. 'I said that our baby witch will be safe with you. If there are pikeys or Good Folk in the forest, they won't try to take Tanith to "pay a teind to hell". Our baby won't be the human sacrifice for the fairies.'

'Emma,' Giles laughed. 'There are no true pikeys left, and the Good Folk wouldn't take a witch's child.'

'This baby will always be ours. Now that she's wiccaned,' Emma hastened to add, seeing the expression on Giles's face.

'We've brought her into the way of the witches, Emma – but remember, the choice of remaining with the ancient religion is hers and only hers. She'll make a decision when she's older and understands.' Emma nodded, but Giles still blocked the pathway. 'Laura is Virginia's child. She's not yours. You may love her and guide her, but you can't have her. Remember that and it'll make it easier for you to part with her when Ashley and Virginia take her away.' He squeezed her shoulder, sensing her unhappiness.

Emma bowed her head and the hood fell forward, covering her face. Taking her silence for acquiescence, he hurried on over the Weald, eager to reach Lyewood before the sky brightened.

━━━◗|❋|❋|❋| V |❋|❋|❋|◖━━━

The waning moon dissolved behind banks of black clouds, and the gravel courtyard was dark and quiet. Only the occasional grating of pebbles betrayed light footsteps walking to the front door of Lyewood.

The great oak door swung open silently and Emma stepped into the flag-stoned entrance-hall. She paused, breathing in the wood-smoke from the fire in the grate. The oak-panelled walls warmed the vast hall and sitting room and Emma listened to the roof timbers creak and groan beneath the heavy Horsham slabs. The sounds comforted her. This greystone house had sheltered the Killick family for hundreds of years and she loved listening to its heartbeat.

Lyewood stood high on one of the rolling eastern Sussex hills near the forest village of West Hoathly. It overlooked almost a thousand acres of sloping fields, woodlands and old hammer-mill ponds, now well stocked with trout.

The gracious manor house had been built by a Killick who made his fortune as a Sussex ironmaster in the sixteenth century. The Killicks were originally a Wealden family of yeoman farmers; they had risen to the gentry through trading in iron dug from the rich deposits in the Weald. Giles still blamed his ancestors for the felling of the great forest trees to feed their iron mills.

Emma tiptoed to the foot of the carved oak staircase. A rumble of snores confirmed Giles's deep sleep. A moonbeam slid through a chink in one of the curtained windows. Emma

29

stretched out her arm and let the light play on the dial of her watch. Laura would not awaken before dawn. The silent house was hers for at least four or five hours.

She buried her face in the huge bunch of herbs and elder-flowers she was carrying. She breathed in the putrescent odour of the white elder. The musk excited her.

'Gathered in the dark and at the time of a waning moon, your magic will be powerful,' she whispered, as the florets tickled her cheeks. 'And the smoke from your burning branches will summon and welcome the dark one I need.'

The tip of her tongue stroked the gap between her front teeth as she hurried past the summer sitting room, the library and Giles's study.

At the end of the passage a rounded door, banded with strips of iron, led into her room. It had been used as a smugglers' hide-out in the eighteenth century, when smuggling was rife in the area. There was a small fireplace with an intricately carved overmantel. When one of the wooden acorns forming part of the frieze was twisted, an oak panel beside the fireplace swung open to reveal a windowless room. It was cool in summer, and in winter was heated by the back wall of the fireplace.

Emma had claimed the two rooms as her own. She used the main room as a study and sewing room. She had detached the acorn and kept it hidden in her desk so that no one could fit it into the frieze and open the panel to the hidden room. It was her witch's room. During the cool winter months the coven often held their meetings and Sabbats in the secret room.

Emma dropped the armful of herbs and flowers on to a chair in the passageway and turned into the kitchen wing.

The large stone-floored kitchen was warm. The bread she had kneaded and baked that afternoon stood high under white dishcloths, filling the room with the smell of yeast. She felt her way across the darkened room to the scrubbed deal table; she did not want a farm-hand to see the kitchen lights and come to investigate the possibility of a burglary. Running her hand down the sturdy leg of the table, she bent and crawled underneath.

'There, there,' she soothed as she found the reeded cat-basket and felt for the kittens, tucked up tightly against their mother's belly.

The brindled cat spat a warning and Emma fondled her torn ears.

'All right, old lady,' she crooned. 'I'm only looking for the puppy you're nursing with your kittens. Don't make such a fuss about your babies. We know that the gardener is going to drown most of them.' The cat relaxed and massaged her cushion in ecstasy as Emma scratched her under the chin.

Emma fumbled in her pocket for the box of matches, struck one and sorted through the cuddled-up kittens.

'There you are,' she said triumphantly as the flame flickered and died. 'Right at the bottom.' She lifted up a black puppy and tucked it into her blouse. 'And you, old girl,' she said to the mother cat as she scrambled backwards and stood up, 'had better stop stalking in the Gravetye woods. That black tom is much too young for you. You're past your prime. You should know better.'

The cat ignored her, intent on licking and placating her sleepy offspring.

Emma retraced her steps down the passage, picked up the flowers and slipped into her room. She turned the key in the lock and breathed a sigh of relief. Drawing the velvet curtains across the leaded windows set deep into the stone walls, she lit the two candles on the mantelpiece. The flowers tumbled on to the tiled floor as she disentangled the elder branches from the herbs. Breaking the branches into small pieces, she blew on the coals in the fireplace and soon pungent smoke filled both rooms.

Emma inhaled the smoke deeply, unbuttoned her blouse and lifted the puppy away from the warmth of her body. The puppy grunted softly and sneezed. 'Shh,' she admonished. She carried it into the witch's room and put it down on the carpet. It shivered and whimpered. She quickly shrugged out of her blouse and let it drop over the whining black bundle.

The puppy curled its blond-tipped tail over its eyes and snuggled happily into the material. She watched it for a few moments and then, satisfied that it would stay quiet, she walked back into her study.

31

Emma felt in the pocket of her long flowered skirt before unzipping it and letting it fall. Her hand closed over a soft, cold body and it quivered as she lifted it out.

'Don't be afraid, my little one,' she murmured.

The anuran sat impassively on her hand. She dropped her lacy black undies on to the skirt and, running her fingers through her pubic hair, she walked naked into the secret room. Skilfully, her fingers played with the toad as it squatted on the palm of her hand.

'Give me your milk, my beauty,' she said, 'and you can go back to your bed under the foxgloves.'

The toad stared up at her, its eyes bright and hard as gemstones, and it exuded the milky poison through its skin for her. Emma trickled a few drops of the hypnotic and deadly toxin into a stone jar of ointment and placed it on the altar in the centre of the magic circle painted on the carpet. She slid the natterjack into a damp, moss-lined box.

'Rest, little one,' she said. 'I'll put you in the garden later.'

She walked across the magic circle, stepping carefully over the puppy. Her breasts swung heavily as she bent down and placed black candles on the pentagrams. She rubbed her nipples between her fingers as she lit the candles on the four cardinal points.

'The south wind is hot and dry,' she chanted, 'so south is fire. The west brings rain, so it's water. The east is cold and dry, so east is for the powers of air.' She always made a private ritual of explaining the powers of the four elements as she struck the matches. 'The north wind freezes, so north represents darkness.'

The flames hung like four golden dewdrops over the candles. Before tracing the circle with her athame and giving it black power, Emma took the pot of ointment from the altar. The acrid smell of smallage tickled her nosrils as she opened the lid. Carefully she blended the toad milk into the mixture.

'Wortcunning you have,' Giles's words echoed in Emma's mind as she stroked the unguent on the pulse points of her body. 'Use it wisely, for knowledge of the secret properties of plants can be as dangerous as misuse of occult powers, Emma,' he warned. 'Don't play with aconite, cinquefoil and belladonna. You know that they are hallucinogenic and can be deadly.'

'You have some knowledge of plants,' she reasoned, as if talking to Giles. 'But I must find and use the powers of my mind. I have only a few hours, and using drugs is a short cut to entering the deeper stage of consciousness which I need.'

She replaced the pot on the altar and swung the censer of incense into the middle of the triangle which she had drawn outside the protection of the magic circle. The dark spirit she evoked would appear in this three-sided polygon. It was only gods who were invoked into the circle.

Silently she justified her actions to her sleeping husband as she continued with her preparations.

You're a good witch, Giles, and a wonderful High Priest. You know the Science and Art of causing change to occur in conformity with will, but you're afraid to look at the dark face of our goddess.

Only woman can identify directly with the Earth Mother. What I'm practising is not the old pagan tradition of witchcraft which we both love, Giles. I practise black magic to control the secret forces of nature. I've tried sympathetic magic: I brought the symbol and the object together. The pins I stuck into the moulded clay image of Virginia gave her pains in her arms and legs; but she still rocks Laura and walks with her. She still mothers my baby. I need Hecate, dark and powerful. The spirit I evoke tonight will bow to the power of my mind and obey me. Virginia will sicken and be unable to care for Laura. The baby must be mine. She heard Giles's deep voice: 'Remember "perfect trust" and "perfect love". The aim of all magic is "perfect love". It must harm no one.'

The origanum she had blended with the incense curled from the copper censer.

Virginia doesn't need Laura as I do, she said, still justifying herself to Giles. You'll never understand my need for the baby. What I have to do I'll do alone. You'll never know that I betrayed your tenets.

33

Satisfied that the spirit she evoked would be able to manifest itself in the smoke, she banished all thoughts of Giles from her mind.

She stroked the skull, 'Old Simon', an ancient symbol of immortality, and straightened the crossed bones beneath the white cranium. Then she picked up her black-handled knife from the altar. Slowly she started to walk widdershins round the circle. As she moved anticlockwise her skin prickled. It was a movement of malevolent magic and she was going to have to control dangerous forces. The ritual continued and the silence deepened.

The room grew still and cold as Emma opened her book of grimoires. It contained all her magical secrets, painstakingly written down in the secret signs of the Theban alphabet. The runes were strengthened by the concentrated thought she had used when writing the unfamiliar letters. The unintelligible words of power, strong and sharp as witches' knives, pierced the silence. Even though the room was warm, Emma's flesh was pimpled and puckered as she intoned the ancient words. The meaning was unknown, but Emma knew that the words were the key to the world of darkness.

'Lamac cahi achabahe
Karrelyos.'

The chanting fevered her mind, and her vision into the unknown was clear. The effect on Emma was instant and potent and strengthened the powers of magic deep within her.

She bent down and shook the puppy loose from the folds of her blouse.

'I offer this animal to thee.'

She carried the sleepy little creature to the altar and his wet nose nuzzled into her armpit.

'O great Adonai, Elohim.'

34

She recited the invocation as she held him down on the cold, marble top. The theta rhythm, usually only present when she was asleep and dreaming, surfaced and she had the key to the world of images. Her eyes were glazed and looked deep into places unknown to man.

The puppy whined softly and his paws scrabbled futilely in the air as he tried to curl into a ball. She uncoiled him and fitted a wreath of verbena over his small head. The candlelight shadowed Emma's eyes into pits and coiled sinuously over her naked flesh.

She moved in a trance. Her fingers caressed the steel blade of her athame. Her voice strengthened and the barbarous words drummed in the small room.

'I spill the blood of this sacrifice.'

The puppy's shriek bubbled away in a bloody froth.

'Grant, Great Adonai, that it be agreeable.'

She touched the knife to her forehead and the blade was scented with the sickly-sweet smell of blood.

'Blood is life,' she murmured. The ointment and the incense continued to seep into her, drugging her body and heightening her consciousness. Slowly she recited the terrible words of power:

'Retragrammaton Olyaram . . .'

The hours crept by as she fought to control and instruct the dark forces she had evoked.

Just before dawn, pale and exhausted, she crept up the oak stairs.

'Please don't wake and cry,' she whispered as she padded past Laura's room. She had to be in the four-poster bed beside Giles when the baby awoke. Giles's day on the farm started at cock crow and Laura's early-morning cries had become his alarm clock.

She pulled back the sheets and froze as he grunted and turned over to face her. 'Emma,' he mumbled. 'Didn't hear Laura cry. What's the time?'

'Sorry I disturbed you,' she said, ignoring his question. His eyes narrowed as he noticed her unbuttoned blouse and skirt. 'Why are you dressed?' he asked, raising himself on one elbow.

Excuses smoked like incense through her mind and vanished. She stared at Giles. She was terrified that he would discover her practising black magic. She knew that she would lose both his love and his respect. 'Laura,' she stammered.

'Is not awake,' he said. Suddenly he smiled. 'I know, you were sneaking out again to collect your herbs before sunrise.'

Emma swallowed loudly. 'You're not angry?' she questioned.

'My little witch,' he said, 'of course I'm not angry. What would my farm-hands do without your herbal remedies?'

'I'm so sorry that I woke you.'

'Then come and prove it,' he said and he pulled her down over him.

Emma lay spread-eagled across his body, weak with guilt and relief. The sudden ringing of the telephone freed her from forcing her limp limbs to respond to his urgent fingers and mouth.

'Hello,' he said, lifting the receiver. 'Ah, Ashley. No, you haven't woken me.' Giles pulled Emma's head on to his shoulder and ran his fingers through her thick crinkled hair as he listened to his brother-in-law.

'Another week,' he echoed.

Emma stiffened and strained to hear Ashley's voice.

'Of course we'll look after Laura. Emma will be thrilled. Give our love to Virginia and tell her that Laura is in excellent hands. She's the most loved baby in Sussex.' He listened in silence for a moment. 'Right, Ashley, I'll speak to you tomorrow. Goodbye and enjoy London.'

'You have Laura for another week, maybe more,' he said, turning Emma over on to her back. 'The doctors want to run

36

another series of tests. They obviously can't decide what's wrong with my poor sister.'

Emma closed her eyes. Her magic was starting to work. 'How sad,' she whispered. 'I'm so sorry, Giles.'

'Don't be,' he answered. 'Virginia may look like a delicate rose, but she's tough. A girl who was decorated for bravery during the war will fight this damn disease and beat it.'

'Of course. Of course she will.'

'And now,' said Giles, glancing at the old carriage clock on the bedside table, 'we have some unfinished business to attend to before the baby awakes.'

Emma grunted as his weight pressed down on her, and she breathed shallowly into his beard as she set about pleasing him.

In the adjoining room Laura lay on her stomach. Her eyes were still lightly closed, but her tiny fist was curled up at her mouth and she sucked it softly. Soon the dark-blue eyes would open and her shrill wails for milk would herald the start of a new day.

───────◙◙◙◙ VI ◙◙◙◙───────

The peacock preened and twirled, fanning his tail into a shimmering turquoise and emerald-green arc. The spots topping the tail feathers stared out, bright as painted eyes, as he strutted past the signpost leading to Horsted Keynes. He stopped once again in the middle of the road to display his finery and impress the dowdy pea-hens pecking for insects in the hedgerows lining the road.

The midnight-blue Land Rover jerked to a halt and Ashley flung open the door.

'The peacocks are not usually in the road. I often see them in the grounds of that old house. Won't be a second,' he called to Virginia as he bounded across the road to the signpost. The peacock eyed him defiantly and spread his tail feathers into a breath-taking display of iridescent blues. Then he snapped them shut and slid through an opening in the hedge to join his unresponsive females.

'There you are,' said Ashley, jumping into the car and starting the motor.

'They're beautiful,' said Virginia, examining the two silky tail feathers he put in her hands. 'But they're very unlucky.'

'Unlucky? Emma has a vase of them in her study and she's certainly a lucky little lady.' He tucked the feathers behind the driving mirror. 'Married to your brother and mistress of one of the finest old houses and farms in the area. Peacock feathers have certainly been good to her.'

He tooted the car horn as a male pheasant scuttled across the road, his plumage a blur of toasted cinnamon, scarlet and green.

'The sun seems to have lured the birds out into the open,' Virginia said, still eyeing the bobbing peacock feathers.

'Tell you what.' Ashley followed her gaze. 'We'll give these to Emma to add to her collection.'

'Good idea,' she answered. 'She's spooky enough to have them close to her.'

Ashley glanced at his wife sharply. It was unlike her to make snide comments.

'Come, she's harmless. Reading tea-leaves in cups and seeing pictures in a crystal is hardly weird. Hundreds of people make a very good living telling fortunes.'

Virginia remained unconvinced and kept quiet. She sat studying the neatly parcelled fields as they sped past, her face turned away from Ashley.

'Her knowledge of herbs is really extraordinary,' he continued. 'And herbal cures are an accepted part of medicine nowadays.'

'As a farmer's daughter I've always believed in the properties of herbs,' she answered. 'But Emma. There's something about her . . .'

'It's because she married your big brother, and in his baby sister's eyes no one could be good enough.'

'Stop teasing,' laughed Virginia. 'Maybe you're right. I may yet forgive her, Giles, and she certainly loves Laura.' She hesitated. 'Perhaps too much.'

'What do you mean?' Ashley asked sharply, immediately concerned about his baby daughter. He had waited for a child for twelve years and was fiercely protective of his baby. 'I couldn't imagine leaving Laura with anyone but Giles and Emma.'

'I agree,' said Virginia, 'but Emma is obsessed with Laura. I never seem to be alone with my baby.'

Ashley squeezed her hand. 'Are you not being a little possessive? Poor Emma will never have a baby of her own. She knows that she'll only see Laura when we come over here, that's probably why she hovers over her.' He looked at Virginia's set face. 'Let's be kind. Allow her to share our baby.'

Virginia sighed and placed her hand on his knee. 'You're right, Ashley. We're so lucky to have Laura. Giles and Emma have always wanted a baby, an heir to Lyewood.' She gave his knee a playful squeeze, making it jump. 'I'll let Emma share Laura, or at least I'll try,' she promised.

'That's my girl,' he answered, swerving to avoid an oncoming truck on the narrow twisting road.

'West Hoathly ahead,' he announced. 'We'll soon be home. I'll be able to see how my daughter's grown.'

'Not much,' laughed Virginia. 'Babies take time to grow into little girls.'

Suddenly she grasped his arm. 'Stop, Ashley. Please stop in the village. Let's have a pub lunch at the Cat Inn. We haven't been there for ages, I don't want to face Emma and Giles just yet. I hate being pitied.'

'What about Laura? You've been longing to see her.'

Virginia looked at the clock on the dashboard. 'Emma will have put her down for her afternoon nap.' She smiled impishly. 'Didn't I receive instructions to share my baby? I'll let Emma have her for another hour or two.'

'The Cat Inn it is,' Ashley agreed. 'You love that old smugglers' haunt, don't you?'

'As children, Giles and I spent hours playing smugglers and

39

riding officers around the farm. We even searched for hidden treasure near the old iron mines and in the forests in this part of the Weald; we lived in hope that we'd find a holloway. We were certain that there were still undiscovered smugglers' passageways across the Weald. It was marvellous fun. One day Laura will play the same games, I hope.'

'If not here, then she'll be able to search for pirates' treasure in the Seychelles,' Ashley said, as they parked the Land Rover and walked towards the inn. 'We'll also teach her to swim, sail and build sandcastles. The islands are a wonderful place for children.'

The sound of raised voices heralded their entrance to the centuries-old inn. They stepped aside quickly as the door crashed open. A stocky, well-muscled youngster lurched out, his face flushed with anger. The young girl at his side dropped her eyes when she saw Ashley and Virginia.

'Damn him to hell,' muttered the youngster. 'We'll have our own party.'

His short blond hair clung to his scalp in tight waves and his eyes were those of a cat: clear, cold and yellow. Virginia shivered as he looked at her blankly. She turned to watch them walk into the grounds of St Margaret's Church.

'That old church must have some stories,' Virginia said. 'It has towered over the village for a thousand years.'

'And had its churchyard walls used as a cache for smugglers' goods,' teased Ashley. He held open the door for Virginia, seated her at an old wooden table near the double-sided fireplace and walked across to the bar.

'What was that all about?' he asked as he watched the innkeeper pour a cider for Virginia.

'Trouble. There's always trouble when that young Bartholomew Faulconer from East Grinstead comes over.'

'Faulconer,' Ashley repeated. 'The doctor?'

'Yes, his father's a fine man. Brilliant plastic surgeon over at the Queen Victoria Hospital. Did sterling work on our airmen during the war.' He pushed a glass brimming with cider across the counter. 'Some say the docs used the burned pilots as guinea-pigs. Practising their skin grafts, as it were. I don't hold with that. They did damn fine work.'

The innkeeper turned to tap a pint of bitter for Ashley.

'But his son is a problem. Proper black sheep of the family,' he continued. 'He's been expelled from two schools. Drinking and impregnating the headmaster's daughter.' He polished the counter in wide sweeping circles. 'Some say it's because he can't live up to the high standards set by the doctor, I say he needs his backside whipped. His father is too busy to do it, and his mother can't handle him. They say the poor lady will never leave her wheelchair. Terrible riding accident that was. Terrible.'

Ashley and Virginia nodded in sympathy.

'Rumour says Faulconer is sending him out to Rhodesia. Apprentice to a white hunter.' The innkeeper grinned. 'Those wild animals will knock the cockiness out of him. Be too scared to open his mouth out there.'

'The girl?' queried Virginia. 'She looks very young.'

The innkeeper looked at her. The Killicks were an old and respected family in the area. He had known Virginia since she was a toddler. 'Has a different one every time I see him,' he answered, dropping the wet cloth on to a tin tray. 'And all of them young, babies. Bartholomew Faulconer likes them innocent and dewy-eyed.'

Virginia gave a small involuntary shudder. There were so many things she would have to teach her daughter. Laura would have to be warned about the Bartholomews of the world she might meet.

'He sounds dreadful,' she said as Ashley set down the beer and cider and pulled back an old black chair.

'Yes,' he answered, 'Faulconer certainly doesn't deserve a son like that. He's a wonderful man.'

'Is he the same surgeon who patched you up?' Virginia asked, sipping the pale-amber drink.

'Yes, the gallery of scars I exhibit are due to his artistic skill,' Ashley answered, wiping a moustache of white froth from his mouth and smacking his lips. Virginia knew that, though

41

the pelt of brown hair covering Ashley's chest and legs now hid most of the scars, Ashley was still conscious of his slight limp and the cicatrices which mapped his body.

She hesitated. He did not enjoy talking about either the part he played as a young pilot in the war or the months he had spent in hospital after his plane, wrapped in flames and smoke, fell from the sky. 'And now, what's it to be: pork pie or ploughman's lunch?'

Their pub lunch was a cheerful affair. Listening to Virginia laugh, Ashley was pleased that they had remained in London for counselling by her neurologist. Her depression seemed to have lifted and her anger at the disease had abated.

Replete and relaxed, they left the Cat and walked to the car. A fresh breeze was blowing across the ridge. Virginia buttoned her pink wool jacket and threw a shawl the colour of moon opals across her shoulders. Her flowered skirt flew around her legs and she bunched it up in her hands, holding it tight against her thighs.

Virginia looked across at the stubby tower and shingled spire of the church. 'You go on to Lyewood, Ashley. I'd like to walk home. The woods are so lovely at this time of the year.'

'But . . .'

'Please, I need some time alone before I tell Giles and Emma about my illness. I'll be back before Laura wakes. I won't be long,' she promised.

Ashley nodded. 'Be careful, the footpaths are muddy.'

'I'll be fine. I haven't lurched at all today. My balance is much better.' She waved, and he watched her walk, tall and steady, past the lych-gate. He knew that she avoided using that entrance to the churchyard because in earlier times corpses were laid out under the roofed gate to await burial.

Her skirt now flew out as she walked and it brushed the banks of daffodils dancing beside the pathway leading to the church.

Ashley turned to the Land Rover. He was satisfied that Virginia would find comfort in the stone church which had rested high on the ridge since the time of the Norman Conquest. She had been christened there, and her daughter would wear the Killick christening robe in the church before they left for the Seychelles.

Virginia sat on a small wooden chair in the church and absorbed the peace. Embedded in the thick walls was the boundless faith and homage paid by people through the ages.

Strengthened and refreshed, she walked down the aisle, then crossed to the little portrait brass of Ann Tree, put up in memory of a parishioner burned as a witch in the sixteenth century.

'Sorry, Ann Tree,' she said, apologizing for the credulity and ignorance which made her Saxon forefathers torture, hang and burn witches.

As a little girl she had been chilled by stories of witch-hunts in the Weald and for years had had nightmares about the women burned to death in East Grinstead's High Street. She still made a habit of touching the brass whenever she was in the church.

Before closing the heavy door behind her, she glanced back at the north wall. As her eyes traced the outline of the bricked-up doorway, she wondered if the same fear of witches and the devil had made her ancestors seal the north entrance to the church.

On impulse she threaded her way through the tilted grave-stones, scattered like playing cards beneath the spreading branches of the dark-green yew tree. She stepped out on to a path, and suddenly the ground dropped precipitously. Valleys, farms and woodlands spread out like a green-and-brown patch-work quilt, edged with blue where the distant downs met the sky. Virginia stood, entranced, her arms folded across her chest.

On the horizon she picked out the dip in the downs, which hid Cuckmere Haven, where the Germans were supposed to have landed in 1940. Her thoughts wandered back to the war years . . . a time when she was young and healthy.

'No, please don't. No, I really don't want to.'

Virginia started. The girl's voice pulled her back from her daydreams; it seemed to come from beneath her. She moved forward a few feet and peered down the slope. A sudden movement in the deep shade of a hedge caught and held her attention. She leaned out over the drop just as a green canvas shoe lashed out, clipping an empty wine bottle which rolled down the grassy slope.

'Oh, yes, you do. You've teased me all damn morning. Now let's see what you've got.'

'No!' The girl's shriek was quickly muffled.

Virginia looked around for help, but the churchyard was deserted. She ran down the ridge, trying to see what was happening, but the couple were shielded by the dense green thicket. Unable to bear the sound of scuffling and hoarse panting, she shouted, 'Hey there!'

There was an immediate silence. A blond head moved into the sunlight and a pair of mocking yellow eyes stared up at her. She started; it was young Faulconer. Watching her, alert and wary, he ran his fingers over the front of his trousers and tugged up the zip.

'I thought I heard someone in trouble,' she said, gesticulating helplessly.

He relaxed and stood, legs astride, with his hands on his hips. He ran his eyes arrogantly over her body. Suddenly she was intensely aware of her skirt blowing between her legs, outlining her figure. As she struggled to control the flying panels, his eyes remained on her, cool and calculating. His lower lip was full and sensual. He pouted and ran his tongue insolently across the pinkness.

'This is none of your business, old lady.'

Virginia's natural politeness vanished. 'I demand to see the girl I heard. Come out, don't be afraid of him,' she called. Nothing moved. 'I'm not leaving until I've spoken to you.'

The bushes parted and the girl stood up. Her hair was garlanded with leaves and twigs and her blouse was incorrectly buttoned. She brushed at her skirt, finding relief in not having to look up at the ridge.

'Are you all right?' Virginia asked. 'You can come with me; I'll take you home. You don't have to stay here.'

The girl shook her head and scuffed at the lime-green grass with her shoe.

Virginia was insistent. 'I heard you call. You sounded upset. Let me help you.'

The girl shook her head again and edged behind the boy. He smiled at Virginia, a mocking, knowing smile. He bent his head and whispered something in the girl's ear. She slipped back into the deep shadow of the hedge.

'You're disgusting.' Virginia's voice quivered with anger.

Not deigning to answer, he followed the girl. At the hedge he stopped, turned, and deliberately unzipped his pants before crawling into the thicket.

The undulating downs swam in front of Virginia. She bit her lip, determined not to let the tears of rage and frustration flow. 'Bartholomew Faulconer,' she muttered, 'I hope the African bush gives you nightmares to plague you for the rest of your life.'

Her heart thudded as she started her walk up to the church, and she forced herself to pause at the wooden bench and read the inscription fixed to the stone wall:

'Friend looking out on this wide Sussex view
Know that they who rest here, looked and loved it too
Pray like them to sleep life's labour past . . .'

Virginia stopped reading. She had always found the words restful, but now they depressed her; she did not want to be reminded of death. Walking slowly, she set out across the fields and woods to Lyewood.

In the thick hedge the girl was quiet and compliant. The fear of being taken home to her parents by the angry blonde woman stifled all her pleas.

Bartholomew Faulconer, panting and triumphant, added another trophy to his list of conquests.

45

A wave of dark crinkled hair brushed the baby's nose and face. Her hands beat the air and her tiny fingers scrabbled to catch and hold the tickling strands. Laura gurgled and chortled with delight as the hair swept across her face again. Suddenly Emma shrieked as Laura snatched a handful of hair and tugged.

'You're becoming too clever, little Tanith,' she admonished, gently opening Laura's fingers and disentangling her hair. 'That hurt.' Laura made soft baby noises and gave Emma a toothless smile. 'I know, it was my own fault for tickling you,' she admitted. 'Now let's concentrate on having you dry and sweet-smelling again.'

She held the baby's feet firmly in one hand, lifted her and shook clouds of white talcum powder over her bottom before pinning her into a clean nappy.

'You'll be a beautiful little witch,' she breathed, as she picked Laura up and kissed the top of her head. She felt the thin patch of scalp beneath her lips and her eyes filled with tears as she held Laura close to her. 'You're mine and I'll never let anyone harm you,' she promised. 'I'll always be there to protect you. That blond man will never come near you.'

'What blond man?'

Emma gasped and spun around. She had not heard Virginia walk into the room. She held Laura tightly and stared at her sister-in-law, speechless. Virginia held out her arms for her child. Reluctantly Emma handed her the baby. Her fingers still caressed Laura's delicate toes. Her touch was the umbilical cord, a thread linking her to Laura. Nervously she straightened the baby's toes, only to have them curl up, as tight as pink shrimps. Virginia waited for her to answer.

'Where's my lovely girl?' A deep voice broke the uneasy silence.

Emma looked up with relief as Ashley strode into the room and put his arms round Virginia and Laura.

'My two beautiful girls,' he said as he hugged them. 'She's

46

exquisite,' he boasted, kissing Laura's cheek. 'Here, Emma, these are for you,' he added, handing her the spray of peacock feathers. 'To bring you more luck.'

'They are beautiful, thank you.'

'No, we must thank you for looking after Laura so well.' He flashed Emma a smile then turned his attention back to his daughter. 'I swear she's grown at least three inches, probably more. And,' he said, taking her from Virginia, 'she weighs a ton. What have you been fattening her up on, Emma?' he teased. 'Must be the stuff Giles uses for his geese!' He swung Laura up into the air over his head.

Emma stroked the peacock's tail feathers across her cheeks, and it seemed as if the feathered eyes patterned on the tips closed and opened with the movement. She did not answer but watched Virginia apprehensively.

Laura squealed and dribbled down Ashley's cotton shirt, and he loved his baby daughter.

'Hasn't Emma done a wonderful job of looking after Laura?' he asked Virginia, as he again lifted the baby high over his head, delighting in her gurgles.

'Yes,' she answered shortly, 'but Emma was just going to tell me about a blond man when you arrived.' She turned to face Emma who was screwing the cap on the tin of talcum powder. 'Weren't you, Emma?'

Ashley gave Laura to Virginia and pulled up a bentwood rocking chair with his foot. 'Sit here with Laura,' he said, noticing his wife's pale face. 'I think the walk home tired you a little.' Satisfied that Virginia was safely seated, he stood behind her. 'Am I allowed to hear the story?' he joked. 'Or is this for girls only?'

'It's nothing, really,' said Emma, trying to evade the question.

'Nothing,' Virginia echoed. 'When it concerns my baby, it is certainly not "nothing".'

'Laura?' Ashley queried, suddenly paying attention. 'What's this about, Emma?'

Emma capitulated. 'You don't believe in scrying, so you won't believe this,' she said.

'Your magic ball again,' said Virginia sharply. 'That hocus-pocus. This is something you saw in your crystal?'

Ashley squeezed Virginia's shoulder, silencing her.

'Yes,' Emma answered quietly. 'It happened a few days ago. Laura had just fallen asleep. She was still holding my finger. I stood watching her, afraid to remove my finger too soon and awaken her.' Emma looked at Ashley, willing him to understand. The silence in the room deepened.

'Go on, Emma,' said Ashley gently.

'Suddenly I had this dreadful foreboding that Laura was in danger. As I stood beside her crib the feeling grew stronger.'

Virginia kissed her baby's little tip-tilted nose and held her close to her body.

'I had to find out more about this sickening feeling, so I ran down to my room. At first my crystal was clouded and I saw nothing. Then misty but unrecognizable shapes swirled on the surface.'

Virginia sniffed. Emma looked at her sister-in-law, but her head was bent over Laura and a curtain of silver-blonde hair hid her face.

'Then I saw him.'

Virginia looked up quickly. Emma's voice had dropped and her wide green eyes glazed and darkened as she relived the event. Virginia lifted her hand and Ashley caught and held it.

'He looked at me over Laura's shoulder. It was Laura. Even though I only glimpsed her face, I knew her. She was a young woman. Her hair swung down her back and brushed the hem of her blue-and-white-striped shorts. She was looking up at him, laughing. Her arms were round his neck.' Emma bit her lower lip. 'She looked so beautiful, so innocent.' Emma's voice was now barely a whisper, and Virginia held her breath, straining to hear. 'He was older than her. A powerfully built man. His hair was yellow and tight waves writhed across his head. It could mean that his hair is waved or that he and Laura were near waves. The sea perhaps.' Emma clenched her hands and her breathing quickened. 'But his eyes. Cold, merciless eyes. Eyes the yellow of a harvest moon. They knew me and mocked me.'

Virginia shifted uneasily in her rocking-chair and it creaked softly.

'He took her. He swung her up into his arms. Laura went with him.' Emma paused. 'The mirror clouded and only his luminous cat's eyes leered at me. Then they, too, were gone. I was left with a cold sense of loss. Not death, but great change.'

The sound of heavy footsteps pounding up the oak staircase saved them from replying, and with relief Ashley and Virginia turned to greet Giles as he swung into the nursery.

'Welcome home.' His deep voice boomed across the room, restoring the air of normality. 'One of my men working in Sweet Briar meadow saw the Land Rover and alerted me. Damn good excuse for a late tea-break.' He turned to Emma and swatted her lightly across the buttocks. 'Please make us a strong pot of tea? Add some scones or muffins. We'll join you in the library.'

Emma smiled. 'I'll bring Laura's bottle as well.' She left the room, thankful for the excuse to escape.

'It's good to have you back, sister mine,' Giles said. As he bent down to kiss Virginia, a pair of baby hands seized the opportunity and dug into his beard with surprising strength. 'Hey, wrestler,' he protested as Virginia freed him. 'I'll have to shave it off if you keep pulling it out in patches.' He clucked Laura under the chin and studied Virginia. 'What's wrong?' he asked, sensing the tension in the room.

Virginia was silent.

'What's happened, Ashley?' he demanded.

'It's Emma,' said Virginia. 'She's been playing around with her crystal again and now she is predicting an unpleasant liaison for Laura.' Virginia put her hand on her brother's arm and looked up at him, her grey eyes wide and appealing. 'Can't you make her stop, Giles? All this magic with herbs and mirrors makes me uneasy.'

Giles ran his fingers through his beard. Answers and excuses raced through his mind as wildly as foxes running before hounds.

'Perhaps it's your book, Giles,' said Ashley. 'Perhaps all your research on witchcraft and magic is influencing Emma.

Women do seem to be more susceptible to these things than men.'

'No,' Giles answered, sitting down heavily on the edge of the bed. 'No, Ashley, women have always been strong.'

He tried to explain to Ashley that, until the advent of Christianity, society had been largely matriarchal and matrilinear. He wanted his brother-in-law to understand that when the goddess, the Priestess, ruled, women embodied all the mystery of Life and its magic.

Virginia started to speak but Giles held up his hand, not wanting to be interrupted.

'They interpreted dreams, knew all about herbs, were queens and warriors, settled disputes in law and were all-powerful. They listened to the subconscious.' He paused. 'That was until the conscious mind gained power and men became dominant.' He reached across and took Virginia's hand. 'Emma is not influenced by my book. She identifies with the Earth Mother and is merely using half-forgotten skills. Don't let her scrying scare you. Emma adores Laura and is sensitive to anything that could harm her.'

Giles's strong fingers stroked her hand and she started to relax.

'Witchcraft scares me, Giles,' she said. 'Lifting the ban on it in 'fifty-one was not a good idea. We also have it in the Seychelles: a form of voodoo. It seems so barbaric.'

'Little sister,' he said, 'witchcraft is as old as man.' He did not want to bore Virginia by explaining that witchcraft had been called devil-worship and was driven underground during the Piscean age when male-dominated monotheism held sway. 'The rites are pagan but not evil. You know the saying, "The gods of the old religions become devils of the new." Witchcraft is the Craft of the Wise.'

'What about black witchcraft and blood sacrifice?' asked Ashley, who had been listening to Giles with great interest. 'I'd call that evil.'

'Right,' agreed Giles. 'It's a perversion. Just as we have murderers and rapists, so we have those who pervert the rituals and deal with dangerous powers.'

'Do you truly believe that there are unseen powers which can be called upon and used?' Ashley asked incredulously.

Giles was about to tell Ashley that in the approaching age of humanism, the age of Aquarius, more and more people would turn to the worship of the god and goddess of Life and Fertility, when Emma's voice rang out.

'Tea's ready.' She rang a silver bell at the foot of the stairs. 'And Laura's milk is getting cold. Come on down.'

'Witchcraft is a fascinating subject,' said Giles, 'but I think we ought to take young Laura for her feed.'

He bent over Virginia, and Laura reached up immediately for his beard.

'Not again,' he laughed, keeping his chin out of her grasp.

Ashley helped Virginia out of her chair and she leaned against him for a few moments.

'I'd like to continue our talk,' said Ashley as Giles led the way downstairs with Laura in his arms.

'We will, but first let me tell you what this young wrestler did last Sunday.' Giles regaled his sister and Ashley with stories of the baby's achievements as they walked down to the library. Witchcraft was forgotten.

'These are delicious,' said Ashley, piling strawberry jam and dollops of farm cream on to a scone. 'You really are a good cook, Emma.' Emma nodded her appreciation and placed another warm scone on his plate.

'Now,' said Giles, easing his large frame into a green leather chair, the armrest polished cream with age, 'what do those boffins in London have to say about your illness?' He stirred his tea, waiting for the sugar to dissolve. 'Just fatigue due to the birth, wasn't it?'

'No,' Virginia answered, holding Laura over her shoulder, patting up wind. 'That wasn't the neurologist's diagnosis.' She looked into her brother's deep-set brown eyes. 'I have multiple sclerosis. It's painless, but there is no cure.'

Giles dropped the teaspoon and it lay, unheeded, on the rich red-and-blue pile of the Persian carpet.

Emma froze, the teapot suspended in mid-air. 'No cure!' Suddenly she caught the heavy scent of elderflowers and incense in the air, and she felt the puppy, soft and warm, under her hands. Virginia would die and Laura would be hers. Keeping her face expressionless, she turned away from the tea-tray and looked at Virginia.

'You need a second opinion,' declared Giles, as he listened to Ashley plot the disease's possible course.

'This neurologist *is* the second opinion,' said Virginia.

'But why has it taken so long to diagnose?' asked Giles.

'Because the disease developed so slowly. We have to accept the diagnosis, Giles, and pray for long remissions.' Virginia stood up and walked over to her sister-in-law. 'I'm feeling fine now,' she added. 'In fact, much better than I've felt in ages.' She lifted Laura from her shoulder and wiped the milky curds from her mouth. 'Here, Emma,' she said, 'would you like to give Laura the rest of her bottle?'

'I'd love to,' replied Emma, surprised, 'and I'm so sorry to hear of the diagnosis, Virginia.'

'I know you are. Thank you.'

Ashley smiled his approbation at Virginia. 'The good news,' he said, 'is that we'll be here until the end of the year. Virginia needs to see the neurologist every month or so.'

Giles smiled widely. 'That's wonderful. I'll be able to teach our young wrestler to ride. I have a pony which we'll break in for her.'

Virginia laughed, a clear, infectious sound. 'Oh, Giles, she'll only be taking her first steps at the end of the year, and you want to make a horsewoman out of her. Ashley wants to take her fishing and scuba-diving. If Laura knew what you were planning, she'd remain a baby for ever.'

'Well,' said Giles, 'perhaps we'll start with a puppy. We have one which is being reared with the kittens. It'll be perfect for her.'

Emma bent her head over Laura and fiddled with the teat on the bottle. She would have to find a very good excuse for the puppy's disappearance. Giles was not an easy man to fool.

Virginia looked at Laura and her heart ached as she watched

52

Emma wiggle the teat into the baby's mouth. She was still a little bemused with the gift she had been given so late in life. Now that her disease had been diagnosed she knew she had to teach her child independence; she had to prepare Laura to face life without a mother.

Grant me enough time to see my daughter grow into a woman, she prayed silently. Let me teach and protect her. Please. She bent over her baby as she lay in Emma's arms. Laura's violet-blue eyes widened and she smiled at her mother, letting the milk dribble down her embroidered bib. Virginia inhaled the warm milky smell of her daughter, and her heart squeezed tight as she kissed her.

CHAPTER TWO

The Seychelles
1966

 I

The tropical sunlight lay like shattered glass on the turquoise waves. White fairy terns hung, as if suspended from a child's mobile, above the water; the sea painted their pearl chests azure, and their enormous black eyes restlessly probed the depths for fish.

Laura exploded from the water, sleek as a flying fish. Her long hair, silvered by the sun, clung to her body. She rubbed the water from her eyes and waved to Virginia sitting in the shade of a hugh takamaka tree. Then, with a strong kick of flippered feet, she was gone. The waves lapped against the wooden jetty monotonously and the heavy midday silence was broken only by the loud twanging call of the fairy terns.

Virginia sighed and lifted her hair from the nape of her neck. Even though it was winter in the tropics and the south-easterly trades were blowing cooler and drier air across the islands, she still found the humidity enervating. She wiped her moist fingers on her cotton print dress.

The intense heat and high humidity of the recent Seychelles summer had made her realize that she could no longer look after Laura without help. She had enjoyed six years' remission, probably helped by the relaxed life she led in the islands. But multiple sclerosis, predatory as a silent shark, had struck again. When Ashley returned from Aldabra, where he had joined a team of scientific observers from London to debate the fate of the island, a stranger would enter their household: a housekeeper. Virginia watched the crystal-clear water swirl over the spot where Laura had dived and she blinked away tears of self-pity.

'Stop it,' she whispered to herself. 'You're being feeble. You've had Laura to yourself for five wonderful years. You've taught her to swim and dive, and now that you can't join her, you're going to make her miserable by crying.'

'Sign of old age,' said Ashley creeping up behind her gaily striped deck-chair. 'Talking to yourself at midday is a sure sign of senility.'

He bent down and kissed Virginia, studying her face carefully for any sign of pain. He tactfully ignored her tear-filled eyes, which she quickly blinkered behind dark sun-glasses. Ashley admired her independence and courage; he was stunned and relieved that she had not become embittered by the debilitating disease.

Virginia smiled at him as he sprawled on the grass beside her chair. 'I didn't expect you home so soon.'

'I missed you and Laura,' he confessed. 'I've only been away for a couple of weeks and it seems like months.'

She leaned over and kissed him, enjoying the roughness of his unshaven chin on her skin.

Ashley squinted in the bright sun as he looked for the familiar hump-back island of Silhouette. 'Coming back to Mahé from Aldabra is like arriving in London from West Hoathly,' he said. His gaze moved to where Praslin, the mythical Garden of Eden, lay like an ink-blot on the horizon.

'We went straight into a meeting. It was as noisy as a local fish-market. Luckily I was able to sneak out. Everyone was shouting and no one was listening. A typical exchange between scientific and government bodies.'

Virginia listened to him intently.

Ashley broke off a blade of grass and chewed at it thoughtfully as he marshalled his thoughts. He admired Virginia's intelligence and enjoyed discussing his work with her. After the war they had gone up to Cambridge together, where they had spent three wonderful, carefree years. She read modern languages and Ashley obtained a double first in the geographical tripos. He had continued and obtained his Ph.D. with a thesis on coral reef communities in the Seychelles. He was now a leader in the field of tropical island ecology.

Ashley had first visited the islands, scattered over twelve hundred kilometres of ocean, when he was a teenager and his parents were farming in Kenya. Their beauty had claimed him instantly and there had never been any question as to where he would settle once he obtained his doctorate.

Virginia had settled into being Mrs Ashley Challoner, but she played an active part in his field studies. She read extensively and was able to understand his research.

Recently, feeling that her stumbling walk on the islands was delaying Ashley's work, she had devoted more of her energies to filing and doing secretarial work for him.

Virginia stroked the thick bleached hair on Ashley's forearm and waited for him to continue.

Ashley was happy with the outcome of the fact-finding mission to Aldabra. Some of the scientific observers had been sea-sick and miserable on the two-week sailing trip down to the island, but he knew they would have a strong case to present to the Royal Society when they returned to England. Apart from realizing the ecological importance of Aldabra, they had also discovered that when the new British colony of the Seychelles had been created the previous year and Britain had annexed the outlying islands of Aldabra, Desroches and Farquhar, the British Ministry of Defence already had plans to use the islands for strategic defence; they planned to build an army base and a concrete runway on Aldabra. This disclosure had not surprised Ashley; he knew that there were usually hidden factors in moves made by governments, and most of them were bone-headed about conservation.

The observers were hoping that when the Society realized that Aldabra and Galapagos were the only two places in the world which had wild giant tortoises, and that Darwin was one of the scientists who pleaded for their preservation, almost a hundred years ago, they would protect Aldabra.

Ashley hoped that the Royal Society would lodge a strong

protest with the Ministry of Defence. He knew that the Ministry dared not ignore a report from so august a body.

Ashley covered Virginia's hand with his and started to describe the expedition. 'I wish you'd been with us, Fody. At one stage I thought the dejected scientific team was going to hand the island over to the British Ministry of Defence. They decided that the only thing the forsaken island was any good for was a military air base.'

He explained how they had arrived at Aldabra at low tide. The lagoon, large enough to accommodate the whole island of Mahé, had been sucked almost dry and lay baking in the sun. The team saw the pitted limestone rocks looking as delicate as lace, but they soon discovered they were as sharp as razors. He described how their enthusiasm for the island waned visibly as they watched the sharks' fins cutting along the overhung-cliff coast line.

'Needless to say, we told them heavily embroidered stories about early sailors who were shipwrecked on the southern part of Aldabra and who drank tortoises' urine to survive,' he said.

'Oh, no,' laughed Virginia. 'That must have nauseated them. You're impossible,' she scolded. 'You were supposed to be showing them how beautiful the island and lagoon are, not how dreadful.'

Ashley's pale eyes sparkled with amusement and he coloured the story, happy to see Virginia so interested and laughing.

He described how the scientific observers fought their way through the almost impenetrable *pemphis acidula* bush as they limped over the rocks. She rocked with laughter as he painted pictures of the team tiptoeing round huge robber crabs at night and having to sweep away wild ants before using the toilet. She listened intently as Ashley described the expedition's exploration of the immense lagoon, freckled with tree-crowned islets. They were both passionately committed to the preservation of the magnificent coral-capped island; the thought of its unique wildlife being destroyed sickened them.

She was delighted to hear that the observers' judgement changed once they saw the tortoises and studied the figures of biomass per square kilometre in relation to the plant life. 'When they realized that the remote and hostile island had more living creatures per kilometre then anywhere else on the whole African continent, they were converted.'

Ashley folded his arms across Virginia's knees and rested his head on them.

'They'll fight for Aldabra, Virginia, I'm sure of it,' he said. 'The Society is powerful, and when it speaks the world pays attention.'

Virginia ran her fingers across his forehead, wiping away the beads of perspiration. She had her reservations. She knew that if the Ministry of Defence lost the fight to build an airbase on Aldabra, their East of Suez defence policy would be jeopardized. They needed this semi-circle of three islands.

'It'll mean an acrimonious end to this year and a lot of infighting in nineteen sixty-seven,' she prophesied. ''Sixty-seven will be an interesting and in some ways a very strange year.' Ashley lifted his head at the tone of her voice. 'We'll have new people in our home and I'll have to learn to share Laura,' she explained.

'Daddy, Daddy, you're home!'

Ashley squeezed Virginia's hand, swung around and opened his arms wide to greet his daughter. She pounded along the wooden jetty, her mask and snorkel banging against her sun-tanned legs as she ran. Dropping her blue flippers on the grass, she hurled herself into his arms.

'Oh, I'm so pleased you're back. I missed you so much,' she said as she covered his face with cold, wet kisses.

'And I missed you, Muffin,' he answered, hugging her tightly, salt water soaking his khaki shirt and shorts.

'Guess what, Daddy. I've just seen a butterfly fish.'

'With orange marks on its flanks?' Ashley teased.

'No, silly,' she answered. 'That's the lined surgeon fish. Mine had black spots on its fin.'

'Clever girl,' he said, wringing the salt water from her hair.

Virginia studied the two faces. Their eyes, Laura's dreaming and filled with wonder, Ashley's piercing and mesmeric, reflected the clear, light blue of the sea they both loved.

'Daddy,' Laura played Eskimo kisses and rubbed her nose against Ashley's prominent one, 'come swimming with me. I think I saw a lion fish, but I'm not allowed to go near them unless you or Mummy are with me. So please come. He was huge.'

'Muffin,' Ashley admonished. 'Are you telling stories again? You know that we don't do that in this family.'

Laura hung her head and laced her fingers. 'Maybe it wasn't one,' she answered, 'but I do want you to come swimming. Please.'

Ashley hugged his leggy six-year-old and wrapped a lime-green and yellow towel round her shoulders. 'Later,' he promised. 'It's lunch-time now and we're expecting a visitor. You run up to the house and shower. Mummy and I'll join you.'

Laura didn't argue. She adored her father, who laughed and teased her, but she knew there was a line which could not be crossed. ''Bye,' she called as she ran lightly up the steps hewn into the huge granite boulders leading up to the house.

'She's more seal than child. She'd sleep in the sea if she could,' Ashley joked as he watched Laura run across the wooden verandah surrounding the old-style plantation house.

'As Emma says, she's a Pisces, a fish, an old soul.'

'Old soul? Is Emma being spooky again?' he teased.

'According to Emma, the Fish is the twelfth sign, a mixture of everything that has gone before. Laura has lived many lives, and that gives her an inner serenity and tranquillity.'

'I suppose Emma would also blame the Fish for Laura's daydreaming, and her habit of embellishing the truth,' mocked Ashley.

'Laura is a gentle, sentimental child.' said Virginia, springing to her daughter's defence, 'and you idolize her.'

'I love both of my women.' Ashley helped her to her feet and handed her a slim, hickory walking stick. 'And after lunch we've to meet the new recruits to our Seychelles family.'

Virginia paused in the shade of the enormous takamaka, a giant which had escaped the axes of the boat-builders. Its spreading branches were streaked white by the roosting terns and its leathery leaves shone dark green in the sun. 'Tell me about them,' she said, glad of the opportunity to postpone the climb up the steps, now baking in the midday sun.

'Both Nicole Daumier and the young boy she mothers, Pierre Payet, have long and very interesting histories.'

'I'd like to know more about her background before we meet,' said Virginia. 'And Pierre Payet,' she added, 'as he'll be living close to Laura.'

'Nicole first. Do we start from the very beginning?' Ashley queried, setting the straw hat on Virginia's head before leading her into the sun.

'How far back is the beginning?' she asked.

'About eighteen hundred and seventy-two.'

Virginia looked at the steps stretching ahead of her. 'Start talking,' she said.

Ashley led Virginia back to 1815 when the Treaty of Vienna ended the Napoleonic Wars. The Seychelles was then declared a British colony, administered by Mauritius, a French island which had fallen to the British ten years earlier. He reminded her that when the British blockaded Mauritius in order to prevent the corsairs raiding British merchant ships, many of the Mauritian planters moved to the Seychelles and set up thriving cotton plantations.

Virginia nodded. Ashley spoke well and she enjoyed listening to him.

'Remember also that, eight years before the treaty, all slave trade had been abolished in British colonies.'

'The slave traders ignored the edict, and the trade continued, especially in the Indian Ocean islands,' Virginia interjected. 'The Seychelles was an ideal port of call for slavers from the African mainland.'

'Who's telling this story?' Ashley enquired, leaning against a boulder and giving Virginia a short rest.

'You, but I'm helping,' Virginia answered, leaning heavily on her walking stick.

Ashley shook his head in mock indignation and tucked her arm into his.

He went on to explain that at that time there were almost seven hundred 'free men' in the Seychelles and over six thousand

60

slaves. The majority of the Seychellois were of African descent. He enjoyed talking about the early days in the islands and he led Virginia through the next four decades, when British ships still sailed the Indian Ocean freeing slaves. All the human cargo found on slave ships sailing north of the equator went to Aden while those found south of the equator were taken to the Seychelles.

'Ah-ha,' said Virginia as Ashley paused in his narrative, 'we're getting closer to the magical eighteen hundred and seventy-two where your story was supposed to start.'

'You would break a storyteller's heart,' said Ashley. He explained that in that same year a British ship released two and a half thousand slaves from Arab dhows. They were apprenticed to coconut plantation owners in the Seychelles – a freedom he considered dubious.

Among the freed African slaves was a young and very beautiful girl of Indian descent, who was employed by a Mauritian plantation owner.

'I thought we were talking about the Seychelles,' Virginia interjected.

'We are. But as I've just told you, Fody, most of the early colonists were from Mauritius. Now let's continue. The lusty Frenchman put this eastern flower to work in his home, and when she turned sixteen be bedded her.'

'Typical male,' teased Virginia, mentally counting the steps still to be climbed.

'She gave him six sons, and at the age of forty-five she gave birth to an exquisite daughter.'

'Women in their forties always produce beautiful daughters,' boasted Virginia. 'Look at Laura.'

Ashley laughed. 'Stop being immodest and listen.' Realizing that the Frenchman's daughter was Nicole Daumier, Virginia listened intently. Ashley painted a vivid picture of the wily old planter, who adored his only daughter. He outlined his dealings from the Second World War, when the price of copra dropped, and the planter went into the production of patchouli oil, cornering part of the Indonesian market. When that collapsed, his daughter was sixteen, but by then he was raping the outlying

61

islands of guano. This paid for his daughter both to be schooled in England and to complete a secretarial course in Paris. Ashley unwound the story of the lovely young girl of Indian/French extraction who returned to the Seychelles from Paris and easily obtained a position in the British Embassy.

Ashley and Virginia reached the wide verandah, and Virginia collapsed thankfully into one of the sturdy chairs carved from the beautifully grained bois de noir.

Ashley fanned her tenderly with her straw hat. He then perched on the white verandah railings to finish his story.

'When our friends at the Embassy heard we were looking for an extremely competent secretary-cum-housekeeper, they suggested Nicole Daumier. I met her briefly before I left for Aldabra and I think she'll be perfect. If you like her,' he hastened to add.

'So,' Virginia mused, 'she speaks fluent French and English . . .'

'And Creole,' added Ashley.

'She can obviously do our secretarial work. Children?' Virginia queried. 'Was she married, does she have any children of her own? I know that she looks after Pierre, but if she's to look after Laura I must be certain that she loves children.'

The slatted wooden door leading into the house swung open and the Creole cook filled the opening. 'Lunch is ready. I've put it on the table under the bois de rose. There's wind on that side of the house.' She wiped her hands on her white apron. 'Laura is making fresh lime juice.' She turned to go. 'Oh, there's someone. Miss Daumier. She's in the small room.' She waddled across the verandah and lowered two of the bamboo blinds, filtering the harsh sunlight.

'Thank you,' Ashley said. 'Please ask Miss Daumier to come out here.'

The door slammed as the cook rolled back into the house.

'She may be abrupt and she certainly lacks social graces, but she's a wonderful cook,' Ashley said.

'Nicole Daumier,' Virginia said quickly. 'Children?'

Ashley was about to answer when a soft cough alerted him.

He stood up quickly, brushed the seat of his pants and held out his hand.

'Miss Daumier,' he said. 'I'd like you to meet my wife.'

Virginia did a quick inventory as the young woman walked towards her. About twenty-seven . . . twenty-eight years of age. Slim. A waist two hands could span. Skin unblemished and pale as milky tea, unusual in a tropical country. Hair a mass of wild, dark waves held back with a tangerine scarf. Hands, delicate with long expressive fingers. Her face a perfect oval with a firm dimpled chin.

'Mrs Challoner,' she greeted, lilting the name with a slight French accent.

Virginia looked up into eyes the spectacular steel blue of a winter sea. Heavy black lashes swept down and meshed at the corners of her eyes. Beautiful. This young woman is too beautiful, she thought.

Suddenly, aware that she was staring, she sat up in the chair and smoothed her creased cotton dress over her knees. 'Miss Daumier. I'm very pleased to meet you,' she said. 'My husband has been telling me a little of your background.'

'Yes,' the young woman smiled. 'I overheard your question about children.'

Virginia felt herself flush.

'I'd like to answer it,' Nicole Daumier continued as she accepted the chair Ashley pushed forward. 'I'm unmarried and happy. I have friends but no special boyfriend.' She leaned towards Virginia. 'Children. I have none of my own, but I do have a twelve-, well, almost thirteen-year-old boy. I look upon him as a son and sometimes as a young brother.'

'Excuse me,' said Ashley, bounding across the verandah. Laura was walking towards them, biting the tip of her tongue as she concentrated on balancing a heavy wooden tray. The glasses, brimming with pale-green lime juice, clinked as she walked. 'Here, Muffin, let me have that,' Ashley said, placing the tray on a low cane table.

'I put two spoons of sugar in your glass, Daddy, and three in Mummy's. Cook says she needs feeding up,' she explained.

Virginia laughed. 'Thank you, Laura. Now come and meet Miss Daumier.'

Laura moved forward a few steps, tucked her long blonde hair behind her ears and studied Nicole with the frank appraisal peculiar to young children.

Two wide smiles marked the end of the scrutiny. Ashley breathed a sigh of relief and Laura welcomed a new woman into her life.

'Mummy, may Miss Daumier stay for lunch?' asked Laura. 'We've tons of espadron and cook's friend brought a heart of palm, so we're having palmiste salad.'

'Certainly,' Virginia answered, surprised and pleased at Laura's quick acceptance of Nicole. 'If Miss Daumier likes smoked sailfish and salad she is welcome to join us.'

Sensing Nicole's hesitation, Laura hastened to explain. 'It's quite all right to have palmiste salad, Miss Daumier. Cook says that, even though they have to kill a palm tree to cut out the heart, new trees grow very quickly.'

'In that case I'd love to join you for lunch,' smiled Nicole.

She watched Virginia ease herself out of the chair but made no offer to help, sensing her need for independence. They walked slowly down the stone steps which swooped up to the verandah. Laura skipped across the lawn ahead of them.

Pale-lemon flowers drifted down from the spreading bois de rose like dust motes in a sunbeam; they patterned the white tablecloth and floated in the jug of fresh lime juice. Laura pulled back a wicker chair for her mother and carefully dusted the fallen flowers and heart-shaped leaves from the seat.

'Now, Miss Daumier,' Virginia said, heaping shredded white strips of palm heart on to Nicole's plate, 'Pierre Payet. I'd like to know something about him.'

Nicole looked at Laura. 'It's a very sad story,' she said. 'When I was fourteen, my father's closest friend and his wife were drowned. They were sailing from Praslin to Mahé. Pierre had been left behind with a friend on Praslin as they didn't want to take a tiny baby on the boat.'

Virginia clucked in sympathy and Laura stopped chewing to listen.

'Was it due to bad weather?' Ashley asked.

'It was in August at the height of the South-east Trades. But as you know the winds are never really very strong here and they were both good sailors . . . certainly good enough to handle a nine knot blow.'

'Was that the same year the *Mary Jane* went adrift?' asked Virginia. 'She was also sailing from Praslin to Mahé, wasn't she?'

'The same journey,' Ashley answered.

'My father's friends died the year before the *Mary Jane* disaster,' said Nicole. 'Two out of the eleven survived aboard the *Mary Jane*. Our friends' boat and bodies were never recovered.'

Laura gulped and her eyes were wide and liquid. Ashley put his hand over hers. Her full lower lip trembled.

'Chin up, Muffin,' he said. 'Pierre was well looked after. He grew up in the Daumier family and they all loved him.'

'My father naturally took Pierre into our home,' Nicole explained, smiling at Laura. 'My mother was getting old; giving birth to seven children had weakened her. I was the only daughter, so I looked after him. I loved having a baby to care for and Pierre grew up looking upon me as a mother and a sister. I missed him when I was overseas.' She paused as Ashley refilled her glass with fresh lime juice. 'When I returned to the Seychelles and applied for the job at the Embassy, Pierre left our family plantation on Praslin and came to live with me. Most of his friends are at the Seychelles College here. The arrangement works very well.' Nicole laid down her knife and fork and looked at Virginia. 'I would like to be part of a family again, Mrs Challoner. It would be good to combine my secretarial skills with looking after children and running a home, especially this home. La Retraite has to be one of the most beautiful old colonial plantation houses in the islands. I would love to live here. That's why I've . . .' She gave a small shrug and looked down at her plate.

Virginia looked at Ashley. A long thoughtful look. Then she turned her attention to Laura, who was chewing a strand of her long hair, her blue eyes fixed on Nicole. Virginia opened her mouth to remonstrate with her daughter. Chewing her hair was a nervous habit, one she hoped had been broken. Before she could speak, Laura stood up. 'Excuse me, please,' she said as she pushed back her chair and walked to her mother. She bent over Virginia with her back to Nicole. 'Mummy,' she said softly. 'Can Miss Daumier and Pierre come and stay with us? Please. I could go to school with him and he could share you and Daddy. He only has Miss Daumier, not a real family.'

Virginia sighed. Laura was so easily moved to pity. Even as a little girl she exhibited a strong desire to help those in trouble.

'I'd love a friend to play with,' she pleaded. She put her arms round her mother's neck and hugged her.

Virginia held her close. Laura had made the decision for her. 'Would you like to be the one to invite Miss Daumier to come and live here and work for us?' she asked.

Laura's unhappiness vanished with the suddenness of a tropical storm burnt away by the sun, and she turned to Nicole. The lunch passed quickly, with Virginia and Nicole discussing the care of Laura and the future running of the home. Ashley sat a little apart with Laura, telling her stories about the expedition to Aldabra. She was a precocious child and showed a grasp of ecology well beyond her years. He enjoyed explaining his work to her.

'It's late,' Nicole said, standing up. 'As I have the afternoon off, I promised to take Pierre to Beau Vallon. He loves the beach and the swimming is so good.' She looked at Laura, perched on Ashley's knee. 'Perhaps Laura would like to join us, Mrs Challoner,' she said.

Virginia smiled as Laura slid off her father's lap, ready to leave with Nicole. 'Virginia, not Mrs Challoner,' she said. 'You're to join our family at the end of the month. I think we can use Christian names.'

'Thank you,' Nicole said quietly.

'May I go with Nicole to fetch Pierre?' Laura pleaded. 'We could meet you and Daddy at Beau Vallon. Please, Mummy. Please say that we can all go to the beach.'

Virginia nodded. 'We'll park in the usual place under the takamaka trees. Behave yourself,' she warned.

'I will. Promise,' Laura said, as she skipped away with Nicole.

The sharp backfiring of a Mini-Moke and the loud roar of its engine told Virginia that Nicole and Laura had left.

Ashley returned from tucking Laura into Nicole's bright red car; he stood in the shade of the wide verandah, studying Virginia before joining her.

Her broad shoulders slumped and he ached for the woman he loved. He knew that by accepting Nicole she had finally acknowledged her increasing weakness and inability to perform the necessary daily tasks. She had opened her family to a stranger. Another woman would help care for her child. For a woman as independent as Virginia, it was a traumatic decision. She had conducted the interview with great self-control, allowing neither Laura nor Nicole to sense her unhappiness and feeling of defeat.

Now she had turned her chair away from the table and was crumbling bread for a dozen tiny barred ground doves. Trustingly they pecked the crumbs which had fallen on her sandalled feet, looking up at her with bright black eyes ringed by brilliant blue. Virginia smiled as a sparrow-sized Fody, sporting the remnants of bright red breeding plumage, flew on to the table, cocked his head to one side, studied her then pecked at the bread on her plate.

'Scruffy little blighter, isn't he?' said Ashley as he neared the table.

'And hopeful,' answered Virginia, grateful that her sunglasses masked her tears. 'Clinging to his red feathers this late in the season, hoping that some little female will find him irresistible.'

'I find you beautiful, my little Fody,' Ashley whispered, leaning over the back of her chair.

'Oh, Ashley,' she said in a small broken voice.

He wiped away a tear which had escaped from behind the dark plastic shield and trickled down her cheek.

'I know,' he said. 'I know.'

The compassion and love in his voice broke the defences she had built up so carefully and she turned, sobbing, into his arms.

As he held her and stroked her hair, sun-bleached to the dead silver-white of driftwood, his reserve crumbled and tears blurred the stark outlines of Silhouette and North Islands, floating on the horizon.

━━━━━►|◈|◈|◈| II |◈|◈|◈|◄━━━━━

Fingers of dark cloud smeared the sun as it dipped slowly into the ocean. The vivid scarlet and gold backdrop that had hung behind the humped shape of Silhouette dulled and the island faded into the dusk. Virginia patted one of the rounded granite boulders blocking the end of Beau Vallon beach.

''Bye, Whale Rock,' she said, running her finger along the crack which formed a smiling mouth in the dome-headed rock.

She and Laura had chosen the rock to mark the end of their two-mile walk along the crescent-shaped beach. They always ran the last hundred yards to win the honour of touching the rock first. Nowadays Laura walked slowly beside her mother, pretending nothing had changed. Virginia placed her palm in the indentation marking the whale's eye and she sighed. Today everything was different.

Laura had declined to come on the walk to Whale Rock, preferring to remain with her new friend, Pierre. She and Ashley had left them digging in the wet sand for tec-tecs. Laura loved the soup made on the island with these little clams. Nicole, slim and vibrant in a coral swimming costume, had remained with the children, offering to hold the plastic bag for the creamy shells.

'Come on, lazy-bones,' said Ashley watching Virginia run her hand over the rough granite surface. 'We'd better stop Laura collecting those clams and take her home or we'll be eating tec-tec soup for a fortnight.'

Virginia grinned, gave Whale Rock a final pat and started threading her way through the tumbled granite boulders. Suddenly she stopped. Ashley, who was following close behind in case she stumbled, bumped into her.

'Oops, sorry,' he apologized.

68

'That is all right. There is no need for an apology.'

The guttural German accent surprised Ashley, and he craned his head over Virginia's shoulder to see behind the rock. The reason for Virginia's abrupt halt was immediately apparent. Leaning back against the sun-baked boulder was a good-looking man in his late thirties. His naked muscular body glowed a deep brown in the rays of the setting sun and his dark pubic hairs and genitals were touched with gold. His eyes sparkled with amusement.

'A lovely day, is it not?' he said, clasping his hands behind his head.

'Ahem, yes. Yes, indeed,' Ashley answered. Virginia was silent, a wing of blonde hair screening her expression. 'Well, we must be going,' said Ashley as he nudged Virginia into leaving. 'Good-day,' he added, conscious of the man's gaze fixed on Virginia's long legs and slim boyish hips.

He managed to catch up with her and walk beside her as the maze of rocks opened on to the curved white beach.

'Well,' he said, breaking the silence. 'Not bad-looking, don't you think?'

Virginia looked at him, and the corners of her mouth twitched. 'I wouldn't know,' she answered, 'I didn't look at his face.'

Ashley was speechless, then he choked with laughter. 'You're impossible. Let's get you away from here immediately!' Ashley tucked her arm through his and, giggling, they walked slowly along the white beach. The pale, lingering light washed over the sea and it gleamed with the opalescence of a green snail shell.

'This must be one of the most beautiful places in the world,' said Virginia, as she waded through the tepid, nacreous water. 'I love these islands so much.' She gazed down the beach to where a few lights, faint as fireflies, revealed the Beach Hotel, tucked tightly into the fish-hook bend where sand gave way to scattered rocks.

'Everyone's dream of a tropical paradise,' agreed Ashley. 'Icing-sugar beaches, palms dripping with coconuts, crystal water . . .'

'Blue skies, hot golden sun, exotic fruit and wonderful Creole food,' added Virginia.

'An indolent lifestyle without feeling guilty,' said Ashley.

'No clothes,' quipped Virginia, and she collapsed with laughter at the look on Ashley's face.

'That nude Adonis has definitely affected you,' he teased.

'Well, only a costume and a beach wrap then. And on the outer islands, those can be dispensed with.'

'When do we visit the outer islands?' Ashley put his arm round Virginia's waist.

She pressed his hand over her stomach. Suddenly she longed for the return of those days when he would take the caress for an invitation and would whisk her into the thick veloutier shrubs lining the seashore. Hidden by the bright green leaves and ivory flowers, they would make love. Closing her eyes, she could feel the sand cool beneath her naked buttocks and see the broad leaves brushing Ashley's hair as he moved over her. She ached for him; but when he came to her now it was with the solicitous care of the healthy for the ill.

She rested her head on his shoulder for a moment then straightened as she recognized the three figures crawling on their hands and knees ahead of them. She scrunched the fine grains of sand tightly between her toes. Her laughter died as she watched Nicole untie the tangerine scarf from her hair and use it to bind Laura's wet hair away from her face.

Control yourself, Virginia Challoner, she admonished herself silently. You cannot and must not be jealous. Nicole and Pierre are here for Laura's good. She and Ashley are not responsible for your illness. They can't share your pain. Smile, girl, smile. She flicked her foot sideways in the shallow water and splashed Ashley's legs. Brace up, she said; pretend you're happy. That's all the future holds for you, pretence.

Ashley laughed and scooped up a handful of water which he trickled down her back, wetting the gaily printed cotton wrap tied round her waist.

'Mummy,' Laura shouted, looking up and recognizing them, as they laughed and splashed in the foamy fretwork of the waves. 'Just look at all the tec-tecs Nicole has in the bag.'

70

Virginia and Ashley made clucking sounds and looked suitably impressed.

'Pierre found most of them. He's really good.'

The lanky young teenager flushed. 'Not really,' he said, dancing the English words to a French rhythm. 'Laura is very quick, especially for a girl.'

Virginia waited for her daughter to react, but she looked up at her gangly new friend in frank admiration.

'Mummy,' she said, 'Nicole makes tec-tec a different way from Cook. She uses ginger. Can we all eat together tonight and then she can show Cook how to make proper soup?'

'I . . .' Nicole stopped, embarrassed by Laura's guileless condemnation of the cook.

'Certainly,' Virginia answered. 'We'd love you to join us.'

'After all,' Ashley said, 'you've spent hours collecting our dinner.'

Nicole smiled, and Virginia caught her breath. The girl was exquisite, a true creature of the islands. She knelt in the sand, looking up at them, and in the crepuscular light she was dainty and unearthly. An ethereal water-nymph. Virginia glanced quickly at Ashley. He was helping Laura knot the top of the bag of clams and was seemingly oblivious to Nicole's beauty. Virginia's shoulders softened and she relaxed.

Listening to Nicole and Virginia discussing the merits of spices in soups, Ashley also relaxed. The first day had been much easier than he had expected. He had been far from certain whether Virginia would accept one so young and so attractive to share the house with them. Nicole's vitality could only make Virginia more conscious of her own physical disabilities. He had watched Virginia covertly all afternoon and could detect no signs of antagonism or jealousy.

Laura accepted the bag of tec-tecs and ran across to show Virginia her hoard. Looking at his wife as she bent over her daughter, seeing the two blonde heads close together and hearing their laughter, he was filled with pain and railed silently against the unfairness of Fate.

Why Virginia? Why choose my wife? he raged.

71

'I think we've lost our daughter, Ashley,' Virginia called. 'She wants to leave with Nicole and Pierre.'

'Please, Daddy,' Laura wheedled, hugging him round the waist, her blue eyes dark and appealing in the dusk.

Ashley stroked her hair. 'Why don't you show Nicole and Pierre the guest cottage near the jetty which will be theirs at the end of the month? They can shower and change and then you and Pierre can help Cook wash the tec-tecs and Nicole can give Cook a lesson in the use of ginger,' Ashley teased. 'Mummy and I will come along later. When the soup is ready.'

'Goody. Thank you, Daddy.' Laura took Pierre's hand and pulled him towards the Mini-Moke. Pierre turned scarlet but did not attempt to disentangle his hand.

'Look after the girls, Pierre,' Ashley called, as they ran up the beach to where Nicole had parked the vehicle beneath the takamaka trees.

Pierre looked back over his shoulder. 'I will, sir,' he answered, proud to be put in charge.

'And now,' Ashley said, leading Virginia to where a pirogue was canted high up on the sand, 'as befits our age, let's sit here and count the stars before joining those restless youngsters.'

Virginia gave him a grateful smile and nestled up against the sun-warmed planks of the fishing boat. Ashley hung their towels over the sharp uplifted end and, favouring his weak leg, settled back against the black hull. The smell of dried fish and salt was strong. He felt for Virginia's hand and placed it in his lap. The soft slap of the rapidly darkening water on the sand and the twittering of fairy terns as they settled uncomfortably on the arched spines of the palm fronds soothed him and he closed his eyes.

Virginia sat quietly beside him, studying the man she loved.

'Ruled by Pluto he is,' Emma had declared on her last visit to the Seychelles. 'Ruler of the underworld, death and reincarnation. A complex birth sign with three symbols, the scorpion, the eagle and the serpent. Ancient astrologers called those born under the sign of Scorpio serpents.' Virginia had objected to having Ashley compared to a snake.

'He's strong and—'

72

'Strong and silent as the sea he loves,' Emma said.

'And intelligent,' Virginia continued, ignoring Emma's interruption.

'Intellect and emotion rule him,' Emma said. 'That calm mask of reserve he wears hides a brilliant mind.' She nodded to herself. 'A mind fascinated by ancient secrets and mysteries.'

'Just because he's interested in Giles's book on witchcraft doesn't mean that he's spellbound by the subject,' said Virginia, eager to dissociate Ashley from anything weird or ghostly.

Emma had bitten back her retort, remembering the many occasions when she had almost been unmasked by Ashley's penetrating questions. 'He's a man of contradictions and mystery,' she said.

Emma's words echoed in Virginia's mind as the darkness softened Ashley's strong profile and blurred his beaky nose.

'You're far away tonight, Fody,' said Ashley, suddenly conscious of his wife's appraisal.

Virginia started. 'I was thinking of Emma,' she answered.

'She hasn't been scaring you again with her horror stories, has she?' Ashley asked.

'No,' said Virginia hesitantly. 'But I'm sure she comes to visit us so often just to make sure that we haven't allowed any blond man near Laura. She dotes on the child.'

Ashley chuckled, a warm deep sound. 'Just as well Pierre's hair is nearly black, or he'd be a prime suspect.' Virginia laughed and wriggled her toes in the warm sand. 'I've never seen such a case of instant hero-worship,' Ashley continued. 'I'm afraid that Pierre Payet has acquired another shadow. Our daughter is fascinated by him.'

'There's about seven years' difference between them, isn't there?' Virginia mused. 'She'll probably drive the poor boy crazy. He'll fall over her every time he turns around.'

'I like him,' said Ashley. 'The poor chap's at the spindly age, where his arms and legs have outgrown his body.'

'He's certainly ungainly,' Virginia agreed. 'I usually don't like people with close-set eyes. But with his high cheekbones and crooked front teeth he's a strangely attractive boy.'

'He has an air of gentleness and concern which I like,' said Ashley, 'and he's very patient with Laura.'

'Well, she's advanced for her age,' Virginia said, eager to defend her offspring. 'Probably being an only child has made her more mature.' She stroked Ashley's arm, rubbing up the thick hair and making it bristle. 'I think he'll be good for her. I'm going to enjoy having another child in the house.'

Ashley leaned over and kissed her on the nape of her neck. The smell of sun-tan oil mingled with the clean tang of sea and his lips lingered on her warm skin. 'You're a very special woman,' he whispered. 'Very special.'

Virginia felt her throat constrict. It was becoming much easier to make Ashley believe that she was happy with the change in their lives.

Keep it up, girl, she said silently.

She squeezed Ashley's hand as they watched two fruit bats soar and dip like swirls of sea mist over their heads before returning to the dark depths of the takamaka trees.

'Two lucky ones who've missed the curry pot,' said Ashley.

'They say the meat's delicious,' Virginia strained to see where the bats had perched, 'but I could never eat them. Too much like munching rats.' She shivered.

'They're fine if you enjoy duck flesh laced with fish bones,' Ashley explained.

'Pierre,' she said, changing the subject. 'Tell me about his parents and grandparents. Do we know who they were?'

'If anything, Pierre's history is even more interesting than Nicole's.' Ashley glanced at the luminous dial of his watch. 'Good, I've time to tell you his story. We don't want to arrive home until Cook has calmed down. She's not going to take kindly to interference in the preparation of her tec-tec soup.'

'I can just see her jowls quivering,' laughed Virginia. 'Let's stay.'

'We go back even further in history for Pierre's story,' began Ashley.

'As the islands have a history of only about two hundred years, you ought to be finished well before dinner,' she said.

Ashley kissed her softly on the lips to quieten her.

He started his story with the first settlers in the Seychelles. They came from France and the French islands of Mauritius and Réunion, plus a sprinkling from India.

He described how Napoleon Bonaparte cleverly used the attempt on his life as an excuse to round up the most blood-thirsty revolutionaries in France and exile them to Mahé. Napoleon's 'Jacobin dogs' started to incite the African slaves to revolt, in order to take over the islands and gain their freedom.

Some of them also consorted with the slaves. The result of one of these liaisons was a lovely blue-eyed daughter who, at the age of sixteen, went to live with one of the most notorious corsairs in the islands.

'Oh, no,' Virginia broke in. 'I think you're trying to tell me something. Pierre Payet. These were his great- or should it be great-great-grandparents? Obviously pirates and revolutionaries made good bedfellows.'

Ashley grinned and held up his hand to silence her, then continued with his story. He explained how despite this corsair's frequent absences roaming the Indian Ocean and looting ships, he fathered eleven children before a British patrol boat finally sent him to his watery grave.

Ashley waited for Virginia's reaction when he told her that the pirate's one and only son then spent the corsair treasure on a coconut plantation and became a wealthy planter.

'Wise man,' Virginia said, unable to resist interrupting. 'Much safer than stealing on the high seas.'

'Wise he was,' Ashley agreed, running his fingers across the sand at the ghost crab which was facing him, waving its front legs in the air like a punch-drunk boxer. It stared at him stalk-eyed for a second and then raced sideways to its cone-shaped burrow, still boxing at him futilely.

Ashley picked up the story where the corsair's son was an old man of seventy and, much to the dismay of his children, sank the money made from the coconut plantation into the production of patchouli oil. The price of the oil suddenly soared and so did his standing with the family.

He then related how the man's son, Pierre's father, inherited the patchouli oil estate when the world prices were dropping.

Then came the tragedy: Pierre's father and mother were drowned. The year after their deaths there was a drastic slump in the demand for the fragrant oil and in 1954 patchouli oil production collapsed. The estate was sold and Pierre, the Payets' only child, remained with the Daumier family and Nicole.

'The poor boy,' said Virginia.

'A sad story,' Ashley agreed, 'but Pierre isn't poor. A trust was set up for him and there's enough to see him through school and university. Nicole tells me that he's studious and very bright.'

'So Laura's new friend has the blood of French revolutionaries and Indian Ocean pirates running strongly through his veins.' Virginia nodded.

'Tempered by the genes of his grandmother, a French schoolteacher from Bordeaux. His mother was schooled in France and was also a teacher.'

Ashley fanned his foot towards the crab, which promptly snapped its legs close to its body and slid into its volcano-shaped retreat.

Satisfied that he had won the territorial dispute with the ghost crab, Ashley stood up. He dusted the sand, thick as cinnamon powder, from his hairy legs and held out his hand to Virginia.

She struggled to her feet and leaned over the pirogue, pretending to examine its ends hewn from solid tree-trunks. Suddenly Ashley spun away from her and ran down the beach towards the water.

'Ashley,' she called. 'Leave that poor crab alone. You'll probably trample on it in the dark.'

'He's challenging me. Look at him. He wants at least five rounds in the ring.' The crab's front claws, like pale-green boxing gloves, were held high. 'He thinks he can hex me with those antennae eyes,' Ashley added.

'Hexing,' Virginia said. 'That reminds me, Emma will be phoning this evening. We'd better be there to temper Laura's descriptions of Pierre, or my sister-in-law will be over here again.'

'Giles will be pleased to hear that we're going to be in

76

England for a few months. He'll be able to keep Emma at Lyewood. She seems to spend more time here with Laura than she does with him.'

Virginia was silent. Ashley still refused to see anything obsessive in Emma's behaviour towards Laura and she did not want to spoil their evening together.

Ashley turned and walked back to her. As he put his arm round her waist the little crab sped away, racing across the sand as lightly as sea froth blown on the wind.

CHAPTER THREE

Sussex
1967

The silver-grey Daimler hummed smoothly along the tangled roads of Croydon. The street lights strobed through the windows, highlighting the crimped blond hair and deeply tanned skin of the driver, as the elegant car flashed past.

Bartholomew Faulconer handled the heavy vehicle with confidence and dexterity. He swung it hard round tight corners and flattened the accelerator on the short stretches of straight road, revelling in the powerful thrust of the engine. His knee jerked spasmodically to the pulsating beat of pop music which battered loudly against the closed windows. An open bottle of beer was wedged between the leather seat and the door, and as he drove he kept a wary lookout for policemen.

He was a few years past his majority but had no wish to be apprehended by the law for driving his father's car while under the influence of alcohol. There had been no major upsets so far on this visit to his family, and he did not want to spoil the record. He had outgrown the need to shock and upset his father. As a youngster he felt inadequate and unable to meet his brilliant father's high expectations. Unable to earn his approbation, he gained the older man's full attention and condemnation by his anti-social behaviour.

Bart relaxed his vigilance slightly as he found and turned on to the A22 to East Grinstead. 'Shouldn't find any cops down this way after midnight,' he said, swallowing a mouthful of beer. 'Damn,' he muttered as the car hit a bump and a fountain of amber liquid splashed over the pale-grey leather seat. 'The old codger thinks I'm using the station-wagon tonight. He'll burst an artery if he finds beer-stains in his precious car.' He scrubbed at the seat with his arm, but his black leather jacket merely spread the liquid over an even larger area.

I mustn't upset the old fossil, he thought. I need him in a good mood when I break the news that I'm giving up hunting. I don't want him to go mad and stop my allowance.

He screeched to a halt at a set of red traffic lights and frowned while he pondered his father's possible reaction. He composed and discarded a dozen openings. There seemed to be no easy way to tell his father that he was going to join the Rhodesian African Rifles. How could he explain that the thought of hunting and killing two-legged creatures was a powerful aphrodisiac that made his blood race and his heart pound wildly?

'Do you know, sir, that Rhodesia supplied more troops per capita, to fight for Britain in the two World Wars than any other country in the Empire? I feel that the time has come for me, a Briton, to repay the debt and help her fight the terrorists.'

He decided that his father would accept the bit about the World Wars – that was his soft spot – but he would be unlikely to accept his son's sudden altruistic feelings.

'The Rhodesians think Harold Wilson's Labour government stinks. It gave independence to Nyasaland and Northern Rhodesia and ignored Southern Rhodesia. I want to do my bit and show them that not all Brits are lousy.'

The piece about the Labour government would work, as Dr Faulconer was a staunch Tory. But Bart's reasons for wanting to join the army at the very beginning of the war were weak. His father was an astute man; perhaps he should just say that in a time of war he felt that bushcraft skills were of more value to the army than to wealthy overseas hunters.

It was also going to be difficult to persuade his father not to buy him the proposed partnership in a hunting concession.

'Even though you may think nothing has changed since

Rhodesia made its unilateral declaration of independence two years ago, I feel that your money would be at risk by setting me up in the hunting business.'

Bart knew that his father had been secretly relieved when he put him on the plane to Rhodesia, almost five years ago. The scandals he had created had hurt his father deeply and were dividing his family.

'He likes me at a distance,' muttered Bart. 'As long as he pays a healthy dollop of money every month into my Salisbury bank account, I'll stay away from East Grinstead and Sussex. Pity about the girls though.' Bart grinned as he thought of the mayhem his surprise visit had caused: suddenly the house was full of young women and the phone never stopped ringing.

'Hang around you, thick as a hatching of mayflies,' his father grumbled. 'And they last just about as long before your attentions stray.'

Bart was certain that his father found his presence exhausting and was looking forward to the end of the month when he would return to his hunting camp. His mother no longer seemed to care; she was wrapped up in her own world of pain and hopelessness: she had finally realized that she would never ride her beloved horses again, nor would she regain the use of her shattered legs.

The traffic lights seemed to stop at red for ever, and as Bartholomew waited for the green lights to release him he again studied the wet patch on the leather seat. It seemed darker now than it had been before he tried to clean it.

'Damn,' he swore as he ran his finger across the stain. 'Blood.'

He ran his hand under the elbow of his jacket and switched on the car's interior light: his fingers were stained red. Quickly he shrugged out of the leather jacket, relieved that there were no cars queueing behind him.

'This'll drive the admirable Dr Faulconer to drink,' he muttered. 'Wonder how I managed to cover the sleeve in blood. The little runt wasn't bleeding much.' He spat on the burgundy lining of his jacket and swore loudly as he rubbed at the pink stain on the seat.

He had driven up to London for a farewell party with his friends. As a finale they introduced him to the masochists' haunt around the Leather Tree on Hampstead Heath. Not wishing to appear ungrateful for the entertainment his friends had provided, he had joined in the orgy of kicking and punching. But he soon found it boring to beat up men who gained sexual gratification only through pain and humiliation; he much preferred the excitement of hunting the formidable and cunning African buffalo.

'Damn runt,' he muttered as the stain refused to fade. 'Putting his filthy blood on my jacket.' Now he remembered smashing his elbow deep into the mouth of one of the sad creatures, who, though hardly able to walk, still begged for further punishment.

The lights changed for a second time and a van behind him hooted. 'Belt up,' he snarled as he roared the Daimler across the road. 'Soap and water, that's what it needs. And my jacket – the blood must be cleaned off before I go home.' He turned off the radio and drove in silence for a few minutes.

'The widow at West Hoathly.' His eyes gleamed in the soft light from the dashboard. 'Haven't seen her for weeks and she's always so grateful.'

He slowed to read a road sign and swung the car off the A22, setting it on the minor road to West Hoathly. As the powerful vehicle sped through the dark, he ignored all signs warning of dangerous bends, steep hills and twisting stretches. His eyes were slits and his mouth compressed into a thin hard line and he tapped out his anger on the steering wheel.

Ahead of him the narrow road plunged down a steep hill and there, haloed in the car's headlights, were a young couple. The man was pushing an old bicycle and holding a laughing girl round the waist as they walked home.

Bartholomew had found something on which to vent his rage. He drove straight at them and smiled wolfishly as they dived, panic-stricken, into the scraggly hedgerow. 'That'll cool you down,' he said as he watched the man stagger up and bend over the girl, then shake his fist in the direction of the disappearing car.

81

The girl had still not moved when he lost sight of them in the driving mirror. He felt a small spasm of anxiety. The man may have seen the number-plate. If the girl was hurt, it would be wise to have an alibi. His father would know that he had been out late, and he usually suspected him of having had a hand in any mishap that occurred within ten miles of East Grinstead.

He was confident he could make the widow believe that it was still before midnight since she never wore glasses when he was visiting and he knew that without them she was as blind as a mole in daylight. He slowed as he turned on to the twisting road to West Hoathly; he did not want to miss the turning leading to the widow's cottage in the dark.

━━━━━●|❀|❀|❀| II |❀|❀|❀|●━━━━━

The leaden Sussex sky looked cold and dead and the silver light filtered weakly through the mullioned windows of the kitchen at Lyewood, bleaching the faces of the family seated round the square deal table.

Laura loved the winter days when they gathered for breakfast in the kitchen, warmed by the huge old Aga stove. She broke up a piece of bacon in her fingers and, checking that Ashley and Giles were still hidden behind the morning newspaper and that Emma was tipping hot rolls from the baking tray on to a plate, she let her hand drop under the table.

Her deception was rewarded with a deep purr and a fluffy tail wound lovingly round her legs. The old brindled cat, her belly once again heavy with kittens, kneaded Laura's leg in ecstasy.

'Ouch,' Laura squeaked, when claws as sharp as thorns pierced her thick woollen trousers.

'Damn cat,' Giles growled, flicking his newspaper under the table. 'Scat. Leave our little wrestler alone.'

Ashley peered at his daughter over the top of his section of the morning paper.

'Feeding her again, were you?'

Laura quickly spooned scrambled egg into her mouth, hoping that by the time she had swallowed, her father would have forgotten his question.

'This little war seems to be hotting up in Rhodesia,' Giles grunted, as he buttered a thick slice of toast. 'Wouldn't be surprised if it turns into another nasty guerrilla war. Violent place, that Africa.'

'For once the British taxpayer won't be paying for it,' Ashley answered. 'Smith took independence, now the accounts fall into his tray.'

'Sad in a way,' Giles said. 'A lot of damn good Brits went to settle out there.'

'Right, but . . .' Ashley stopped speaking and smoothed out the page he was reading. 'Nasty,' he murmured, 'and only a few miles from here.'

'What?' Emma asked, putting the hot rolls on the table and trying to read over his shoulder.

'A hit-and-run. Large luxury car, but too dark to read the number-plate.'

'The girl's in hospital with a fractured collar-bone. Poor thing,' exclaimed Emma.

'Do they give any names?' Giles asked. 'We know so many families in the area.'

'Night before last,' Emma read. Quickly she looked up at Giles. 'That car, Giles. The Daimler that almost forced us off the road, just after the Hoathly turn-off.' Emma failed to see warning in Giles's eyes. 'It could have been the same car.'

'What?' Ashley smiled. 'This happened at about two-thirty in the morning. What were you two doing, driving around at that time?'

Emma paled. Since Ashley and Virginia's arrival with Laura, they had been holding their witches' meeting at the home of a member of their coven.

'Friends, we'd been visiting friends. Had glue smeared on our bums and couldn't get up to leave,' Giles joked, smiling at Laura.

Laura giggled and quietly dropped another piece of bacon rind on to the flagged tiles.

Emma sighed with relief. 'Fair,' she said. 'He had fair hair, didn't he, Giles?'

'Too damn busy keeping the Land Rover out of the ditch to look at the idiot,' he answered.

'Would you recognize him if you saw him again?' Ashley asked.

Laura looked at Emma, her eyes huge with excitement at the thought of Emma identifyiing the hit-and-run driver.

'Maybe,' she said hesitantly. 'I'm not sure. It was only a glimpse in the headlights.' She paused and glanced at Ashley. 'I seemed to know him.'

Blond, Emma thought, as she passed Laura the honey. Blond and familiar. Laura, could it be the same man? I must scry. I must know.

'Probably a neighbour's son,' Giles grunted.

'I thought . . .' said Emma, and paused.

'What?' Ashley looked up from the paper.

'I thought it might be Faulconer's son.'

The paper crackled in Ashley's fist. He remembered the arrogant young boy barging out of the Cat Inn. 'Ought to be easy enough to check up and see if he owns a Daimler.'

'His father, Dr Faulconer, probably does,' said Giles.

'Oh, Aunt Emma,' said Laura, 'you'll be able to catch him and your photograph will be in the paper.'

Emma shook her head. 'One has to be very certain before going to the police, Laura. I'm not absolutely certain that it was him.'

'That Bartholomew Harden Faulconer will come to a bad end,' Giles prophesied. 'My head groomsman is looking for him.' Ashley raised an eyebrow. 'His daughter has had to visit relatives in Scotland for nine months.'

Laura opened her mouth but closed it when she saw the look on Ashley's face. This was obviously adult talk and she would be reprimanded if she joined in.

'I don't like this Bartholomew,' Emma said. 'I hope the police catch him.'

'Let's hope they catch the culprit,' Giles said. 'It may not even be Harden Faulconer.'

'I hope not, for his father's sake,' Ashley replied, as he folded the newspaper and placed it neatly beside his plate. The wooden legs scraped loudly on the tiles as he pushed back his chair. The cat darted out from under the table and her belly, distended with kittens, slapped at her legs as she ran into the scullery.

'Come, Laura,' Emma said, putting a flowered teapot on a tray. 'Let's take breakfast up to Virginia.'

'Try to keep her in bed today.' Ashley swung Laura up into his arms as if she was still a baby. 'It's miserably cold and she needs to rest.'

'I'll stay home today.' Laura broke in quickly. 'I'll help Aunt Emma and I'll read Mummy some stories.' She wrapped her arms round Ashley's neck.

'And miss school?' Ashley asked sternly.

'Only for today.' Laura snuggled her face into his neck. 'And I know the work they're doing. It's easy, Daddy. It's not as if this is my real school like the Regina Mundi on Mahé.'

'It may not be the convent, young lady, but remember: the only reason you are allowed to come over here while Mummy visits her doctor and I attend the meetings to save Aldabra is on the understanding that you go to the local school.'

Laura kissed him.

'Right, but just for today,' he capitulated, kissing her on the cheek. 'Be careful not to tire your mother, she's not very strong at the moment, Muffin.' He lowered her to the ground and watched as she carefully stood a silver toast rack on a plate and followed Emma out of the kitchen.

'Don't worry about Virginia,' Giles said. 'Go on up to London. Your meetings are important. We'll look after her.'

'Emma's doing a marvellous job,' Ashley said, 'but I can't bear to see Virginia like this. I wish we could leave for the Seychelles immediately. She's so much better out there.' He closed his eyes and pinched the bridge of his nose between his thumb and forefinger. 'Hopefully I'll be able to get back to the islands fairly soon and then return here only towards the end of the year. Stage One in the battle to prevent Britain and the United States ruining Aldabra is almost over.'

Giles stroked his beard and studied his brother-in-law, noting for the first time the shadows smudged beneath his eyes and the fine tension lines straining at the corners of his mouth.

'How's the conference progressing?' he asked, his voice soft with compassion.

'Conference?' Ashley echoed. 'Oh, yes. They've finally reached a decision.'

'That's a major step.' Giles laughed, trying to distract Ashley from worrying about Virginia.

Ashley nodded but was silent as he thought of all the scientific and protection parties that had actually been involved in putting an end to the secret agreement between Britain and America. Mentally he ticked off most of the important ones: the United States National Academy, the Smithsonian Institute and the Seychelles government, working through the Organization of African Unity. As he put his foot up on the seat of the wooden kitchen chair to tie a loose shoelace, he remembered the months of flying between London and the Seychelles to attend meetings and plan ways of forcing the superpowers to leave the islands alone. He understood the strategic importance of refuelling bases in the Indian Ocean, but he was certain that if enough pressure was brought to bear globally, alternative sites would be found.

'At the meeting today they'll make public the fact that Aldabra is unique and the one place in the world—' he grunted as his foot slipped, 'where an air force base should *not* be built.' He knotted the bow and stamped his foot on the tiles to allow the trouser cuff to drop over his shoe. 'Then all hell will break loose. It'll be a war waged in words and business suits.'

'Who do you think will win?'

'We will . . . I hope. That huge eroded coral sponge deserves to be protected. There are certainly enough people fighting to have it turned into a nature reserve.'

'I'm all for protecting wildlife,' Giles said, wiping buttery crumbs from his mouth and beard. 'The delicate balance of nature depends on the diversity of species. Look at the mess they've made down here by ploughing up the hedgerows.

86

Butterflies, hedgehogs and insects, all facing possible extinction because their habitat has been destroyed.'

Ashley hid a small smile. Giles was so much like his sister: they both become eloquent and angry when talking about the abuse of the planet. Starving millions were a problem, but a raped and polluted Earth took priority.

'And the replanting programme,' Giles continued. 'Are they replacing the good old native oak trees? No, they're putting in shrubs and exotics, things more suited to a suburban garden.'

'If you're right, we're about to see a revival in concern for our Earth,' Ashley said. 'We're now in the age of Aquarius, where our attention will be focused on the holistic side of things. Isn't that correct?'

'Well,' laughed Giles, 'you and dozens of others are over here fighting to protect an island which is only a speck of dust in the immensity of the Indian Ocean.' He dropped his crumpled newspaper on to his chair and padded across to the back kitchen door.

'Touché,' Ashley smiled.

'I know that I'm right.' Giles paused as he bent down to pull on his muddy wellington boots. 'I'm off to a meeting tonight to protest against the continued destruction of our hedgerows and forests.' He grunted as he stamped his foot and wriggled his toes into a more comfortable fit in the green rubber.

'Strength to the holistic age then,' Ashley teased.

'Strength to our desire to listen to our unconscious side and get back to living in harmony with the Earth,' countered Giles. 'And that's something I'm about to do right now.' He pulled his flat plaid cap well down over his shock of hair. 'Check that my men are clearing out mud-filled ditches and filling potholes on the farm roads. Must be able to reach the livestock if the predicted snow falls.' He opened the door and a blast of icy air cut into the kitchen, sharp as a steel knife slicing into warm bread.

'Whew,' Ashley whistled, buttoning his overcoat. 'Those tropical islands have thinned my blood. I don't envy you a day out in the fields, Giles.'

Giles's answer was muffled as the door slammed behind him and all Ashley heard was, 'Back to the earth. Close to Mother Nature.'

He smiled and walked through to the entrance hall to collect his umbrella. These would be a busy few days in London for him, and he looked forward to the fight that the board's decision would bring.

━━━●|❀|❀|❀| III |❀|❀|❀|●━━━

The wind moaned and beat at the windows, but it could not shake the panes of glass held firmly in the thick walls.

Laura was seated cross-legged, leaning back against the carved oak pillar of the four-poster bed. Her long hair swung forward around her face as she puzzled over a word in the book she was reading. Absentmindedly she pulled a handful of hair across her lips and chewed thoughtfully at the splayed tip.

' "Branchial?" What are branchial chambers, Mummy?' she asked, still studying the book. 'It says that ghost crabs aren't air-breathers so they carry a bit of seawater in these chambers. That's why they run down to the sea so often; it's to replace the water.'

Suddenly she brushed the hair away from her mouth and wiped her lips guiltily. She looked across the bed at Virginia and waited to be reprimanded, but Virginia's eyes were closed.

'Mummy,' Laura said softly, but only silence answered her. She unfolded her long legs and slid off the bed, careful not to disturb Virginia. She tip-toed to the bedside table and pushed aside the white porcelain planter holding a miniature poinsettia plant. Its pointed bracts spread out like scarlet fingernails and tapped against her hand as she put the book down on the glass top.

She glanced at the euphorbia and saw the same scarlet bushes growing tall and in wild profusion in the garden at La Retraite. She saw Pierre chasing her down to the jetty with a poinsettia bract hanging from his mouth like a bloody tongue.

Let's go home, Mummy, she said silently. You never stay in bed when we're on the island. I know you'll be better there.

She bent over Virginia to kiss her cheek, then hesitated. Virginia was not breathing. Laura froze, not daring to move, as if caught out in the childish game of 'statues'. Her face hung a few inches above her mother's, and she stared at the pale skin in horror. Panic closed her throat and she could not scream. Her stomach muscles contracted.

A sudden sourness in her mouth released her from her petrified position. As she turned and scrabbled for tissues on the bedside table, Virginia sighed softly and turned over on to her side.

Laura sank to her knees. Her mother was still with her. She hadn't left her. She put her hand on the mint-green blanket and was comforted by the warmth of her mother's body.

Please don't leave me, she pleaded. I love you so much.

She examined her mother's face, not noticing the sunken cheeks and the blue veins lacing the white eyelids.

We all love you, Daddy and Uncle Giles and Aunt Emma.

Emma. She wanted to be held and soothed. She needed to hear Emma's low voice calling her Tanith, her special baby name, and telling her that she was loved. She stood up, patted the blanket then crept from the room.

Lyewood seemed cold, dark and menacing as she ran from one empty room to another looking for Emma. Even the cat lying in front of the stove offered no comfort. She hissed a thin warning as Laura tried to lift her, and she grumbled deep in her throat as she watched the girl wander out of the kitchen.

Laura walked past the rounded door studded with iron bands, paused, then turned and tried the iron ring handle. The door swung open smoothly and she stepped inside. She had never been alone in Emma's study. She had realized with the instinctive insight of children that this was her aunt's private retreat and she had kept away.

Now she examined the room with all the curiosity of a cat. Her blue eyes widened as she saw and recognized the shepherd's crowns on the mantelpiece above the fireplace.

She picked up one of the fossilized sea-urchins and held it in the palm of her hand: it was an almost perfect heart shape, and she carefully traced the outline of the five-pointed design on the top. It thrilled her to hold something which had lived millions of years ago.

She wondered if Emma had picked these up in the fields. She herself had spent months searching for a shepherd's crown after Virginia had told her that if a farm-worker found one while digging, he would spit on it and throw it over his left shoulder to avert bad luck. She ran her hand over the top of the fossil, then replaced it on the mantelpiece.

A watery ray of sunlight pierced the window-pane and silvered a collection of glass balls suspended from the ceiling, swinging like glittering decorations for a giant's Christmas tree.

The flashing light caught Laura's attention and she moved to examine the reflecting balls. She was turning a large glass ball filled with thousands of coloured threads when a muffled cry startled her. The ball swung out of her hands and clashed loudly against the dark-green, gold and silver balls.

She held her breath, hoping they would not break. She watched until the witch balls stopped swaying and hung motionless once more, then she moved to the panelled wall beside the fireplace.

Cocking her head to one side, she stared at the oak-lined wall. The silence deepened and she chewed the inside of her lip nervously. Suddenly the sunbeam retreated behind a cloud, darkening the corners of the study and blending the blackened oak into the gloom.

Laura shivered; the room was no longer friendly, and as she turned to leave a touch as soft as a cobweb brushed the back of her neck. She fled towards the door, panic-stricken and flailing wildly at her neck. Her throat constricted and her tongue stuck to the roof of her mouth. Her fingers felt something soft and silky on her shoulder and it floated to the floor as she crashed into the door. A dark eye, nestling in iridescent green, stared up at her.

She rested her head against the oak door and the iron bands were cold against her cheek. Slowly the pounding in her ears

90

subsided and the raggedness left her breath. She bent down and picked up the peacock feather.

She would have to replace it in the jar of feathers on the mantelpiece. The walk across the room seemed endless. Something had changed. She felt nauseous and apprehensive.

'Don't be a baby,' she admonished herself. 'Mummy would be so ashamed of you. Look how brave she is.'

She stretched up on tiptoe to replace the feather in the tall pottery vase, and as it slid into place it quivered and the emerald-green and turquoise tail feathers swayed hypnotically over her head. It seemed as if all the eyes were moving and were glaring balefully at her.

She stepped back quickly – and the heel of her shoe caught in one of the uneven old tiles. She lurched sideways and flung out an arm to steady herself. Her hand hit the oak panel beside the fireplace and she felt the wood move.

She screamed silently and screwed her eyes closed. Purple and gold whirls filled her vision and red tooth marks were indented deeply into her fingers before she dared open her eyes.

The opening was outlined by a soft yellow glow and the light helped to calm her. She leaned forward and peered through the crack. A sigh of relief edged past her lips and she relaxed.

She pushed at the panel. It swung open silently and she stepped into Emma's secret room.

She wrinkled her nose at the strong smell of burning incense and tiptoed towards her aunt, who was seated at a narrow table with her back to the secret panel. Two red candles stood in tall brass stands behind Emma and the flickering light danced a stately minuet over the altar and the round crystal in front of the woman.

Laura resisted the urge to call out; it would be more fun to creep up and surprise her aunt. She rubbed her nose hard, the smoke was making it tickle.

Don't sneeze, she warned herself silently. You'll spoil everything.

When she was close enough to touch Emma, she hesitated, puzzled. Her aunt was wearing a black cloak and was staring at a shiny transparent ball. She was whispering, but Laura was unable to hear the words.

'Look,' said Laura, 'it's a lady. How clever, there's a picture in the ball.'

Emma was stunned. The air hissed through the gap in her front teeth as she drew in her breath. Careful, she cautioned herself. Don't scare her. Make her feel secure. Then she must share the secret.

'Tanith,' she said, turning to Laura. 'What a surprise. I thought you were spending the morning reading to Virginia.'

'I was, but Mummy fell asleep and I was lonely, so I came to look for you,' Laura answered, edging closer to the table.

'I'm delighted that you did. You know how much I love having you with me,' Emma crooned, looking round the room quickly, hoping that there was no paraphernalia on display which could alarm Laura.

Her athame was lying by the side of the crystal. As she swung a fold of her cloak over the alter to slip the knife into her pocket, she dislodged a fine porcelain mug, slopping the tea on to the floor.

'Oh,' Laura exclaimed, as she steadied the mug on the edge of the table. 'May I have a sip? I'm so thirsty.'

Emma gulped. The tea was an infusion made with the young aromatic leaves of the 'mother of herbs'. She often used mugwort tea as an aid to clairvoyance. 'I don't think you'll like it, Tanith,' she warned. 'It's not proper tea. It's a sort of herbal tea.'

'I love herb teas. In the Seychelles we drink citronelle tea after dinner. Mummy says that the lemon grass helps us to digest our food.'

Emma capitulated. 'Just a little then, because it's a very strong tea.'

Emma watched Laura sip the infusion and she relaxed as Laura put down the mug and wrinkled her nose.

To cover her dislike of the mugwort tea, Laura turned her attention to the crystal ball. 'What's this?' she asked.

'Here,' said Emma, 'come and sit on my knee and I'll show you.'

Laura straddled Emma's leg and rested her elbows on the altar.

'It's crystal, a semi-precious stone. This one is very old and very valuable,' Emma explained, running her fingers through Laura's long flaxen hair.

'It's icy-cold,' Laura exclaimed, stroking the crystal. 'What do you do with it? Why was there a picture in it just now?' She rested her chin on her hands and stared at the ball, now devoid of figures.

'This crystal was probably used hundreds and hundreds of years ago by a wise old woman. She would have given it to one of her daughters, who also became a wise old woman, and so it was handed down through the ages.'

Laura was silent for a moment. 'But what did the wise old woman do with the ball?'

'She looked deep into the heart of the crystal, Tanith, just as you're doing, and it showed her pictures. She was then able to tell people what was going to happen in the future and—'

'Just like a fortune-teller at the fair,' Laura broke in excitedly.

'Well, almost. But a lot of fortune-tellers at fairs don't really see the future; they make up stories to please the people who are paying them.'

'Mummy says it's a lot of nonsense,' Laura said, unconsciously copying Virginia's voice.

'As you grow older, little Tanith, you'll find that people usually scorn things they don't understand.'

'But Mummy's very clever,' said Laura. 'Daddy says she has a fine brain, and he knows lots of things.'

Emma wisely retreated to safer ground. 'You're right. Your parents are both very clever.' She hesitated. It was necessary to have Laura's co-operation in keeping the secret of her room, but she was well aware of the dangers of initiating one too young into the ancient religion of Wicca. She knew that young people need to establish their own sexual identity firmly before awakening their contra-sexual side.

Emma agreed with Giles that, if introduced to Wicca too soon, the young could use their interest in spiritual growth to avoid growing up and facing the responsibilities of life; they could retreat into a life of fantasy. She had received many a lecture from Giles on what Jung called the individuation process, the bringing together of the 'conscious' and 'unconscious'. It was not a task for the young.

She did not want Laura to regress, to escape from the demands of life. She wanted her to develop fully, but she also wanted her to follow the pagan religion.

She continued to gentle Laura, stroking her hair softly. Somehow she had to win Laura over to her side, so she sat as quiet as a spider and wove a web of stories to explain the room to Laura and enmesh her in sticky strands of secrecy.

'Aunt Emma?' Laura shook her aunt's arm.

'Sorry, Tanith, I was day-dreaming. What did you say?'

'Where have the pictures gone? Where is the lady?' Laura tried to lift the crystal and look underneath, but it was heavy and it dropped on the table with a dull thud.

'Lady?' Emma queried, steadying the crystal.

'Yes, the one with long hair like mine. She was wearing pretty white shorts with bright blue stripes.'

Emma gasped and struggled to keep her expression neutral.

'Didn't you see her? She was walking away. She looked so sad and alone.'

'No, Tanith,' Emma lied. 'Did you see anyone else?' she asked quickly, anxious to know whether Laura had seen the man with yellow cat's eyes. His presence in the crystal once again had terrified her.

Laura shook her head. Losing interest in the crystal, she studied the objects on the altar table. Her gaze fastened on the skull, as white as a dead man's flesh, and she shuddered.

'That's only Old Simon,' said Emma, putting her arms round Laura and rocking her on her knee. 'He's very old too. For hundreds of years people believed that he was the symbol of death and rebirth.'

'Like Jesus,' Laura broke in, pulling away from Emma. 'He rose again.'

'Well, similar,' said Emma hesitantly.

Laura ran her finger round the empty eye-sockets in the

94

bony head. 'You've lots of very old things, Aunt Emma. Mummy doesn't have things like this. I like this room.'

Emma took a deep breath; now was her opportunity. She would have to explain witchcraft and the reason for the secret room to Laura. She kissed Laura on the cheek and her frizzed hair brushed across Laura's eyes, closing them. Emma placed her fingertips on Laura's lids.

'Keep your eyes closed, my Tanith,' she said. 'It'll help you to concentrate on what I'm saying. I'm going to tell you a secret.'

Laura's eyelids quivered but she kept her eyes closed.

'Long, long ago,' Emma began, her voice low and lulling, 'people lived in cold, dark caves. They were afraid of many things: dangerous animals, ghosts at night, storms and lightning.'

Laura loved stories. She curled her hands into her armpits and leaned back against Emma, nestling her head in the hollow of Emma's neck.

Emma's arms tightened round her and she cushioned her cheek on the silky hair. 'The sun and the stars guided them,' Emma continued, 'a fire in their cave warmed them and made them feel safe. When they were ill or very afraid they went to the wise woman. She listened to the voices in the wind, she spoke to the trees. She knew which herbs to use to cure them. This wise woman threw stones and bones to foretell the future and she gave them charms to drive away the ghosts. She was a very, very important person.'

The warmth of Emma's body soothed Laura. Her hypnotic voice drew vivid pictures of the Stone Age wise women who later became the religious and magical witches of the Greek age.

As she held Laura in her arms, Emma explained how the early Christian Church did not understand the wise old witches, so they had to practise their witchcraft in secret. She described how, in the Dark Ages, the wise witches were tortured and burned alive because they loved their old pagan religion and refused to give it up. A single tear, clear as a crystal, rolled down Laura's cheek. Skilfully Emma played on Laura's sensitivity and pity for the weak and underprivileged. She successfully stilled

Laura's fears about wicked witches on broomsticks cuddling frogs and weaving black spells. She made her believe that there were no bad witches or black witchcraft.

'So you see, little Tanith, if I had lived long, long ago, people would have called me a wise woman. I would have been a witch.'

'Are you a witch now, Aunt Emma?' Laura asked, suddenly sitting up straight and fixing her liquid blue eyes on Emma's face.

'The answer to that must be our very own secret, Tanith,' answered Emma seriously. 'As I explained, even though they no longer burn witches to death, people are still scared of them and believe that witches worship the devil. You will be told that people who practise witchcraft are evil.'

'But you're not bad,' Laura said, tucking Emma's hair behind her ear and watching it spring out sideways.

Emma paused. Virginia was unexpectedly mirrored in Laura's perfect oval face and swinging blonde hair. 'I hope not,' she answered quietly.

Laura studied Emma in silence for a few moments then slid off her knee. 'I promise I'll never tell anyone that you're a wise woman-witch.' She licked her finger and drew a line across her throat.

Emma laughed. 'I've a much better and stronger promise for us to make, Tanith. We'll do something which will bind us together forever and we'll never be able to break the promise.'

Laura's eyes widened. 'Will it make me a witch as well?' she asked.

Emma gulped and pushed her tongue hard against the gap in her teeth, a habit she reverted to when worried. By her answer to the child's question she could either win Laura to their pagan beliefs or she could lose her for ever. This was her chance to ease Laura away from Ashley and Virginia and bind her to herself and eventually to the craft of Wicca.

'Would you like to be one?' she responded lightly. She held her breath, and her smile became fixed as she waited for Laura to answer.

'It would be fun to have a room like this,' said Laura. 'I'd like to see pictures in a ball like you do and tell people what was going to happen.'

Emma exhaled. It had worked. The secret room and its accoutrements had not frightened Laura. Instead of being terrified and revolted she was fascinated.

'One day you will, little Tanith,' she said, cutting the exultation from her voice. 'But it takes a long time to become a wise woman. There are so many things to learn.'

Laura's mouth drooped. 'That's what Mummy says when I don't feel like going to school.'

Emma grinned and held out her arms to Laura.

'The things we'll learn are all fun, Tanith. Until you have a secret room of your own, you and I will come to this one and I'll start teaching you all the skills the old wise women knew so long ago.'

Laura ran into Emma's arms and kissed her. 'Would you, Aunt Emma? I'd love that.'

'But first,' warned Emma, 'we must seal our promise to keep this our very own secret.'

'Can't we even tell Daddy or Mummy?' Laura queried. Suddenly the thought of excluding her parents made her uneasy.

'You have wonderful parents and they are both very clever, but they have been trained to deal with facts. They would not understand these things. Remember, Tanith, that the wise women were simple country people. They lived very close to the earth and their skills were learned by listening to voices that we don't hear in our modern world.' She tilted up Laura's chin and looked into her eyes. 'This has to be our secret. Yours and mine. Not even Giles can know about it.'

Laura stood silent for a moment, then nodded. 'It's a good secret, isn't it, Aunt Emma? Mummy says I must never keep any bad secrets.'

'I would never do anything that was bad for you. I love you, Tanith.'

As she spoke she snapped open the lid of a carved trinket box, the ivory now yellow with age, and took out a silver needle. It gleamed in the candlelight and Laura looked at it apprehensively.

Emma stood up and her cloak, black as well water, swirled round her legs. She wafted the needle through the candle flame and the splintered light wavered across Laura's pale face.

'Just a tiny prick,' said Emma as she reached across and took Laura's thumb. 'You won't even feel it.'

Laura flinched as the steel point pierced her skin and she stared at the ruby drop of blood which Emma squeezed from the hole. Noticing her white face, Emma quickly drove the needle into her own thumb and waited until the blood oozed out.

'There, little Tanith, it's all over,' she said. 'You're a brave girl and you're going to be a wonderful witch one day.'

She took Laura's thumb and pressed it to her own. The blood mingled. This will unite us, Tanith, she thought as she watched the red drop swell. This will form a psychic link between us, just as the drops of blood I feed to old scarface cat heighten her psychic perceptions. 'Now our secret is sealed,' she said.

Still holding their two thumbs together, she walked Laura over to Old Simon and, as she squeezed their thumbs hard, a few drops of dark blood dripped on to the skull.

Theatrical Emma, she admonished herself silently. But in the eyes of a seven-year-old it'll make the oath of secrecy all the more binding. She smiled at Laura, who was staring at the blood, hypnotized.

'Say after me,' she said, her voice breaking the tension, 'I, Tanith, swear never to reveal any of the secrets I have seen today.'

Laura repeated the words, her voice faint and wavering.

Emma separated their thumbs. 'Suck your thumb,'she said, 'then it won't ache.' Emma laughed, eager to restore an air of normality. 'We look like two big babies sucking dummies,' she teased. 'Come, I have a present in my study for you.'

Laura's eyes lit up and she followed Emma out of the secret room without a backward glance.

Emma switched on the desk lamp. The red and yellow glass in the Tiffany shade caught and reflected the light, and the room became instantly gay and welcoming.

She slid open the bottom drawer in the oak desk and scrabbled through the contents. Laura left her side, drawn back to the witch balls, now licked the colour of flames.

'What are these, Aunt Emma?' she asked as she spun the balls on their chains.

Emma lifted her head from behind the desk and pushed her crinkled hair away from her face. 'Witch balls,' she answered. 'They were hung in dark corners or in the windows of cottages to avert the "evil eye".'

Laura looked puzzled.

'Those shiny ones were meant to reflect the evil look of a passer-by straight back at him, and the one you're holding, with all the coloured cotton twisted inside, was to make the glance follow the entangled cotton.'

Laura stroked the ball and the threads tumbled inside. 'What's an evil eye?'

'It's a very old belief which is found in nations all over the world,' Emma answered, once again ducking down behind the desk. 'They believed – and many people still believe today – that if you hate someone and stare at them with bitterness in your eyes you put the "evil eye" on them. It can bring them bad luck or they can become very ill.'

'Does it really work, Aunt Emma?' breathed Laura.

'If you believe in something then you lay yourself open to its influence,' explained Emma as she placed a small red box on her desk. 'In the olden days many desperately poor people kept themselves alive on handouts. The villagers believed that they would have the evil eye put on them if they didn't help.'

Laura was quiet for a few moments. 'Is that why we always buy heather from gypsies when we see them in London? Mummy says one must, otherwise they'll wish bad luck on us.'

'Right.' Emma laughed. 'Now come here and see what I have for you.'

Laura skipped across the room and leaned over the desk. As Emma flipped open the lid of the box, Laura gasped. 'It's lovely. It looks just like a cross with loops,' she said.

'That's what it is.' Emma was pleased with Laura's reaction to her gift. 'It's an Egyptian ankh. This looped cross was thought to be the key of life. They used it both as an amulet to protect the wearer from danger and as a talisman to attract good fortune.'

'So it's a very, very lucky cross,' said Laura.

'This one is a rare and precious cross, Tanith. I know that you will treasure it and never lose it,' said Emma. Carefully she lifted the cross and chain from its faded red-silk bed and slipped it over Laura's head.

Giles had found the crux ansata years before in an antique shop. They had bought it to give to Laura once she expressed the desire to be initiated into the religion of Wicca. Witches considered it to be the key of initiation which opened the door to everlasting life.

Emma lifted Laura's hair so that the chain rested on the soft skin at the nape of her neck. It may be too soon to initiate you, Tanith, she thought, but now you have the key.

'Mine,' breathed Laura. 'It's for me.' She lifted the small ankh and her eyes squinted as she examined it. 'It's beautiful. I'll look after it carefully for ever and ever.' Still cradling the cross in the palm of her hand, she twined her arm round Emma's neck and hugged her. 'Thank you,' she whispered. 'Thank you for my lovely present.'

'Wear it with love, my little Tanith,' said Emma. My little witch, she added silently.

'Can I go and show it to Mummy?' Laura asked happily. Seeing Emma's expression harden, she quickly amended her request. 'I won't wake her if she's still sleeping.'

Emma forced herself to smile. Virginia still commanded her daughter's love and loyalty, even though she was weak and ill. That would change when Virginia was gone. She thought quickly. The ankh should not raise Virginia's suspicions. Many people wore them on charm bracelets. Virginia was accustomed to her showering gifts on Laura.

'Of course,' she said, 'and when Virginia has seen it, come down to the kitchen and help me bake raisin scones. Your father will be hungry when he gets home.'

She listened to Laura's footsteps ringing on the tiles as she ran to her mother. Emma shrugged her black cloak from her shoulders and hung it in her witch's room.

As she bent over the candles to extinguish them, she stared into the yellow tongues of light and she suddenly remembered the blond man she had seen in the crystal just before Laura surprised her. She wished that the crystal would show her his face, but she saw only his eyes and hair.

Her skin prickled. She had the feeling that he was close, very close to them. She hurried from her room, the acrid smell of guttering candles tickling her arched nostrils.

She inserted and turned the acorn in the frieze, firmly shutting the secret panel. Quickly she switched off the desk lamp and walked out of the door, leaving the room streaked with shadows and the pallid light of winter.

<hr>

IV

The Land Rover left deep tread-marks in the rich red mud as it ground slowly down to Lower Pond, lying deep in the fold of the hills. A chilly breeze corrugated the surface of the water but failed to penetrate the wild rough hedge of holly and yew at the southern end of the lake.

The bare oaks circling the hedge hung over a sheltered dell, their huge, gnarled trunks helping to protect the picnic spot from the wind.

'Well.' Ashley laughed as the car lurched to a halt at the end of the rutted road. 'Who would have thought that we'd have a day like this at the end of the year? Clear skies and a watery sun.'

'I did,' said Virginia. 'I was determined that we would have a picnic lunch here before we leave for the Seychelles.' She stretched out her arms and Ashley swung her down from the car. 'It's one of my favourite places on the farm.'

Ashley kept his arms round her waist. Her grey eyes were clear and sparkling and the cold air had painted a false glow of health on her cheeks. Her face was framed by the hood of her deep-blue duffel coat and a matching mohair beret warmed her ears.

'You look like a bluebell in spring,' he whispered as he led her to a fallen oak.

They were returning to the islands at the end of the week. The fight to save Aldabra had been successful and they could now return to their beloved islands. Since Virginia had heard the news the improvement in her condition had been extraordinary.

'Spring will soon be in the air and I feel that I could gambol like a lamb,' she replied.

'Don't,' Giles broke in, lowering the wicker hamper from his shoulder. 'It's far too muddy and spring's a long way away.'

They all laughed except Emma, who busied herself opening out the striped deck-chairs. She was upset at the thought of losing Laura and was determined to bring up the sensitive subject of the girl remaining in Sussex at Lyewood.

'You were here at the beginning of the year, when it was winter and cold and wet,' she said, snapping open the last deck-chair.

'We left in the middle of the year, when it was summer. Cool and wet,' teased Ashley.

'And now you're leaving at the end of the year, when it's winter again,' Emma continued, ignoring Ashley's interruption.

She sat down heavily on one of the chairs and the wooden frame squeaked.

'Don't you think that it would be wiser to settle Laura in one place? You move around more than a diplomat's family,' she said to Virgina. 'All this travelling is disruptive. Now that she's almost eight, her schooling is becoming more important.'

Virginia's chin squared and her breathing quickened.

'We have excellent schools here,' Emma pressed on, 'Giles and I would care for her. After all, Lyewood is Laura's home.'

'Laura's home is with us,' Virginia snapped.

Ashley blanched. Virginia seldom lashed out at people, but when she did her temper flew with all the uncontrolled rage of a child's tantrum.

102

'The Regina Mundi Convent in the Seychelles maintains an excellent standard. If it didn't, Laura wouldn't manage the school work here.' Virginia paused for breath. 'Not only does she manage, she does so with ease . . .'

Emma's eyes slitted and darkened, like a crack-line in an emerald. She laced her fingers tightly, fighting back the words she knew she could never say. You will die, she determined mutely. She felt no pity for her sister-in-law. When Virginia was dead, Ashley would give her the responsibility for bringing up Laura. Then she would at last possess the child.

She would make certain that Laura left the Seychelles. It was in the islands that the blond man would enter Laura's life. She had to prevent it. She sensed that, when he did, she in some way would lose her hold over Laura. Tanith will be mine and she'll stay where she belongs, here at Lyewood with me.

Giles glanced from Emma to Virginia and broke in.

'Right, our little wrestler is a smart girl and, as Emma says, we'd love her to live with us. But, if telephone calls to the Seychelles are a reflection of Laura's wishes, then it seems that she's missing her friend Pierre and, I think, Nicole.'

It was a masterly stroke. He had reminded both his wife and his sister that Laura was present. She was looking anxiously at the two women she loved and trusted. The mention of Pierre Payet successfully channelled Emma's attention away from Laura's nomadic lifestyle and centred it on this new contender for Laura's affections.

'It's cheaper to fly to the Seychelles than to pay for my daughter's telephone calls.' Ashley laughed as he tweaked Laura's hair.

Virgina smiled. 'She's used up all of next year's pocket money on the calls.'

Laura grinned, relieved that Virgina was no longer angry. 'May I go to Sweet Briar Meadow?' she asked. 'I want to see if that squirrel is still nesting in the oak near the stile.' She smiled at the adults. 'Please. I won't be long.'

'If you are, I'll have finished all the gingerbread,' warned Giles.

'I'll be back before Mummy cuts it,' she promised, and she bounded away, her red rubber boots flashing as she ran.

103

'Talking of young Pierre,' said Giles, opening a folding table. 'How is he progressing? Laura seems to idolize him. I do look forward to meeting him when we come over next year.'

Emma bristled, but silently flapped a yellow-checked cloth over the table and busied herself setting out the picnic lunch.

'Turning into a fine young man,' Ashley answered, sneaking a piece of shortbread from the table. 'He's becoming very involved with the new Seychelles People's United Party.'

'New?' Giles queried.

Ashley paused. Giles was correct. The People's Party and the Democratic Party had been in existence for over three years. The wave of political consciousness which was sweeping across the islands worried Ashley. The islands were indescribably beautiful but had few economic resources, and he felt they should remain under the care and protection of Britain. They had been a Crown Colony for about one hundred and fifty years and he saw no reason for a change. He licked biscuit crumbs from his lips. 'Pierre is fascinated by the idea of an independent Seychelles, and the People's Party seems to be committed to independence. They appear to be determined to cut their ties with Britain.'

'Isn't he a bit young for politics?' asked Giles.

'He's approaching the age when most young people want to change the world and they feel they have solutions to all its problems,' Virginia said, warming her hands round a mug of soup. 'It's only natural that Pierre should take an interest in the government of his country.'

'I hope he doesn't involve or influence Laura,' Emma said, slicing into a large chicken pie. 'His ancestors were a rather unsavoury lot.'

Virginia wondered what Emma would say if she knew that among the seventy Jacobin deportees sent to Mahé was the notorious Corchant, who sent almost two thousand people to the guillotine without a single trial, Rossignol, who stormed the Bastille and said that 'heads would fall like hailstones and the streets would be strewn with guts', and Boniface of the September massacres, whose wife drank the victims' blood. She was tempted to tease Emma by saying that Pierre's ancestor was probably Parein or Corchant, who were responsible for the executions in Lyons.

Ashley laughed at Emma's description and held out his plate for a slice of pie.

'You may laugh,' Emma said grimly. 'Those deportees were all revolutionaries and murderers. Pierre Payet has their genes in his blood.'

'You're being discriminatory,' Virginia snapped, forgetting her own initial reaction when hearing about Pierre's antecedents.

'Come, Emma,' Ashley said. 'We're not much better on this little island. We too have some unsavoury genes.' He thought for a moment, rubbing his hand on his chin, before reminding them of English kings who had been pagan sympathizers and practised sorcery.

'How can you equate revolutionaries with witchcraft?' exploded Emma. 'Having the genes of a witch is not the same as having the genes of a murderer.'

'Sorry,' Ashley said, realizing that Emma was truly angry. 'My analogy was misguided. I was merely trying to point out that one finds strange ancestors in the most unlikely places.' Eager to make amends, he took Emma's hand in his. 'Come back with us. Come and see Pierre. Come and judge for yourself. Satisfy yourself that he's a good companion for Laura.'

Ashley spoke persuasively and Emma softened. Virginia frowned. She had hoped to have her daughter to herself in the Seychelles. Emma monopolized Laura when they were at Lyewood.

'You're like an old mother hen,' Giles said to his wife as he stood up to have his soup mug refilled. 'You'll give yourself grey hairs over Laura.' He towered over Emma, with his back to Ashley and Virginia. He stared at her, his face as hard as a slab of Sussex marble, and she accepted his silent message.

'I'm sorry, Virgina and Ashley,' she said, as Giles moved away. 'I'm afraid that I'm a little touchy because you're going away.' Her mouth drooped as she looked at Virginia and she willed her eyes to fill with tears. 'I miss you so much, especially little Laura. The home seems so empty without her.

105

Perhaps if I'd been able to have a . . .' She let her voice trail away.

'We know, Emma,' Virginia said, immediately sympathetic. 'But we'll be back soon and you know that Laura will always love you.'

'It'll soon be much easier and quicker to visit us,' Ashley said. 'I hear that contracts will be out next year to build an international airport on Mahé.'

'Oh, no.' groaned Giles. 'That means I'll be a permanent widower.'

They all laughed at Giles's mock misery as they accepted plates laden with salad and wedges of chicken pie from Emma.

'He's there, he's there.' Laura's voice, high with excitement, heralded her arrival. 'My squirrel's in the oak and I'm sure he knows me.'

'The same as everything else on Lyewood.' Giles laughed, relieved that the tension had been broken. 'You've named the fowls, the ducks and the pigeons. My men tell me that you've even started naming the sheep.'

Laura laughed. 'Oh, Uncle Giles, you're so funny.'

She moved across to Emma, ready for her lunch. As she waited for Emma to fill her plate, she ran the ankh up and down the chain round her neck. Playing with the talisman was a new habit of Laura's and one which irritated Virginia almost as much as the old habit of chewing her hair. Virginia was a little uncertain about Emma's gift to Laura. She felt that the looped cross was a heathen symbol, but did not want to upset Emma by decrying it. She had wondered whether she should tactfully warn her daughter about Emma, make her aware of her aunt's strange interests. But she decided not to mar the innocence of Laura's childhood and her love for her aunt by raising spectres.

Giles solemnly topped and handed around four champagne glasses. He then poured a few teaspoonfuls of golden bubbles into a liqueur glass for Laura. She balanced her glass on her plate and went to sit beside Virginia. Giles stood up, sweeping back the mop of hair from his forehead, and the pale sunlight gilded and accentuated the strong planes of his face.

106

'Brother mine, you look like one of the old druids in his grove of sacred oaks about to make a libation,' Virginia said.

Giles looked at his sister sharply, then smiled.

'I am in fact a hard-working farmer who is about to make a toast to his sister and brother-in-law.' He coughed and drew himself up to his full height. 'I want to congratulate you on the success of your tremendous fight to have Aldabra protected. It is an achievement of which you deserve to be very proud. We drink to you.'

He raised his glass and myriad bubbles sped through the champagne like tiny shooting stars. Laura spluttered. She pulled a wry face at the dry taste and carefully spilt the champagne as she placed the glass under her chair.

'Thank you,' Ashley answered, 'but we do have to share the credit with the present British government.'

He listened in silence as Giles exploded into a denunciation of the government. He listed its failings: the country was facing its worst financial crisis in twenty years. The pound had been devalued again. Bank Rate was up to eight per cent. Two hundred million pounds had been added on to taxes, and Britain was reduced to pleading for foreign loans. He ended his diatribe by declaring that Britain needed a change of government before it was forced to join the queue of little nations with begging bowls.

Ashley nodded his head as Giles stabbed at his pie crust. He agreed with everything Giles had said, but the economic mess the government was in meant that the plan to take four Indian Ocean islands and create the British Indian Ocean Territory as an East of Suez defence base had collapsed. They had been obliged to abandon the project. Aldabra would not be destroyed by concrete runways. It would never be an aircraft support base.

Virgina lifted her glass of champagne, determined that the picnic was going to be a happy occasion. 'Now that the Royal Society has stated that Aldabra is one of the most important islands in the world, they have to do something about it. So . . .' she paused and sipped her champagne, 'they're setting up a research station on the island next year.'

'Wonderful news, wonderful.' Giles smiled.

'This victory will of course draw attention to the other coral islands in the Aldabra group,' Ashley said, biting into a slice of winter berry tart. 'It'll hopefully mean that the other three islands in the Aldabra group – all of which had giant tortoises and flightless rails up until about five hundred years ago – will no longer be exploited.'

Laura stood up to take Virginia's empty plate and put it on the table. 'Pierre says that when the Seychelles are independent all of the islands will be safe because they'll look after them,' she said.

'A nice thought, Muffin,' Ashley replied, 'but protecting places is a very expensive business, and tropical islands are not noted for their booming economies.'

Laura's face fell. 'Pierre says—'

'Pierre won't have to worry about that problem until, and if, the Seychelles become independent,' said Virginia. 'Now, my baby, would you pass me a slice of Emma's berry tart?'

Laughter punctuated the remainder of the picnic lunch. As the family busied themselves packing the hamper and piling the chairs in the Land Rover, Giles put his arm round Virginia's shoulders. 'We had some good times here as children, didn't we?' he said.

Virginia saw the dell carpeted with periwinkles and wild strawberries and the holly hedge garlanded with open-petalled dog-roses and virgin's bower. 'We had a special childhood, Giles,' she answered, smiling up at him as he walked her slowly to the car. 'I only wish that I'd been able to have a son, then Laura could have experienced the joy of a brother.' Giles squeezed her shoulder. 'But it's too late now,' she whispered.

'You've produced an exceptional daughter. Laura will have a brood of youngsters and they'll fill this dell, Lyewood and La Retraite to overflowing.' He swung Virginia up into his arms as easily as shouldering a sheaf of wheat, and tenderly sat her down on the car seat. 'You and I will be up to our ears in grandchildren.'

Virgina held her brother's hand and he felt the sadness in her.

He caught and cupped her hand. 'Little sister,' he whispered, 'don't give up. You have to keep fighting it.' Virginia winced as he pressed her fingers together. 'We all have untold powers deep inside ourselves. Use the incredible strength of your unconscious mind. Make it work for you. You have powers which can overcome this illness, if only you'll use them.'

'Oh, Giles,' she answered. 'I pray so hard. So hard and so often.'

Giles stroked his beard. 'Prayer can be very powerful,' he conceded, 'but one usually prays to saints who have led perfect lives, to the Virgin Mary or to the Godhead.' He ran his hand through his thick hair. He would have to be very careful not to upset or antagonize Virginia. Her faith was strong; he did not want to break it, but he had to try to make her influence the outcome of her illness by using the power of her mind. 'I want you to tap into and use the capacity of your mind, little sister. I know the force of prayer, but please trust me, the powers we have in ourselves and don't use are so much stronger.' Virginia opened her mouth but he forestalled the words. 'Believe me,' he said quickly. 'Pray, but rely on yourself. Use the strength of your unconscious to strangle this multiple sclerosis.'

He glanced over his shoulder. Emma and Ashley had helped Laura untangle a paper napkin from the thorns of a wild raspberry bush and were walking towards the car.

'Think yourself well,' he said softly and dropped a kiss on her cheek.

Virginia smiled and watched him shepherd the family into their seats.

As the Land Rover climbed slowly up the glutinous road to Lyewood, Virginia pressed her cheek to the window. The fields were alive with children yet to be born, grandchildren she knew she would never see.

CHAPTER FOUR

The Seychelles
1972

I

The rough sisal was looped in a double-hitch round the reptile's speckled flippers. Slowly the ropes tightened and bit deeply into the green turtle's flesh. The muscles of the two fishermen leaning over the wooden island schooner bulged and knotted as they strained against the creature's weight.

The turtle swung and bumped helplessly against the side of the boat and its heavy lids drooped wearily over its eyes. Sharp commands rang out in Creole and the men balancing in the small pirogue tied to the side of the fishing boat hastened to hold the paddle-like flippers and steady the swaying turtle.

The fishermen narrowed their eyes against the blinding reflection of the sun, mirrored on the sea, and sweat oiled their armpits and ran down their arms, soaking the ropes and splattering the turtle's ivory belly.

The dull grumble of a speedboat's engine alerted the men and they glanced anxiously in the direction of the approaching vessel.

'Hurry, Pierre,' urged Laura, holding the grip-rail tightly as the orange and white speedboat they were on bounced over the waves.

They hit an unexpected swell and, before Pierre could ease back on the throttle, the small boat fell back into the trough with a jarring crash. Laura lurched into the centre console and her knee crashed sharply against the fibreglass.

'Ouch,' she screamed and bent over, rubbing her knee.

Pierre jerked the control throttle to neutral and the boat rocked gently on the water.

'Don't stop,' Laura shouted, pain sharpening her voice. 'We must save the turtle. Look what they're doing to that poor old thing. It'll die in the sun.'

'It'll die in any case,' Pierre answered, kneeling down to examine her knee. 'They're catching them for meat.'

'But it's illegal,' Laura protested, and winced as he flexed her leg. 'They're not allowed to capture green turtles any more.'

Pierre patted her leg then stood up. 'You'll live,' he pronounced. 'It'll be bruised for a few days but nothing's broken.'

'The turtle,' insisted Laura. 'Let's go and stop them. Please, Pierre.' She looked up at him, her blue eyes wide with concern.

He hesitated. He had never been able to resist Laura's pleas. Even though he would be going to France the following year to study business management and tourism, this blonde schoolgirl could still command his attention and time. He slapped the boat into gear and moved slowly towards the fishermen.

'It's a very unpopular ban, Laura,' he said, as they neared the schooner. 'Turtles have been a traditional source of food for the islanders for centuries. For years it was the only red meat they had.'

'Traditions have to move with the times,' Laura replied primly, mouthing Ashley's sentiments.

Pierre grinned. 'Think, little girl,' he said.

'I'm not little! I am only one year away from being a teenager,' flashed Laura.

'That shouldn't stop you from thinking.' He pulled her long pigtail gently. 'These men are poor fishermen.' He slowed down to come alongside the pirogue. 'They eat what they catch. The few turtles they take will make very little difference. It's the people who sell the meat to restaurants and who export them who are dangerous.'

'But, Pierre,' she wailed as she leaned out and caught hold of the raised curved end of the pirogue, 'look how sad and afraid the turtle is.'

Pierre cut the engine and peered into the tarred boat. The

111

fishermen were standing on another two turtles which had been up-ended, exposing their soft undersides to the grilling rays of the sun. Their wrinkled necks were stretched back and their heads lolled in the slopping bilge-water. There was something obscene in their defenceless, spread-eagled position and Pierre looked away.

Laura gulped and swallowed back her words of remonstration. Ashley and Virginia had taught her the difference between a protectionist and a conservationist. She was trying hard to remember to consider the species as a whole and not become emotional over the isolated few, but it was a difficult task.

'Why don't you eat fish?' she pleaded with one of the fishermen. 'Why do you have to eat turtles?'

The man looped a piece of rope and slipped it over one of the turtles. 'Take her away,' he said to Pierre without looking up. He tightened the rope and a flipper beat in the air, vainly feeling for the water. 'They don't understand our ways.' He quickly secured the other flipper and tossed the two ropes up to the men on the schooner.

The white weatherboards dipped into the sea as the pirogue canted to one side. The men lifted the turtle and then jumped back quickly to balance the boat. The creature craned its neck forward as its hard convex shell smashed into the wooden planks and it stared at the men in bemusement.

'Oh no,' Laura whimpered as she turned away. 'He looks like an old professor who has lost his glasses. It's so horrid.' Pierre squeezed her arm. 'Can't you make them release the turtles? Say we'll tell the police,' Laura urged.

Pierre shook his head. 'By the time we return to Mahé and phone the police, these boats will have vanished. There'll be no trace of any turtles.'

Laura's eyes filled with tears. 'But – '

'Be sensible,' Pierre broke in. 'You and I alone can't force them to free the turtles. They're tough fishermen and won't brook any interference from us.'

Laura studied the five men, who were stripped to the waist, heaving and tugging at the turtles. She realized that Pierre was right.

'Come,' he said briskly, 'fend off the pirogue while I start the engine.'

Laura pushed at the pirogue. She glanced up sharply as the turtle slid over the schooner's rail and thudded on to the deck.

'Why are they transferring the turtles from the pirogue to the schooner?' she asked in a small voice, as the speedboat swung away in a wide arc, rocking the pirogue.

'Probably because it's easier to conceal them under the fishing gear and nets or because the schooner is faster.'

Pierre glanced at her face and opened the throttle. Soon the pirogue and schooner were lost on the horizon. Laura's attention focused on the silver flying fish streaking over the waves, gliding away from the predators lurking in the indigo-blue waters. She smiled as the slim fish propelled themselves from the water. The lower lobe of their tails blurred, whirling faster than rotor blades as they shook off the restraints of gravity and for a few seconds skimmed the water with the seabirds.

Laura watched the flying display for a while. Then, squaring her shoulders, she took a deep breath and turned to Pierre. 'Pierre,' she said, but her voice was lost in the hum of the engine.

He stood, tall and slim, legs astride, riding the swells and chop of the waves easily.

Pierre knew all her childish secrets and fears. Usually she found it easy to confide in him, but now, suddenly, she was uncertain. 'Pierre.' She tugged at his salt-stained shorts.

'All right,' he said, smiling at her. 'You take over, but keep the speed down. Try not to take off like your flying fish.'

'No, thanks.'

Pierre stared at her in surprise. She loved being allowed to pilot the speedboat.

'I want to talk to you.'

'And that's new?' he teased. 'You never stop talking.'

'This is serious.' Pierre swallowed back a glib reply. Laura's straight dark brows were drawn together and her face was set. 'It's about Mummy.'

He cut the engine and the boat see-sawed in the warm water.

'Come and sit beside me,' he said, 'but put on a hat. Your nose is as red as a fody.'

Laura obediently pulled on a woven straw hat.

'I know that Mummy is getting weaker, Pierre. Usually she is so much stronger in the Seychelles, but not this time.' She plaited her fingers together nervously and ran her tongue over her dry lips. 'I'm afraid. Last night I heard Daddy and Aunt Emma talking on the verandah. Aunt Emma was saying that she thought she would stay here longer, as the family would obviously need her when Virginia was gone.'

Laura sniffed and Pierre put his arm round her shoulder and held her to him.

'She also said that Daddy would have to consider letting me stay in Sussex.' She rubbed the underside of her nose hard and looked up at Pierre, but his eyes were shaded and black behind his dark glasses.

'I want Mummy to be with us always. I can push her wheelchair and read to her.' Her voice broke. 'Oh, Pierre. I don't ever want to leave you and Nicole.'

He patted her shoulder gently. His eyes smarted as he stared at two frigate birds majestically riding the thermals, startling white against a sky the colour of forget-me-nots.

'Virginia will always be with you, Laura,' he comforted, 'even – '

'Oh, Pierre,' she said, throwing her arms round his neck and hugging him hard. 'I knew you'd say that. I knew you wouldn't say that Mummy was going to leave me.'

Pierre rested his chin on her head and her hat was rough against his skin. Let her believe that, he thought. Don't endorse Emma's opinion.

Emma had been one of the first tourists to arrive at the newly completed airport and Pierre feared that she would now become an even more regular visitor to the islands. He sensed an antagonism in her. At first it hurt him. He had tentatively broached the subject to Nicole, but she had merely laughed, saying that barren women were always possessive of children. He had accepted the explanation, realizing that Emma resented the time he and Laura spent together. But he was still uneasy in Emma's presence.

'You take over,' he said, kissing Laura softly on her cheek and sliding her behind the steering-wheel. 'Nicole is preparing a surprise lunch for everyone. She's spent hours ferrying everything from the mainland to Praslin Island, and she'll be mad if we're late.'

'Wait, Pierre. I must tell you something.' Pierre merely smiled and pressed the starter. 'It's about the bonhomme du bois.'

Pierre froze. 'Laura! What have you been doing with gris gris? Your parents will be furious if they know that you've become involved in island witchcraft. Are you crazy?'

Laura bit her lip anxiously. 'I haven't done anything yet, Pierre,' she answered. 'But Cook knows a very good bonhomme who can give us a gris gris to make Mummy better.'

She paled as Pierre stood up and put his hands on his hips, but she was determined to make him listen and help.

'Please, Pierre, please come to the bonhomme with me.' Seeing his lips compress, she hurried on. 'Charms work. I know they do because Aunt Emma has shown me -- '

Suddenly she broke off, remembering dark-red blood dripping on to a skull. She was betraying a solemn secret. She looked up at Pierre aghast, torn between her need to confide in him and her fear of divulging forbidden things.

Seeing her consternation, Pierre took her hands in his. He knew her so well. From their first meeting they had understood each other and thus knew with astounding accuracy what the other was thinking and doing.

He realized he would have to coax her into telling him about Emma. 'Bonhommes are powerful people for those who are superstitious, Laura. They know all the black magic of Africa, and some of it is bad.'

Laura heard the gentleness in his voice and she relaxed and held his hands firmly. 'I know, Pierre, but we only want the good magic. The magic to help Mummy.'

'You know that the practice of gris gris has been banned in

115

the islands, just like the killing of green turtles. You were furious with the fishermen, but now you want to break a ban yourself.'

Laura was silent for a moment.

'Yes, it's wrong,' she whispered, 'but I have to do it.' Her full lower lip drooped. 'Please, Pierre. He lives on Praslin. Cook knows this bonhomme well and he's a good one.' She pulled at his fingers in agitation. 'When we've had Nicole's surprise lunch, the grown-ups will all go back to Mahé on Daddy's big boat. We can say we want a last snorkel at St Pierre Island.' Sensing Pierre's disapproval, she gabbled on quickly. 'The bonhomme is expecting us. Cook sent him a message.'

Pierre was silent and stared down into the surging water as if seeking an answer in its aquamarine depths.

'Laura,' he said finally, 'if I do go with you, I shall need to know about Emma.' Seeing her shoulders stiffen under her thin yellow shirt, he hardened his voice. 'You can't expect me to be part of this secret visit to the bonhomme if you hide things from me.'

Laura was silent and ran her bare foot up and down the white floorboards.

'Don't you trust me, Laura? Have I ever broken a promise?'

Laura swallowed. She could not hurt Pierre and he had always kept her secrets. 'You have to cross your throat and swear to die if you ever tell anyone.'

Pierre solemnly licked his finger and drew a wet line across his sunburned throat.

'Well,' Laura began, 'Aunt Emma is a witch. But a good one,' she hastened to add. 'She says that people think of witches as being bad people, but they're really only wise women.'

Pierre was stunned, but he merely nodded, willing Laura to continue.

'She gave me this ankh.' The looped cross swung in the air between Laura's fingers. 'It's a good-luck charm and will protect me. It's – '

'Then why doesn't she give you a gris gris for Virginia?' Pierre snapped.

Laura stared at him open-mouthed. 'Of course,' she laughed.

'Aunt Emma can help.' Then her smile vanished. 'Oh dear, she can't. She needs her special room at Lyewood with all the magic things in it.'

'Do you often go into her special room?' asked Pierre, coaxing the story from Laura as skilfully as a fisherman trailing plastic streamers in the sea to lure and entangle sailfish.

'Oh, yes,' Laura replied happily, 'I'm going to learn to make medicines with plants and all sorts of things.'

Pierre shivered involuntarily. He had grown up on a coconut plantation on Praslin and was familiar with the bonhommes du bois. Their art fascinated yet frightened him. He did not want Laura caught up in the blackness of magic.

'Laura, I promised to keep your secret, now I want you to promise me something.'

'Of course,' she answered, relieved that Pierre knew about Emma and happy that he was not angry.

'I want you to tell me everything Emma teaches you.'

'Why?' Laura asked. 'Do you want to learn witch things too?'

'No, and I don't think you should either.' Her face darkened. 'You see, Laura,' he hastened to explain, 'my grandmother used to consult and believe in a gris gris man here on Praslin. When I was born he told her that those born in the sign of water should swim hard to keep away from the current of black magic or they would be sucked into it and drowned.' He drew in a deep breath. 'You are also a water sign. I want to look after you, so promise that you'll keep no witch secrets.'

'Silly,' said Laura. 'I promise.'

Pierre smiled; but as Laura clung to the wheel, piloting an erratic course to one of the hidden sandy coves on Praslin, he wrestled with his conscience. Virginia and Ashley should know about Emma. It's my duty to tell them, he agonized silently. If I do, Laura will never forgive me.

He looked down at the tall slim girl at his side. Her hair lay on the wind behind her and the sunlight danced across her tanned nose and cheeks. She stood, balancing on the balls of her feet, smiling and licking the salty spray off her lips.

No, he thought. I can't betray her trust. She'll be safe.

She'll tell me exactly what Emma does. I'll be able to protect her.

'Watch out,' he warned, as a thin line of white foam signalled the presence of the coral reef.

Laura bit down on the tip of her tongue as she concentrated on guiding the boat over the reef.

A burst of clapping from the shore greeted their arrival. Pierre dropped the anchor overboard with a splash, and he and Laura waded through the warm shallow water, scattering shoals of tiny silver fingerlings.

'About time,' scolded Nicole in Creole. 'Another ten minutes off the coals and my surprise would have been ruined.'

'Sorry,' Laura said, hugging Nicole, mindless of the fat-spattered white apron.

'Smells good,' sniffed Pierre. 'Can I go and see what you're cooking?'

'Not a hope,' laughed Ashley. 'None of us has been allowed behind those rocks.' He wriggled his empty beer bottle deep into the sand. 'Now that you two have returned from your fish cinema at St Pierre, perhaps Nicole will relent.'

'Oh, Daddy, we saw a black-spotted puffer. Pierre said it was only a model toby. But as he wouldn't let me go near it, it must have been a black-spotted,' Laura said, walking across to her parents who were sitting in the shade of a palm tree.

Emma shuddered as she watched Laura sit down cross-legged on the sand beside Virginia. Ashley had explained how the black-spotted was called *fugu* in Japan and was eaten as a form of bravado. It needed only a tiny piece of the intestine or liver to be left in the flesh and death would result within minutes. The poison was more deadly than cyanide and there was no antidote.

'I hope that puffer is not on the lunch menu, Nicole,' teased Emma. She liked the young island woman with the sparkling eyes and infectious laugh.

'Come and see for yourself,' invited Nicole. 'My kitchen is now open to the family.'

Ashley and Pierre bent down, crossed arms and gripped

each other's wrists, forming a chair for Virginia. She put her arms round their necks and they lifted her easily. She now felt as light as a young child.

The heat from the coals in the drum which Nicole had wedged between huge granite boulders popped out the sweat on their foreheads. They followed her to the trestle table set out for lunch and stared in amazement at the concave carapace resting on a bed of palm leaves on the sugar-fine sand.

'Caille!' said Pierre.

'How did you ever get permission to have green turtle?' asked Ashley.

'Through old friends at the Embassy,' Nicole answered happily. 'They obtained a permit. I wanted something very special to celebrate the inauguration of Aldabra as a research station; you worked so hard to save that island.' She smiled at their astonishment. 'We're also celebrating the fact that Virginia will now be able to follow you down to Aldabra for the opening ceremony.'

'We should have invited the secretary who gave up his seat on the old Grumman Albatross seaplane for Virginia,' Ashley laughed.

'Not such a good idea,' said Virginia. 'He didn't give it up willingly. Half the island is trying to get down to Aldabra. I was just lucky.'

'Lucky?' snorted Ashley. 'You deserve to be there. You've been involved in the project from the start.' He put his arm round her shoulder and seated her on a flat rock. 'Let me bring you some caille.'

'No, no,' said Nicole. 'One eats the rarest dish in the Seychelles in traditional fashion, with your fingers.'

Laughing and jostling, the family settled down on the beach round the turtle shell.

'Mmm,' said Ashley, closing his eyes in mock ecstasy, 'you're a wonder, Nicole. This is a feast fit for the gods.'

Nicole smiled at Ashley and her cheeks flushed a deep rose. She quickly dropped her eyes and concentrated on scraping a wedge of turtle fat and meat from the shell.

Emma glanced quickly at Virginia, but she was squeezing a chunk of red meat and rice between her fingers and was not looking at Nicole.

A frail and crippled wife, a handsome husband and a vibrant and beautiful woman do not make a good ménage à trois, thought Emma. Her eyes slitted as she studied Nicole and Ashley. No, she decided, Ashley was not aware of Nicole's feelings for him. She glanced at Virginia. Laura was curled up against her mother. Emma had noticed that whenever Laura was troubled or unhappy she needed the physical comfort of Virginia. Her sister-in-law never smothered the child with love but she had a wonderful ability to turn tears to laughter and to calm troubled young minds. I'll do that for Laura, mused Emma. One day I'll be the one she runs to for comfort. And that day is almost here, she vowed, looking at Virginia's skeletal wrists and fingers as she dug into the caille.

Laura tried not to look at the layer of turtle fat and meat which had roasted in the shell for most of the morning.

'Muffin,' said Ashley, 'you're not eating. Here, have some, it's delicious.' He scopped up a mixture of rice and vegetables which had been cooked in the molten turtle fat and popped it into his daughter's mouth.

Laura's face mirrored the white of the beach. She scrambled to her feet and ran, gagging, into the coconut plantation.

'I'll go to her,' volunteered Pierre. Sucking the fat from his fingers, he quickly followed Laura.

'I'm sorry, Pierre,' she snuffled, wiping her mouth with the back of her hand. 'I'm a ninny. It's just – '

'I know,' he said. 'I know.'

'Please don't tell them about the old turtle this morning. Daddy'll be so ashamed of me.'

'I won't,' he said as they walked back, stepping carefully over the piles of decaying palm leaves. 'I'll say that caille is an acquired taste and you just don't like it.'

'Thank you,' she whispered. 'I really don't want to spoil Nicole's surprise feast. I'll just eat fruit. As long as I don't look at the turtle meat, I'll be all right.'

The meal dragged on interminably for Laura. The sting in

120

the sun's rays had eased to a gentle warmth by the time the family had cleaned up the picnic spot and the adults settled into Ashley's boat.

'Don't be late,' Virginia shouted, as the twin propellers beat the water into a white froth.

'We'll be back well before dark,' Pierre promised. He and Laura waved and watched until the boat rounded the headland. Then they quickly waded out against the incoming tide and clambered on to the speedboat.

'You're certain that Cook's sister will be at the point to meet us?' Pierre asked.

'Yes, and the bonhomme is waiting.'

'He'd better be. We haven't that much time if we're to be back in Mahé by sunset.' he grumbled.

Laura crossed her fingers behind her back. Time was not an important concept on the islands. Cook's sister could easily decide to stroll down to the point tomorrow instead of today. Please be there, begged Laura mutely. We won't be back on Praslin again before Mummy leaves for Aldabra, so this is my only chance to get a gris gris. She squeezed her eyes tightly shut. I must have the charm to protect Mummy now. I must. I must.

'Laura!'

She started and opened her eyes.

'Are you all right?' Pierre asked, peering at her solicitously.

'Yes, just some dust in my eye,' Laura lied.

'Dust, on the sea?' queried Pierre.

'Oh, look, isn't that her?' Laura changed the subject. She pointed to a tiny figure standing on a jumble of wet rocks which arrowed into the sea. 'Yes, it is!' She squirmed impatiently as Pierre found a good spot to anchor the boat.

They scrambled hastily across the rocks, afraid that she would be angry because they were late. But when they reached Cook's sister, she merely grunted, turned and walked back to the beach.

'She's about as talkative as Cook,' Pierre whispered as they left the red granite rocks behind and wound their way through a grove of latanier palms.

Laura giggled and covered her mouth with her hand. Just as

she was about to reply she tripped over one of the palms' stilt roots and lay sprawled on a thick bed of dry fronds. Their guide paused for a moment, looked down at Laura dispassionately, then plodded on. Pierre bent forward and helped her up.

'Awful latannyen lat,' said Laura, using the Creole name for the endemic palm and kicking the enormous stilt root. She spat on her finger and wiped her skinned knee, then hurried after Cook's sister. Pierre grinned but was silent.

They came to a clearing and walked quickly past a cluster of homes. The women, neat in their clean cotton-print dresses, looked up as they passed then continued to sweep the wet red earth with their grass brooms. They brushed the ground in stately rhythm, keeping one hand behind their backs, formal as dancers in a French minuet.

The palm forest retained the heat of the day beneath its tall fringed canopy and the air was humid and oppressive. They breathed a sigh of relief when their guide darted off the path, brushed through a grove of banana trees and stopped in front of a corrugated-iron home, set up high on pillars of broken granite. The house had once been painted blue, but it was now streaked red with rust and patterned green with moss and mildew.

'Here,' she said. 'The gris gris man is inside. I will wait here.' She pulled a wooden chair into the shade of a mango tree, took off her wide-brimmed straw hat and closed her eyes.

Laura turned to Pierre apprehensively. He held out his hand and his irregular teeth flashed in a familiar grin. Laura took his hand gratefully and together they walked up the path lined with climbing vanilla vines. At the foot of the wooden stairs Laura paused briefly then walked resolutely on to the small wooden verandah.

Only the sound of their breathing broke the silence. Gingerly Laura moved towards the green-and-orange-striped curtain which drooped in the open doorway. She started as it swung open and stood transfixed as the bonhomme emerged from the gloomy interior.

The witch-doctor was tall and lean and he had to stoop to pass through the opening. His stomach was as rippled as an old zinc washboard and his khaki shorts hung down to his knees. Tight white curls clung closely to his head and his eyes were set deep in dark wrinkled skin.

'I know of you and what you want.' He spoke with the crackle of dry palm fronds. 'Come.'

He led them around to the back of the tin house and sat them on upturned petrol drums in a circular enclosure shaded by an ancient takamaka tree. The area was ringed with thorn-apple shrubs and the perfume of the white trumpet-shaped flowers made Laura feel giddy.

'Why is he picking devil leaf?' Laura whispered, watching the bonhomme selecting poisonous leaves from the thorn-apples.

'They contain daturine,' Pierre answered. 'It's a hallucino-genic drug,' he added, seeing Laura's puzzled look. 'It helps them prophesy.'

'But we only want a gris gris,' said Laura.

'Ssh, here he comes,' warned Pierre as the bonhomme re-entered the circle, carrying a red rooster under one arm and the devil leaves. He placed the leaves upright in an old jam tin and, satisfied that the juice was leaking out from the cut stems, he stretched the rooster across his knees. Holding its feet in one hand, he ran his fingers rhythmically up and down its throat and the bird closed its eyes and lay still.

'*Donnez moi*,' he commanded in Creole.

Pierre looked at the old blade set into a wooden handle that was lying beside the jam tin. Sensing what was about to happen, he stood in front of Laura and handed the bonhomme the crude scalpel.

With one sure, swift stroke the bonhomme sliced through the fowl's neck and the head dropped to the soil. The rooster's yellow eye stared up at them for a moment and then blinked. Kicking the severed head aside, the bonhomme held the bird's body in his hands like a soda-siphon and squirted the dark-red blood into the tin.

Satisfied, he dropped the fowl. The headless bird zigzagged round the circle, flapping its wings wildly. A fountain of blood pumped up from its neck and blazed its path. The bonhomme leaned forward and intently studied the bird and the pattern painted by the blood. When it finally collapsed and lay still in front of Laura, he frowned and muttered under his breath.

Pierre had been unable to shield Laura from the bird's gyrations, and she sat pale and still. Before he could move back to sit at her side, the bonhomme beckoned to her. She walked to him blindly and sat in the dust at his feet.

'You have brought me a piece of your mother's clothing?' he growled.

Laura nodded. Delving into the pocket of her shorts, she pulled out a lime-green scarf which Virgina often knotted over her hair when out on the boat.

A faint perfume of stephanotis trailed behind the scarf as Laura handed it to the bonhomme. For a brief moment she saw Virginia's smiling face as she sprayed the flowery fragrance behind her ears. The perfume strengthened Laura's resolve. She sat up straight and looked into the bonhomme's eyes, ignoring his bloodstained fingers.

He twisted the scarf round the jam tin and tightened it with an intricate knot. Stretching out a skeletal leg, he dragged the rooster to him and, bending down, pulled a long crimson feather from its tail.

Laura swallowed convulsively but did not turn away as he stirred the mixture of blood and leaf sap in the tin, using the devil leaves as a spoon. She shuddered slightly as the stained leaves were thrown on top of the fowl. The bonhomme passed the jam tin under his nose, savouring the aroma with all the delicacy of a master perfumer.

But her resolve to be strong did not allow her to watch as he dipped the feather into the mixture and ran it across his tongue. His muttering grew louder as he licked the feather a third and fourth time.

Pierre perched on the edge of his seat, ready to snatch Laura and run if the bonhomme became ill or violent. But the gris gris man's eyes stained and clouded. He merely rocked a little on the tin drum, digging his cracked heels into the sand to stop it overbalancing.

Suddenly he picked up the tin drum and set it down in front

124

of a makalapo. Pierre recognized the old musical instrument based on a bow, though he had not heard one played since he was a child. The bonhommes du bois had been forbidden to practise their skills in a vain effort to stamp out black magic in the islands, and the weird music of the makalapo was now seldom heard. Pierre studied the piece of tin nailed to the wooden bow. It was half buried in the sand and old tree stumps held down the two sides. He watched as the bonhomme stretched his thin legs out on either side of the tin. He picked up a stick and made the tin shriek and clang. He started chanting in a high cracked voice. The words were lost in antiquity and Pierre understood none of them.

Singing to the spirits, he mouthed at Laura as she watched him. Laura shivered. Her feet prickled and ached in her cramped position, but she remained as unmoving as a granite rock wedged deep into the sand.

Suddenly the bonhomme threw back his head and his eyes rolled until only the veined whites were showing. 'Trop tard,' he whistled thinly. 'Too late.'

Laura glanced at Pierre and he shook his head, warning her to remain still and silent. It can't be too late for Mummy, Laura pleaded dumbly. He can't mean Mummy.

She breathed a sigh of relief as once again he leaned forward and picked up an old coco de mer palm nut. He rummaged in its pelvis-shaped interior and pulled out a round black object with a hole in it. Pushing the huge nut aside, he dropped the black disc into the jam tin.

Laura stared at him aghast as he handed her the tin. Sweat trickled down her neck and stained the front of her swimming costume.

'Untie the scarf,' he commanded.

With trembling fingers she undid the knot and handed him the tin and the material.

He wedged the tin under his arm and, hunched over like a blind man, he stumbled to the middle of the enclosure and built up a small fire of dried devil leaves and twigs from a cinnamon tree.

When the flames were licking skywards he dumped the

125

green scarf on the fire. Before it turned black he quickly speared the disc out of the tin with the feather. He then dripped the blood and sap on to the flames. The fire spluttered as he held the disc, still swinging on the feather, in the thick smoke.

As the tendrils writhed round his head and reddened his eyes, again he chanted in a language Pierre could not understand.

Laura longed for the ordeal to end. She wanted to plunge into the sea, to feel the wind in her hair; she needed to leave this clearing deep in the forest. The trees and huge leaves seemed to be smothering her and she couldn't breathe. The oily smoke hung low in a black cloud over their heads and the sickly-sweet smell nauseated her. She wanted to be at home with Virginia, far away from the gris gris man and his magic.

She tried hard to think of good things. 'When you're lying awake in the dark after a nightmare, think of good things, they'll chase the bad ones away.' Virginia had once told her this when she was small and crying in bed.

Her mind was frozen and she could conjure up no good thoughts. Too scared to move and too squeamish to stay, at first she did not hear the bonhomme.

'*Prenez-la*,' he said, handing her the black disc. 'Here, take it. It's a strong gris gris.' He paused and scratched in his curls. 'Strong. But I do not like what I feel. It is bad.'

Laura took the disc gingerly and dropped it into her pocket. She wiped her fingers surreptitiously on the seat of her shorts.

'Your mother must keep the gris gris with her always. On her body by day, and at night on her bed.'

'*Merci*,' said Laura, struggling to pull a crumpled envelope out of the front of her costume where she had tucked it for safe keeping. It contained all her savings plus some rupees she had borrowed from Cook.

'Thank you,' she said again, backing out of the enclosure.

As they rounded the house, Cook's sister opened her eyes. There was a knowing gleam in them. 'De power is in de haid,' she crackled. She settled her straw hat firmly on her head,

126

wriggled her feet into her plastic thong sandals and led the way back through the undergrowth.

'What does she mean?' Laura whispered.

'If you believe in something then it'll work,' said Pierre.

Cook's sister looked over her shoulder and Laura was silent until they were once again in the boat.

'Oh, Pierre,' said Laura as the speedboat skimmed over the sea and Praslin faded into a misty blur behind them. 'That was horrible. I had the feeling that something awful was about to happen. I was so scared.'

'Keep away from magic and witchcraft, Laura,' he answered sternly. 'Strange things happen when you become involved with people who practise those crafts.'

'But Aunt Emma isn't scary like the bonhomme,' argued Laura. 'I love her. She's fun and she's so nice to me.'

'Of course she's nice,' said Pierre. 'But my grandmother always said, "Turn the rupee over." There's always another side – and it's usually dark.'

Laura listened to Pierre but was silent. She fingered the gris gris through the fabric of her shirt. She would thread it on her silver chain and give it to Virginia to wear. She would say that it was a present to celebrate saving Aldabra. At night she would hang it on the foot of Virginia's bed and it would be her duty to see that Virginia wore it every day.

The gris gris man must have meant that it would be bad if Virginia did not have the charm on her. She would make sure that it was always round Virginia's neck.

The sea had flattened to a sheet of pearlized glass, and the towering cumulus clouds edged in peach and silver looked down at their reflections, mirrored to an endless horizon.

Laura leaned back against the canopy and watched the boat's wake shatter the perfect, tumbling, gleaming clouds.

The first rays of dawn slipped through the wooden shutters guarding the humid darkness of the bedroom. Overhead an old punka fan creaked as it shifted the warm air round the room.

Virginia moaned softly in her sleep and turned on to her back. The sheet wound itself as tight as a straitjacket round her thin body and she kicked out feebly against the constriction. Her damp hair lay streaked across the pillow and her eyelids flickered restlessly. 'No, Ashley, no,' she pleaded helplessly.

He lifted his arms and she saw the muscles move under his deeply tanned skin as he clapped his hands round Nicole's tiny waist and drew her down over him.

'You can no longer fly, Fody,' he sneered. 'You're sick and useless.'

His eyes were soft with love for Nicole and she could hear his breathing hoarse and ragged. Nicole flung back her head and her hair washed in an arc of dark waves across her shoulders. Her mouth was open and she lowered her eyelashes seductively as she straddled Ashley.

'No,' groaned Virginia as she saw Laura run into the room. 'Laura,' she called. 'Laura.' But Laura ignored her and ran to Nicole and Ashley. 'My parents,' she laughed, 'these are my new parents.' They opened their arms to her and three pairs of steely-blue eyes stared accusingly at Virginia.

The sudden clash of shutters and the music of birdsong jolted Virginia awake. She lay, dazed and nauseous. Her heart pounded with fear at the thought of losing Ashley and Laura. She rested her hand on the empty pillow at her side. Ashley was already at Aldabra. She would be with him by lunchtime.

''Morning, Virginia. Sleep well?' Emma greeted her as she clipped back the shutters and bustled into the bathroom. She dragged Virginia's stool under the shower and turned on the cold water. 'It's a lovely day. No rain showers are forecast so the flight to Aldabra should be marvellous.'

Emma had taken over the daily task of helping Virginia

shower and dress. Virginia found that she usually looked forward to Emma's bright chatter and the scandalous stories she gleaned from Cook. She found Emma more acceptable in the islands, probably because she did not have the same control over Laura that she had at Lyewood. Laura spent most of her time out of doors with Pierre and Nicole.

'You're so lucky to be going to Aldabra. I wish I could take your place,' said Emma. She gabbled on, not waiting for a reply. She found that her talking helped Virginia to disguise her weakness when dressing in the morning. 'Giles and I feel so much a part of the struggle for the island.' She snuggled her shoulder under Virginia's arm to form a crutch. 'I'd love to see that atoll lying in the middle of nowhere. How did Ashley describe it in his article for the Society?'

'The island lies outlined on dazzling turquoise like a bearded corsair, forever gazing up into the blue vault overhead,' Virginia said.

'I think that's a beautiful description,' Emma said, leading Virginia to the bathroom.

'It's a very special island,' Virginia said dreamily. 'Out there the ocean seems scrubbed, polished and limitless. It's like being at the end of the world. The sea and sky blend. One is enclosed in a translucent ball of the purest blue.'

Emma kept quiet and let Virginia talk. It was a long time since she had shown such enthusiasm.

'I'm sure you would enjoy Aldabra. Perhaps Ashley could arrange a trip. I'll speak to him.'

'Thank you. Do you know what I'd really love to see?' Emma said, helping Virginia out of her nightdress. 'The bird that can't fly. The only one that hasn't gone the way of the dodo and the elephant bird.'

'The flightless white-throated rail,' Virginia said. She held on to Emma's shoulder and wriggled out of her slippers. As she looked at her toes she remembered the pretty little rail pecking at her red nail varnish, completely unafraid. She sighed. The trust between living creatures and humans had been long broken on all the other islands. The wonder of Aldabra was the abundance of living things and their acceptance of humans.

'Perhaps you'll even see that black dronga that was discovered only a few years ago,' Emma added as she settled Virginia on the plastic-topped stool and closed the door of the shower.

'Perhaps,' Virginia said. She closed her eyes and let the jet of cold water wash away her nightmare.

As she relaxed, her excitement at going to Aldabra returned. She longed to see that awe-inspiring island once again. This time she would be in a seaplane and be able to look down on the deep-water channels throbbing like massive arteries as they pumped sea water into the lagoon.

She could no longer scuba-dive. She would not be able to fin down deep and ride out on the strong currents as the lagoon emptied. She well remembered the thrill of being sucked out to sea with the barracudas and sharks.

Perhaps if she had Ashley beside her she would be able to lie on the surface with a face mask and snorkel and let herself be sucked through one of the smaller passes. Perhaps Passe Femme.

She smiled and wrapped a large lemon towel round herself. 'Emma,' she called, 'I'm ready.' She waited impatiently for Emma to help her dress.

She was eager to leave for the island. She wanted to float in a dinghy on the lagoon. She wanted to weave between the mushroom-shaped islands and look up at the balconies of boobies. She had a sneaking sympathy for these gentle sea gannets who sat with their bright-red feet wrapped round the branches like leg warmers. The great frigate birds lay in wait for the boobies to return from their fishing expeditions; they then bullied them into vomiting up the day's catch, which they promptly caught and ate. She wanted to trail her fingers in the shallow crystal waters and try to touch the black-tip sharks, looking as harmless as Disney models. She was eager to see Ashley and feel his strong arms round her. She needed to hear him say that he loved her.

Laura came bounding down the granite steps, with Pierre close on her heels. She raced to reach Virginia first and claim

130

the honour of pushing her wheelchair to the car. Pierre pretended to trip and Laura flung her arms breathlessly round Virginia. 'I touched you first, Mummy. I push the chair today.'

Virginia laughed and buried her face in her daughter's hair, breathing in the fresh tang of coconut oil shampoo. She flicked the heavy blonde pigtail back over Laura's shoulder and kissed her. Her baby had grown into a lovely young girl and soon she would be a very beautiful woman.

Laura stroked her mother's hair, surreptitiously feeling for the silver chain and gris gris charm.

'It's there,' said Virginia softly. 'I wouldn't forget to wear your gift on the day I leave for Aldabra.'

Laura hugged her mother, relieved that she would be protected.

'Give Daddy a big kiss and come back soon,' she said as she stood back for Pierre to help Virginia into the red Mini-Moke.

Nicole swung into the driver's seat and Emma squeezed into the back seat under the arms of the wheelchair.

'You may have to wait for me after school,' Nicole called as she turned the key in the ignition. 'I'm taking Emma down to the south of the island to visit some herbalists.'

Virginia put on her dark glasses and studied Nicole as she was speaking to Laura and Pierre. The nightmare flooded back: she saw Ashley hold Nicole's naked body, she saw the love and desire in Nicole's eyes, she heard Ashley's voice raw with desire and excitement. Virginia twined her fingers through the chain Laura had given her and she fought to remain calm.

'Herbalists?' Pierre and Laura echoed in unison.

'Yes,' said Emma, trying to wedge herself more comfortably into the small back seat.

'You're not taking her to the bonhomme, are you?' Pierre asked Nicole in Creole. He and Laura exchanged quick glances.

'No, of course not,' she answered, then quickly broke into English. 'Emma is interested in the properties of plants on the island.'

Virginia shook her head. It was only a bad dream. Nicole was sweet and gentle; she did not have to fear her. Nicole had

131

never shown any interest in Ashley – her illness was making her fanciful. 'We must go, or we'll miss the old Sea Turtle,' she broke in, placing her hand on Nicole's arm.

'Sea Turtle?' said Emma.

'Our name for the Grumman Amphibians. The old seaplanes look so much like turtles as they labour out of the water and roll on to the runway,' explained Virginia.

'They'll probably be an endangered species too, now that the new airport has opened,' said Emma. 'You had better enjoy this trip. It could be your last.'

'Don't say that,' said Pierre and Nicole together.

Virginia laughed before Emma could answer. 'Don't be pessimistic. Seaplanes will be wallowing around for years to come. It'll take forever for the outlying islands to build airstrips.'

Nicole put the car into gear, and Laura swung herself on to the running-board and held Virginia's hand as the Moke rolled slowly to the gate.

''Bye, Mummy,' she said, jumping off. 'I love you,' she whispered as the Moke stuttered round the corner in a cloud of exhaust fumes. She stared at the empty road and blinked hard. Don't be a baby, she admonished herself. Pierre will think you're just a silly kid. You can't always travel with Mummy.

She bent down to pick up a ripe mango from the driveway and took the opportunity to brush her hand furiously across her eyes. Then, smiling brightly, she ran back to where Pierre was waiting and offered him the ripe fruit.

<hr>

III

The bamboo blinds had been lowered against the slanting rays of the late afternoon sun and the verandah was shady and cool.

Cook placed the tea tray on the table in front of Emma and Nicole. Her tears blotched the rose-pink tea cosy and tray cloth. She made no effort to wipe them away.

'Cook,' said Nicole, 'sit down. Have a cup of tea with us. It'll help.'

Cook shook her head. Her eyes were red and swollen but her face was expressionless as she waddled back to her kitchen.

'A cup, Pierre?' Nicole asked.

'No, thanks. It's time I left to collect Laura,' he replied heavily. 'It's almost five. Her music lesson will be over and she'll be waiting outside.'

'Yes, poor little girl,' sighed Nicole.

Emma nodded in agreement but kept her eyes lowered over her teacup. It had been a long wait, but the dark ones had at last obeyed her commands. You're nearly mine, Tanith, she thought happily.

Laura was standing outside the Regina Mundi Convent, waiting for Pierre. The classroom windows were concertina'd open as if gasping for air and the dark-grey granite walls held the day's heat.

Three Seychelles College boys, neat in their khaki shorts and white shirts, were talking to her. Pierre noticed the red flashes on their epaulettes. They belonged to Hilary House, his own house at the college. His mind concentrated on details, unwilling to deal with facing Laura. The boys scattered as he pulled up at the kerb. Laura jumped into the Moke before it had stopped.

'They're lying, Pierre. They're stinking liars. It's not true, is it?' she asked, shaking his arm violently.

'Who? What?' he replied, trying to delay answering. Nicole and Emma had decided that he would bring Laura home and then Emma would break the news quietly and soberly. They would be able to comfort her in the privacy of her own home. This had not been planned, and suddenly he felt very young and inadequate.

'One of the boys whose father was on the plane to Aldabra has just been collected by a government car and taken home.' She clung to Pierre's arm and her eyes were dark with fear. 'They say that the Grumman has crashed into the sea.' Her voice broke. 'It's not true, is it, Pierre? Is it? Mummy was

133

wearing the gris gris. I know she's safe.' The words trailed away.

'Yes, Virginia had the gris gris.'

He was desperate to get Laura away from the groups of children waiting to be collected after their extra lessons. He would have to tell her that the rumour was true, but he needed somewhere quiet. There would be no time to get her home. He swung the open Moke into the traffic. The car climbed up the sharp blind bends of Le Niol before dropping down to Beau Vallon Bay, and he was grateful that the roar of the racing engine and the wind whipping through the open Moke made talking difficult.

'Come,' he urged as he parked the car in the deep shade of a takamaka which leaned precariously over Beau Vallon beach. 'We need to talk. Let's go to our place.'

Listlessly Laura swung a leg over the side of the car. Her brown sandal beat a tattoo on the bodywork. 'But, Pierre, why did they say that, then? It's a cruel thing to say.'

'Give me your shoes and book bag,' he commanded. 'I'll lock them in the boot.'

Laura tugged at the strap of her bag. The buckle was wedged tightly in the side of the seat. She dropped the strap and stared at a family crawling around on the wet sand collecting tec-tecs.

'Here, let me do it,' said Pierre, worried by her unnatural quietness.

As he ripped the strap away from the seat-cushion a small black disc flew out and cracked against the windscreen. Laura jumped as if stung by the poisonous spines of a lion fish. She caught the delicate silver chain before it fell to the floor.

'Mummy,' she breathed. 'It's Mummy's gris gris. Why isn't she wearing it? It was round her neck when I said goodbye.' She turned the disc over in her hand and ran her fingers along the broken chain. She looked up at Pierre, silently begging him to say that Virginia was safe. 'Then they weren't lying. It's true,' she said when Pierre didn't answer.

Pierre looked at her pale set face and nodded. She stood and

134

stared out to sea to where the island of Silhouette was resting beneath her crown of clouds.

Laura spun away from Pierre and fled along the beach. Her feet flew across the deep sand as effortlessly as a tern skimming the waves. Pierre threw the keys under the seat of the Moke and pounded after her.

Laura's footsteps dragged as they neared Whale Rock and the nearby cluster of granite boulders, which had been their secret place for years. Suddenly she threw herself against the boulder and pounded her fist into the open gaps forming the whale's mouth. The rock skinned her knuckles and shattered the black disc.

'Laura, stop it. Stop it,' Pierre shouted as he caught up with her. She twisted away from him and hurled pieces of the disc into the sea. The chain twisted and sparkled as it sank beneath the waves. She plunged into the sea after it. Her green-and-white-striped school uniform rode high above her waist as she struck out strongly for the open water. Pierre stared at her aghast. She was going to drown herself. He dived in after her. Together they swam through the darkening water and their flailing arms sliced into waves stained apricot and oyster by the setting sun.

The hotel lights were flickering faint as starlight across the sands, and the sea and sky had become a dark warm womb, when Pierre finally persuaded Laura to turn and swim back towards the shore.

As her feet touched the sandy bottom, she doubled over.

Pierre turned away, waiting for the paroxysms of vomiting to end. He put his arm round her and steadied her as they walked to the rocks, now black and indistinct. She stretched out and hung over one of the boulders as limp as wet seaweed, and Pierre sat at her feet.

'Daddy?' she said softly.

'Ashley is still at Aldabra.' Laura shifted restlessly on the rock. 'But I hear the government are trying to find another amphibian to fly everyone out,' Pierre hastened to add. 'So he'll probably be here within a day or so. You know that he'll come

135

the minute he can find some means of getting off Aldabra.' He looked at her and struggled to find words of comfort. 'I'm sure that Virginia—'

'I don't want to speak about Mu—' said Laura.

But her mother's name turned the key and released the tears which would eventually dilute her pain. She drummed impotently at the rock with her fists and heels while Pierre tried to hold her and calm her. He murmured words of sympathy but was helpless to ease her anguish.

Finally Laura was quiet; only the odd hiccup shook her body. Pierre sat on the rock beside her with his arm round her shoulders and stared out to sea, as the clothes dried on his body.

'Aunt Emma,' said Laura, sitting up and tugging at the end of her pigtail. 'Does she know?'

'Yes, she and Nicole are waiting for you at home.'

Laura slid down from the rock. He laced his fingers through hers and they started walking up the beach.

'You're very lucky to have known a mother, Laura. Remember that you had twelve years with Virginia, and you still have Ashley.' He felt her fingers stiffen and then relax in his hand. She nodded but remained silent.

A pair of fruit bats swooped unnoticed over their bent heads as they walked along the dark beach. Ghost crabs adopted defensive attitudes, then scuttled out of their way. They walked on, oblivious to the night creatures round them.

The backfiring of the Moke alerted Nicole and Emma, sitting on the dark verandah.

'It's them,' Nicole said, jumping up.

Emma closed her eyes in relief. The goddess Diana had protected her own. Tanith, her witch child, was safe. She moved across to the door and switched on the outside lights.

The harsh glare trapped the two exhausted youngsters as they stood, barefoot and pale, on the steps.

'Laura!' Emma exclaimed, staring at the girl's skinned hands and blood-streaked legs and heels. 'What has—?'

136

In response to a mute appeal from Pierre, Nicole moved forward. She ran down the steps lightly and squeezed Emma's arm. The sour smell of vomit was strong as she enfolded Laura in her arms. Laura rested her head wearily on Nicole's shoulder and for long moments they stood in silence. Then Nicole released Laura and Emma held her niece closely.

'Oh, my little Tanith,' she whispered as she kissed Laura's damp hair. 'My little girl.'

Laura put her arm round Emma's waist, smearing Emma's crisp white blouse with blood from her grazed hands.

'I'll run a hot bath,' Nicole said, 'and Emma can tuck you into bed.'

Pierre watched them lead Laura into the house. He sank down on the step and dropped his head into his hands.

Nicole and Emma fussed tenderly over Laura. They washed and dried her hair. Nicole brushed it until it shone like sheet lightning and Emma dabbed her cuts and grazes with scarlet mercurochrome. Laura winced as the cotton wool rubbed over her raw flesh, but she made no sound. Nicole found Laura's favourite pink-striped nightie, slipped it over her head and led her to her wickerwork bed.

Laura paused at her bedside table and ran her fingers lightly across the silver frame holding a photograph of her and Pierre winning a sailing race. They were standing on the jetty at the Yacht Club and Pierre was holding up her arm in a victory salute. It was a happy picture. She looked at it briefly then climbed into bed.

The two women drew up the thin cotton sheet and plumped up her pillow. Nicole fumbled in her pocket as Emma pulled a turquoise wicker chair up to the side of the bed and settled down in it.

'Here,' Nicole said, pulling out another silver photograph frame. 'I thought you'd like this beside you tonight.'

Laura took the frame and her eyes filled with tears. It was a picture of her and Virginia taken on the beach: she had her arm round Virginia's neck and they were smiling at each other as if sharing a wonderful secret. It was Virginia's favourite picture and always stood on her desk in her study.

'Thank you,' Laura said finally, lifting up her arms to Nicole.

'Virginia will always be with you, Laura. Remember that. You'll never lose your memories of her and the things she taught you,' Nicole whispered as she bent down over the bed. 'Hold on to that love, it'll make this awful time a little better.' She pinched Laura on the cheek and walked quietly out of the room, pausing to turn on the punka fan.

Emma made no attempt to break the silence once Nicole had closed the door. Laura lay, quietly studying the photograph, then she put it face down on her chest and folded her hands over it. Emma shuddered. Laura's hands, streaked red with antiseptic lotion, clutched the photograph like the bloodied claws of a bird of prey.

Emma was delighted that Virginia no longer stood in the way of her eventual control over Laura, but she wanted to take Virginia's place immediately. Laura had to stop crying for her mother. Emma studied Laura. She would have to take away the ugliness of death. 'Little Tanith,' she said, 'I promised you that I would teach you all about witches.'

Laura blinked but did not answer.

'Well,' Emma continued, her voice low and conversational, 'there are certain things that witches believe in implicitly. One of them is reincarnation.' She caught the flicker of interest in Laura's eyes and hurried on. 'We don't believe that there is only one life, followed by hell if you've been bad or by heaven if you've been good. Neither do we believe that when you're dead that's the end.'

Laura's eyes widened, and Emma smiled inwardly. She had Laura's attention.

'We do believe that the body can die and be buried. But the person, the spirit, the intelligence cannot be destroyed. That goes on living.'

'Even when you're drowned and locked in a plane at the bottom of the sea?'

'Even then.'

Laura's hands relaxed on the photograph frame and a little of the tension eased away.

138

'We believe that when the body dies the soul goes to the Land of Faery.'

'Is that also up in heaven?'

'No, Tanith. We believe it's a whole world we can't see. It exists with the world that we do see. Sometimes we are able to visit it when we dream, and when we wake we occasionally remember a little about it.'

'Do only witches believe in the Faery Land?'

Emma shook her head. 'For thousands of years people have believed in reincarnation. Reincarnation is still part of the religions of Asia and India. The Ancient Egyptians, the Romans and the Greeks, all believed that the soul could never be destroyed.' She leaned closer to Laura and rested her elbows on her knees as she searched for the name of an early philosopher whom Laura would recognize. 'Pythagoras. You'll know the name from your maths lessons. He taught that the soul is immortal.

'So you see, Tanith, we aren't the only ones who believe that the soul rests and then comes back to Earth again.'

'Mummy will come back?' Laura said, sitting up and staring at Emma.

'Virginia's soul will return, but in a different body and as a different person.' Laura flopped back on her pillow and tucked the photograph under the sheets as if holding Virginia closer. 'You see, Tanith,' Emma said, resting her hand just above Laura's skinned knuckles, 'even though we can't have Virginia with us, we must be happy knowing that her spirit is resting and one day it will have a new, strong body.'

Laura nodded and bit down on her lip.

'Turn over now and close your eyes,' Emma said. 'I'll stay beside your bed until you're asleep.'

Laura humped herself on to her side and placed the silver frame on her pillow. The metal pressed into her cheek and comforted her.

'Aunt Emma,' she whispered as Emma bent over to kiss her, 'why didn't you make a magic charm to help Mummy? You are so clever and know so much about magic.'

Emma hung over the bed. Silence draped itself over them

like a billowing mosquito net. Laura opened her eye. and stared up into dark emerald depths just a few inches above her face. 'I did,' Emma said, and she again smelt the sickly-sweet smell of elderflowers.

'But it didn't work,' Laura said softly.

Emma brushed her lips over Laura's cheek. 'Sleep, little Tanith,' she whispered. 'Sleep, and everything will be all right.'

Emma closed the bedroom door quietly and tiptoed down the passage. She walked quickly through the quiet home, glancing into the rooms as she passed, looking for Nicole. She wanted Nicole on her side when Ashley returned. She was determined that Laura would leave the islands to live with her and Giles at Lyewood.

The verandah was dark and empty, and Emma walked down the stairs and out on to the tourterelle grass. The dainty leaves meshed tightly together, forming a pale-velvet carpet in the bright moonlight. The sea lay heavy as mercury at the foot of the garden. Emma walked slowly down the path to the jetty.

The night was still and airless. Death seemed to have hung a silver shroud over the house and gardens. Even the sea swells scaled in silver moved round the rocks in oily silence and the ripples barely whispered as they touched the wooden jetty.

Emma lifted her face up to the moon, and her wide-set eyes were deep and dark as sea caverns as she gazed at her moon goddess. Great Diana, you are all beautiful and all powerful, she mouthed.

A slight movement at the end of the jetty alerted her. As she walked across the wooden planks, she smelt Nicole's perfume: a rich blend of patchouli oil and frangipani. Straining her eyes, she saw the shadowy outline of a figure sitting in the deep shadow of the bulwark.

'Nicole,' she said.

Pierre answered, and Emma cursed silently. She wanted to speak to Nicole. She wanted to point out that, with Laura away from the Seychelles, Nicole would be able to devote more time to Ashley. Nicole could not fail to see the advantages of such an arrangement.

'Nicole?' she queried.

'I'm here,' Nicole replied. She held out her hand and Emma saw her leaning against the wooden post. She had been masked by Pierre. 'Is Laura asleep?'

'Yes, she's exhausted,' Emma answered, sitting down beside them. 'I sat with her for a while in case she woke up. I left the passage light on.'

They sat in silence, watching the sea heaving beneath them, each lost in thought.

'Nicole,' Emma said, finally breaking the silence. 'I think we ought to have a talk about Laura.'

Nicole looked up quickly, but Emma's face was pure and serene in the opalescent light; her eyes were wide and guileless. Pierre coughed and made to get up.

'No,' Nicole said. 'Stay, Pierre, you are probably closer to Laura than any of us.'

Emma clenched her teeth and then smiled thinly. 'Of course you must stay, Pierre. We all know how fond Laura is of you.'

Pierre detected a scraping of sarcasm in her voice but he merely nodded.

'Now that Virginia has gone, we must consider Laura's future,' Emma began.

'Isn't that for Ashley to decide? asked Pierre. 'After all, he is her father.'

'And I'm her aunt, also a relative,' snapped Emma. She quickly sweetened her voice. 'But, as you say, Ashley is now her only guardian, and we'll obviously also discuss this with him when he returns from Aldabra. Hopefully tomorrow.'

'Perhaps after the funeral,' Nicole suggested softly. 'He adored Virginia and—'

'He did,' Emma agreed, 'but one has to look to the future. I want us to agree on some points before we speak to Ashley.' She smiled at Nicole. 'As you say, he'll be very upset and it'll be a help if we can present him with a plan for Laura's future schooling.'

Pierre started to speak, and Nicole cut in quickly. 'What do you suggest, Emma?'

'Well,' she answered, pleased that Nicole was deferring to her. 'The island school was fine while Laura was young, but she now needs superior schooling. We have excellent schools in our area.'

Pierre stirred restlessly and Nicole tapped him lightly on his leg.

'It wouldn't be necessary for Ashley to live in England. He could continue his work here. He has you to run the home and look after him. Pierre will soon be in France, so it would just be the two of you in the house,' she added meaningfully. Nicole's face was still hidden in the shadows. Fortunately Emma did not see her expression. 'I would of course bring Laura to the Seychelles for the school holidays.'

'I see,' Nicole said, 'and you think that Ashley will be happy with this arrangement?'

'Men seldom know what's best for them. I'm relying on you to help me convince him that this will be for Laura's good.' Taking Nicole's silence for assent, she congratulated herself silently. It took a few seconds before she realized what Nicole was saying.

'Virginia wanted Laura to grow up enjoying the freedom and beauty of the islands. She felt that there was time for the sophistication of city life later. She would not want Laura to be taken away from the Seychelles.'

'But,' said Emma, 'you don't even begin to understand.'

'I do,' Nicole replied firmly. 'In fact, I understand only too well what you want. I'm sorry, Emma, but I can't support you.' She turned to face Emma. 'I know how much you love Laura and she adores you, but I feel we would be betraying Virginia.'

Emma stared at Nicole then turned her face away, but not before Pierre had caught the expression in her eyes. He shivered in the hot, humid night air. Nicole would have to be careful. Even in the moonlight he had not mistaken the hatred which flashed and then vanished as swiftly as a shooting star in Emma's eyes.

'It's been a dreadful day,' said Emma, standing up and dusting off the seat of her cotton dress. 'I'm going to bed.' She yawned theatrically. 'I'll leave you to the peace of the sea and the night.'

'Goodnight, Emma,' Nicole answered gently.

''Night,' Pierre added.

Enjoy your island while you can, fumed Emma as she climbed the steps leading up to La Retraite. Virginia did not stand in my way; nor will you, she vowed. I'm prepared to wait.

She looked up at the moon before she closed the slatted door leading into the house.

'Diana the light, and Hecate the dark,' she whispered.

The door slammed shut behind her.

CHAPTER FIVE

England and the Seychelles 1977

 I

The rain beat a steady drum-roll on the roof of the Daimler, parked hard against the brick wall of the parking lot. It was high summer, but the London skies were overcast and it had rained intermittently all day.

Bartholomew Harden Faulconer slid into the car, slammed the door and dropped the safety locks. He glanced quickly round the dark interior and grunted his satisfaction. The rain-streaked windows would soon mist over and the car was hidden from the pub by a bright-orange tow-truck. The truck driver had a couple of hours to spend before going off duty. He had just settled down to a game of darts and a few beers with his mates.

Bart shrugged off his damp leather jacket and tossed it into the front seat, then he turned to the woman at his side. She was well past the age he usually chose, but the years he had spent fighting in the vicious Rhodesian bush war had taught him not to be selective. He took women where and when he could find them, the way he took catnaps when out on recce. He put an arm round her waist and pulled her across the seat.

She laughed throatily as her mini-skirt rucked up high. Her deeply henna'd hair hung in corrugated waves to her waist and her plum-coloured lipstick was daubed across her mouth. As he lifted her face to his, the smell of sweet sherry was strong on her breath. He covered her mouth with his lips, and as he felt her questing tongue he hooked his fingers into the elastic of her panties. She squirmed and beat at him with her fists, but his weight held her pinned to the seat. It excited him when women protested.

'No,' she grunted as she wrenched her mouth away from his.

'Oh yes,' he contradicted, breathing heavily. 'You were ready in the pub. You were in the starting blocks, eager to go.'

'But not in the back seat like a bloody teenager,' she retorted, writhing helplessly beneath him.

'Come, baby,' he cajoled, switching suddenly from arrogance to charming persuasiveness. 'You're so damn attractive. You'd drive any man crazy.' She stopped struggling and he smiled down at her. Few women were able to resist Bart Faulconer. He exuded power and excitement and it was a potent aphrodisiac.

She ran her fingers through his beard, yellow as an overripe corn-cob, and she opened her mouth wide to taste his lips.

'That's my baby,' he murmured as he tugged her skirt up round her waist.

When he was finally satisfied, he grunted and rolled back on to the seat, still panting lightly. 'What now?' she asked.

His eyes, clear as golden topaz, ran over her dishevelled clothes and smudged make-up. 'Now I go back to my pals and get on with the serious business of drinking,' he answered, tucking his shirt-tails deep between his legs and zipping up his pants.

'And me?'

'I suggest you clean up and head for home. Unless you feel like looking after my friends as well.' He released the car locks and swung the door open. 'Don't try tearing the leather or smearing lipstick on the seats. Remember, I know where to find you and I have an awful temper.' He grinned and kicked the door closed behind him.

She watched him stride into the darkness, his walk jaunty and arrogant. 'Swine,' she whispered as she groped for her underclothes on the floor. 'Like all bloody men, lusting swine.'

A middle-aged man lifted his head, shiny and round as a bullet, as the pub door swung open. His eyes narrowed while he studied Bart. He had waited for him for over an hour. He was known only as Top and masterminded a crack mercenary army who were much in demand in the shadows of international politics. He was not accustomed to being made to wait for new recruits. He had been wary of Bart when they first met in Rhodesia, where he was scouting for mercenaries, but Bart had all the necessary qualifications for the counter-coup they were planning in the Seychelles, so he had stilled his misgivings and hired him.

Randy, he thought, looking at Bart as he swaggered through the doorway. His jacket was slung over his shoulder and his shirt was plastered to his muscular body. Randy, but a damn good fighter. Give them a taste of blood and death and they either puke or clamour for more. This one's a glutton. Been in Africa for ten years now and is still eager. Some of my best men have come from the African bush wars.

He took a mouthful of beer and watched Bart thump on the stained counter to order a drink. Probably high time we pulled him out of the bush. Three years with the Selous Scouts and there's not much left to teach him. Have to keep a watch on him, though. There are signs that he's a killer. He's forgetting he is a soldier. He smiled thinly as Bart whacked a pal on the back, almost knocking him off his feet, and threaded his way through the tables.

May the Lord help those poor blighters in the Seychelles, he thought. Hope the new president can manage this one when he arrives under the guise of training his personal guard and security forces. For a moment he wondered whether he had been wise to arrange a position so close to the president for Bart. Then he smiled. The president was tough, he had taken power by a coup d'état. He should be able to handle Bartholomew Faulconer.

Top kicked back a chair and Bart dropped into it, feigning exhaustion. 'Hot,' he said, wiping at non-existent perspiration on his forehead. 'That bitch was hotter than chillies.'

The man grinned, hiding his irritation well. 'You'll wear it out if you're not careful.'

'No way,' Bart laughed, leaning forward to put his mug on

146

the table. 'Just practising for those babes in the Seychelles. Roll on palm trees, white beaches and girls with long blonde hair.' He licked his lips and rolled his eyes theatrically.

'You leave the day after tomorrow.'

Bart sat up as though an FN rifle had been jammed into his back. His eyes slitted into the cold, calculating stare of a hunting lion and he leaned forward. 'It's all arranged, then?'

'Yes. I have your papers with me. You'll not be going in as Bart Harden. I understand you don't want to keep the name you used in the Selous Scouts.'

'It was OK in the bush. My old man's a stickler for human rights and all that crap. When there's killing to be done I prefer my second name, Harden. It keeps Faulconer pure and my father can't gripe.' Bart drained half of his drink in one long swallow. 'I'll be close to the president in the Seychelles, so let's keep it respectable. I'll use Faulconer.'

The man nodded and lifted his glass. 'A word of advice,' he said. 'Generally the islanders are a happy, fairly indolent lot. The coup on the fifth of June this year put an end to the coalition government. It deposed the president and put the Democratic Party out of power. It brought in the Seychelles People's United Party and the former prime minister now heads the new government. Needless to say, there is a lot of unhappiness in the democratic ranks and we are going in to restore the former president to power. We aim to make our move before the new government have settled down and closed all the loopholes.' Delicately he licked the foam off his neat grey moustache. 'Remember, until now the only uniforms the islanders have seen belonged to the police force. Damned good crowd, those police,' he mused, 'trained in the best British tradition at the Police College in Hendon.'

He tapped his glass and chose his next words carefully.

'The Seychellois are not too happy with the soldiers who have been brought in from Africa. They don't like strangers lording it over them.' He dropped his voice and his demeanour changed to that of a man in supreme command. 'Keep your nose clean. The civilians do not want you or your men. Keep out of the politics, both military and civil. Remember, your

147

cover is that you know African soldiers. You've worked and fought with them for years. You are there only as an instructor. Don't forget it.'

Bart heard and recognized the steel in the man's voice.

'You'll give all the information you glean to our agents. They'll contact you periodically and at their discretion. There will be two agents on Mahé. You will know them as Job and King. They will be posing as English brothers, fairly wealthy, looking for a place to while away the English winters. You will obey their orders and not question them.'

'How long before the counter-coup takes place?' Bart asked unwisely.

'How long does it take you to track up a group of terrorists in the bush?' countered the man in command. 'You are no longer under the protection of the Rhodesian army. Cross me, disobey orders, endanger this operation of mine – and you will vanish. Job and King are highly skilled men.'

Bart accepted the rebuke.

For the next two hours, under cover of the drunken laughter in the pub, they discussed Bart's participation in the forthcoming counter-coup. Finally, satisfied that Bart would play his part to perfection, the bald man stood up. Clutching each other's shoulders and laughing raucously, they staggered out of the pub, giving an excellent imitation of a couple of drunks.

━━━━●|❀|❀|❀| II |❀|❀|❀|●━━━━

The study door was firmly closed. There was a rich aroma of beeswax and its polished surface spoke of loving care.

Nicole raised her hand to knock, then hesitated. Old doubts returned like roosting birds to plague her. She frowned and the fine lines marking the passage of time deepened on her forehead. Nervously she knocked loudly.

'Come in,' Ashley called.

She turned the gleaming brass doorknob and stepped into

his study. He was sitting at his desk with his back to the open double doors, and the warm breeze ruffled his hair. He smiled at her and returned to his phone call. She settled into a cane chair near his desk and crossed her long, slim legs.

She studied him surreptitiously, as if seeing him for the first time. She noticed that the hair which spilled from his open shirt-front was now sprinkled with grey, and the sun-bleached streaks on his head had silvered with time. The lines which bereavement had etched lightly on his face six years ago had deepened. But he was still very attractive. He seemed to have lost none of his tremendous vitality, and when he laughed at something he sounded like a young man.

He rubbed the side of his nose with a yellow pencil as he listened, and he raised his eyebrows at her in mock resignation. She watched him and loved him.

Eventually he replaced the phone on the receiver. 'Whew,' he whistled, running his fingers through his hair, leaving it standing up like the spines of a sea urchin. 'That has to be the craziest idea of all to raise money for the protection of Aldabra.'

Ashley was worried. Since 1976, when the Seychelles had voted for independence from Britain, the cost of continuing the research on Aldabra rested with the islands. No one realized how expensive it would be to meet the bills which the British government and the Royal Society had paid for the last ten years.

'Since Aldabra was handed back to the Seychelles, the wires have been burning with wild ideas to finance the place,' Ashley laughed. 'Now, enough of that. Tell me what the problem is.' He smiled at her and she felt her resolve waver. 'Is Cook sulking again? Has Laura turned down yet another invitation from one of her hopeful suitors? Are Pierre's political dissertations driving you crazy?' Ashley teased her gently and was relieved to see a glimmer of a smile tilt the corners of her mouth.

'No, no. I have something very serious to discuss.'

Ashley put down the pencil, laced his fingers and leaned forward over the desk, waiting for her to continue.

'This is not a sudden decision of mine, Ashley. I've been

wanting to talk to you for some time.' Nicole bit her lip. Telling Ashley was going to be even more difficult than she had thought. 'It concerns my future.'

Ashley felt the first cold fingers of apprehension stroke the back of his neck, and suddenly he did not want to hear what Nicole had to say.

'Ashley.'

'Daddy.'

Two voices rang out in unison as Pierre and Laura pounded down the verandah to his study. Thankful for the interruption, he swung his chair round to face them as they burst into the room.

'Daddy,' Laura pleaded breathlessly, 'please make Pierre take me with him to the meeting tonight.'

'Ashley, please keep her here,' begged Pierre. 'She's only a distraction. The guys won't keep their minds on politics when she's there.'

Ashley stifled his laughter. Pierre had always been interested in politics, but since the Seychelles People's United Party had taken control in June that year, politics had become an obsession.

'Muffin,' Ashley said, 'are you going to these meetings to cause mayhem or because the socialist policies of the new government really interest you?'

Laura looked down at Ashley from under her long lashes and her full lower lip quivered. 'Both,' she said happily. 'Pierre is just a grouch. He doesn't like the guys talking to me.'

'Talking!' Pierre exploded. 'They drool over you. It's disgusting.'

Nicole smiled. Pierre was still fiercely protective of Laura, and he had every reason to be worried. She had grown into a remarkably beautiful seventeen-year-old. She had inherited Virginia's slim willowy body and flowing walk, but her eyes were still filled with dreams, and she had the implicit trust usually found in babies. Laura was blessed with the body of a sensuous woman and the carefree innocence of an island child.

Ashley and Nicole had won the battle against Emma and they kept Laura at school in the Seychelles. Laura chose not to

150

accompany Ashley on all his trips overseas; she was content to stay at La Retraite with Nicole and Pierre, who had moved into the main house after Virginia's death.

Emma hid her anger well, but made a point of returning to the Seychelles with Ashley whenever he visited England. She was content to wait; she knew that Laura would come to England once she had finished her schooling on the islands. She would then have Tanith to herself at Lyewood and could initiate her into the old pagan religion. She had no doubts that one day Laura would wear the witch garter.

'Laura,' said Ashley. 'will you promise not to break any hearts and to pay attention only to the speakers if Pierre agrees to take you?'

'Promise,' she answered demurely.

'Do you think you could give her another chance, Pierre?' Ashley asked formally.

Pierre stared at Laura, but she kept her head bent and her hair curtained her face in bleached silk.

'All right,' he relented, 'but she has to behave. And she's not to make any more remarks during meetings.'

'I only said that coups were sneaky and that people should be allowed to choose their own government,' she flashed.

Ashley caught Nicole's eye and they quickly composed their faces into masks of solemnity.

'Muffin,' Ashley admonished. 'When you're a tax-paying member of society, then you can have a say in the running of the country – '

'But Pierre does,' she protested vehemently.

'Pierre has been a working man since he returned from France two years ago, and he is about to be offered a good position in the new Ministry of Tourism.'

Pierre glanced at Laura's woebegone face and he put his arm round her shoulders and hugged her. 'We'll be late. Let's go.'

Her face lit up. She kissed Nicole and Ashley goodbye and followed Pierre from the room. As they walked down the steps, her voice floated back to the study. 'You're wrong. Taking power was not the only way of ensuring that everyone would have equal rights . . .'

Pierre's low answer was lost to them.

'And the slogans! "We shall never forget 5th June." "The future lies in the liberation of its youth." Why must we have banners and slogans everywhere?'

Ashley shook his head and smiled. 'The impetuousness of youth! Patience is a dirty eight-letter word to them. They believe they have the immediate answers to everything.'

Nicole nodded. 'Everyone on the island is embroiled in politics at the moment.' She paused. 'Except you.'

'I find it a messy business. It's best left to those who can tolerate soiled hands and numerous bed partners,' Ashley replied, dismissing the subject lightly.

'Oh,' said Nicole quietly and looked down at her hands. 'I was thinking of becoming involved.'

Ashley looked at her sharply then sat back in his chair and tapped at his thumbnail with the yellow pencil. Nicole realized that he was waiting for her to continue.

'Since Virginia's death I've had a great deal of time to spare, and soon I'll have even more. Next year Laura will be in London starting her art course. Pierre is away at work for most of the day and there is no longer much for me to do at La Retraite.' Nicole paused to gather her thoughts. She watched the clouds bruise over Silhouette as the sun slipped away, leaving them dark and purple. Ashley waited patiently. 'You are very involved with the research station on Aldabra and will have the additional burden of trying to raise funds.'

Ashley nodded but offered no encouragement.

'Cook can manage the home perfectly well. I know that she can be uncommunicative and surly, but she is very loyal and is an excellent worker.' Nicole nervously twirled the antique ruby gypsy ring which Virginia had given her. 'Please understand, Ashley. I love living here, but I'm now thirty-nine and I have to consider my future. If I become involved in the political field, I'll not be able to fulfil my duties here, so—'

'I always thought you were happy with us, Nicole,' said Ashley softly.

'Oh, I am! I'll always love Laura and the home and everyone. I'll miss living here dreadfully. The decision has not

152

been an easy one to make, but I have to do something with my life.'

The sun was setting and the shadows thickened in the study while they were talking. Nicole could no longer see the expression on Ashley's face.

'Nicole, you came to us at a time when we needed you desperately. You gave up your job with the British Office and devoted yourself to our family.'

His voice was warm and low, and Nicole felt tears in the corners of her eyes. She pressed her knuckle hard into the bottom of her nose to stop them.

'I can never repay you for the comfort you gave Virginia or the love you've given Laura.' He coughed gruffly. 'I have to respect your decision and I wish you happiness and fulfilment in your new life.'

Nicole felt nauseous: Ashley had accepted it; he was not going to plead with her to stay, even though they had grown so close since Virginia's death. Well, she admonished herself silently, obviously he doesn't share your feelings. You've just been a good friend and a shoulder to lean on. Don't let him see you cry. Leave with dignity.

'Thank you, Ashley,' she said quietly as she pushed back her chair. 'Thank you for having accepted me as part of your family for so long. I'll keep you informed of my plans.'

She left the room, closing the door quietly behind her. Ashley sighed and pushed himself up heavily from his chair. He walked out on to the verandah, and his steps were those of an old man. Leaning his head wearily against a wooden post, he closed his eyes.

A sound as high and burbling as a singing kettle attracted his attention. He sat down slowly on the verandah rail. A tiny fody, his scarlet chest and head now only a dull smudge of colour in the fading light, swung lightly on the rope stay of the bamboo blinds. He finished his territorial song, warning everyone to keep away from his area and his mate. Then, cocking his head to one side, he studied Ashley cheekily.

'Virginia,' Ashley whispered. He could see her blonde hair swinging away as she cocked her head to the side to listen to

153

him. But he could no longer see her clear grey eyes. He could hear her high laughter but he could not find her lips. He closed his eyes tightly, blotting out the scarlet bird, but Virginia's features would not cohere.

Instead, a mass of wild dark waves flew round a perfect oval face, and silky lashes met and mingled at the corners of striking steel-blue eyes. A generous mouth tilted up at the corners in a permanent smile and a voice soft with the lilt of the islands called his name.

He shook his head, splintering the face. The fody chirruped shrilly and flew away. She's gone. Virginia's gone, he thought. And Nicole? Will she go too? He groaned softly.

Losing Nicole would leave a vast and aching emptiness in his life. She had become his trusted friend and companion. She was a mother figure to Laura. Her confidante. In the bleak sad months after Virginia's death when he withdrew, haggard and heartbroken, it was Nicole who gave him strength. She made him finally accept the sea as Virginia's grave. She stood firm beside him and resisted Emma's efforts to take Laura away to Lyewood. She comforted him and she calmed Laura's fears and soothed the pain. Nicole had waded with his only child through the currents and the backwash of puberty. He owed much of Laura's happiness and his own contentment to her.

For long hours he sat, staring vacantly at the black sea and sky. As the moon cut a silver crescent into the inkiness he reached a decision. He could not lose Nicole. He would have to plead with her to stay. He needed her.

The door to Nicole's room stood ajar. She still left it like that for Laura. For months Laura had run into Nicole's room after a nightmare and Nicole would stroke her hair and murmur softly to her until she fell asleep. The childish habit had become a custom, and now she sat on the end of Nicole's bed almost every night and discussed the day's events before she went to sleep. Without realizing it Laura had come to accept Nicole as her mother. When they discussed Virginia, it was with warmth and love. The searing pain had gone. Nicole had led Laura to happiness.

154

Ashley tapped tentatively on the door.

'Come in, Laura,' Nicole called. Her voice was muffled and broken, and Ashley frowned.

He walked into her room. The familiar scent of frangipani flowers and patchouli oil made him catch his breath.

'Nicole,' he whispered, 'may I talk to you? It's important.'

Nicole sat up and reached for a handful of tissues.

'Please don't be alarmed,' he said quickly. 'If you don't mind, I'd like to talk to you here.'

She quickly dabbed at her eyes, but fresh tears soaked the soft paper and oiled her thick lashes.

'May I sit down?' he asked. As Nicole nodded silently he settled himself on the edge of her bed.

A soft breeze waltzed the curtains across the open windows and moonlight flickered over her face and shoulders. Ashley started in surprise. He leaned across her and held back one of the curtains while he studied her face.

'Oh, Ashley,' she sobbed brokenly, 'I'm sorry.'

He released the curtain and awkwardly folded his arms round her.

'Don't cry,' he said gruffly. 'Please don't cry, Nicole. It's all right.'

He rocked her in his arms and as her sobs died away he lifted her head from his chest and tilted up her chin. She looked up at him and her dark brows were arched high above her large, liquid eyes. Her full lips looked soft and vulnerable and the lower one still trembled.

'You're beautiful, Nicole,' he breathed, wiping the tears from her cheeks with his thumb. 'So beautiful.'

Tentatively she raised her arms to him and her small breasts stood high and dark-nippled beneath her thin muslin nightdress. His breathing quickened. As he tasted the salt on her lips, compassion and contrition gave way to desire. She felt as light and as delicate as a tiny tern in his arms. He stroked the silken smoothness of her skin. He tried to force himself to be gentle, but he had waited too long and his need for this woman was too great. His fingers fumbled at the straps of her nightgown,

155

and as the soft material fell away he laid her back against the white pillows. She cried out beneath him and the old house echoed their fulfilment.

'Nicole,' he whispered into the dark waves of her hair as she lay resting in the crook of his arm, 'I've been such a fool. I've taken you for granted for so long.'

'Ssh,' she answered, running her fingers lightly over his lips. 'We have each other now and that's all that matters.'

'I want—' The backfiring of the Mini-Moke drowned his words. Ashley threw aside the sheet.

'Don't go,' Nicole said, and she kissed the pulse throbbing in his throat.

'The children. Laura,' he protested.

'You closed the door. She never comes into my room if it's closed. I want you with me tonight, Ashley. I've waited for you for so many years. I need to know that this isn't just a dream.'

'Tonight and every night.'

They were silent as Laura's footsteps stopped outside the door. Nicole felt Ashley stiffen and she held her breath. Don't let tonight be the exception, she thought. Laura waited for a few moments and then they heard her patter down the stairs to her bedroom wing.

Ashley relaxed and turned to Nicole. She felt his kisses, fleeting as fairy footsteps across her body, and her nipples puckered as his lips passed over them. His mouth played with her body until she trembled to his touch.

'Love me again,' she mouthed in his ear. 'Please, love me now.'

Ashley looked down at the delicate woman beneath him. He moved over her and saw her lips wet and her face soft with desire. He knew that his life was once again complete.

The jarring quack of fairy terns circling the waves near the jetty awakened Nicole. The sea breeze had freshened, lifting the curtains and allowing her a glimpse of the pale-lemon freshness of dawn. She turned her head and looked into a pair of eyes sparkling as the sun-spangled sea.

156

'You're awake,' she whispered.

'For the last hour,' he answered. 'I've been lying here looking at you, marvelling at how lucky I am to have you.' He combed her tumbling hair away from her face with his fingers and searched her eyes as if trying to read her heart. 'I realize how much Laura and I owe you. Laura loves you deeply and I now know that I need you beside me always.'

Nicole tried to speak and choked.

'Join us at Lyewood for Christmas. We could be married quietly. We could finalize the arrangements for Laura to start college in the New Year and then fly back to the Seychelles for a tropical island honeymoon.'

'Marry?' Nicole said quietly.

'Yes, Nicole. Will you? Will you be my lover and my wife? Mrs Challoner?'

She was silent for a few moments, her eyes wide and questioning, as if waiting to hear that he was teasing her. Then she nodded and her smile was as radiant. 'Yes. Oh, yes, Ashley.'

Ashley stretched out to embrace her. Suddenly she pulled away and sat up, the sheet slipping from her naked body.

'Oh, Ashley, I can't spend Christmas at Lyewood,' she said dolefully. 'It's my mother's birthday on Christmas Day. It's a very important day.' Ashley looked puzzled. 'You see, she believes that she'll die before her eighty-fifth birthday next year. None of the women in our family have celebrated their eighty-fifth year. It's an old gris gris curse. So she's having a family reunion on Praslin this year. I must be there.'

'Not a particularly good curse,' Ashley said. 'Eighty-four is a very good age.'

Nicole laughed. 'We say that the bonhomme had too much toddy to drink. He meant to punish by grandfather by saying no woman in his family would live beyond the age of twenty-five but he slipped up and made it eighty-five!'

'Strong stuff, that palm wine, especially the three-day-old vintage,' Ashley grinned. 'Never mind, we'll have an island wedding. I'll fly back with Emma, Giles and Laura after Christmas and we'll be married here at La Retraite.'

His eyes crinkled at the corners when he saw her delight.

Spanning her tiny waist with his two hands, he swung her over him.

'I now expect a good-morning kiss from the future Mrs Challoner,' he teased.

Nicole laughed, throwing back her head. Her hair swept back in tumbling waves. Her open mouth was warm and inviting and her eyes were seductive beneath the lowered black lashes.

III

The apple logs spluttered in the old iron fireplace and the ones which had been brought in from the slushy ground outside steamed as the flames dried them. The Christmas tree stood, tall and green, in the middle of the panelled room; the silver star on its tip scraped the high ceiling. The festive smell of resin was strong.

'Ouch,' squeaked Laura, backing out from under the spreading branches on her hands and knees. The glass balls and silver bells jingled as her head bumped a low branch. A sprinkling of dead pine needles patterned the rich Persian rug. 'Oh no,' she moaned, sitting back on her heels. 'Just when I'd swept up the last lot.'

Emma grinned and busied herself replacing ornaments which had been brushed off the tree or which now hung askew.

'The needles seem to be falling sooner than they did last year. I certainly don't remember sweeping up as many.'

'You'd better hurry,' Emma admonished, ignoring Laura's complaints. 'Giles and Ashley will be down from London soon. Hopefully they'll have Nicole's dress. I'm dying to have a peep at it before we leave for lunch at the Cat.'

'She'll look stunning,' said Laura dreamily, thinking of the tight pearl-encrusted bodice and floating skirt which was being made in a London boutique for Nicole's wedding.

'Yes, she's very lovely,' Emma agreed, kneeling on the floor beside Laura to tie a porcelain angel back on the tree.

'Tell me, Tanith,' she said, her voice low and confiding, 'are you happy that Ashley is remarrying?'

'Yes,' Laura answered slowly. 'Daddy has been unhappy and very lonely for so long. It doesn't mean that he's forgotten Mummy,' she quickly defended him. 'He'll always remember and love Mummy. So will I.'

'I know.' Emma knotted the white satin bow round a branch, sending another shower of needles on to the rug.

'You see, nothing will really be different. Nicole has always been there. She and Pierre seem to have been part of the family for ever and I love them both very much.' She paused and her voice was muffled as she crawled back under the tree. 'It must be lovely to fall in love with someone like Daddy,' she mused. 'He's so super.'

Emma stood up and brushed the snippets of ribbon and tinsel from her grey tweed slacks.

'One day you'll meet someone like Ashley,' she said. 'You just have to be very careful that you give your love and yourself to the right person.'

'And how,' said Laura sliding out on her stomach to avoid bumping into any further branches, 'do I do that?'

'Aha,' Emma answered. 'That's where you're lucky to have a clever witch for an aunt.'

'Oh, Aunt Emma,' Laura laughed, 'not your magic spells again.'

Since her visit to the bonhomme du bois on Praslin, Laura had been reluctant to enter Emma's secret room. Emma realized that something had frightened her and was content to wait. She was certain that, once Laura lived at Lyewood, she could rekindle her interest. She had hoped that the time was ripe when Virginia died, but her plans had been thwarted. On reflection, Ashley's news that he was going to marry Nicole pleased her. Perhaps Nicole would be more useful alive. Ashley would probably now be content to spend more time in the Seychelles with Nicole. Emma would not have his influence to contend with while Laura was at Lyewood. Laura would study art for three years and she, Emma, would at last be able to start moulding her into the ways of Wicca.

'Love potions, Love charms, my Tanith,' she said as she took the dustpan and brush from Laura. 'Charms to bring you anyone you desire. No man will be able to resist you.'

'Oh, you're a horrid tease,' Laura said, but Emma had pricked her interest. 'What sort of love charms?'

Emma wriggled her hips, parodying a vamp singer. 'When I need love,' she crooned the popular song and rolled her eyes. Laura grinned. She adored her aunt. She now looked forward to living at Lyewood. 'All I need is a potion,' Emma ad libbed and Laura clapped her hands.

'Love potions,' said Emma, sinking into an armchair to regain her breath. 'Let's see, we could use the blue periwinkle. Picked at full moon and placed under your pillow; words of magic recited before you go to sleep and your lover will appear to you in a dream.'

'A dream,' Laura laughed, 'only in a dream!'

'Well, we could of course make cockle bread. Give it to the gorgeous hunk you're mad about and, once he eats it, he's yours.'

'Cockle bread?' Laura queried.

Emma's eyes sparkled with mischief. 'You don't use your hands to work the dough, instead you lift your skirts and—'

'Aunt Emma!' Laura's cheeks reddened. 'You don't mean it.'

'The old people said it worked,' Emma teased, 'so, when you've found a hunk—'

'No, no, stop it! You're dreadful, Aunt Emma.'

'My feelings exactly,' Giles boomed.

Emma and Laura spun around to face the door. Their laughter had drowned the sound of the car and the men entering the house. Emma pounced on a large white cardboard box which Giles was cradling.

'The dress,' Laura squealed. 'Nicole's dress.' She ran to join Emma.

'Careful,' he warned. 'And a kiss before you open it.'

Emma stood on tiptoe and he pressed her quickly to his body, delighting in the feel of her breasts flattening against his chest.

160

'And one from my wrestler,' he demanded, putting his arm round Laura. She put her hand on his beard to press it down and kissed him quickly before the hair sprang back and tickled her.

Then she turned and flung her arms round Ashley. 'Daddy, isn't this exciting? I can't wait for the wedding,' she said.

He smiled, delighted with her happiness.

'You men wait for us in the hall,' Emma commanded. 'You're not allowed to see the dress.'

'We won't look,' Giles growled, rubbing his hands in front of the fire.

'Lesson number one,' Emma warned, giving Laura a gap-toothed grin. 'Never trust a man.' She put her hands on her hips. 'Out, the two of you. We'll meet you in the hall in three minutes.'

'Good,' Ashley agreed. 'I'm starving.'

'Pork pie and a pint of light will fix that,' said Giles, clapping Ashley on the shoulder, 'We'll give you girls three and a half minutes, then we're off to the Cat,' he threatened.

'Or we'll sneak back and look at the dress,' Ashley teased.

'Out,' Emma said, and she waited until the door had closed before opening the box.

'Oh,' breathed Laura. The pearls gleamed beneath her fingers like a beach bathed in moonlight. 'My new mother will look stunning in this. She's so beautiful.' She held the floating white chiffon to her cheek.

'Mother?' Emma echoed thinly. Her eyes narrowed to shards of emerald.

'Yes,' Laura answered happily. 'I think I'll call her mère Nicole. Don't you think she'd love that?'

Emma busied herself packing the dress back into its box, paying exaggerated attention to the folding of the layers of chiffon. Her mind seethed as she searched for an answer. She had underestimated the little French islander. The woman's hold over Laura was strong. The child really loved her.

'Mother? Isn't that a little much?' Emma asked gently. She jiggled the lid down on the box and took Laura's hand in hers. 'Nicole is sweet. And of course her attention will now be

161

centred on Ashley.' Laura opened her mouth to protest, but Emma squeezed her hand and hurried on. 'I had always hoped that you would look upon me as your mother, Tanith. I held you in my arms when you were only a few days old.' She looked at Laura, willing the tears to well up in her eyes, but they remained obstinately dry. 'I've always looked upon you as my daughter.'

Laura laughed and hugged her impulsively. 'Oh, Aunt Emma, you could never be my mother. You're so much fun. You do those crazy witch things and I love being with you. You're my very, very best aunt.'

Emma forced herself to return the embrace, but a cold fist kneaded deep into her stomach. She would have to use Hecate's dark minions once again, and she was afraid. The forces she commanded to do her bidding were powerful and baleful. Each time she unleashed their terrifying potency she found them more difficult to control. Each ordeal drained a little more of her strength and she knew the black forces were held in check only by her immense willpower. She could not turn to Giles; she was alone in this ordeal. If she weakened, she would be engulfed.

Tonight, she decided, as she kissed Laura lightly on the cheek and ushered her out of the sitting room. Tonight they will bend to my will once again.

She dropped the cardboard box over the back of the sofa. 'Remain in the box,' she hissed, 'unseen and unworn.' She closed the door and ran lightly down the passage after Laura.

Emma's mood was distracted on the cold walk across the bare fields to the Cat, and her participation in the excited conversation about the wedding was minimal. Giles hung back as Ashley ushered Laura into the pub. 'Anything wrong with my little witch?' he asked softly.

Emma started, then smiled up at him. 'No, no. I'm just a little cold,' she joked. Giles was astute and intuitive. She did not want him disturbed. She did not want him prowling round the house late at night because he was worried about her. 'It's old age,' she said.

Giles laughed as they walked into the pub. It was warm with the smell of hops and spilled ale and blue with tobacco haze. 'Never. You'll be young for ever,' he said. He pulled back two bar stools beside Ashley.

The landlord beamed when he saw Laura and made a great fuss of pouring her a glass of apple juice. 'I hear you'll be staying with your aunt and uncle for a while.' Laura nodded, her face buried in her glass. 'That will have the young men steeplechasing over the fields to Lyewood, Giles. They'll be knocking down your fences in the stampede!'

Laura flushed and looked to Ashley for help.

'She'll be studying.'

'Never knew bookwork to stand in the way of stirring blood,' the landlord guffawed.

'Daddy's right,' Laura said, putting down her glass. 'I'll be working very hard, and I'm spending the holidays in the Seychelles.'

'Ah-ha, the Seychelles,' he repeated, wadding up a damp cloth and scrubbing at a ring mark on the bar counter. 'I hear that's where old Faulconer's son is.' He rubbed his nose on the stained cloth then dropped the cloth under the counter. 'Was in here earlier on in the year. Great bear of a man now.'

'And arrogant,' added his wife, squeezing behind him to draw a pint of light.

'What's he doing in the Seychelles?' Ashley asked, popping a handful of nuts into his mouth. 'I thought he was hunting, somewhere in Rhodesia.'

'Was,' answered the woman, mopping up the foam as it trickled down the side of the mug. 'Then he joined the Rhodesian army and he was in that crack team that had the terrorists in Rhodesia running.'

'Selous Scouts,' continued the landlord as she hurried away with the beer. 'Right job for him. Looks a right bloody killer.'

'Who is he, Daddy?' asked Laura. 'Do you know him?'

'No, Muffin, but Virginia and I saw Bartholomew Faulconer here briefly, many years ago. In fact, just after you were born. Mummy didn't like him at all.'

'Could sense trouble, could Virginia,' said the landlord as

163

he leaned over the counter and took an empty mug from a customer. He continued to speak as he filled it. 'Now Smith is talking about black majority rule in Rhodesia. To the wrong guys, mind you. It's those guerrillas he should be chatting up, not the moderates. Young Faulconer has cut and run.' The landlord snorted. 'Not enough excitement left in Rhodesia. He's probably going to start his own war in the Seychelles.'

'Wrong place,' laughed Giles. 'They may have had a bloodless coup, but there's no war.'

'What worries me,' said Emma, joining in the conversation to prevent Giles becoming suspicious of her silence, 'is that one coup usually leads to another. They seem to foment suspicion and dissatisfaction. I can't bear the thought of those beautiful islands becoming a battlefield.'

'They're the islands of love, not death,' said Giles. He drained his glass and pushed it across the counter for a refill. 'You'd have to wake the islanders up first before you'd get them to fight. It's something to do with that heavy tropical air.'

'Untrue,' defended Ashley.

Giles roared with laughter and slapped Ashley on the back. 'Thus speaks a man about to marry one of the most beautiful women in the Seychelles.'

'Indeed?' said the landlord.

'Yes, Nicole is lovely and we all love her,' cut in Laura.

'In that case, it's drinks on the house,' grinned the landlord, 'and my congratulations. Will we get to see the lady?'

'Oh, yes,' said Laura. 'Nicole and Daddy are coming over when I start college. They'll be married by then,' she added.

The landlord smiled and pushed another apple juice across the counter. 'I look forward to meeting your new mother,' he said. 'Cheers, congratulations and much happiness in the future.'

Emma raised her glass in response, but the ale was bitter as it slid down her throat.

' What's it like there now?' asked the landlord, turning to Ashley and Laura. Like all good publicans, he loved to gossip

164

and was a repository of scandals and trivia. 'Hear it's going to be run by a bunch of commies.'

'It's calm at the moment, though rumours are having the same effect on the people as a fox in a pheasant pen,' Ashley replied.

'Mummy always said that communism is a wonderful idea but it needs capitalists to realize the dream,' said Laura.

'Damn right,' agreed the landlord. 'Someone has to pay for all the free services.'

'But Pierre says the new government is socialist, not communist.'

'Same difference to me,' grunted the landlord as he deftly replaced the dirty ashtrays lining the counter.

'Oh, no.' Laura shook her head. 'Pierre knows, because he works for the government. He'll probably be in charge of the bureau for tourism soon. He's very clever.'

The landlord winked at Ashley as he scrubbed at the patches of ash that had stuck on the bottom of the ashtrays.

'Is this Pierre your young man out there?' he asked.

Scarlet crept up Laura's neck and rouged her cheeks. 'No,' she gasped. 'He's my very best friend and he's going to be my stepbrother.'

Ashley adroitly turned the conversation back to the political situation in the islands to save Laura further embarrassment.

'They seem to be committed to the uplifting of the general population and the growth of industry. There's talk of French involvement in a massive fishing industry. They'll start using those damn drift nets, and the Korean longliner boats are sure to follow.' He sipped his beer thoughtfully. 'And of course there'll be the everlasting search for black gold. Treasure-hunting is an endemic island illness; now it'll be oil they hunt. I'd prefer them to concentrate on tourism and off-shore banking. Oil rigs, fuel bunkers and factory ships have no place there. What worries me is that, when all the great industrial ideas have proved to be impractical or uneconomical, the damage will be irreversible. The tuna shoals will be gone. The tourists who are about to be "controlled" will find other tropical

165

resorts.' He sighed. 'Islands have such a fragile ecology. One just hopes that the pressing need for finance to support the socialist ideas will not mean the rape and ultimate death of the islands.'

'Don't worry, Daddy. Pierre says that the islands will be better protected under the new regime,' soothed Laura. She reached out for her glass. 'This is strong apple juice,' she said, wrinkling up her nose.

'Let me taste it,' suggested Emma. 'It's cider,' she exclaimed, 'not apple juice. We'll have you dancing on the bar counter if you finish it.'

'Real witches' brew, that stuff,' warned Giles, his eyes twinkling.

'Do witches drink it?' Laura asked, eyeing the amber liquid suspiciously.

'In early times they probably did, and as the fermented juice made them tipsy they thought it was magical,' Emma answered.

'The apple is still a magical fruit,' added Giles, crunching a mouthful of peanuts. 'Its core is a five-pointed star and that's a pentagram, a magic symbol in witchcraft.'

'How's your latest book progressing?' asked Ashley, beckoning to the landlord, who had moved away to replace the cider with apple juice.

'Not much chance to write during the summer months, but I'm hard at work on it now,' said Giles, dusting off his beard.

'We had a case of witchcraft in the Seychelles recently. A man was brought to court for practising gris gris illegally. The case interested me and I read up on the subject,' said Ashley nodding his thanks to the landlord. 'A point I found fascinating was that the revival of the cult of Wicca was apparently brought about by two men, Gardener and Crowley.'

He watched Laura sip the juice, worried that the landlord had again made a mistake and poured cider. 'Apparently Crowley used his fertile imagination to devise the strange rituals.'

'What absolute rot,' fumed Emma.

Giles tapped her on the leg with his large hand. 'All religions and cults have their detractors,' he said.

'I believe that Wicca is probably the oldest religion in the world; it is a pre-Christian Nature religion.' Giles set out to explain the religion of Wicca to his brother-in-law. He could prove that carvings and paintings depicting witches and their rituals dated back to the Stone Age. He agreed that the invocations and rituals had obviously changed through the ages. He was even prepared to admit that Crowley may have refined the rituals and gilded some of the old invocations and evocations, but he was adamant that the roots of Wicca were firmly embedded in Nature worship and had not changed.

Laura listened to the conversation avidly. She admired Giles; he was a good and colourful speaker and he was agreeing with what Emma had told her about witches.

Giles completed his explanation and then launched into a dissertation on an inherited collective consciousness. Seeing Laura frown, he tried to simplify Jung's concept. He explained that, no matter where people lived or what their culture was, they would all have similar myths and beliefs.

'One finds traces of the old religion across the world, from Mexico to Europe,' added Emma, unable to keep quiet.

Laura nodded but still looked puzzled. The landlord leaned over the counter and listened intently. Giles tried to explain how witchcraft worked with this inherited psyche. 'Witches deal with the divine force in themselves and also those forces which exist in the ether, in the fifth dimension,' he said.

He pushed his mug across the counter for a refill and tried to clarify the theory for Laura by telling her that there is another plane, and that it has higher vibrations than the physical plane people are attuned to on this planet, only people have lost touch with it.

'That must be the same plane that Cook says small children know,' mused Laura. 'Cook says that we beat the knowledge out of them; we tell them they're making up stories. We narrow their minds.'

Giles smiled. 'Cook's probably right.'

Ashley cleared a space on the counter for the plates of pork pie being brought in by the landlord's wife. He then related his fears about Wicca, which seemed to be the 'in' religion at the

167

moment. What worried him was that the unseen forces could be evil, so what started off as simple Nature worship could end with horrific rites and people being possessed by black spirits. Instead of controlling the forces, they in their turn could become controlled.

Giles was grave as he carefully sliced his pie into neat sections. Emma kept her eyes down, concentrating on her salad. Giles agreed that if the rituals were not carried out correctly and with respect, harm could be done. He also agreed that there were forces of evil and that they were clever and powerful and were best left severely alone.

'There have always been laws against the use of black magic. It has been denounced since earliest times,' he said, trying to spear a piece of hard-boiled egg on his fork. He stabbed at the egg as if to emphasize that seekers and doubters would be well advised not to dabble in Wicca because great care had to be taken when dealing with divine forces.

'So witchcraft *is* dangerous?' said Laura softly, looking at Emma.

'No, little wrestler. Wicca is a good and honest religion, but those who deal with the black side for evil reasons of their own are dealing with death,' Giles answered, catching the sliced egg neatly in his mouth before it could drop off the fork. He scrubbed at his mouth and beard with a paper napkin.

A shiver cold as an unseen presence iced Emma's spine. She put down her knife and fork. 'Let's have a slice of chocolate cake,' she suggested.

'That was good,' said Ashley, patting his flat belly. 'But we should be getting back to Lyewood. Nicole is phoning at four.'

'We'll be able to tell her about the wedding dress,' said Laura, sliding off her stool and picking up Emma's paper napkin which was lying on the floor.

'Right,' Emma agreed, forcing her mouth into a smile.

'Only two weeks left before the great day,' teased Giles, punching Ashley lightly on the arm.

'And just as well. Any longer, and everyone on the island would be invited. The guest list lengthens by the day,' laughed Ashley.

168

'Everyone's so excited,' said Laura. 'Pierre says that we're having a traditional island feast and a sega band. Everyone will dance the moutia.'

'A fitting dance for a wedding,' Giles grinned wickedly. 'Those swivelling hips should set the mood.'

'And caille?' added Emma.

'Yes, they lifted the ban on male green turtles last year. There will certainly be caille,' Ashley confirmed, and he looked at Laura. 'Hopefully a certain young lady won't display her dislike of the dish by throwing up in a coconut grove again.'

'Daddy, I was only a kid then,' Laura protested. Her eyes clouded for a moment as she remembered the feast on Praslin and the bonhomme du bois. Well, she reassured herself silently, I won't need a gris gris this time. Everything is going to be wonderful. 'Aunt Emma,' Laura went on, tucking her hand into Emma's, 'could we go up to London tomorrow? There's a brooch in Burlington Arcade that—'

'Ah-ha,' nodded Ashley, 'so that's why you needed your pocket money three months in advance.'

Laura smiled at him. 'It's a lovely hummingbird and it looks just like the Seychelles sunbird. I'm going to buy it for mère Nicole as a wedding gift. She'll love it.'

Ashley felt his throat constrict. He knew that Laura loved Nicole, but he had not realized that she accepted her as a mother. He hugged her to him. 'Mère Nicole will treasure it,' he said, and suddenly the urge to be back at La Retraite with Nicole was overwhelming.

'Laura,' said Emma as she slung her bag over her shoulder, 'could we postpone the visit to London until the day after tomorrow instead? I have some things to do and will probably be very tired tomorrow.'

'Of course,' answered Laura, waving goodbye to the landlord and his wife. 'Can I help you, Aunt Emma?'

'No thanks, Tanith,' Emma demurred. 'It's something I must do alone.'

A painted pentagram, large and dark, filled her vision and she shuddered.

'Last one to reach the stile at Briar Meadow remakes the

fire in the sitting room,' called Giles, holding open the pub door.

'Not me,' squealed Laura, and they all bolted out of the Cat, seemingly as carefree as children on a school outing.

━━━●|✦|✦|✦| IV |✦|✦|✦|●━━━

The noonday sun beat down on the fanciful Victorian clock tower in the centre of Mahé and the silver paintwork flashed back blinding signals to the burning skies.

Bartholomew Harden Faulconer sat in a small beige car at the street stop sign and waited impatiently for a stooped Seychellois, thin as the barracuda he was carrying, to cross the road. The fish's tail thumped on the tarmac, leaving a trail of slime and flies.

'Another toddy drinker,' Bart muttered, dabbing at the perspiration on his forehead with the back of his hand. 'On a diet of palm wine until he fades away.' He hooted impatiently. 'Bloody fool,' he cursed as the old man continued to shuffle across; he glanced neither to right nor left, his face buried beneath the brim of a palm-fond hat.

Bart revved up the car and swerved towards the pedestrian as he drove past. He grinned as he saw the man jump on to the pavement and drop the fish in the gutter. 'That got you moving.'

He circled the clock tower and slowed down as he drove along the main road. It was lunchtime, and the office girls were window shopping. They were a bit thin for his taste. He preferred to dig his fingers into curves. But they were young and willing, and they made the boredom of the island bearable.

He was tired of waiting for the counter-coup. He had spent months training the presidential guard in unarmed combat and guerrilla tactics so that the president was now surrounded by men who could protect him in any situation; but there was no excitement in this assignment. Bart missed the thrill of the hunts, the gut-jarring exhilaration of the fire-fights and, most of all, the eyes of the prisoners as they felt the muzzle of the FN at their temple. He was a trained killer and as dangerous as a leopard confined in a circus cage. He circled and paced, waiting for his opportunity to be set free. He needed to exercise his skills.

On Mahé the agents Job and King had realized this and contacted London. 'He's a disaster waiting to happen,' they warned.

But it was too late to change the game-plan. Bart Harden was a key figure and had to stay: he was the one man who had free access to the president and his trust. On the day of the counter-coup he would take the president into custody and hold him until the previous head of government had been reinstated.

He whistled at two young girls walking into the grounds of the Yacht Club. The younger one, secure in her youth and prettiness, looked at him over her shoulder and called out to a group of island boys working on a glass-bottomed tourist boat. Their roars of laughter reflected the girl's wit, and Bart reddened. He had picked up sufficient Creole in the army camp to know that she had called him a sweating pig, plus some other, equally uncomplimentary names.

'Bitch,' he said and, throwing the car into top gear, he roared recklessly down to Le Chantier roundabout and turned on to the airport road to Cascades. 'Should have been in my camo,' he fumed. 'The sight of a uniform soon shuts them up. Scared to hell of soldiers.'

Scared? The young girl he'd picked up a few nights ago on his way down the La Misère road, she'd been scared. Too scared to refuse the lift he offered her. Too scared to scream when he pulled off the road and walked her up the mountain. Too scared to report him or tell her parents when he dropped her off afterwards at her home in Cascades. His breath quickened as he remembered how he made her hold him on the way back.

'She'll do it again,' he said out loud and punched a tape into the cassette player. 'One of the few perks in the place,' he groused as the heavy beat of rock filled the car. 'Pity the

governmental purse-strings still don't include air-conditioning.'
He hung his arm out of the window and the air dried white salt
rings round the wet patch under his arm.

The road to Cascades and the airport was wedged between
the edge of the sea and the steel-hard granite rocks that tumbled
down from the mountains. Blue, green and pink wooden houses
wearing peaked iron roofs were wedged into every available
clearing. Mango trees grown huge with sewerage hung over the
houses, their falling fruit crashing down like thunder on the
rusted iron sheets. Ferns and moss grew wild in the stone stilts
holding up the wooden structures, and chickens and children
scratched and played in the shade under the houses.

Village life centred round the little trading stores that
balanced between the deep concrete storm-water drains drying
the road and the sheer drop-off into the sea. Children flitted in
and out of the dim interiors, running errands, and teenagers
propped up the walls outside.

When he had first arrived in the Seychelles, Bart found the
road picturesque, but constantly having to swerve on blind
bends, to avoid oncoming traffic, and the long waits behind
cars parked on the side of the narrow road now irritated him.

He was now stuck behind a van offloading crates of sugary
orange and green drinks at one of the stores. An unending
stream of cars filed towards him, driving from the airport into
Victoria. Angrily he wrenched off his dark aviator glasses and
wiped his face across his shirtsleeve. He glanced at his watch.
He'd miss the girl if he had to wait for the men to finish
offloading. She would have had her lunch and returned to work.
The sound of her voice begging him not to hurt her excited him,
and he revved the car, racing the engine.

Suddenly a gap appeared in the oncoming traffic; he spun
the wheel and swung out into the middle of the road. A yellow-
and-black soccer ball bounced in front of his car, closely
followed by a young boy. Honed by war, his reflexes were
excellent: he wrenched the wheel over and swung back in front
of the van. A high screech betrayed the meeting of the two
bumpers.

172

'Damn, damn senseless people,' he cursed as he glanced in his rear-view mirror to assess the damage.

Looking once again at the road in front of his car, he froze. Everything seemed to be moving in slow motion. It was as if he was back in the Rhodesian bush and had walked into an ambush: time hung suspended.

The parked van had blocked a bright red Mini-Moke from his view and now he was driving too fast to stop. A woman was climbing up into the Moke and even in his panic he noticed her thighs, slim and brown, beneath her hitched-up skirt.

An island bus, bulky and belching black fumes, came rocking towards him. He might just be able to scrape between the bus and the Moke.

Options flashed through his mind with the speed of gunfire shattering the silence. 'My skin or yours,' he muttered between clenched teeth. 'It's the bus or the Moke. At least I'll stay alive if I take the Moke.'

The woman swung to face his car. Her eyes widened in horror and dark hair swirled round her head like a satin cape. He hit her with a sickening thud. Putting down his foot, he swung the car round the bend and raced for Cascades. Though he was a soldier and accustomed to death, he had never killed a woman, and he felt somewhat nauseous.

Gradually his heart stopped pounding and he wiped his palms on his pants. No sirens wailed behind him and the road was clear. 'You've done it!' He punched the steering-wheel, light-headed with relief. 'You've got away with it.'

Ahead of him was the fishing village of Cascades and he relaxed. The sea stretched clear and blue to the islands in the St Anne marine park. The village women on the opposite side of the road were draping the grey rocks of the milky inlet with freshly soaped clothes for the baking sun to clean. The printed material lay draped across the granite like sprays of brilliantly coloured bougainvillaea.

The peaceful scene reassured Bart. The woman's death would be accepted as just another unfortunate road accident. He would not have to face Top's wrath. Top had a formidable reputation for ruthlessness. Bart knew that by joining his mercenary force he had placed himself completely in the man's power, and it made him uneasy.

He took no notice of the white car which pulled out of the road outside the police station and fell in behind him. He would soon be turning off the main road and bouncing and jolting up a red soil track to a house which hugged the mountain hard. He stroked his beard into shape and combed his fingers through his hair.

'Now what?' he muttered as he rounded a bend, to find a car slewed across the road. 'Another fool who can't drive?' He slowed down and stopped. Concentrating on the car ahead, he did not notice that the white car had driven up behind him and blocked the way back. The doors opened and policemen stepped out of both cars and walked towards him. They were impeccable in their tropical dress of navy trousers and crisp white shirts. Bart watched in disbelief as they approached, their highly polished black shoes scuffing up the leaves on the road.

'The shopkeeper must have phoned and alerted the Cascades police,' he muttered. 'Damn him to hell.'

The sun polished their cap badges, set on navy-and-white chequerboard ribbon, and their faces were unsmiling as they bent down and opened his door. Act innocent, he cautioned himself, you know nothing. He composed his face into his most charming smile. The army will get you out of this, he reassured himself as he stepped out of the car. You're the president's favourite. They have to help. If they can't, Top will have to, or it's bye-bye counter-coup.

<hr>

V

The hinges on the grey suitcase creaked and groaned and the lid bulged over the tightly packed clothes, but the catches refused to click. Laura and Emma climbed off the suitcase lid and looked at each other.

'We'll just have to take out some of the clothes,' Emma

decided. 'Perhaps we can sneak them into Giles's suitcase. He always has plenty of room – he never takes much to the Seychelles.'

Emma left Laura's bedroom, her arms piled high with clothes, and Laura snapped the catches closed on the suitcase. With a sigh of satisfaction she eased the tip of the luggage strap through its silver buckle and pulled it tight.

'There,' she said, as she trundled the case out of the way. 'Uncle Giles or Daddy will have to help me carry it downstairs tomorrow.'

The case was heavy and, as she tried to position it against the wall, the phone rang. She ignored the first few rings, concentrating on moving the case.

'Answer that, Tanith,' Emma's voice rang out from the next room. 'I have my arms full.'

Laura abandoned her struggle with the case and lifted the phone. 'Pierre,' she said, her voice high with pleasure. 'I didn't think you'd phone again before we left. This is a super surprise.'

'Laura,' he said quietly, 'is Ashley there? I must talk to him.'

'He's down at the stables. It'll take ages to get him here. I'll have to ask him to phone you back,' she answered.

'Please hurry, call him now.'

'Oh, Pierre, don't fuss. I have something to tell Nicole. It's important,' Laura said, pulling the phone across the glass-topped table so that she could settle down on her bed for a long talk to mère Nicole. 'I have to tell her about the shoes we've found to go with her dress.' She chattered on happily, tickling a strand of hair across her lips and not noticing the silence at the other end of the phone. 'Oh, Pierre, the whole outfit is fantastic; she's going to look wonderful. Just wait until you see it.'

A strangled sound, harsh as the cry of a seagull, answered her, and she frowned.

'Pierre,' she said. 'Pierre, what's wrong?'

'Nicole,' he choked. 'I must speak to Ashley now.'

'Why? What's Nicole done?' Laura demanded. 'Oh, Pierre,' she said, losing patience, 'whatever it is, let me talk to Nicole quickly and then I promise I'll run and call Daddy.'

'I can't,' he whispered. 'Nicole's not here.' His words hit her as hard as a punch in the stomach. 'There's been an accident. A hit-and-run.' He paused. 'Nicole's gone. She's dead, Laura.'

She was winded and wanted to vomit. She stared at the phone and shook it wildly. She smelt the wild tang of the sea and saw once again a seaplane locked in its dark depths. Virginia and Nicole had become one.

'No,' she screamed, and her voice echoed the cries of the insane. She could not accept this second death. She could not lose both mothers. 'No! No! No!'

She smashed the phone down on the tabletop, each blow emphasizing her denial of Nicole's death. The glass smashed as completely as Pierre's words had shattered her world.

The door to her room burst open and Emma and Giles rushed in.

'Laura,' Giles shouted.

'Tanith,' Emma screamed, 'stop it, stop it.' Giles locked his arms round Laura and carried her, screaming and kicking, away from the phone.

Emma ran and picked the receiver up, heedless of the glass crunching into the carpet beneath her feet. Her face paled as she listened, but the gleam in her tilted eyes was that of a cat crouching over a bloodied bird; it gave the lie to her words of sympathy. 'Bartholomew Faulconer!' she said. 'Oh, Pierre, how dreadful. His father is the surgeon who saved Ashley when he was shot down in the war. I can't believe it's his son who . . .'

Giles squeezed Laura tightly, as if his strength could stop her screaming. His heart cracked with compassion as he held her to him.

Emma replaced the receiver and turned to help Giles. Time will heal the hurt, Tanith, she thought. This is best for you. It frees you to follow the path of the wise. I will at last be able to mould you in the Way of Wicca.

'Ring for the doctor,' Giles commanded, holding his face out of the way of Laura's butting head. 'Then go and get Ashley,' he shouted, trying to make himself heard over Laura's screams.

Emma ran to comply. Although Laura's pain and shrieks

176

cut her with the swift deep strokes of an athame, Emma's heart sang with joy. Both women were now out of Laura's life. The future was hers.

══════◄◙◄◙◄◙| VI |◙►◙►◙►══════

The grey suitcase stood against the panelled wall of Laura's room and a film of dust coated its surface. They had left it where she could see it, hoping that it would awaken some interest in her in returning to life. But she refused to return; life had ceased to exist for her. Perhaps in the Seychelles Pierre could rekindle her interest in people and her surroundings, but it had been months since the phone call and she still moved through the house, silent as a secret vow, answering only when spoken to and then in monosyllables.

'Depression,' diagnosed the family doctor. 'It's quite common after a shock. It'll pass. Youth bleeds easily but heals quickly, and the scars fade completely.'

Laura continued to bleed. She lost interest not only in her surroundings but also in herself. Emma made her bathe and change her clothes; she washed her hair and cut her nails; she watched over her at mealtimes, coaxing her to eat. She collected her from dark corners where she sat silently weeping and took her for long walks. Laura was compliant but apathetic.

'Her emotions are so flat,' Emma whispered to Giles and Ashley.

Ashley buried his own grief, and the shock at learning it was Dr Faulconer's son who had killed Nicole, in his concern for Laura. He spend hours sitting with her. He talked about her baby days and childhood. He reminisced about Virginia and, in desperation, about Pierre and Nicole. But nothing he said could awaken her interest. She was emotionless and lost to him.

'St Francis Hospital,' the family doctor announced finally, 'they have experts to deal with this. Laura needs help.'

'St Francis,' said Ashley, 'isn't that a mental hospital?'

'Wonderful old Italianate building,' the family physician elaborated, misreading Ashley's reaction. 'First ever purpose-built mental institution.'

'Doctor,' Giles cautioned, looking at Ashley, who had gone pale.

'My daughter is not mad,' said Ashley, spitting out the words as sharply as electric shocks.

'Of course not, Mr Challoner. Of course not,' soothed the doctor, realizing his mistake. 'Laura has just sunk into a deep depression. She's still at a sensitive age and cannot accept this double blow. I suspect that some of the grief she buried at the death of her mother has resurfaced now. We need to help her and we can't do it alone.' He smoothed down his bushy eyebrows. 'St Francis is run by dedicated and caring people . . . by people who are trained to bring Laura out of the state she's in. I know that you love Laura dearly and want to see her happy and restored to health, Mr Challoner.'

Ashley nodded and unclenched his fists, relaxing slightly.

'This is the only way to do it. Please believe me, we must commit Laura. She must go to St Francis.'

Emma stepped up to Ashley and put her mouth close to his ear. 'There's a history of depression in the Killick family,' she whispered. 'Remember the eldest girl, the one who died when Virginia was still young. *She* suffered from depression. Perhaps it's genetic. You cannot leave Laura like this.' Ashley glared at Emma, but she persisted. 'Ashley, we owe Laura her health and happiness. Let the doctors there get it back for her. Please.'

Ashley stood, silent and unyielding.

'Do it for Nicole and Virginia. The two women she loved,' said Giles.

Ashley started, a pulse beating in his jaw the only sign of his agitation.

'Nicole would do anything, anything at all, to help Laura. She would never allow her to remain like this, living a shadow existence.'

Ashley spun on his heel. He had lost two women he loved.

He couldn't let his daughter slip away into a twilight world of despair. 'Make the arrangements,' he said as he left the room.

That evening a small blue case stood beside the dusty grey one and Ashley sat at his daughter's bedside, watching her sleep. Loving her and grieving silently.

Pale light proclaimed another cool spring day. Ashley pinched the skin over his nose hard and stretched in the chintz-covered armchair. His shoulder-blades cracked and he rubbed at the tension nodules in the back of his neck.

It had been a long night. But he knew that his vigil would end only when Laura once again ran, laughing, along the crescent beach of Beau Vallon and struck through its turquoise waters, sleek and lovely as a flying fish.

Laura opened her eyes and for a moment they remained clear and untroubled, then the familiar blinds were lowered.

'Good morning, Muffin,' said Ashley lightly as he leaned over her. 'I want to have a talk with you before Emma arrives.'

Laura nodded and stroked a thick hank of hair that lay across her cheek.

'I'm taking you to Haywards Heath this morning, Muffin. There's a hospital there which has doctors who can help you. I want you to do this for me, Muffin: I want you to stay there, talk to the doctors and take the medicines they give you. Will you?'

'If you want me to, Daddy,' she said spiritlessly.

Ashley swallowed and kept his voice light. He cupped Laura's face in his hands and stared into her vacant eyes. 'You're all I have left, Muffin. Please smile for me.'

He dropped his hands as the door opened, and he turned to greet Emma.

'We'll leave after breakfast,' he said. 'There's nothing more I can do.' His shoulders slumped and his feet dragged as he closed the bedroom door quietly behind him.

179

Laura's fingers plucked at the strand of hair, but her expression did not alter as she watched him leave.

Ashley drove slowly but the car ate up the miles relentlessly. He was hoping for a miracle . . . praying that Laura would suddenly laugh . . . longing for an excuse not to leave her at St Francis.

'I'll come and see you every day,' he promised. 'You'll only be there for a few weeks.' He ruffled her hair. 'Time will pass very quickly.'

Laura merely nodded. She made no attempt to smooth down her tousled hair. Her gaze was fixed sightlessly on the rolling farmlands.

'Pierre is missing you dreadfully. He is very lonely at La Retraite.' Ashley watched Laura closely, waiting for a reaction. She turned to face him for the first time since leaving Lyewood but said nothing. 'And I want you to come diving with me. There are so many old wrecks we haven't yet explored.'

Ever since her sixteenth birthday she had pleaded to be allowed to dive on wrecks, but he had always demurred, saying that it was too dangerous and she was too young. Now the carrot dangled limply. Laura rubbed her hair across her lips and cheek.

'Soon, Muffin,' he whispered as he removed the coil of hair from her fingers gently. 'Soon we'll be back in the Seychelles.'

He turned his attention to the road and, as he slowed down for a car in front of him to turn off to Horsted Keynes, he half expected to see a strutting peacock fanning its exotic tail beneath the white signpost.

'Pierre says that there's talk of a one-party state being declared,' he announced, hoping to interest her. 'He says you ought to be at the meetings with him. He has a whole lot of new slogans to try out on you. Plus the usual *Liberté, Egalité, Fraternité* one.'

Laura stared ahead, her hands lying limply on her lap.

'I don't think I'm very happy with single-party states,' Ashley mused. 'Any government needs a strong opposition

180

party to keep the scales balanced.' He glanced at her, but even this subject awakened no interest. Yet only a few months ago meals under the bois de rose had been loud and noisy with her and Pierre's opposing views on the new government.

He stopped talking as the traffic became heavy and tangled near Haywards Heath.

'Phew,' he breathed, as they found and turned into Colwell Road. 'I didn't think we'd ever find the place.'

He stopped the car at the entrance to the hospital, momentarily taken aback by its size and Victorian grandeur.

'It looks as though they built it out of red and yellow candy sticks,' he joked, putting his arm round Laura's shoulder.

She looked at the sprawling building, banded with horizontal bands of red bricks, and her indifferent gaze centred on St Francis's chapel, raised high on a hillock of green shrubs and flowering plants.

'Not as large as our old St Margaret's,' said Ashley, 'but if you like, I'll come on Sunday and perhaps we can attend a service.'

A slight nod greeted his suggestion and she returned her vacant gaze to the main building.

A white station-wagon pulled out of a parking place near the front entrance; their family doctor leaned out of the window and beckoned to Ashley to follow him. Puzzled as to why they were leaving the large hospital, Ashley drove down the road behind him. They stopped near a rather modern brick building cubed in bright blue panels and squares of glass. The doctor slammed the door of his wagon and walked across to open Laura's door. He dispensed with joviality when he saw Ashley's pale face and set jaw. 'There we are then, young Laura. Out you jump,' he said. 'This is the villa where you'll be staying for a while.' He took her hand and turned to Ashley. ''Morning, Mr Challoner. Would you bring Laura's case, then we can settle the young lady into her room.'

Laura walked between the two men and her feet dragged as she climbed the steps. Glancing round the utilitarian entrance-hall, a wave of panic threatened to drown Ashley. The rubber-tiled floor swam across his vision in swells of bilious yellow.

'Good morning, Mr Challoner, Miss Challoner, Doctor,' said a brisk voice.

'Nurse,' the doctor returned the greeting.

'Let's go down to the ward and take your details,' the nurse said, taking Laura's arm. 'You can join us, Mr Challoner,' she invited. 'I'll give any jewellery and money to you for safe keeping. Our doctor will then make a routine physical check-up on Miss Challoner, followed by a chest X-ray in a day or two.' She smiled at him reassuringly. 'We'll meet you in the lounge. I'll give you the phone number of the ward and the visiting times before you leave.'

'I've arranged for you to meet the consultant, young Redvers,' the family doctor whispered as they walked down the stairs to the wards. 'Still looks wet behind the ears, but he's brilliant, quite brilliant. We'll leave for his office as soon as they start the medical. It's best if the nurse is left to introduce Laura to the other patients. Redvers will then want to take her case history.'

Ashley glanced at the closed doors lining the corridor and quickly dropped his eyes to the bitter-chocolate linoleum that covered the floor. He did not want to see faces with unfocused eyes and bodies with twitching limbs; he did not wish to see the inmates he was committing his daughter to live with.

'Here we are,' said the nurse cheerily. 'Would you put the case on the bed, please, Mr Challoner?'

Ashley looked up when a middle-aged woman walked into the room. 'Good morning, nurse,' she said. 'I've just come to fetch my book.'

'Reading today, are you? That's good.'

'Is this a new one?' the patient asked as she sidled out of the door, her book under her arm.

'Yes, she'll be in your ward,' answered the nurse.

'That's nice. It'll be a change to have someone young in here. Perk us up,' came the answer and she shuffled off down the corridor.

The nurse saw Ashley's look of amazement as he watched the patient leave. 'We have some lovely patients,' she said. 'I'm sure that Miss Challoner will soon make friends and be very happy with us.'

Laura made the leavetaking easy by giving Ashley a perfunctory kiss. Ashley was relieved and a little guilty to escape so lightly. He had steeled himself for tears and entreaties. 'It's not at all what I expected,' he said, following the family doctor out to the car. 'It all seems so normal.'

'What did you expect?' The doctor smoothed a straggly hair in his thick eyebrow. 'Barred windows and iron railings?' He chuckled. 'Twenty-odd years ago that's what you would have seen here. But with the new drug discoveries in the 'fifties, asylums changed from being places of custody to places of healing. That's what I tried to explain to you at Lyewood. A mental disorder is merely another disease. It can be treated.' Ashley listened in silence. 'Doctor Redvers has a meeting in the old building, so we're meeting him there. Follow me.'

They stopped in the parking area near the front steps and Ashley followed the doctor up the stairs to the entrance of the massive edifice.

'We have a meeting with the consultant,' the latter called out, poking his head through the hatch into the small reception office.

A round face framed by a heavy fringe and straight curtains of dull black hair peered at him. 'I'll phone. Wait for the secretary to come and collect you,' she replied, and disappeared.

The doctor smiled. 'Still strict on security here. Lock their doors every time they leave their rooms.' Ashley looked surprised. 'One of the inmates could wander in and get the place in a right mess.' He smiled. 'Not as bad as in the old days, though. The staff then faced instant dismissal if they lost or mislaid their keys. You should find time to have a look at the museum here. The inmates may have been mentally unstable but they weren't stupid.' He took off his heavy tortoiseshell glasses and wiped them carefully. 'One of them pinched a tablespoon. Somehow the clever blighter managed to make an imprint of the warder's key. He then fashioned a perfect replica of it out of the handle of the spoon.' He stood at the head of the stairs and rocked back and forth on his heels, his hands clasped behind his back.

Ashley joined his family doctor and gazed out of the front

door. The chapel gleamed like a freshly licked striped lollipop. 'It all looks so lovely. It's difficult to believe that institutions existed where they were so tormented.'

'It's easy to be critical and condemnatory of the early practitioners – after all, they had no wonder drugs. They believed that if they could induce sufficient pain and nausea and were able to make it last long enough, the disturbed mind would have a new set of sensations to deal with, and the original complaint would be cured. Even today, with all our scientific advances we don't understand these damn mental illnesses completely.' The doctor chattered on, taking Ashley's mind off the coming meeting with the consultant.

He broke off as the click of high heels heralded the arrival of the secretary. The doctor nodded affably at Ashley and they set off down the corridor to the consultant's room. When Ashley smiled back, the doctor was relieved to see him relax. He would be more receptive to what the specialist had to say. 'Ah, here we are,' he said. He held the door open for Ashley and smiled his thanks to the secretary. Doctor Redvers surprised Ashley, he looked so young, scarcely older than Pierre. When he stood up, he had a scholarly stoop to his narrow shoulders, but his handshake was firm. 'Mr Challoner,' he greeted Ashley. 'Do sit down. I have taken the liberty of ordering tea.'

'Thank you,' said Ashley, choosing one of the four brown chairs that stood round a square, dark, wooden table.

'Now,' said Doctor Redvers, seating himself opposite Ashley and lighting up a heavy black pipe, 'your doctor has given me Laura's case history, but I'd like to hear the story again, in your own words.' He sucked at the pipe as eagerly as a baby pulling at a teat. Satisfied that it was drawing well, he settled back in the hard chair.

'Well,' Ashley hesitated.

'Begin some time before the death of Laura's mother,' Redvers suggested.

Ashley was a non-smoker, but as he spoke he found the rich tang of tobacco and the soft sucking noises strangely comforting. The consultant listened in silence. His eyes, dark and

184

piercing behind the gold-rimmed spectacles, never moved away from Ashley's face.

'And that,' said Ashley eventually, 'is the whole story. My daughter has sunk into a deep apathy. I'm afraid that I'm losing her. Each day she seems to move further away. It's like being on a treadmill: no matter how fast I run, I just can't reach her. I can't touch her.' He closed his eyes and massaged his forehead.

You've certainly had your fair share of hardships, thought the registrar as he leaned forward and tapped his pipe into the ashtray. 'What we propose to do, Mr Challoner,' he said aloud, leaning back and putting the empty pipe back into his mouth, 'is to examine and assess Laura. Once that is complete, we'll start her on a course of anti-depressant drugs.'

'Drugs?' said Ashley.

'Yes. I'll probably be prescribing a course of tricyclic drugs.' Ashley moved uneasily in his chair. 'I want you to disregard the stories published in the popular press about drugs. Without the discovery of the extraordinary properties of chlorpromazine, we would probably still be using plant extracts and simple chemicals ... substances like arsenic, cyanide, datura and camphor. Hardly "safe" drugs.'

'Are any drugs safe, doctor?' queried Ashley. 'Side effects are usually discovered by testing drugs on animals. How do you test drugs that are to be used for mental illnesses on animals? Do we have schizophrenic rats and manic cats?' Ashley broke off as the secretary walked in with tea for them. 'Please excuse me if that sounded rude,' he said as she left, 'but Laura is my only child . . .'

'I understand,' the consultant answered. 'The side effects of drugs are discovered only after long years of use and clinical studies. We believe in the rational use of drugs, Mr Challoner. These psychotropic drugs offer our patients the hope of being cured, of once more living a full and normal life.' He flicked open a tin of tobacco with his thumbnail and refilled his pipe. 'What is the alternative?' He rested his elbows on his knees and fondled the unlit pipe. 'Either Laura remains as she is, a flat shadow who could become suicidal, or you allow us to try drug therapy.'

185

Ashley visualized Laura as he had last seen her in the ward, her shoulders slumped and her face blank. 'You have to try,' he said wearily.

'It's difficult to judge the depth of a person's depression,' Doctor Redvers said briskly, 'but we will probably give Laura a tricyclic anti-depressant such as Amitriptyline. If she doesn't respond, we'll try Nomifensine.' The names sounded chilling, but Ashley continued listening intently. 'She'll stay on each of them for three to four weeks. She'll be very closely observed. The nurses and therapists will spend a great deal of time with Laura. Her case will be fully discussed on the weekly ward round. I will then be able to determine the efficacy of the drugs.'

'She's young and healthy,' broke in Ashley. 'She should respond well.'

'Hopefully we'll be able to discharge her after a fortnight,' said Redvers comfortingly. 'She'll continue to take anti-depressant tablets for a few weeks, and within three months or so we'll wean her off the tablets.'

He smiled at Ashley, and his grin was as crooked as Pierre's. Ashley suddenly warmed to him.

'You'll soon have your daughter back. This may seem like a nightmare, but it will be as easily forgotten.'

'Doctor Redvers, you have been very frank with me and I appreciate it,' Ashley said, slowly stirring his tea. 'But I have one further question. If the drugs don't work, what then? My doctor has mentioned the possibility of shock treatment,' Ashley continued.

Redvers tightened his mouth and shook his head. 'A term we dislike intensely, Mr Challoner. It has been used by the press and certain religious sects to whip up a hornet's nest of misunderstanding in the general public. Electroconvulsive therapy has been in use for fifty years. At one stage it almost had to be discontinued because of adverse publicity. But I assure you that it's a very effective form of treatment.' Redvers stole a quick look at his watch. 'In Laura's case we would consider ECT only if the drug treatment failed completely.'

'But what about brain damage, doctor? As I understand it, the electrical impulse which is passed through the brain changes

186

the chemical status, causing loss of memory and, possibly, irreversible damage.'

The phone rang. Redvers leaned across to his desk and lifted the receiver. 'Yes, I'm still with her father . . . No, I'll be a little late . . . Good. Thank you.' He replaced the receiver.

'They're waiting for me to interview Laura, but first I would like to set your mind at rest about ECT. The main aim of ECT is to produce a convulsion. In the early days, they used to convulse the patient with insulin or camphor. Today, electricity is used, simply because it's more convenient.'

Redvers pulled down his shirt cuffs, shrugged on his jacket and stood up.

'You said you were worried about brain damage, Mr Challoner. It's still a controversial subject. There is very little proof of irreversible memory loss due solely to the use of ECT – especially now that we use the modified form and oxygenate the patient before and after the treatment.' He picked up a folder from his desk and slipped a pen into his shirt pocket.

Ashley pushed back his chair and stood. 'Thank you for your time. It has been most informative.'

Redvers picked up his tobacco tin from the table and stood twirling it between his fingers. 'Mr Challoner, we seldom use ECT in cases of reactive depression like Laura's. It's really not a cure for sorrow. Please don't worry.' He ushered Ashley to the door, and Ashley waited while the consultant locked his door and pocketed the key. 'I understand that you have a home in the Seychelles,' he said as they walked towards the entrance hall.

'Yes. That's where I'll be taking Laura as soon as she's . . .' Ashley shrugged, his hands held out in supplication.

'. . . well,' said Redvers, completing the sentence. 'And she will be.' At the top of the steps he held out his hand to Ashley. 'We'll be seeing more of each other in the next few weeks, Mr Challoner, and perhaps I'll have the pleasure of meeting you and Laura in the Seychelles.'

'Ah. You're planning a tropical island holiday?'

'No,' Redvers laughed. 'A group of us have been chosen to visit and lecture at island institutions round the world. For some reason, islands seem to be neglected; they are seldom included in conferences. Les Cannelles has invited me to spend a few months on Mahé. I'll be working in the hospital, and of course giving some lectures. It should be interesting.'

'Yes,' Ashley agreed dubiously, 'but be prepared for—'

'A shock,' said the consultant with a broad smile.

'Well, it's certainly nothing like this,' Ashley answered, thinking of the small asylum set up high on a hill in what had once been a cinnamon plantation.

'So I understand,' said Redvers, patting his pocket for his pipe. 'Mr Challoner,' he called over his shoulder as he ran down the steps, 'you did the right thing, bringing Laura here. Go home. Relax. Leave her in our hands. They're pretty capable.'

Ashley watched the young doctor stride across to the villa, and for the first time in weeks he felt hopeful.

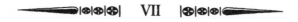 VII

Bartholomew Faulconer was worried. He sat alone on one of the wooden benches lining the side wall of the elegant colonial court house.

The men and women waiting their turn to be called into the law court avoided catching his eye. Those who were sitting on the bench when he arrived slid off the green leather seat where he sat down and moved to another bench.

Local gossip sped through the islands with the speed and heat of a plantation fire. 'Radyo banmbo' had told them all about this hard-faced blond who had killed Nicole Daumier. The islanders were convinced he was guilty. There was even talk that Nicole's family had consulted a bonhomme. A gris gris was going to be smeared on the blond's doorstep. Each time he trod on it he would be a step nearer death.

A few of the older women studied him surreptitiously from beneath the side brims of their hats. There would be many stories told that night about the man with the yellow eyes.

Bart folded his arms across his chest and scowled at the sun-

188

baked tourists. They were bargaining for local crafts at the makeshift stalls that lined the stone boundary walls of the court buildings. Not even the young girls, exposing the cheeks of their buttocks as they bent over to examine the shells and coral beads, aroused his interest.

He rolled back his cuff and looked at his watch, then stared at the Victoria Clock Tower. There was no chime to help him – the clock had remained silent ever since the dockers unloading it had dropped the pendulum overboard. But the numerals were large and clear.

Bart crossed his legs. The humidity was setting creases into his cotton trousers. He smoothed the material out and felt sweat trickle down the back of his knees. Running a finger round the inside of his damp collar, he loosened his tie.

'Mr Bartholomew Faulconer.'

Bart stood up, flexing his shoulders.

A murmur of interest, soft as surf lapping the beach, rippled through the people attending the court that day. They leaned forward on their benches to watch as he struggled into a beige-and-white seersucker jacket and walked through the high dark doors into the courtroom. Then they turned to one another in excitement. Voices rose and were immediately silenced by a glare from the court usher before the doors closed.

The air-conditioning was turned up high in the courtroom. The back rows were packed with islanders, some of whom had slipped into the court to escape the heat – it was a perfect place in which to relax between bouts of shopping.

Bart sat, immobile, in the defendant's raised dock, studying the room and the people. 'Always assess a strange situation. Don't move until you are familiar with the terrain.' His commanding officer's words guided him, and he once again absorbed the mood of the court. He was surprised to see the court so full. His lawyer had said it would probably be almost empty by the third day. The people sat shoulder to shoulder on the hard benches, as straight and as expectant as participants in a High Mass.

Bart let his gaze rove across the people, then it returned to the lanky young man seated near him. The man's eyes were

189

small and they seemed to cross as they bored into Bart; his high cheekbones gave him an eastern air, as did his straight black hair, cut just above his collar. The first barbs of warning prickled the back of Bart's neck: hate. It was hate which darkened those brown eyes. Probably a member of the woman's family, he thought. If only the fool woman had not parked in the road, I wouldn't be in this mess.

Pierre stared up at Bart, and he felt nauseous. He had sat in the court for three days among the other islanders and had listened to Bart Faulconer lie, and lie extremely well. Pierre was certain that the judge and spectators were now convinced that Nicole's death had been nothing worse than a regrettable accident.

But today, the final day of the hearing, he had come early and found a seat as close to the dock as possible. For days he had wanted to witness the killer's face pale; he had needed to see his head drop in despair as he realized he would spend the rest of his life in prison. Pierre had needed those things to help him live with his grief. But deep inside himself he realized that these things would not happen. Faulconer would be judged only for failing to stop, failing to render assistance, and probably for not reporting an accident. Faulconer would not be found guilty of causing death by dangerous driving but simply of negligent driving, the lesser offence. Bartholomew Faulconer might not rot in prison, but her relatives would arrange for Nicole's death to be avenged. The older family members still believed in the power of the bonhomme du bois.

Bart was bored. The proceedings had been long and tedious. He listened for a while, but the prosecuting counsel was reciting the same facts and making the same ridiculous demands. Bart had taken an intense dislike to the bewigged prosecutor; it seemed to him that the man was waging an island vendetta and was persecuting him mercilessly merely because he was an outsider. I could break you in half, he uttered silently. The thought of the prosecutor's spine cracking beneath his hard fingers brought a smile to his lips.

Once again his lawyer frowned and flashed him a warning look. He did not enjoy having Bart as a client. Even though he

190

was excellent under cross-examination, he was unrepentant and seemed to believe that he was above the law. Bart understood the visual message but ignored it.

He felt confident. 'It's just like being in a school for the mentally handicapped,' he had quipped to his pals back in barracks. 'The old crow in black says a few words then waits for the judge to write it down. Every damn word is written down by hand. You'd think the courts would have caught up with the twentieth century by now.'

After a chilling two-day silence his secret contacts on the island had informed him that he would not have to serve a jail sentence. 'But Top is furious with you for putting the coup in jeopardy. Your orders were to keep a very low profile. You were told to stay out of trouble – not take centre stage in a court case. Top says that if you so much as squash a cockroach before the coup, you're dead. And,' they added with glee, since Bart had been almost impossible to handle and control, 'he means *dead*.'

Bart had fumed at the message. He had no desire to meet with a fatal accident on Mahé, so he feigned contrition and gratefulness. He turned his attention back to the prosecutor.

'Rather than risk colliding with an oncoming bus, the accused chose to take the life of an innocent woman.' The words burned Bart as deeply and painfully as the barbs of a lion fish. His dislike seethed and churned and he itched to quieten that unctuous voice. 'That is tantamount to murder. He made a deliberate choice: he chose to kill her.'

Bart moved restlessly on the hard wooden stool. He fumed at the possibility of the prosecuting counsel convincing the judge at this late stage that he was guilty. As the prosecutor reached the end of his closing address, his voice rose and his condemnation of Bart became even harsher. Bart gripped the edge of his stool. He could feel the hard beat of his heart as it pumped his racing blood. It was an accident. How dare the prosecutor insinuate otherwise?

The prosecutor came to the end and inclined his head slightly towards the bench. As he turned to sit down, he looked straight at Bart and his tight smile mocked and taunted him.

191

'Bastard!' Bart roared. And he picked up his stool and hurled it at the prosecutor with all the speed and accuracy of a fast bowler. The stool missed the man's head, but it crashed into his shoulder with sufficient force to knock him off his seat.

The courtroom erupted with a thunderous roar. The judge hammered at the bench with his gavel, but in the furore it was as useless as the silent chimes of the Victoria Clock Tower.

Bart's temper subsided as quickly as a boiling pot when the lid is removed and he stood quietly while the orderlies pinioned his arms. He grinned inwardly as the prosecutor was helped to his feet and led from the courtroom to await medical attention. The man did not look at him again.

The hall doors were closed. The crowd outside clamoured to know what had disturbed the peace in the normally quiet courtroom. On a bench near the back two men sat, shocked and silent. Job shook his head and held his face in his hands.

Gradually order was restored. As his lawyer pleaded for the court's indulgence and understanding, Bart suddenly realized the enormity of his action. He looked for the two agents at the back of the court, but they sat with their eyes closed, listening to his lawyer.

'M'lud, although my client's action is reprehensible, I crave the court's indulgence.' Bart's lawyer spoke earnestly and well. 'I present to you an innocent man. A contrite man. An honest man. A man driven to this act solely by the tension of the last three days. A man driven to the brink of despair by Miss Daumier's death.'

Bart studied the judge but could read nothing on his inscrutable face. The judge remained impassive as the defence lawyer pleaded, and Bart's unease gave way to fear. He had been warned. Top was a hard man. He could pay with his life for the moment's revenge.

The judge peered at Bart from beneath his curled silver wig. He eased the grey sash round his waist and patted the slashed white tabs at his neck before speaking. 'It is the order of this court that Bartholomew Faulconer be committed to Les Cannelles for ten days' observation.'

Bart gasped and Pierre smiled. At last something had

192

shattered that overwhelming air of condescension and self-assurance.

But it's a mental asylum, Bart wanted to shout. I'm not mad, I'm not a lunatic. Bart had all the layman's fear of mental illness. Physical pain and deprivation he understood. Mental disabilities terrified him.

The sharp rap of the gavel signified the close of the session and the court stood in silence as the judge departed in a swirl of crimson robes.

Bart's lawyer crossed to the dock. His black gown floated over the benches like a widow's veil of mourning. 'I'll accompany you to Les Cannelles,' he said shortly. The court orderlies' restraining arms were as unyielding as a straitjacket.

'But I won't . . .'

'I cannot guarantee to keep you out of prison unless your behaviour is exemplary for the ten days that you are under observation.'

'But it's a mental hospital,' protested Bart.

'Correct. It's where they put people who behave irrationally,' said his lawyer pointedly. 'I suggest that you knock your head on the ground three times when anyone up there speaks to you.' He nodded to the orderlies and they turned Bart around to lead him out of court. For an instant he resisted and his biceps bulged, straining the seams of his jacket. 'Remember, your behaviour determines your freedom,' warned his lawyer.

Bart nodded and walked docilely into the blinding sunshine.

VIII

The treatment room was small and bright. Doctor Redvers stood, looking out through the large plate-glass window, sucking thoughtfully on his empty pipe. He had his back to the two medical student observers. He turned around as trolley wheels squeaked on the highly polished grey-and-white-streaked linoleum floor.

The ward nurse swung the trolley into position and clicked

193

on the wheel locks. 'Patient is ready for treatment,' she announced and stood back, waiting to wheel the trolley into the recovery room after the treatment.

The students glanced at the patient then jolted into attentiveness. They found a good position near the trolley.

'I'm delighted to see you two gentlemen are paying attention,' said Redvers as he crossed the room. The young girl gazed up at the faces hovering above her; her face was calm and serene. Her mauve nightdress hung over the side of the trolley like the faded petals of an iris. She had been given a drug to relax her and she smiled faintly as Redvers lifted her hand. The nurse applied the cuff and inflated it, to take a recording of her blood pressure.

'Good-morning, Laura,' he said, stroking her fingers gently. 'Today should be our last treatment.'

He continued talking to her while he quickly stuck the electrocardiogram recording discs on her shoulders and connected the leads. He ran his eyes along the rhythm strip. Satisfied that it was recording her heartbeat properly, he picked up the electroencephalogram electrodes and held out his hand for the electro jelly.

'After this it'll be Lyewood for a few weeks,' he continued.

The nurse in charge cleaned Laura's forehead with alcohol. She tucked away a few tendrils which had escaped from the band that held Laura's thick hair away from her face.

'Seychelles,' Laura whispered, running her tongue round her dry mouth.

Redvers bent low to hear whatever she was saying. His fingers were busy smearing jelly on the EEG electrodes.

'Right, and I'll be waiting there to meet you,' he answered as he slipped the brainwave monitoring electrodes under the rubber band and tightened it round her forehead.

The nurse parted Laura's hair, a few centimetres above her ear hole. She rubbed the clear patch with conductive gel, then handed the steel EEG treatment discs to Redvers.

As he tested the thickness of the conductive gel on the silver electrodes, he explained to the students that he would be using these unilaterally since it caused less confusion and memory loss than the bi-lateral version, which used more electricity. He held their attention while he placed the first disc a few centimetres above the midpoint between the angle or orbit and the ear hole. He then positioned the second disc where the nurse was holding back Laura's hair. He placed both electrodes on the non-dominant side of the head, reminding the students that this was the side which did not affect speech.

The medical students nodded and turned their attention back to Laura's face, each trying to catch her eye. 'Gentlemen,' Redvers rasped, 'you're here to study the technique of electro-convulsive therapy.' Guilty as Peeping Toms, their eyes swung back to look at Redvers. Holding the upper electrode firmly in place on Laura's scalp, and satisfied that the students under-stood the importance of having a good clean contact, Redvers nodded to the anaesthetist.

The anaesthetist scrubbed at the inside of Laura's arm. 'Just a small prick,' he murmured soothingly as he inserted the needle to open the intravenous line. One student sidled over, trying to read Laura's name taped to the pentothal syringe that lay on the tray.

'All right, my lovely,' said Redvers to Laura. 'You start counting to a hundred for me.' Laura began to count, but as the pentothal took effect she mumbled then stopped. 'Carry on, Laura,' said Redvers. 'Laura, answer me.'

'She's gone,' the anaesthetist decided. 'Now the scoline.' Deftly he replaced the empty syringe with the muscle relaxant and shot it into her vein.

Redvers helped him insert the airway into her throat and connect the oxygen tank. They clamped the rubber mouth-guard between Laura's teeth, distorting her mouth as gro-tesquely as a boxer's wearing a mouthpiece.

Redvers glanced up at the students and explained how important it was to oxygenate patients before, during and after the treatment: it minimized confusion after the treatment and lessened memory impairment. He studied the tremor in the muscles of Laura's neck and shoulders as the relaxant worked it way down her body. As he watched and waited for the nerve tremors to die away in the small muscles of Laura's foot, he told the students about Bowlig's experiments with rats the previous year. Bowlig had used the modified ECT with muscle relaxants and oxygen and found no neuropathological changes. Redvers agreed that there was still some fear that ECT treatment led to irreversible brain damage. He went on to explain that, though changes had been reported, it was uncertain just how much was as a direct result of ECT; a lot could be accounted for by other factors. 'We believe that any damage is reversible,' he said, tapping Laura's patella and watching her leg jump. He signalled to the anaesthetist, who stopped the oxygen flow. 'She's ready.'

He checked once again that the EEG leads were connected properly and would start monitoring her brain activity as soon as he depressed the ECT treatment switch.

The anaesthetist helped the nurse stretch out Laura's neck and hold her jaw tight shut. Redvers did a last visual check-up of the instruments and depressed the treatment button. The stimulating current coursed through Laura's brain. Her muscles suddenly contracted strongly then relaxed as the two-second electrical impulse ended. As the tonic phase began, her arms and legs gradually flexed and became increasingly rigid. Her feet humped up into high arches and her toes bent back stiffly.

The students waited and watched for the twitching of the small muscles round her eyes and the twitching of both thumbs and both big toes. This delayed twitching was one of the signs of a successful treatment. As the rhythmic movements of the clonic phase began, Laura's body jerked and shook as uncontrollably as teeth chattering with cold.

'How much? How long?' both students asked together, then stopped in confusion.

Redvers smiled faintly. 'We used only a pulsed current, gentlemen. The square wave pulses are almost ideal. We find that one can produce a full convulsion using thirty J of electricity. The confusion should last for at least twenty-five seconds to be effective.'

'Thank you, sir,' they replied.

Redvers watched Laura as the spasmodic twitching died away, then he turned to look at the EEG monitor which still

196

showed convulsion activity in the brain. They waited in silence for the few seconds it took for the seizure finally to end.

The anaesthetist discontinued the use of oxygen and turned Laura on to her side. He listened to her breathing. Redvers helped the nurse in charge to remove the headband and electrodes. Satisfied that she was breathing easily, the anaesthetist motioned to the nurse to wheel Laura into the recovery room.

'She'll soon be ready for a nice cup of tea and her breakfast,' said the nurse cheerfully as she released the wheel locks. 'She was up and about in no time after the last treatment. There is no nausea or vomiting with this one.'

Redvers smiled at the nurse. He leaned over the trolley and ran his hand tenderly over Laura's head. Her eyelids flickered imperceptibly. He smoothed her dark arched eyebrows. 'She's responded magnificently,' he said, turning to the students. 'I wish all our cases were this simple.'

The students ran to open the door for the departing trolley. Redvers waited until they had reluctantly closed the door and returned to where the nurse was setting out a new tray of labelled syringes for the next patient. 'Would you gentlemen care to spend fifteen minutes in the recovery room observing the patient's progress?' he suggested.

'Yes, sir. Thank you, sir,' they chorused, and the door banged loudly behind them.

Redvers and the nurse in charge exchanged amused glances.

'Hard to believe that they will eventually become sober, hard-working doctors,' laughed Redvers.

'But always susceptible to a pretty face,' teased the nurse, and Redvers busied himself with his empty pipe.

CHAPTER SIX

The Seychelles 1978

 I

The silver-grey Boeing crested the forest-clad mountains of Mahé then dived down towards the sea. Just offshore, the islands in the St Anne Marine Reserve lay, as green and rich as uncut emeralds in the shallow sapphire and turquoise water. Laura sat with her nose pressed to the cabin window as if seeing the beauty of the islands for the first time.

'It's strange to think we have the only granite islands in the world, Daddy.'

'And the most beautiful,' he answered, looking over her shoulder.

'Look, there's St Anne, and Round and Cerf,' she said, pointing to the islands.

The plane turned out over the sea to line up with the runway. The wheels seemed to be rolling on the water as it skimmed the white-capped waves. Suddenly brown earth appeared beneath the wheels and Laura turned away from the window and reached for Ashley's hand. 'When the airstrip was first built, I was terrified that the plane would overrun it and we'd land in the sea,' she said, gripping his fingers tightly. 'I'd close my eyes as we approached the runway and start praying. And I'd only open them when I felt the plane taxi on to the apron.'

'Well, old lady,' teased Ashley, 'I'm pleased to see that you've outgrown that fear.'

'Almost,' Laura confessed, disentangling her fingers and plastering her nose back against the window.

The little houses, which had once edged the sea and now edged the land reclaimed for the runway, sped by. Laura examined them all eagerly. 'It's so good to be home,' she said as they waited for the health inspector to board the plane and check that it had been sprayed for mosquitoes. 'Thank you for allowing me to spend the last six months of this year here with you, Daddy,' she said, stuffing a book down the side of her bag. 'I wouldn't have enjoyed starting my art course in the middle of the year. I know that staying with me in Sussex for so long has interfered with your work, but I'll help you on Aldabra and try to do your typing.' She paused and her mouth drooped. 'My typing won't be as good as Nicole's,' she said with the semblance of a smile.

'We'll both miss Nicole very much, Muffin, but the memory of her love and laughter will always be with us.' He squeezed her hand. 'And we do have Pierre.'

Laura flicked her hair back over her shoulders. 'I want to talk to him. He seems to have adopted some strange political policies since we've been away.' She picked up her canvas hand-luggage and slung a leather tote-bag over her shoulder. 'He'd better come up with some good reasons for this single-party state or I'm not giving him the diving watch we bought him.'

'Laura,' Ashley admonished, following her down the steps, 'you can't withhold a gift for someone just because you disagree with his political beliefs.'

'Can't I?' Laura answered, squinting in the bright sunlight. 'Come on, Daddy.' She tugged at his arm impatiently. 'I can't wait to see Pierre and La Retraite and Cook.'

Ashley followed her through the terminal and stood back, smiling, as she recognized Pierre. With a shriek she dodged past laden trolleys, sweating tourists and waiting families and threw her arms round his neck. 'Pierre, I've missed you so much,' she said breathlessly. 'Oh, it's so good to see you. We have a super present for you. I chose it. You're going to love it.'

'I've missed you too,' he answered, holding her to him tightly. 'It's been very lonely at La Retraite.'

For the first time in months he felt complete. His family had returned. Looking down into Laura's clear untroubled eyes, he realized that deep mental pain had replaced the long-legged school-girl with a mature and very beautiful young woman. He realized how tightly he was holding her, and relaxed his grip and kissed her lightly. Her face was thinner and her hair now swung below her waist.

Laura clung to his arm as he walked across to greet Ashley and take the luggage trolley. 'There's someone waiting for you in the Moke,' he said as he swung Laura's hand-grip on top of the suitcases. 'It's the bright pink one.'

'Where's the red– ?' Laura asked. Then she remembered and was quiet.

'It's new,' said Pierre quickly. 'If you're very good I'll let you use it for your driver's licence exam. That's if you still remember how to drive.'

'My licence? Oh, of course, I can have one now. Thanks, Pierre,' she said gaily. She looked in the direction he was pointing and spun away. She raced across the concourse to where a familiar figure sat wedged uncomfortably in the front seat of a candy-floss-pink Moke. 'Cook,' she called as she ran. 'Cook, it's you!'

Pierre turned to Ashley. 'How is she? She seems to have recovered completely.'

'Redvers and the staff at St Francis have been wonderful,' Ashley answered as they zigzagged the trolley through the crowd. 'When she didn't respond to the drug therapy, I thought that we'd lost her. Pierre, you would not have recognized her. Then, as you know, we tried electroconvulsive therapy.' Ashley's eyes clouded as he remembered the acrimonious arguments he had had to weather with Emma; she was convinced that his consent to the treatment would damn Laura to the life of a moron. 'It worked. They are weaning her off the anti-depressant pills. Redvers is now here at Les Cannelles. He has suggested that Laura visit the hospital three times a week and that she does some voluntary work among the patients.'

'Will she?'

'She became very fond of the nurses and therapists at St Francis,' Ashley answered, slowing up as they approached the Mini-Moke. 'She idolizes Doctor Redvers and is delighted at

200

the prospect of helping him. He's also young. Mid-thirties, I'd say. His youth probably helps her relate to him.'

Pierre felt a swift and unreasoning dislike for the doctor.

'At first I wasn't happy with the idea of Laura working up there. It's not as . . .' Ashley paused, not wanting to denigrate the little island hospital, '. . . progressive, as advanced as St Francis,' he finished lamely. 'But Laura was adamant, and Redvers feels it'll be therapeutic. It also gives him the opportunity to monitor her progress and lessen her dependency on him.'

'Dependency?' Pierre queried tightly.

'Laura has accepted him as the mother-figure she needs. Apparently patients often do this. The psychiatrist then has to lessen that dependency without plunging the patient into another state of depression.'

Pierre bent down to lift the front of the trolley over the kerb. 'So Laura could become depressed again?'

Ashley nodded and manoeuvred the trolley closer to the Moke. 'Redvers feels that six months of rest in the islands will stabilize her. She'll be ready to start art school at the beginning of next year.' Ashley dropped his voice. 'I'm betting that with our love and a little island magic we can cut that down to three months.'

'How long is this doctor going to be at Les Cannelles?' Pierre asked, keeping his voice neutral.

'Oh, a couple of months,' Ashley replied. 'I thought we'd take him out fishing and diving. You'll like him. He even looks a bit like you. Now that you've cut your hair,' he added, looking at Pierre's short haircut with approval.

Pierre ran his hand over his brush cut and grinned. 'They tell me in the office that it looks like a lavatory brush,' he confessed.

Ashley exploded with laughter, and he was still laughing when he greeted Cook.

The return to La Retraite was easier than he had expected, and he was relieved. He had been worried about Laura's reaction to Nicole's empty room, but Pierre had thoughtfully moved into

201

it; now it was filled with fishing and diving paraphernalia and framed tourist brochures of the islands brightened the walls. A pair of parakeets swung in a cage at the open window. The African beat of island music came from a record player resting on top of an old oak roll-top desk. It was a man's room and there was no trace of Nicole left in it. Pierre was on his knees under the bed, looking for a piece of coral he had found to add to Laura's collection.

Ashley clenched his teeth as he stood in the doorway. He could still smell Nicole's evocative perfume and could see her kneeling over him, her slender body framed in the light from the open window. He squeezed his eyes tightly closed. Stretching a smile across his lips, he turned to Laura, ready to comfort her, but she had run across the room to the parakeets and was cooing at them in Creole.

Ashley offered up a small prayer of thanks to Redvers; his therapy was working. Laura was obviously ready to face up to life and accept the loss of her two mothers. 'It'll take some time,' Redvers had warned Ashley. 'She blames herself for their deaths. That's certainly unreasonable, but not at all unusual. It's my job to have this feeling resolved.'

Ashley watched Laura put some sunflower seeds between her lips and hold her face up to the cage for the parakeets. Emotion thickened his voice. 'See you downstairs in ten minutes, Muffin. If you're late for her special dinner, Cook will never forgive you.'

'We'll be down right now,' she said, splattering seeds all over the floor of the cage. 'It's tec-tec soup. I can smell it.'

With a grunt of satisfaction Pierre backed out from under the bed, holding a delicate spray of gorgonian fan coral.

'It's beautiful, Pierre,' Laura said, examining the spectacular spray. 'When can I come and dive with you? You and Daddy promised to take me on a deep dive.'

Pierre and Ashley exchanged glances over her head and they grinned. The carrots which had dangled limply for so long were now being taken. Laura was ready to start living.

'Next weekend,' Pierre suggested and Ashley nodded.

'Super!' Laura shrieked, looking up from the coral. She had

not expected them to agree. Her eyes sparkled as she looked up at Pierre.

Ashley left the room and they didn't notice his departure. The sound of their laughter followed him down the passage. To his surprise he found himself happy. He had his daughter back, and perhaps a son.

Dinner was over. Laura had praised Cook's tec-tec soup and had been rewarded with a rare smile. The old house creaked and groaned as it settled down for the night. Laura sat in front of the dressing table and brushed her hair until the ends danced up to greet the brush. On the hundredth stroke she put her hairbrush down and sat staring at the bare glass top: her photographs were gone. She looked across at her bedside table. It, too, was bare, but for a glass vase of delicate lime-green tree orchids.

Cook. She must have put them away, thought Laura, as she pulled open the drawers of the dressing table and scattered their contents. But there were no silver frames. She pushed back the stool and paused. Then, jumping up, she flung open the lid of the stool. There, nestling on a bed of tissue paper, were the frames. Laura picked them up and arranged them carefully on the glass table top. She kept the last two and walked across to her bed.

A young girl of eleven sat with her arms entwined round her mother's neck. Laura looked at Virginia and kissed the photograph gently. There was no longer any pain as she studied her mother's face . . . only warmth. Carefully she wedged the deep-blue velvet stand open and stood it on the bedside table, then she lifted the second frame and turned it over.

Nicole laughed out at her; she was sitting on the granite steps at La Retraite, leaning back against Ashley. She was holding down her flowered skirt against the wind, and her dark hair whipped round his face. Laura held her breath. The pain came in short sharp stabs. Holding the photograph to her chest, she ran out of her room and down the dark passage to Nicole. Outside the door she stopped. It was closed. Nicole was gone.

She flung open the door. 'Pierre,' she whispered brokenly. 'Pierre, it's Nicole.'

Pierre switched on the bedside light and tightened his lips as he saw Laura clutching the silver frame. Wordlessly he held out his arms and Laura rushed forward and buried her face in his shoulder. He covered her shivering body with the light sheet and cradled her to him. Gradually the warmth of his body stilled her shivers and she lay, dry-eyed, in his arms.

'We both miss Nicole dreadfully,' he murmured into her ear. 'But now the time has come for us to think of Ashley.' He felt Laura's breathing quicken. 'He planned a future with Nicole. Now he has only us. There can be no happiness in his future if he sees us sad.' Gently he stroked Laura's cheek. 'We must be strong for him, Laura. Do you think you can be?'

Laura gulped then nodded. 'Yes. Daddy has done so much for me.'

'Now you can repay him. Smile and laugh for him and for Nicole.' Laura stiffened momentarily against him, but he carried on speaking. 'Nicole would want us to make Ashley happy. She loved him so much.'

'When I feel very sad, can I share that with you?' she asked, her voice as small and uncertain as a child's.

'Yes, Laura, my door will always be open for you, just as Nicole's was. I'll always be here.'

She sighed and cuddled up against him, holding his arms round her. Pierre tucked a pillow under her head and brushed her hair away from her face. He listened to her breathing deepen. As the long hours passed and his arm under her head grew numb, he understood that his love for Laura had changed. He now loved and wanted her as a woman, and the realization frightened him.

The rainclouds, blue and black as putrescent fish, lay in bloated piles in the sky. A light south-westerly breeze whispered through the open windows but did little to dispel the heat, baked into the white walls of the little office.

The rich, sweet smell of tobacco swirled slowly round the room and eased through the half-open door into the cement-floored passage. Doctor Redvers sat at the wood-veneer desk. A pile of case histories was stacked in front of him and he held his pipe against the side of his head as he studied the topmost file. Bartholomew Harden Faulconer, he read.

A diffident tap on the door broke his concentration. 'Yes,' he called out.

'Good afternoon, sir,' said Bart Faulconer. 'I'm sorry to trouble you, but it does look like rain. I'd like to move the patients to the other side of the lounge and lower the blinds.' Sensing Redvers' annoyance at being bothered by trivialities, Bart quickly explained. 'I'm sorry to trouble you, but some of the nurses are busy in the laundry and the others are with the new arrival who set his mattress alight.' Bart stepped out of the doorway and turned to leave. 'I'm sorry, sir. I'll wait until one of the nurses is free.'

'No, no,' said Redvers, leaning back in his chair and studying Bart. 'It'll save the nurses a lot of trouble if you move them now.'

'Yes, sir,' Bart acknowledged and his face lit up in an engaging grin. 'I'll move the table across as well.' Redvers looked puzzled. 'Henri has been rolling on it all morning. He'll be difficult and will upset the others if I lift him off.'

Redvers nodded and made a note to check the medications. 'How long have you been here, Faulconer?'

'I was here for ten days, sir,' Bart answered politely. 'For the next six months I'll be here on Saturdays and Sundays. It's community service, sir.'

'You were committed for psychiatric observation,' mused Redvers, thumbing through Bart's file.

205

Bart edged closer to the desk, hoping to read some of his file, but Redvers was holding it upright. 'Yes, sir. A very foolish mistake on my part. There is no excuse for my behaviour, sir,' said Bart humbly. 'I threw a stool at the public prosecutor. I was in court because of an accident. I was found not guilty,' he added quickly as he saw Redvers reading.

'According to this, there was insufficient proof of intent to convict you of manslaughter. Not quite the same thing,' said Redvers, putting his pipe in his mouth and lacing his fingers together at the back of his head.

'No, sir. Yes, sir,' Bart agreed. 'But I swear I'm innocent.'

'Yes,' said Redvers.

'I'm here because of the public prosecutor.' Redvers remained silent and Bart plunged on. 'He was trying to make the court believe that I caused the accident deliberately.'

Bart searched Redvers' face for a reaction, but the psychiatrist's eyes remained dark and enigmatic.

'I've certainly learned my lesson, sir,' said Bart. Suddenly he was eager to be away from Redvers' calculating stare. 'Excuse me, please. I must return to work.'

He backed out of the office. The lesson is, never get caught, he said silently as he passed the heavily barred rooms reserved for violent patients. The door to the one cell stood open and the smell of wet ash was strong. For a split second it took Bart back to his recce patrols in Rhodesia. That smell heralded excitement; it told of a recently doused camp-fire and the proximity of enemy guerrillas.

Bloody idiot ever to have left, he thought as he looked into the cell. The nurses had hosed out the room, and scraps of charred mattress-ticking plugged the hole, set low down in the wall. The fire had etched weird figures on the cement wall above the bed and the purple light of an approaching storm bruised the shapes. Bart felt and heard the misery of the tormented people who had paced, mumbled and screamed obscenities inside the cell, and he needed to be outside. His shoulders shook involuntarily and he stepped into the courtyard just as the first fat drops of rain splashed on the tin roof.

*

206

Redvers sat, puffing contentedly on his pipe for a few minutes after Bart left. Then he turned his attention back to the file. 'Let's see what the doctor here thought of Faulconer,' he muttered as he turned the pages.

Thirty-four years of age. Classified duties in Seychelles army. Comes from very successful family in Sussex. Mother invalid, Father brilliant surgeon. Home atmosphere one of conditional acceptance. 'That would have put some pressure on him as a youngster,' he muttered. 'He was rewarded only for what he achieved.' He ran his finger on down the page. 'Possible psychopathic tendencies. Strong narcissistic streak. Shows little moral responsibility. Enjoys brutality of war. Capable of committing violent acts. Contemptuous of critics.' Redvers read on. 'Persuasive . . . charming . . . attractive to women . . . manipulative . . . tendency to drink.' He flipped over to the last page. 'Shows little remorse for death of woman . . . Feels no guilt.' Redvers paused and tapped the file with his fingers, then read the last paragraph on the page. 'Suggest a probationary period of community service attached to a social worker.'

Redvers dug deep in the file and found a summary of the court proceedings. He read it slowly and carefully, pausing frequently to digest the details.

'The judge obviously accepted this recommendation. So Faulconer will be here over the weekends,' he said quietly. He tucked the summary back into the file and bent to look under the desk for the waste-paper basket. 'He knows how to present himself as both sincere and likeable,' he mused. 'I'd agree with the doctor's assessment: he is both persuasive and manipulative. He certainly managed to convince his lawyer and the court that hitting the woman was a terrible accident and that driving away from the scene was pure panic. He has to be good to get away with that.' He tipped the contents of the ashtray into the straw basket and rested his pipe on the clean glass. 'Wonder what he does in the army that's classified? Should have thought that life in the islands would be too tame for the likes of Faulconer.'

Redvers looked up as an inmate stumbled down the open-air corridor. Sweat had polished his skin to the deep ebony found in wet turtle-shells and his eyes were rolled back, white and huge, in his shaven head. Behind him walked Faulconer and a nurse. She barely reached Faulconer's shoulder and her uniform belt doubled round her tiny waist.

Redvers shook his head. It amazed him that the slender island girls had the strength to handle the inmates. Yet in the short time he had spent in Les Cannelles he had seen them physically deal with patients twice their size. The nurse unconsciously smoothed her uniform over her hips and fluffed up her hair as she smiled up at Bart.

Redvers sighed. Society was flooded with psychopathic Faulconers; they just didn't commit enough crimes to be locked up. He closed the file on Bart and replaced it at the bottom of the pile. Tucking his pipe into his shirt pocket, he went in search of the head nurse. They were going to Victoria to meet government officials and try to obtain a promise of financial help for improvements to Les Cannelles.

The loud clanging of the bell hanging inside the sealed front door to Les Cannelles attracted Bart's attention. He smacked the nurse lightly on her small tight buttocks and walked towards the door that was set into the high boundary wall.

'Some idiot standing at the entrance,' he said. 'I'll let them in the gateway.' The nurse opened her mouth to protest. 'Go on,' urged Bart. 'I won't be long. See if you can get your patient to water the vegetable garden instead of the outside walls of the lavatory.'

The inmate turned his huge cannonball head towards Bart and grinned foolishly.

'Yes, you,' said Bart. 'I'm sick of cleaning up your pee.'

'Bart,' admonished the nurse, pronouncing his name as if the 't' was silent, 'it's not his fault. He does not know. We must help him.'

Sure, Bart agreed silently. An overdose of Pentothal would be a great help.

'I'm trying,' he laughed. 'I'm trying.' He watched her bottom swing under the tight skirt as she walked to the dusty garden, and he filed her away for future attention.

The bell clanged again and Bart hurried through the gate.

*

208

Laura stood under the small cement portico. For a second time she pulled the wire which ran through a hole in the door to the bell.

'If no one answers now, I'll leave,' she comforted herself.

It had taken her almost half an hour to find Les Cannelles. She was conscious of her new licence and had driven slowly. Each time she stopped the Moke to ask for directions, she had been greeted with suspicion or feigned incomprehension.

Over the years the village homes had crept up the steep hill and now they rubbed shoulders with the small hospital. The locals paid it as little attention as they would flatulence at a social gathering. The place was an embarrassment to them.

Laura stepped back from the door and looked at the stone walls. The name 'Les Cannelles' was etched in the cement beside the door, patches of grey mould festered on the white paint and the hairline cracks were green with moss. She stood on tiptoe, but all that was visible were grey roof sheets.

'It'll be easier to come in through the gate,' said a deep voice. 'You won't see much from out here.'

Laura spun around. Bart had padded up behind her, soft-footed as a feline. He stood with his hands on his hips, laughing at her discomfiture; she was abashed at being caught out trying to peep over the wall, and her usual politeness vanished. 'Had the bell been answered the first time I rang, it wouldn't have been necessary to . . .'

She turned to face him and her hair was caught and held in a net of sunlight. Bart caught his breath. This girl was beautiful. 'Sorry,' he said, now anxious to present a good image. 'I should have come sooner.'

She took off her sun-glasses and twirled them in her fingers. His apology doused the fire in her bright blue eyes and she smiled at him tentatively.

Bart appraised her quickly. Slender, but curving in the right places, he decided. A full, sexy bottom lip and skin glowing with the first kisses of the sun. Her cotton dress moulded her body as she moved and his fingers itched to untie the bows on her shoulders and let the dress fall. Cool it, Faulconer, he cautioned himself. This one is classy. A thoroughbred English

209

filly and probably not yet broken in. His blood rose, but he kept his voice neutral. 'We were busy with one of the inmates. I'm sorry that you were kept waiting.'

Laura was immediately contrite. 'I must apologize,' she said. 'It's just that I was a little nervous. It took so long to find the place and then it seemed deserted.' She looked up at Bart, noticing for the first time his muscular build, soft curving lips and tightly waved blond hair. He was an attractive man. His voice betrayed a good public school and he was obviously a gentleman. 'Are you one of the doctors?' she asked, trying to decide whether his eyes were yellow or pale lime-green.

'No,' Bart replied, thinking fast. 'I do voluntary work up here. Over weekends mostly.'

He moved into the shade of the wall. He wouldn't be missed for some time: Redvers and the head dragon had left and the rest would think that he was still in the garden with the nurse and the patient.

'Oh,' said Laura, immediately warming to him. 'That's very unselfish. It's not always easy looking after people with mental illnesses.'

'It can be trying,' he answered, motioning for her to join him in the shade. Like to wring their bloody necks, he thought. 'But we owe it to them. One should help those less fortunate than oneself,' he added aloud.

Laura moved across and leaned against the wall beside him. 'I've come up to see Doctor Redvers,' she volunteered.

My luck, thought Bart. Just when I've found something decent on the island, she turns out to be a loony.

'He suggested that I should come and help here. They're always grateful for voluntary workers,' she explained.

Bart immediately exuded charm. 'That's wonderful,' he said. 'We'll be able to work together. You'll brighten up both this place and my weekends.' He glanced at his watch. Redvers would be away for at least two hours. 'Doctor Redvers had to go out on business,' he said, 'but I'd be delighted to show you around Les Cannelles.' Bart sensed her hesitation. 'I'm not as knowledgeable as the doctor, but I'm sure you'll find my guided tour more interesting than sitting waiting in his office.'

210

A half-smile warmed his face and he pulsed with eagerness.

He suddenly reminded Laura of Pierre when he wanted to show her a rare shell or coral he had found. She felt the same repressed excitement, the same need.

'Thank you,' she said, accepting his offer.

He took her arm lightly, careful not to exert any pressure which would cause her to pull away. 'My name is Bart,' he said. 'Bart Harden.' When he had first arrived at Les Cannelles, he had asked the doctor in charge if he could use his second name, Harden, instead of Faulconer. He explained that he wanted to start afresh and he feared that he would be prejudged if he used the name of Faulconer. The doctor had agreed, and Redvers was also sympathetic. Looking at the young girl, Bart silently congratulated himself on his foresight. The island was small and she might have heard of the court case.

'Laura,' she responded. 'Laura Challoner.'

The name trickled through his memory bank like a faulty current, but it failed to spark a connection. 'A beautiful name. It suits you,' he said.

Laura felt her cheeks redden and she bent down to remove a non-existent stone from her sandal.

As they entered Les Cannelles Laura was pleased that Redvers was away. She would be able to spend some time with this man. Bart was so different from the island boys. He made her feel very grown-up, and she liked the sensation. Laura paused at the entrance and studied the jumble of buildings. They lay scattered across the dusty slope like children's building blocks, the edges chipped and the paint flaking.

'It looks so sad,' she said, pointing to the stained and mud-spattered walls.

'There's never much money to spare on islands,' answered Bart, 'and these patients don't know or care what the place looks like. So.' He spread his hands and shrugged his shoulders, straining his turquoise shirt at the seams.

'But the staff do,' said Laura. 'They should have a decent place to work in. It's no wonder they can't get help up here. It's depressing.'

'That's the fate of mental asylums.'

Bart led her down the covered passageway in front of the offices, pointing out the small treatment room and the staff lounge. Then he let her peep into the cavernous kitchen. Great cauldrons of fish stew and rice were bubbling on the stoves and the heat steamed up the screened windows. Two inmates were scouring out a stainless-steel cauldron that was large enough to accommodate their curled-up bodies. The cook looked up from the steaming pots only long enough to wipe his face with his sodden apron.

Bart led her outside. 'It's terribly dry up here,' she said as the heat rose to meet them from the baked soil.

'There's very little water,' he explained. 'It was a typical desk jockey's idea to build an asylum on the top of a dry hill in the middle of an old disused cinnamon plantation.'

Laura replaced her glasses and lifted her heavy hair from her neck. Her skin was pale where it had been shielded from the sun and Bart ached to sink his mouth into it.

'Where are the wards?' Laura asked.

'There's a men's dormitory,' he said, pointing out a rectangular block. Laura moved across to the closed dark-brown door. 'The rooms are kept locked, once they've been cleaned,' said Bart. 'It stops the patients messing them up and keeps them outdoors in the fresh air.' Bart winked. 'It also gives the male and female patients a chance to unroll a mat under a tree and become acquainted.' Worse than bloody rabbits, some of them, he added silently.

Laura nodded, not grasping the innuendo.

'And here comes one of them,' he warned.

Laura turned to watch a portly islander bouncing across the short yellow grass towards them. His arms were windmilling frenziedly and he was singing in a high cracked voice.

'He's manic,' said Bart. 'He's coming down from one of his highs. You should have seen him yesterday. He was swinging from the mango trees.'

As the inmate approached, the words of the song became distinguishable, and Laura glanced quickly at Bart. With a small sigh of relief she realized that the inmate was singing in Creole and Bart didn't understand the bawdy lyrics.

212

'Come on,' urged Bart. 'Let's get out of here before he starts talking. That one has found the secret of perpetual sound.

'Hey,' he called over his shoulder as he and Laura walked quickly towards the main building, 'Nurse wants to talk to you. She's in the garden.

'It worked,' he grinned as the manic patient turned and headed for the unsuspecting nurse. That'll keep her busy, gloated Bart. I don't need her ordering me around, not in front of Laura.

He caught Laura's hand and, giggling like truants, they walked back to the main building. They strolled through the open-sided common room which had a long dining table stretched across one end. Bart had Laura helpless with laughter as he described the antics of the inmates. He kept his stories touching and humorous and was rewarded with peals of laughter. Get them laughing and you're half-way there, he thought as he embroidered yet another story.

Bart hurried Laura across the cement courtyard, past the barred rooms for violent patients. He didn't want her to see the newest inmate. It was his task to make the institution look as attractive as possible. He wanted this young blonde to be up at Les Cannelles every weekend.

They were almost opposite the last room when Bart heard the distinctive clatter of the old minibus grinding through the gateway. Damn! Redvers is back, he cursed silently. I can't let him see me with Laura. He'll warn her away from me.

The door to the fire-blackened cell still stood open, and he whisked Laura inside. He half closed the door with his foot. 'Almost missed this one on our tour,' he laughed.

'But it's only a bare and rather ugly room,' said Laura, looking puzzled.

'It's where the violent ones are kept until the drugs have quietened them,' he explained. 'The last patient in this room set fire to his bedding. Nearly barbecued himself.' Laura paled and moved towards the door. 'I only showed it to you so that you would avoid these rooms when you come up to help.' Bart hoped it had not been a mistake to show her the barred rooms. She was looking quite ill.

'They don't have places like this at St Francis,' she whispered. 'There, someone stays with the patient and the room is . . .' she hesitated, '. . . nice.'

'St Francis? Isn't that the name of the mental asylum in Sussex?'

'Yes. It's the hospital for mental disorders,' Laura corrected him.

'Were you working there?'

Laura was silent. She realized that she didn't want this man to know about her illness.

'I'm sorry,' said Bart, sensing that she was reluctant to discuss the institution. 'It's none of my business.'

'Oh no,' Laura answered, thinking quickly. 'It's where I met Doctor Redvers. It's not far away from where we live.'

Bart laughed and took the opportunity to rest his hand on her shoulder. 'I didn't think for one moment that you were in there with all the crazies.'

Laura swallowed hard. He doesn't mean that mentally ill people are crazy. He wouldn't be giving up his weekends to help them if he did, she comforted herself.

'I'm only teasing,' he said, seeing her face fall. He looked at his watch. Only half an hour to go before my stint is over; I should be able to keep out of Redvers' way, he thought. 'Miss Challoner,' he said.

'Oh, please call me Laura.'

'Thank you . . . Laura,' he amended. 'I have to leave now, but I shall look forward to seeing you tomorrow.'

'Tomorrow?' said Laura.

'Yes. It's Sunday. Doctor Redvers is off duty and it's more relaxed around here.'

Ashley and Pierre were taking her diving tomorrow. They had decided that she was now ready to dive at Shark Bank, the deepwater rocks on the way to Silhouette Island. The thought of seeing a great spotted whale shark and the enormous grey stingrays, which claimed the diving site as their own, had excited her all week.

'I leave here at four. We could go down to Anse Royal. The

214

swimming and snorkelling near Ile Souris are marvellous.' Bart could see that she was wavering. 'On the way back to Victoria we could stop at one of the beach restaurants and have turtle coconut curry.'

'No kitouze for me,' laughed Laura. 'The restaurants are not allowed to sell turtle.'

'Octopus curry, then,' Bart decided, 'followed by—'

'Ladob,' cut in Laura. 'That's breadfruit, yams and sweet potatoes simmered in coconut milk and sugar,' she explained.

'You've sold it,' said Bart, peering round the door and hoping that he could slip away to the garden before Redvers or the head nurse saw him. 'So you will join me?' he asked with an engaging grin. 'It'll be great fun.'

Thoughts of Shark Beach, where Pierre had collected the white fan of gorgonian coral, faded. She could always ask Ashley to take her diving during the week, and she would persuade Pierre to sneak a day off work.

'All right,' she said, 'I'll see you here tomorrow.'

Bart smiled. It had worked. She had been lured into his trap as skilfully as fish were led into woven palm-leaf caiziers. 'Wonderful,' he said. 'I look forward to tomorrow.'

Bart put his hand on her waist to guide her to the door. Laura felt as flustered and excited as she had when as a schoolgirl she had given away her first kiss at a birthday party.

Bart stopped in the doorway. 'Don't tell Doctor Redvers that you've met me.'

'Why ever not?'

'I'm sure he would like to show you the hospital and grounds himself.' Bart leaned towards her and lowered his voice. 'They say he's also a bit of a stickler about work. He doesn't like his workers to stroll around sightseeing.'

'Oh, no. He's very understanding, Bart,' Laura protested.

'Absolutely. But this place has to be one of the centres for island gossip. What do they call it? Radio coco or coconut?'

'Radyo coco or banmbo,' she giggled and walked out into the cement courtyard.

Eager to leave Les Cannelles before Redvers introduced

Laura to the staff, Bart humbled himself. 'Please, Laura, I'm a very private person. I'd rather not let the staff know that I find you a very attractive woman.'

Laura lowered her eyes, then nodded.

Well done, Faulconer. It worked again, Bart congratulated himself.

'I understand,' said Laura, his words singing in her eyes. It was exciting to be called a woman. Pierre still treated her like a child. 'I'll tell no one that we've met.'

Bart pressed her fingers gently. 'The blue door over there is Redvers' office. Until tomorrow.'

Laura turned to look for the door, and when she turned back Bart was gone.

A coarse chuckle came from the fire-blackened cell. Unable to resist it, Laura walked back to the cell and copied the laugh. A leaf-green gecko appeared between the rusted iron bars. Beady eyes stared at her through the opening in the lower eyelid. It watched her fingers slowly walking up the wall. The gecko waited until she was almost within touching distance, then with a quick flick of its tongue to clean the viewfinder in the fused lids it vanished back into the dark cell.

'You disappeared as fast as Bart,' she said as she walked away.

She glanced back at the barred cells and they were no longer ugly and depressing. The cluster of old buildings was suddenly picturesque and full of charm. The thought of the blond man lightened her step and she hummed under her breath as she set off to greet Doctor Redvers.

<hr>

III

The sea sparkled as if sprayed with silver glitter. The two boats swayed and bumped together lightly as the water felt the rocks of Shark Bank and drew back.

Laura leaned over the side of the boat and spat into her face mask. She rubbed the saliva over the plate then trailed it in the sea, watching the saline water dilute her saliva and clean the glass.

Pierre and Ashley straightened up from their inspection of the oxygen tanks.

'Ready, Laura?' called Pierre.

Laura emptied the water from her mask and pushed it up high on her forehead.

'Let's hear the checks,' said Ashley as he handed her the equipment.

'You've already cleared the valve orifice and checked that there's enough air supply,' she said. 'I saw you.'

Pierre grinned and shook his head at Ashley.

'Always check your own diving equipment,' Ashley admonished. 'Remember—'

'A safe diver is a live diver,' Pierre and Laura chanted together.

Ashley laughed. 'Right, so let's have those diving checks.'

'It's taken us over a month to drag her away from Les Cannelles and bring her diving,' said Pierre in mock indignation. 'And she wastes time arguing.'

'What's the attraction up at the institution?' teased Ashley. 'The doctor or the patients?'

Laura felt herself blushing and she bent down to pick up her weight belt from the deck of the boat.

Pierre noticed her embarrassment and frowned. 'It must be Redvers,' he said, still pretending to be flippant. 'We never see you on Sundays. You leave at daybreak and are never back until after dark.' He turned to Ashley and helped him tighten the cylinder strap. 'I think you should check up on your daughter,' he said.

'Doctor Redvers isn't . . .' retorted Laura, then lapsed into silence. She didn't want Ashley to know that Redvers was not at Les Cannelles on Sundays. He might stop her going, and the thought of missing her Sunday outings with Bart dismayed her.

Ashley looked at his daughter's red face and took pity on her. 'We're only teasing, Muffin,' he said, strapping a knife to his leg and checking that it was within easy reach. 'I'm delighted that you enjoy helping out at the clinic. I saw Doctor Redvers in Victoria last week. He says that your help in the occupational therapy classes is invaluable.'

'But is it necessary to go up three times a week and then again on Sunday?' asked Pierre. He missed having Laura with him over the weekends. Suddenly it wasn't much fun sailing and fishing alone.

'I'm at home on Saturdays,' Laura retorted. 'If you cut down on all those boring meetings, we could do things like this more often.'

Pierre grinned; he wasn't going to let anything spoil the day. After the dive, he was taking Laura to Silhouette. She had never attended a real moutia. The workers from the coconut plantation were holding the traditional dance on an isolated strip of beach near Anse Lascars. The administrateur, an old family friend, had invited him to attend. He had also managed to get invitations for Giles and Emma, who were spending a few days on Silhouette visiting a herbalist.

'Here,' said Pierre, whipping her thick beach towel off the scuba cylinder, 'let me help you on with this.'

Pierre and Ashley watched carefully as Laura opened and shut the cylinder valve rapidly, clearing the orifice. Her fingers were deft and sure as she fitted and secured the demand regulator to the cylinder and checked for leaks.

'Good girl,' said Ashley as she went through her pre-dive checks methodically.

'We'll make a diver of her yet,' teased Pierre.

Laura finished taking slow breaths from the mouthpiece, checked the clearing button then pulled a tongue at him.

'Muffin!' Ashley admonished her in mock horror. 'Aren't you a little old for that?'

Laura laughed. 'He deserves it, Daddy. He still treats me like a baby.' She switched her reserve air supply to the closed position. 'And I'm not.'

'Well,' Pierre defended himself, 'you certainly don't look like a baby but—'

'Come on, you two,' Ashley grinned. 'Let's go. You can squabble after the dive.'

Laura smiled up at Pierre. She opened the cylinder valve

218

fully and let him settle the cylinder on her back and tighten the straps. 'You're still my best brother and I love you,' she said, tweaking his short hair.

He bent down and pulled her weight belt out of her diving bag. He no longer wanted to be loved as a brother. Perhaps there would be another opportunity at the moutia to tell her of his changed feelings.

Ashley was sitting on the edge of the boat. His eyes were crinkled against the glare and he was hot and uncomfortable in his black wetsuit. He was about to shout to Laura when Pierre straightened up and handed her the weight belt. Ashley swallowed as he caught the look in Pierre's eyes: it was one of naked longing. Pierre was in love with his daughter. He wanted Laura. Ashley felt his heart racing and he breathed in deeply. He had lost two women and was not ready to lose a third. Laura was still a child; she had to be protected from men.

'Hey!' Pierre's voice, like sea water surging under a face mask, shocked him. 'You're hyperventilating. And before a dive?'

'Daddy!' Laura looked up, surprised. Her father had warned her of the dangers of flushing carbon dioxide out of the lungs and blacking out in a dive.

Ashley studied Laura as she stood, legs astride, riding the swells easily. Her electric-blue-and-black wetsuit moulded her body, emphasizing its curves and hollows. Her hair was scraped away from her face, leaving a pale strip along the hairline. It hung in a heavy plait over her shoulder. As she waited for Ashley to respond, she twisted the splayed end of the plait round her finger. Suddenly he realized that he was looking at a woman – Laura was no longer his little girl.

Pierre stood beside her as attentive as a bridegroom. One hand was under her elbow ready to steady her if she overbalanced with the weight of the cylinder.

'Ashley,' he said, worried by the vacant look in the other's eyes and his silence. 'Are you all right?'

'Sorry,' Ashley replied, forcing himself to respond. 'I must have been daydreaming.' He smiled at Laura. 'The habit is obviously catching.'

Pierre chewed at his lower lip; something was wrong. Like sensing a storm long before the clouds tumble up into the sky and darken, he knew that Ashley was troubled.

'Right,' said Ashley, sitting up straight. 'Checks all done?' Pierre nodded. 'Good. Now, Laura, this is an outer dive and more interesting than the ones you've done so far. As it's your first dive at Shark Bank, there are a few things you should know.'

Laura sat down beside Ashley, balancing carefully on the edge of the boat. Pierre remained standing in front of them.

'This'll be your deepest dive. There are massive granite boulders which go down to one hundred and fifty feet.' Seeing Laura's eyes widen, he hastened to add, 'But we'll certainly not be diving to those depths.' He broke off and looked up at Pierre. 'Pierre and I will be close to you at all times. Remember to stay within touching distance. Don't go off chasing sea bass like you did on the last dive.' He looked at her thoughtfully then added, 'We've seen sharks on every dive here. They're usually grey reefs and are only curious!'

'I'll stay near you, Daddy.'

'There are stingrays,' added Pierre. 'Huge ones live around here.' He moved slowly towards Laura with his arms outstretched. 'They'll wrap you in those shawl-like fins and whip that tail around, burying the spine in your body.' He pounced on her and wrapped his arms round her waist. 'We'll have to use Ashley's knife to cut out the spine and stop the pain—'

'Stop it,' Laura shrieked, pushing him away and almost overbalancing herself. 'You're just trying to frighten me.'

'And succeeding,' Ashley laughed, unscrewing the cap on a bottle of Val Riche mineral water. 'Here, Muffin,' he said, handing her the water. 'Have a good drink then give it to Pierre.'

He watched in silence, making sure that they were both well hydrated, then he drained his own bottle.

'The currents are often strong at Shark Bank and, judging by the surface waves, we'll have to begin the dive against the current. That'll make it less tiring at the end of the dive.' Laura nodded. 'If for any reason you want to surface before I signal the end of the dive, make sure that we know and come up with you.'

'Oh, Daddy, I'd never ascend faster than my smallest air bubbles. That's one of the first things you ever taught me.'

'Today: on this dive I want you to be even more conservative. We'll use Spencer's Tables. So, Muffin, your smallest air bubbles are still too fast. Understand?'

'Yes, Daddy.'

'You follow me. Pierre will come in last,' said Ashley, peering at the bezel of his diving watch through the plano-convex lens glued to his mask. 'Remember, hard swimming burns up oxygen in the bloodstream. No racing down there.'

Laura nodded again.

He's getting old, thought Pierre. A magnifying lens on his mask. No more bounce dives to haul up the anchor. Aspirin and water before dives? The thought saddened him. As a boy he had idolized Ashley, and now as a man he admired and loved him. He wanted his hero to remain young for ever. He watched as the water swirled and calmed over Ashley's body.

'Hold on to your mask,' he cautioned as Laura pressed her palm against the face plate.

She paused on the edge of the boat and crossed her eyes at him through the glass. Then holding on to her scuba tank firmly, she let herself fall back gently into the water.

Her world became instantly blue and silent. She felt weightless, slim and fast as the myriad fish silhouetted against the splintered white face of the sun. There were no boundaries or horizons in this world of water. The deep turquoise was limitless and she felt a sense of freedom and excitement never equalled on land. The water was warm and silky. She floated in it, as cushioned as a foetus held in the amniotic fluid of its mother's womb.

Pierre signalled to her and she swam across to him. Her eyes grew huge as she gazed at the sea garden of gorgonian fan coral he had found. The pristine sprays glowed with the creamy opalescence of pearls. Tropical fish – ruby, emerald, topaz and sapphire – hung from the coral fans like precious gems. She

221

finned slowly round the fans, wanting to imprint their beauty on her memory for ever.

She started as Pierre shook her arm to get her attention. Looking in the direction of his pointing finger, she caught her breath. Suddenly her vision was starred by vertical black and primrose streaks. She swatted at a school of Moorish idols swirling round her head.

As they finned away to regroup for another foray in front of her face plate, she saw what Pierre was watching. She felt for his hand. The water darkened to cyanine as a floating mass, larger than an airship, swam lazily above them.

Pierre and Ashley exchanged glances and, signalling to Laura to ascend, they swam up to meet the creature. As they came up beneath the dark mass it seemed to Laura that a piece of the reef had broken away from the sea-bed and was floating above them.

Ashley kicked strongly and caught hold of the edge of the huge dorsal fin, signalling for Laura and Pierre to join him. Laura swam up and Ashley caught her arm, helping her to cling to the dorsal. It felt like hanging on to the outside window frame of a moving bus. Pierre swam under the fin and alongside the broad blunt head. He hooked his fingers into the side of the immense mouth. He hung on to its lips as the whale shark continued to move slowly through the water, paying no attention to them.

Laura's heart pumped wildly. It was every diver's dream to swim with the largest fish known to man. This one had to measure at last fifty feet in length. As the water sped past, she dug her fingers into its fin and studied the gentle creature. The whale shark's ridged dark-green back was blotched with pale spots and stripes as if freckled by the sun to camouflage it while basking on the surface of the sea. The tiny eyes seemed ineffectual in so large a mass. Looking up at the gaping gill-slits, Laura shivered; they seemed large and deep enough to engulf a diver. She imagined the rush of water drawing her into their black depths, and she tightened her grip on the fin.

All of a sudden, seeming to tire of the human parasites that were clinging to its body, the gigantic shark sounded. The water whirled and boiled as the fish drove almost forty thousand pounds of body weight down through the water. Thinking that the giant fish was angry, Laura panicked. She turned and sped away from the whale shark. As she descended, she swung her legs powerfully from the hip and she swam on blindly, not thinking of Ashley or Pierre, wanting only to distance herself from the whale shark.

The drag of her cylinder and the density of the water soon tired her and she slowed. Gradually her breathing became less ragged. She realized that she was now alone. She trod water, spinning in a slow circle, searching desperately, trying to penetrate the indigo blue which closed round her. Her eyes burned as she searched for Pierre and Ashley, for the tell-tale sheen of rising bubbles. She strained her eyes; the water was pressing down on her, she felt that she was suffocating and her heartbeats thudded loudly in her ears. As she sniffed back her tears, she heard Ashley's words: 'Keep within touching distance. Don't surface without letting us know. Dive alone and you die alone.'

She forced herself to remain calm, fighting back the surging waves of fear and panic which threatened to swamp her. The fish towed us away from Shark Bank, she reasoned. So if I continue to swim in this direction, I must find our dive site. Daddy and Pierre will return there. They'll find me.

As she finned through the water she searched hopelessly for the earlier fantasia of colour and movement. She needed to find the reef fish which would herald Shark Bank. But she moved alone in the dark-blue void. Her flutter kicks propelled her on through the water. She checked her pressure gauge and blanched. She had only fifteen minutes of air supply.

'Panic and swim hard, and you'll push up your air intake from twenty-five to sixty litres a minute,' Ashley had warned. 'Your air supply is your most precious asset when diving. Don't abuse it, never allow your tank pressure to approach ambience. When the pressure is down to 2.3 megapascals, end your dive and surface.'

Laura swam on. Indecision and fear tore into her self-control with all the frenzy of feeding sharks.

'If you lose sight of me, don't swim around, searching. Don't be a fool. Circle slowly a few times, then go up. I'll meet you at the surface.' Laura swallowed. She had forgotten one of the first rules Pierre had taught her. Ashley and Pierre would be waiting on the surface. They wouldn't swim back to Shark Bank. If she surfaced now, they wouldn't know where to look for her. She would be as discernible as a gull's feather floating in the immensity of the ocean.

The realization that she could die seeped into Laura and horrified her. Until now she had been cocooned in the immortality of youth. She was having to kick harder to move forward, and it took a few moments for her to realize that she was in the current. The reef, she thought. I must be near Shark Bank. I've hit the current.

Relief sickened her and she swallowed hard, trying to clear the sour taste from her mouth. She scissored her long legs powerfully, eager to see the reef. The current became stronger and she felt the ache deep in her thighs as she moved against it.

The grey reef sharks swam easily and silently in the current. Alerted by their sensitive lateralis system to vibrations, they cut swiftly through the water, accurately locating the low-frequency movements of a swimmer. They were active predators and, of all sharks, had the most highly developed macula neglecta organs in their ears.

The five greys saw and smelt Laura long before she was aware of them. She had stopped kicking and lay motionless in the water, resting her tired legs. Slowly she rolled over, searching the murky depths for the reef. Her eyes narrowed and she blinked hard. There were dark shapes in the periphery of her vision. In her need, she fashioned them into the rocks of Shark Bank . . . but as she watched, the rocks grew and moved. She squeezed her eyes tight closed. She was tired. Rocks could not move.

She jack-knifed into an upright position as if struck by a yellow-bellied sea snake. Her brain recorded what her eyes refused to accept. Grey reef sharks, it told her, as the stocky predators became recognizable. They were now close enough for her to distinguish the wide black bands edging their tail fins, and their stomachs were the colour of sour cream. To be treated with great caution, her brain warned her. Inquisitive and can be very aggressive.

Laura had seen many sharks, but Pierre or Ashley had always been beside her; she had had the security of a hard back pressed firmly against hers when the sharks became too inquisitive. She looked around quickly. There were no rocks for her to back up against. No matter how fast she spun, she could not face all of them. Some would swim up behind her. She felt a strong sense of detachment as if she was an observer, not a player. Time seemed to hold its breath; everything moved in slow motion. Her vision became startlingly clear.

As their long rounded snouts cleaved through the water, she could see the funnel-shaped nostrils just in front of their mouths. She knew that water was rushing through the openings on the outside of the nostril flaps, carrying smells to the detection cells inside. She believed that she could see the water spilling out again from the inside openings, having carried her scent to the predators. Knowledge gleaned from Ashley that hungry sharks responded to smells in dilution of one part in ten billion only served to strengthen her terror.

Laura tried not to look into the rigid lenses of their eyes. Behind their cold, implacable stare was excellent eyesight. A reflecting layer of silvered platelets under the retina had caught all the available light and enabled them to see her while she was still peering uncertainly into the indigo screen surrounding her.

She kept as still as possible, not wanting to irritate or excite the grey reefs. She did not want to be mistaken for a fish in distress. The leader was now only a body length away. He swam with his mouth partially open as if suffering from a sinus affliction. His serrated upper teeth, sharp as the blade of a band-saw, extended the width of his jaw. Laura shuddered and stared transfixed at the rows of teeth folded into the gristle in the shark's lower jaw. There was no gap in the formidable array of ice-white teeth. Replacements rotated into place when necessary, keeping the predator fully armed. She forced mental images of severed limbs and bloody intestines oozing from gaping wounds from her mind and concentrated on the sharks.

The leader swam to within three feet of her and, silent as a sigh, vanished. Laura searched for it out of the corner of her eye. She was too scared to turn away from the others. She stared in horror at the mouths that were slowly opening and closing as they gulped in seawater to aerate their gills. Like hounds baying silently, they closed in on her.

She screamed soundlessly and kicked out violently in the water as the leader bumped against her. The rough placoid scales on its body rasped the skin on her hand and she instinctively crossed her arms over her chest. They taste you first, Ashley had teased. They rub those tooth-like denticles over your skin to see if you're worth eating.

Her frenzied kicking alarmed the sharks. With a thrust of their powerful tails they swirled, tangled as grey seaweed round her. She closed her eyes, waiting for the searing pain as their teeth tore through her wetsuit. Adrenalin surged through her. The hair stood erect on her arms. Her breathing became sharp and shallow. Seconds were a lifetime and her whole being screamed out for a man with yellow eyes. She did not see the sharks, obedient to some hidden signal, swing away into the ultramarine depths. Nor did she see the leader circle back and face her, arching his back as high as an angry cat's.

Ashley and Pierre swam on, peering into the gloom, starting at every dark shape. They were searching for a slim body in an electric-blue-and-black wetsuit.

Just as Ashley glanced at his watch he felt the first tug of the current. They were near Shark Bank. He breathed a short prayer. Let her be here. Let her be safe.

Ashely started as Pierre kicked his leg to attract his attention. He hesitated as Pierre turned away sharply and dived down, then he followed. Almost immediately he saw the shapes which had attracted Pierre's attention. Laura's blonde hair shone with a green hue in the aqueous light. The stripes on her diving suit marked her as clearly as peacock lines identify a parrot fish. Relief drained him, weakening his legs. His flippers flopped down loosely in the water and he breathed in deeply.

Then he recognized the hunched shape confronting her. An iron fist knotted and twisted his stomach and squeezed his lungs. He held his breath.

'Move, Laura!' he screamed silently. 'Get out of its way. It's about to attack.'

The grey reef shark zig-zagged in front of her, throwing its head from side to side. The pectoral fins were lowered to the stiff-legged stance of a threatening lioness. The shark's lifted snout displayed an armoury of teeth, each one sharp enough to shave a baby's head.

The sight of Pierre circling round the shark in order to reach Laura electrified Ashley into action. As he moved, the shark seemed to hump its back even higher and its swimming became more erratic.

Why isn't she moving away? Pierre thought as he powered his way through the water. She knows that it's madness to remain facing a threat display. As he neared Laura, the reason for her behaviour became clear: her eyes were tightly closed behind the mask. He quickly glanced across at the shark. The swimming pattern had become frenzied. Pierre lunged for Laura, grabbing her arm and pulling her to him.

Laura steeled herself as she felt her arm being wrenched to the side. Let it be quick, she thought. Don't let them tear me apart slowly. Then she realized that she was being towed through the water and there was no pain. Hesitantly she opened her eyes. Pierre! she shrieked dumbly. It's Pierre!

She wanted to stop and talk to him with hand signals, but his face was set and hard and he held her arm in a steel grip. He forced her to swim fast. She twisted her head, trying to find Ashley, and for the first time saw the shark. It was a few feet behind them, still in its threatening position. Fear gave her legs the strength of piston rods and she kept pace with Pierre easily.

As the two figures ascended, the grey reef shark resumed its normal swimming posture, satisfied with its victory. Ashley had remained near the shark, ready to confront it and, if necessary, divert its attention from Laura. He watched the angry creature relax and he swam slowly after Pierre and Laura. As he followed them up to the surface, he glanced behind him frequently, wary of a sneak attack. But the grey had disappeared.

Ashley checked his pressure guage. They had reached ambience. He looked up – Pierre and Laura had vanished. Damn, he swore. Why is Pierre surfacing so quickly? He knows that Laura will have extra air in her tank as she rises and the pressure decreases. He opened the valve of his reserve air supply and swam up after them.

Pierre watched Laura carefully as they rose. She was on reserve air supply and seemed to be breathing normally. He had pointed to her tank and mouthpiece as they started surfacing and she had formed a circle with her fingertips on top of her head, assuring him that she was fine.

Suddenly, like a cork popping from a bottle, she flew up ahead of him. For an instant he froze as he watched her disappear, then he sped after her. Flare, he pleaded silently. Your tank is empty and you have excess buoyancy. His black flippers thrust him through the water with the force and ease of a shark's tail. Flare out, Laura, it'll stop your runaway ascent, he pleaded as he struggled to reach her.

As if in reply to his mute appeal, Laura's spreadeagled body appeared above him. Bend back even further, he urged. He breathed out in relief. The brush with the sharks had not prevented her from acting quickly and correctly in a runaway situation. She was presenting the greatest resistance possible.

He swam up beside her and caught her shoulder. She turned her head towards him and slashed at her throat with her hand. She needed air. Pierre signalled acknowledgement. He breathed in deeply then dislodged his mouthpiece. Laura wedged it into her mouth and breathed in the oxygen eagerly.

Pierre held her hand tightly, controlling her ascent. As they rose to where the sun probed sparkling fingers into the water they shared the mouthpiece as contentedly as children sucking an iced lolly.

The two boats toasted beneath the grilling rays of the tropical sun. They lay like breadcrumbs on the vast blue tablecloth of the ocean. Ashley and Pierre worked in silence as they erected a shade canopy over the centre of the larger boat and stowed the scuba tanks in its shade. Laura busied herself opening the picnic lunch Cook had provided. She kept her head bowed, glancing up only occasionally to look at Ashley's expressionless face. She realized she had made him very angry. She blinked back her tears as she waited for the lecture which she knew must come.

The boat gave a sudden lurch as Ashley was about to sit down under the canopy; it threw him against one of the scuba tanks, and a bright red line opened across his shin. The blood welled up and trickled down his leg. Laura lifted her hand then let it drop.

Ashley stretched across her and took a paper napkin from the cold-box. He tore off a strip and stuck it on the cut. 'I was obviously mistaken about your diving readiness and capabilities,' he said as he dabbed at the cut, staining the paper red. 'You broke every safety rule. You endangered not only yourself but us as well by your irresponsible and reckless behaviour.'

Laura twirled the end of her plait round her finger and hung her head. She was unable to meet the disappointment in her father's eyes.

'Visibility was only twenty-five yards. We trusted you to stay with us.' Laura fixed her eyes on the blood, now congealing into deep maroon lumps on Ashley's leg. 'Searching the ocean for a diver who has panicked is as futile as looking for . . .' Ashley paused, gathering his thoughts, 'a contact lens in a cazier full of fish.'

Pierre busied himself stowing away the diving gear. He could feel Laura's misery and humiliation and he longed to comfort her.

'I'm—'

'Don't say you're sorry,' Ashley interjected. 'Sorry divers are usually dead divers.'

Two tears, as fat as rain drops heralding a tropical storm, plopped on to Laura's cheeks. She dashed them away with her pigtail.

Ashley was unmoved by tears. 'It's a hostile environment down there,' he continued. 'It may be breathtakingly beautiful

229

and exciting, but it's dangerous for those of us without gills.' Ashley looked at his beautiful daughter and longed to hold her in his arms and rock away her fears, as he had when she was a child. But the surge of adrenalin which had driven him through the murky depths searching for Laura had drained away. The relief of finding her had left him nauseous and angry.

The certainty that he would never see her again had sickened him. The thought that she would die of anoxia when her brain no longer had enough oxygen to retain consciousness terrified him. The knowledge that she had lost her normal buoyancy due to compression of her lungs during the dive, and that her body would sink as she died and she would be eaten by sharks, horrified him. He now lashed out at the child that he loved. 'So, Laura, I have no option but to—'

Sensing that Ashley was going to ban Laura from diving again, Pierre broke in. 'She'll never behave like that again, Ashley. She's been lucky to have had this dreadful experience so early in her diving career. Laura will now be a very safe and cautious diver. I know it.'

'Please,' said Laura, speaking for the first time. 'Please, Daddy.'

There was a long silence. Pierre held his breath and Laura crossed her fingers surreptitiously.

'We'll dive here again tomorrow,' Ashley said finally. 'I'll be watching you very carefully.'

He knew that she had been unnerved. The next dive would tell whether she had the courage to be a good diver.

'Thank you,' she whispered.

Ashley glanced at his daughter's slumped shoulders and miserable face, and relented. He dug into the packet of sand-wiches and found a bacon and egg one, which he handed to Laura. She smiled and accepted the peace offering.

As they ate their sandwiches and the wind dried their hair, Ashley spoke idly about sharks. Laura gasped when Ashley said that some modern sharks had a family history which could be followed back about one hundred and thirty million years to the Jurassic period. It was difficult to trace their history, since sharks' fossils were seldom found because their skeletons are made of cartilage; the only hard parts are the teeth and teethlike scales.

'Aunt Emma has two fossilized teeth in her secret—' Laura gulped. 'In her study,' she amended. 'She says they were used as charms against poison.'

'Your aunt believes every object in nature either attracts or repels evil,' answered Ashley.

'Yes, but the teeth she has are huge.'

'So were the extinct sharks. They were probably about forty feet long. The tooth enamel was about twice the height of that found in a present-day white death shark.'

Laura crossed her legs and settled back against the console. She loved listening to Ashley. She closed her eyes and mentally filed away the facts as Ashley spoke.

Sharks were not mindless, prehistoric eating machines. They could learn as fast as white rats and had been trained to respond to signals and to obey commands. They also had an extraordinary sensitivity to the electric field that encircles all animals. Definitely the most highly developed of any marine creature.

'So it's not surprising that divers seldom see the shark which attacks them,' Ashley concluded.

'They looked like hunters, Daddy. Like salivating wolves. Those huge mouths opening and closing . . .' Laura choked and kneaded her fingers in her lap.

Ashley covered her hands with his. 'Remember that picture whenever you're tempted to do something silly underwater. Remember that hunting pack of greys. Treat sharks with extreme caution. Always.'

Laura nodded and, wriggling one hand free from his grasp, she smoothed down the hair on his arm.

A sudden gust of wind flipped the plastic wrapping paper into the water. Pierre and Laura lunged for the plastic sheet before it sank.

Ashley laughed. 'Another strange thing about sharks,' he said as they dropped the sodden paper into the basket. 'Sharks should sink like that paper. Their bodies are heavier than water and they don't have an air-bladder to keep them buoyant.'

'They have flat pectoral fins,' said Laura triumphantly.

'And a tail fin in which the upper lobe is bigger than the lower one,' added Pierre. 'It gives them lift.'

'And?' teased Ashley.

Pierre and Laura looked at each other and shook their heads.

'An oil-filled liver. That's their air-bladder.' Ashley smiled and dusted away breadcrumbs caught in the hairs on his legs. 'Now let's clean up here, then you two can take the other boat to Silhouette.'

He handed Pierre a plaited palm-leaf basket.

'This is from Cook to thank the administrateur and his wife on Silhouette for putting up with the two of you for the night.'

'Thanks,' smiled Pierre, stowing the katayia away beneath one of the seats.

'Give Giles and Emma my best, and warn Giles to take his own drink to the moutia. That toddy is strong stuff.'

'The first time he drank calou he was sick for days,' Pierre remembered.

'Yes, but it *was* a two-day-old brew,' Laura defended him, 'and that would make anyone sick.'

'It didn't make Emma ill,' teased Pierre.

'She probably counteracted the effects with one of her potions,' said Ashley. 'Now, off you go and enjoy yourselves.'

'I wish you were coming, Daddy. Do you really have to spend the evening with that old grouse from London?'

'That "grouse" happens to be an eminent professor, Muffin, and I most certainly am going to have dinner with him.'

Laura threw her arms round Ashley's neck and rubbed her cheek against his, before stepping across into Pierre's boat. 'We won't be late tomorrow, Daddy. I promised to be up at Les Cannelles by ten o'clock.'

Pierre's face hardened. He had hoped that Laura had cancelled her appointment at the hospital. It doesn't matter, he thought as he untied the second boat, once she knows how I feel about her, she'll forget Les Cannelles.

'Tomorrow we dive,' said Ashley.

Laura's face dropped then she smiled quickly. 'Of course. Sorry, Daddy.' She would have to get a message to Bart. She

232

ached at the thought of not seeing him, but Ashley was still a stern father and was not to be disobeyed.

Pierre smiled and hummed under his breath as he readied the boat to take Laura to Silhouette.

Laura and Pierre sat in silence as the boat skittered across the wavelets. Laura trailed her hand over the side and watched the water explode into silver streaks as it met her fingers. Excuses to make Pierre return to Mahé raced like two-winged flying fish across her mind. She needed to talk to Bart. She wanted to hear his voice reassuring her that they would meet on the following Sunday. But when she looked up at Pierre and he grinned at her, she knew that she would attend moutia with him. He had propelled her away from the shark and almost certain death. She could not hurt him.

She answered his engaging, crooked smile then turned away to look at the sea. It stretched out ahead of her, as bare and empty as her weekend without Bart.

Pierre spun the wheel, narrowly avoiding a bobbing coconut. He hummed an old island sega tune as he basked in the warmth of her smile.

As they approached the island Pierre looked up at Mount Dauban, thrusting its granite head up over two thousand feet into the sky. It claimed the right to wear its wreath of cloud, now tinted peach and mauve by the sinking sun. Yes, he thought as he eased back on the throttle, it's certainly one of the most beautiful of all the islands. My corsair ancestors probably buried treasure and hid from the British fleet here. This is the perfect place to tell Laura that I love her. As he lowered the anchor and waited for the administrateur to come and ferry them across the shallows in a flat-bottomed boat, he was tense with anticipation.

There was a cathedral-like hush beneath the spreading takamaka and breadfruit trees at the jetty. The thick canopy cut out the dying rays of the sun. Laura lagged behind Pierre. She stood, studying the old colonial plantation house near the slipway.

'Come on, slow coach,' Pierre called as he strode towards the copra plant processing the pieces of shelled coconut. 'Cook

233

will receive a complaint about our manners if we're late for dinner.' He kicked out at a chicken pecking the ground close to his toes. 'We still have to shower and change for the moutia down on the beach.'

'I wish that the pillars in La Retraite had been built with capucin,' she replied. 'It's such a lovely wood.'

'You're lucky to live in a beautiful old house – there are so few left on the islands,' Pierre replied, sending a shower of fine beige sand over the persistent fowl. 'Now, do come on.'

The rich smell of drying copra hung on the hot air. Before he could stop her, Laura darted into the drying room of the corrugated-iron and wood shed.

'Laura!' he admonished her and ran after her.

She turned away from one of the wooden trays as she heard him come in and popped a piece of warm coconut into his mouth.

'This is my best thing ever,' she said, stuffing the warm pieces of copra into the pocket of her shorts.

Pierre's mouth was full and he was unable to reply. He followed her from the shed helplessly. As they climbed the wooden steps leading to his friend's house, Laura stopped suddenly. 'A new sign of the times,' she mumbled, her mouth stuffed with half-chewed coconut.

Pierre looked at the collection of old jars and tins lining the steps. Flowers and ferns tumbled over the chipped enamel and rusted iron in colourful disarray. 'What is?'

'This,' she said, nudging a box filled with bright yellow portulaca flowers.

'It makes an excellent flower box,' Pierre replied, looking at the empty AK ammunition box.

'Russian guns and ammunition in the islands. It's a disgrace. These islands have never needed an army and now—'

'Well, you know the motto on our coat of arms,' he whispered quickly. '*Finis coronat opus*.'

'The end justifies the means,' she translated. 'It all depends on whether you like the end or the means.'

'Sometimes seemingly harsh measures have to be taken for the good of the people.'

234

'Yes, like having a government which has not been elected by popular vote. The people weren't even given the opportunity to say whether they wanted a change. Overnight they were just presented with a new set of rules.'

'Laura,' Pierre sighed, wishing that the conversation had never started. 'The rules are for the good of the people. There are going to be better amenities. The copra workers and fishermen will now have a fair deal.'

'I've heard this a hundred times at your meetings. Explain to me where the money is coming from. Tourism is discouraged and businessmen are leaving the islands. Daddy's friends—'

Laura broke off as the blue floral curtain covering the doorway swung aside and their host appeared. Pierre introduced Laura and they gratefully accepted the fresh coconut milk he offered them. She smiled at Pierre over the top of her coconut. He lifted the corners of his mouth, but a small frown was stamped on his forehead.

He worried about Laura. Instead of acknowledging the good that the government was doing for the people, she insisted on equating it with all the single-party states on the African mainland, where corruption and inefficiency raced neck and neck to win the prize for disaster.

Laura tried to protest when she was given the administrateur's bedroom for the night. Like the tail-end of a tornado, she pushed through the curtain separating her room from Pierre's. 'Pierre, I can't take their bedroom. They're going to sleep on the verandah. It's not right.'

'Laura, Laura,' Pierre soothed, unzipping his tote bag. 'They'll be so hurt if you reject their offer. They consider it an honour to have you in their home.'

'All right,' she finally acquiesced, 'but we have to send them a gift when we return to Mahé.'

'We will, we will,' agreed Pierre. 'Now hurry up and change.'

Laura returned to the bedroom and studied the cross hanging on the wooden wall above her bed. She then examined the brightly coloured pictures of the Virgin Mary beside it and finally the family photographs, displayed on the polished dressing table.

'Laura,' Pierre called. 'Are you getting ready?'

Guiltily she put down the plastic photograph frame. She pulled a flowered skirt and a strapless red top from her bag and ran across to the shower room.

'About time,' said Pierre in mock indignation as Laura stepped out on to the verandah.

The full skirt swung in tiers from her slim waist and the red cotton-knit top clung tightly to her high breasts, leaving her bronzed shoulders bare. She had washed her hair and it cascaded like a golden waterfall down her back.

'You look lovely,' he said softly.

Laura smiled up at him impishly. 'So do you. Those new white pants and the blue striped shirt will drive the island girls crazy.' She jumped out of the way and ran to the steps as Pierre lunged at her. 'I'll have to watch you tonight, my big brother. They say strange things happen at moutias.'

'Don't let me hear any dirty talk from you,' teased Pierre. 'If I know you, the roles will be reversed. I'll be the one searching for you in the bushes as all the guys make complete fools of themselves.'

Laura laughed. She enjoyed Pierre's protectiveness. 'Let's eat and then go and dance the moutia,' she said. 'I'm dying to see Uncle Giles try the steps. He can't even sega.'

'No, but Emma can. She's as good as the islanders.'

'Better,' Laura corrected him.

A picture of Emma dancing the tantalizing, hip-swinging, yet faintly crippled sega step flashed before Pierre, and he had to agree with Laura. He nodded. She laughed and twirled away, swinging into the sega as she moved to the dining area. Watching her imitate the provocative movements, Pierre frowned, wondering whether he had been wise to bring Laura to a moutia. The church had tried to stop the sensual dance for years, decrying the gatherings as orgies. Well, it's too late now, he consoled himself. And anyway I'll be there to look after her.

Pierre's friend had gone on ahead, taking the musicians, Giles and Emma in the flat-bottomed dinghy.

Laura had wanted to walk to Anse Lascars, and she and Pierre hurried along the cliff path. Laura turned to look back at La Passe. The beach lay like a spill of mercury in the bright moonlight. 'It's so beautiful, Pierre. We're very lucky to live here.'

Pierre took her hand. 'You too are beautiful, Laura,' he said softly, 'and I'm lucky to live with you.'

Laura's eyes widened in surprise. Pierre fought to control the urge to take her in his arms and kiss her; as he stared into her clear blue irises, now shadowed indigo, he lost the battle. His lips settled on Laura's, lightly as a warm sea breeze.

She pulled away. 'Oh, Pierre, you silly thing. What movie did that come from?' She laughed, certain that Pierre was teasing her again. Pierre swallowed hard and stilled the quaver in his voice. '*Casablanca*, I think. Or was it *Gone with the Wind*?'

'You're so funny. I love being with you,' she said. She ran ahead of him then stopped. 'Come on. I'm sure I can hear the drums. We'll be late.'

'You're never too late for a moutia. It'll go on till daybreak,' Pierre answered, hurrying to catch up with her.

Emma rested her back against Giles's bent legs and sipped thoughtfully at a cup of toddy. 'Tastes like flat ginger beer with a squeeze of old lemon in it,' she said.

Giles surreptitiously dribbled his palm spirit into the sand and reached into his back pocket for his flask of whisky. 'That stuff ferments to eighty per cent alcohol. It's dynamite,' he said.

Emma's crinkled hair swung across her face as she turned to Giles. She carefully flicked at a few strands pasted to her lipstick. 'I love it. I wish we could tap palm trees for our Sabbats. The coven would love toddy.'

'You'd have the most raucous coven in Sussex,' laughed Giles. 'We'd attract every newspaper reporter and policeman in the district.'

Emma laughed throatily. 'But think of the loving we'd have.

237

It would please our great mother, Diana.' She looked up at the moon and her eyes were soft with love.

Giles cupped her full breasts as he leaned forward to kiss her throat. 'My lovely witch,' he breathed into her ear.

'Aunt Emma.' Laura's voice broke them apart. They watched as she stepped into the firelight and walked towards them.

Then Pierre called and she turned back to where he was talking to a musician. 'She looks so like Virginia,' said Giles.

Emma nodded. 'But even more beautiful.'

Giles watched Pierre take Laura's arm and pull her closer to where the musician was heating his tambour. As the ray skin warmed it tautened over the circular hibiscus frame. The musician tapped on the skin, listening to the tone.

'A decent young man,' said Giles, watching Pierre beat a few soulful notes on the tambourine.

'But not for Laura,' Emma interjected.

She watched as Laura turned her attention first to the tambour then to the tam-tam and tried to beat out a rhythm on the drums.

'Emma, you cannot expect Laura to remain virginal and untouched for ever. One day she'll fall in love and—'

'She's too young,' protested Emma. 'People in her star sign fall in love irrationally. She'll not use her intelligence in her choice of a man. It'll be a terrible mistake.'

'You were eighteen, almost nineteen, when I met you. Remember?'

'Yes, but—'

'No buts. Laura is young and lovely, and someone will attract her. Be prepared for it. She's no longer a child.'

'Well, it won't be Pierre,' said Emma firmly, as Laura and Pierre left the musician. 'He'll be blond. I know that she hasn't met a man with the yellow eyes of a cat, so she's safe.'

Laura and Pierre flopped down in the sand. 'Phew, that walk has made me thirsty. May I have a mouthful of your drink, Aunt Emma?' Before Emma could reply, Laura lifted the cup and drained half of it in a gulp.

238

Pierre thumped her on the back as she spluttered and gagged. 'Idiot,' he said, 'you sip toddy, you don't guzzle it.'

'Didn't know it was toddy,' said Laura, wiping at her eyes.

'Here, have some lime,' said Giles. 'We've brought two bottles.'

Gratefully Laura drank the juice then studied the setting for the moutia. 'But nothing is happening,' she complained. 'Everyone is just sitting talking—'

'And drinking,' Giles broke in.

'That old man has been singing to himself for ages,' said Emma, pointing to a skeletal figure leaning against a palm tree playing the zez, a traditional instrument fashioned from a calabash.

'He's good,' said Pierre, watching the player hold the instrument to his mouth as he plucked the strings on the carved piece of wood to which the resonating calabash was attached. The groups of islanders sitting near him rocked with laughter and slapped one another on the back.

'What's he singing?' Emma asked.

'Don't ask,' grinned Pierre. 'It's a particularly bawdy song about his neighbour's wife.'

'I wish I could speak Creole,' said Emma.

'They are going to make it the main language of the island, with French and English as second languages,' said Laura, looking at Pierre. 'It's a great way to make certain that English and French are not spoken correctly and that the islanders are unable to travel or work anywhere except where Creole is spoken.'

'Well,' Pierre retaliated, 'that's tough talking, even for you. Creole is the people's language and should be acknowledged as such.'

'Why aren't all three given equal status?'

'Come on, you young firebrand,' Giles soothed her. 'Creole is part of their culture, just as this moutia is. Let's enjoy a very special evening. If you two start one of your political arguments, we'll be kicked out and never invited to another gathering.'

Laura laughed. 'Sorry, Uncle Giles. You're right, I'm—'

'Here we go,' Pierre broke in as two islanders dressed in loose shirts and shorts moved leisurely into the firelight.

They faced each other in silence for a moment then one clapped his hands and broke into a long-drawn-out shriek. The musicians had warmed and tuned their drums. The beat was becoming insistent. The first singer shuffled his feet in the sand and recited the words to the tune in a monotone. His partner then repeated them in song.

'Everyone seems very listless,' murmured Giles.

As he spoke, the men sitting in the circle joined in the refrain. The drums grew louder. Their voices strengthened and their shuffling steps became a swaying dance.

Laura listened to the song carefully, but the words were African in origin.

'Do you understand what they are saying?' Emma asked, holding out her cup for a refill of palm wine.

Laura shook her head. 'The early slaves brought these songs with them from Africa,' she explained. 'They're tribal songs with a smattering of Arabic from Madagascar and a few French words.'

'Did they have moutias in the early days?'

'Yes. The plantation workers would sneak away to some remote place after the day's work and sing the songs of their homelands. That's probably why so many of the songs are sad.'

'And scurrilous. They made up songs and stories about their employers and people they held a grudge against,' Pierre added. 'They still compose songs and words as they dance. And they are often very funny.'

Suddenly the two men changed the song and the new words sounded like an entreaty. They stretched out their arms and approached the seated women.

'What are they doing now?' Emma whispered.

'The men, the cavaliers, are enticing the women to join them,' explained Pierre.

'Not having much success,' Giles grunted.

As the two singers stood swaying in front of the chosen women, the rest of the men scrambled to their feet and joined in. The women ignored the men at first, then, moving as slowly as an early-morning stretch, they unfolded their legs and pushed themselves up from the sand. They shuffled towards their partners, their faces devoid of animation in the flickering golden light.

The deep chanting of the men was now answered by the high voices of the women as they swayed into the circle. Holding their upper bodies as upright and controlled as ballroom dancers, they seemed to ignore their partners as they moved into a sensuous and provocative routine. Even though their bodies never touched and they seldom faced each other, their movements were charged with sexuality. It was a slow and alluring mating dance.

Emma wedged her cup deep into the sand and leaned forward to watch. Her tongue, pink and pointed, licked at her lips and her eyes glittered in the firelight. 'Flames and wine, music and dancing,' she whispered. 'A celebration of life by people who live close to the earth. They would love Wicca.' An isolated sandy beach in the Seychelles became a secret clearing on the Weald. The islanders were her fellow witches. 'Come,' she breathed, taking Giles by the hand.

'Emma,' he protested. 'Bonfires and dancing in the tropics are for—'

Her long nails dug into the palm of his hand. Taking a mouthful of whisky, he followed her into the firelight.

'Aunt Emma looks about sixteen,' said Laura, turning to Pierre.

The soft wash of light erased the lines on Emma's face and bleached her grey hairs into blonde highlights. She lifted her skirt above her knees, imitating the island women, and her legs seemed to be as slim and smooth as a young girl's.

'She acts like one,' Pierre answered, watching Emma rub herself against Giles yet barely touch him.

'You still don't like her, do you?'

'I don't trust her, Laura. I know you say that she's a good witch.' He paused as he remembered the look of hatred in Emma's eyes when Nicole had refused to try to persuade Ashley to let Laura live in England. 'But I feel she has powers which are evil. I'm afraid that while you are studying in England she'll

241

try to control you. Try to involve you in her "bonnefemme du bois" crafts.'

'Oh, Pierre,' said Laura, resting her head on his shoulder, 'Emma's not like that at all.'

'I've seen her look at you. A jealous, hungry look.'

'That's toddy talking. Let's dance. Aunt Emma's wine is making me sleepy and I refuse to miss the fun of my very first moutia.'

'Right. Up then,' said Pierre, twisting her long hair in a hank round his fist. 'Giddup, let's prance.'

'We haven't played at horses since we were children,' laughed Laura as she broke into a childish gallop and led him into the circle.

Pierre's breathing was heavy as he danced with Laura. She imitated the movements of the moutia easily; but there was a freshness and an innocence to her thrusting hips which made him catch his breath. He knew that he had to tell her of his love.

Emma was dancing with her back to Giles. The deep eerie beat of the drums throbbed through her body. She had thrown her head back and her wide eyes were fixed on the waning moon. As she danced she worshipped Diana, her goddess.

Giles moved to face her and whispered her name. She looked up at him and ran her fingers through his wet beard, wringing out the perspiration. His open shirt clung to his body like sea-fret to sand, and his skin glowed.

'We must honour the Great Mother,' she said.

Giles smiled down at his witch. 'There is no wapping thorn, but I am sure our goddess of light will accept a coconut palm.'

Emma twined her fingers through his and called to Pierre and Laura. Pierre was dancing with his back to Laura and Emma did not see the look of naked adoration on his face. 'We're walking back to the village. See you tomorrow before you leave.'

'It's almost tomorrow now,' shouted Laura. 'We'll take the boat back. Pierre says the musicians will stay till sunrise and then they'll all walk back. 'Bye.'

Emma waited until the bonfire faded behind them before

branching off into the coconut grove. The beat of the drums and the wailing chants pulsated in the dark shadows and her fingers trembled as she struggled out of her skirt and blouse and laid them over a mat of fallen palm fronds. She ran her hands over her body, anointing herself with the sweat trickling between her breasts. Then she turned to Giles.

He picked her up and laid her on the fronds. She heard the urgent scurrying of night creatures as the leaves crackled and settled beneath her weight.

She trickled her fingers over Giles's back. She traced the deep cleft of his buttocks with her finger, delighting in the oiled wetness of his skin. As he pressed down on her, she licked the salty skin round his small, hard nipples. The taste of perspiration and the soft sucking sounds of their wet bodies meeting and parting excited her and she cried out, raking his back in her need. Her eyes stung as beads of perspiration dripped from Giles. She shut her eyes tightly, exulting in the pain.

She was oblivious to the crabs, scratching the brittle fronds as they fled on raised legs, or to the ants, buzzing in agitation as their nest was flattened. She was conscious only of Giles: his body smothering her and his weight compressing her lungs. She held him tightly, gasping for breath. Only when the soft light fingers of dawn parted the horizon from the sea did she relax her hold.

'Pierre,' said Laura, watching Emma and Giles walk off into the night, 'if we're taking the boat back, could we look for a nesting turtle on the way?'

'You're ever the optimist,' he answered. 'Let's sit down for a while, I'm dying of thirst.'

'Could we?' Laura insisted as they sprawled on the sand and watched the islanders rock and sway tirelessly on a beach plated silver by moonbeams. A sudden wash of sheet lightning, blinding as a photographer's flashlight, spotlit Laura's face. Fatigue had smudged mauve rings beneath her eyes and her eyelids drooped.

'You've had a long, hard day,' he said gently. 'And we're

diving again tomorrow, I think we should go straight back and get some sleep.'

'Please, Pierre. I do so want to see one actually laying her eggs. Please.'

'Ashley says that, at the most, only ten females actually nest in these granitic islands. It's not like Aldabra, where thousands nest. Your chances of seeing one are dismal.'

Laura hung her head, and before her hair curtained her face Pierre caught a glimpse of a drooping mouth.

'All right,' he conceded, 'but we must leave now as the tide's turning; if there is one nesting, she'll leave on the outgoing tide.'

Laura jumped up, brushing the sand from her skirt. 'Thank you, Pierre,' she said and gave him a quick hug.

He kept his arm round her waist and together they walked down the beach and paddled through the luke-warm water to the boat.

The bow carved cleanly through the inky water and phosphorescence hung like fireflies in the white lace of the wake. Laura lifted her face gratefully to the breeze when the boat shifted the air as effortlessly as a punka fan.

Pierre shone his flashlight across the wet darkness, searching for hidden reefs and solitary rocks. Laura scanned the strips of white sand that gleamed like teeth beneath the dark moustache of casurinas and palm trees. With each flash of lightning she expected to see a dark shape lumbering slowly up the beach. Her eyes smarted as she stared at the rocks, willing them to move, to become turtles. Then she closed her eyes for a moment to rest them.

Suddenly Pierre cut the motor. She lurched forward, stubbing her toes on the spare petrol can as Pierre leaned across her to pick up an oar, motioning for her to be silent.

Laura hung over the edge of the boat, her heart pounding, trying to spot the turtle. She prayed for a streak of lightning to illuminate the beach, but the sky remained obstinately dark.

She knew that it would be no use pleading with Pierre to shine the flashlight on the beach. The turtle was very wary and would return to the safety of the sea with surprising speed if she was disturbed before she started digging out her nest in the sand.

Laura bit her lip in a fever of impatience as Pierre poled the boat to the beach. The sand grated on the steel bottom and she held her breath, but Pierre seemed unperturbed. He held out his hand and they eased themselves out of the boat and sat down on the dark beach.

'She's at the far end,' Pierre whispered. 'We won't disturb her here. We'll give her half an hour, then crawl up to her nest.'

Laura hugged her knees in glee and settled down to wait. They were sitting beside a 'broccoli' shrub and the moist air absorbed the heady, perfumed white flowers. Laura reached up, broke off a cluster and tucked it into her cotton top. 'Look where the Southern Cross has gone to,' she whispered, leaning towards Pierre. 'It was lying on top of the palm trees when we arrived at the moutia.'

'It hasn't gone anywhere,' Pierre corrected her. 'The Earth rotates and we see the cross from a different angle, that's all.'

'Why are you always correct?' teased Laura.

'It must be genes from my ancestors. They roamed the seas, and the stars were their guides,' he answered. 'Now see if you can find your stars, Pisces. Remember, they lie between Cetus and Pegasus.'

'Daddy says my sign has no bright or interesting stars,' Laura complained as she rested her head on Pierre's shoulder and gazed up at the heavens.

Time passed quickly as Laura and Pierre studied the japanned sky sequined with stars.

'Let's go,' said Pierre finally. He massaged his arm, which was numb from supporting Laura.

They moved silently through the sand, warm and soft as dough. As they walked they listened for a splash above the sighing of the incoming tide. It would herald the flight of the turtle. But all was silent on the perfumed beach.

A weak flicker of light from a distant thunderstorm showed them marks, as deep and uniform as tyre treads, rolling up the beach. Pierre paused with his foot raised over the tracks. 'It's her.'

Laura nodded. Together they crawled up the turtle's pathway, scarcely daring to breathe. 'I hope the electric storm doesn't die down. We'll see nothing if the lightning stops again.'

A shower of damp sand hit Laura in the face. She gasped and rubbed her eyes, then carefully lifted her head over the rim of the crater. The green turtle lay spreadeagled in the basin she had carved out of the sand with wide sweeps of her powerful front flippers. Her squared carapace filled Laura's vision and she quickly positioned herself directly behind the turtle to escape the stinging sand.

The female stopped her strong sweeping and tilted her huge body sideways. Laura tensed, ready to flatten herself into the sand should the turtle turn and see them. The reptile stretched her back flipper deep into the hole she was digging. The speckled flipper curled round the sand like a beggar's hand. As she lifted her body, the opposite flipper immediately scooped up and threw out the sand with one deft movement. Laura moved closer to Pierre, away from the flying sand.

The green turtle's sweeping movements became slower, as if the strength in her flippers was ebbing. She grunted and the pauses between scooping the sand out of the hole became longer. With a deep sigh she stopped digging and rested her head on the wet sand. Her rounded nose was buried in the side of the crater and loose sand trickled over her head.

'Oh, Pierre, she's so tired,' said Laura, her voice quivering with compassion.

Pierre nodded. 'It's tough going, having to scoop out this crater and then dig a hole deep enough for hundreds of eggs.'

'Ssh,' Laura cautioned him, 'she'll hear you.'

'Nothing will disturb her, once she's in her nest and ready to lay. It's like childbirth. Only death can stop her procreating.'

'Death,' echoed Laura. 'They used to catch laying turtles in the early days.'

'They were easy prey,' answered Pierre. 'One quick flip on to their backs and they were helpless.'

'Look,' whispered Laura urgently and pointed to the convulsing folds of white flesh above the turtle's back flippers. 'She's going to lay.'

246

The turtle positioned the white and wrinkled edges of her genital organ exactly over the hole. Her ovipositor opened and lowered. From its point two eggs, white and shiny as ping-pong balls, thudded on to the wet sand. Silver mucus dripped on to them. Laura was silent; only her eyes, wide and glistening in the moonlight, betrayed her excitement.

Pierre sensed something behind them in the dark. A robber crab sidled across the sand, intent on reaching the eggs as the turtle lay helpless in the iron grip of contractions.

Pierre bent down and picked up the crab carefully, avoiding its powerful front pincers. His outstretched hand was not large enough to cover its carapace and he held it tightly as it swung its claws.

'Ugly thing,' said Laura, turning her attention away from the turtle. 'It looks like a new scab.'

'It does look as if dried blood is streaked across it,' grinned Pierre, amused at Laura's description of the sweet-fleshed crustacean.

'Well, that's one who won't be eating fresh turtle eggs tonight,' she exulted as she watched it scuttle away backwards with its thick tail tucked well under.

Laura and Pierre turned back to crouch beside the hole as fast contractions squeezed the turtle. She sighed deeply and flopped her head on to the sand as a set of eggs dropped out of her after each spasm.

Eventually she lay still, exhausted and empty, stretched across the crater as if tied to the rack. She lifted a flipper and it flopped back, barely able to move the sand. Then, with an enormous effort, she lifted her head high. With a wild surge her back flippers beat at the sand like shovels, as she covered and hammered down the damp sand over her breeding spot, protecting her eggs from robbers.

The turtle's head was still lifted to the heavens as a flash of lightning froze her expression. 'That was beautiful to watch, but she's so tired and sad,' Laura whispered, longing to reach out and brush away the sand that was clotting in the female's eyes. Water ran down the turtle's cheeks and her pupils were clouded as if by cataracts of the aged.

'No, happy,' Pierre contradicted her. 'She's done her job. Her eggs will hatch—'

'And be eaten by crabs and birds as they try to reach the sea,' added Laura.

'Nature isn't kind. It's practical. The fastest and strongest will reach the water and survive. They in turn will breed good, strong turtles.'

Laura sat back on her heels to watch the weary female sweep wide circles inside the rim of the basin, concealing the position of the underground egg locker.

Pierre knelt behind Laura and rested his chin on her shoulder. 'Thank you, Pierre,' she whispered. 'I'll never forget this evening. Watching her nesting has been very special.'

'Laura,' his voice cracked and his pent-up feelings spilled over. He covered her mouth with his and, as he felt her lips soften in a tentative response, he lay back on the sand and pulled her down gently beside him.

Laura's emotions had turned full circle: the terror at Shark Bank had changed to an almost light-headed relief while dancing the hypnotic moutia and drinking toddy, followed swiftly by a feeling of reverence and awe at the turtle nest. She responded to Pierre's embrace with all the innocence of a child snuggling into its mother's arms. But as his kisses became deeper she breathed in short shallow gasps. She held his head tightly to hers as his hands ran lightly over her body, and the blood pounded in her ears. Bart, sang Laura silently, moulding her body to Pierre. In her desire and imagination she heard Bart's deep voice murmuring in her ear and it was the spice of his after-shave lotion which filled her nostrils.

She loves me, Pierre exulted, as he felt her body press against him and her mouth open to his kisses. Laura is mine, his heart sang. He rolled down the red cotton-knit top and cupped her firm breast in his hand. Her skin puckered and the whisper of a sea breeze caressed and cooled her nakedness.

'Laura, my Laura, you're so beautiful.'

Pierre's voice jarred Laura back to reality. She pulled away from his embrace as if touched by fire coral. Pierre! It's not

Bart. What have I done? She agonized silently as she struggled to sit up. She dragged her top up over her breasts.

'What's wrong?' said Pierre, his breathing hard and ragged. 'Laura, I love you.'

Laura froze. She wanted to hear those words – but not from Pierre. Pierre was her friend, her brother.

'No, Pierre,' she said. 'No, not you.'

Pierre dropped his hand as if Laura had hit him. He stared at her in silence. Who? he agonized. He raced through a list of their friends and discarded them all as possible suitors. The doctor . . . it had to be the doctor at Les Cannelles. He would find someone who worked in the hospital; they always gossiped. They would tell him if Redvers was after Laura. He fought back his feelings of outrage. Laura would not respond to the doctor. He had to convince himself that Redvers was too old for Laura.

'Laura, I'm so sorry,' he said gently. 'But I can't help loving you.'

'Oh, Pierre.' She threw her arms round his neck. 'You're my brother. You're my friend. I don't want that to change.' Her tears soaked into his thin shirt, cleansing away her tangled emotions.

'It won't change. I'll always be your friend, Laura.' He patted her back lightly. 'I promise you that.'

Laura hiccuped and tucked her hair behind her ears. They sat down together in silence with their shoulders touching.

'Laura,' whispered Pierre. 'Is there anyone else?' His only answer was the soughing of the surf and the grating of sand in the turtle nest. 'Please, I must know. Tell me, as your friend.'

Laura hung her head. When Pierre saw her stroke a hank of hair across her mouth and chew the splayed end, he knew she would lie.

'No. No, Pierre.'

His damp shirt clung to his body like a soggy ice-pack and his dark eyes were cold and dead as he watched the turtle clamber out of the basin and rush to greet the waves.

Soon the female would be encircled by males, all awaiting their turn to impregnate her. Then she would once again

249

undertake her lonely journey up some dark beach and bury her round white treasure beneath the warm sand.

'She's gone,' said Laura.

'Yes.'

CHAPTER SEVEN

The Seychelles, Christmas
1978

The flames licked eagerly at the brandy. The Seychellois cook scrunched up his toes in the hot sand and walked quickly to a large table set in the shade near the bar. A drunken cheer greeted his arrival and a space was cleared in the nest of empty beer bottles. He caught up the edges of his apron and scooped the beer bottles into it, eager to have his pudding admired.

'Wonderful, bloody wonderful,' slurred Bart, reaching out and digging his fingers into the steaming pudding. The cook blanched. He put down the knife and plates and returned to his kitchen. 'Traditional English pud on an island in the middle of nowhere.'

'Not nowhere, but a thousand miles from either India or Africa,' corrected one of his army officer friends, snapping the cap off a fresh bottle of beer.

'As I said,' Bart hiccuped, stuffing the hot fruit pudding into his mouth. 'Christmas Day on the bloody equator. Humidity at one hundred per cent and temperature probably ninety.'

'Six to eleven degrees south of the equator,' said the officer, throwing back his head and draining his beer.

'Who bloody cares? It's snowing back home.' Bart dug out another handful of pudding and stuffed it into the mouth of a heavily muscled man slumped in a chair beside him. 'That's a proper Christmas. Christmas in England. Log fires. Holly. Mistletoe. Roast turkey.'

The man shook his head as he swallowed the pudding.

251

Crumbs were caught in his chest hair and rested on the strip of red cotton which served as a swimming costume. 'Why are you not at home, then? Why are you here with us?' He tried to hold Bart's face in focus as he flicked the crumbs from his lap.

'Got a girl who won't have him,' a senior officer sitting opposite Bart jeered. 'He's lusting and can't leave.' His belly jogged on his lap as he roared with laughter at his own wit.

'She'll have me all right,' said Bart, caressing himself. 'Haven't found one yet who can resist this.' The island girl who shared the officer's knee with his hefty belly looked at Bart's hands. 'See what I mean. Gets them every time,' he said coarsely.

The officer stopped grinning and clamped his wet mouth over the girl's, proving that she was his property.

'My girl has her aunt and uncle here from Sussex,' continued Bart, idly picking raisins from the pudding. He remembered Laura's hurried phone call saying that they were taking Giles and Emma on a tour of the outer islands for a few weeks, and he frowned.

'What's wrong?' taunted the soldier in red. 'Aren't you good enough to join her family for Christmas?'

'Do you have nothing in that thick head of yours?' asked Bart, struggling to sit up straight. 'You never meet the family till you've had her. That way they can't stop you!'

The men bellowed and slapped their thighs. 'More beers,' shouted the hefty officer, snapping his fingers at the barman. He stood up, spilling the girl from his lap. 'Come, I've arranged something for us up at the house.' The men picked up their beers and lurched after him. 'You wait here for me,' he called to the girl over his shoulder.

'*Cochon*,' she hissed as she watched the men toil up the sandy path to the island house perched on the hilltop.

'Why do you go with him?' asked the barman curiously as he cleared the bottles, cigarette butts and dirty plates from the tables.

'Why do you and all these people sit here and laugh with them?' she retorted. Her sweeping arm embraced the lunch tables filled with islanders. 'Because they're army,' she whispered.

The barman flicked his towel at a pair of barred doves pecking eagerly at the crumbled Christmas pudding. He placed the unused dessert plates and the knife on his tray and shook his head. 'Come,' he said. 'Have a beer at the bar.'

The harsh tropical light filtered through the drawn curtains, bleaching the colours on the screen. The film was old and grainy and the soundtrack worn, but the men sprawled around on the seats watched avidly.

They shouted encouragement to the porn star as his white buttocks bobbed up and down on the screen. They cawed, their voices harsh as crows', when the girl thrashed beneath him, screaming, 'Enough, enough!'

'Again,' they demanded as the film ground to a close. 'Again.'

The fat officer lumbered to his feet and rewound the film. He swung a bottle of brandy off the table and buried the neck of the bottle in his mouth. Coughing and hawking, he handed it to Bart, who drank deeply then passed it around.

'In two weeks' time I have a few days' leave,' said Bart. The bodies writhed over each other on the screen and he watched their gyrations idly. He preferred participating to watching.

'I have the use of a house.' The officer's eyes never left the screen. 'It's isolated. We could take girls.' Suddenly he had their attention.

'The weekend would be good,' grunted his friend, adjusting his red costume.

'No, not the weekend,' said Bart. 'I have plans for the weekend. But during the week, it's easy to arrange an exercise or meeting on Praslin.'

'Done,' said his friend.

'No!' countermanded the most sober officer. 'Have you forgotten? We all have to be here on Mahé for the second week in January.'

253

'Why?' asked Bart. 'Are you having some party? If so, I haven't been sent an invitation.' He grinned and lay back on his elbow.

The officers looked at one another and glanced away before their eyes could meet. Tension like an electric storm pulsed through the room.

Bart's hunter's instincts were aroused. Excitement cleared away the stupor of alcohol, exposing the skill and cunning of a predator. 'It's all right if you guys don't want me at your party.' He grinned and waved the brandy bottle round his head. 'Thought we were brothers. Comrades in arms.' He lifted the bottle but plugged the neck with his tongue. 'So much for love and trust and dying for your friends.' He thumped the bottle on the floor and lay down, throwing his arm over his eyes.

He grinned inwardly as he studied their faces from under his arm. They are falling for it, he gloated. He tried to clear his head and marshal his thoughts. He sensed that the next few minutes would be very important.

'Brother,' wheezed the large officer. 'Sit up and listen.'

'If you repeat anything that you hear in this room you will die,' slurred his friend. 'One of us will find and kill you, no matter where you run.'

The hair prickled on the back of Bart's neck as he listened. These men held good positions in the army. They were trusted, but they had tasted power and it was a potent aphrodisiac.

As their plans to overthrow the government and install a military junta unfolded, Bart's initial excitement turned to rage. His army pals had to be stopped. If they went ahead they would jeopardize *his* plans. An army coup could not succeed – certainly not the way they had planned it. He paled at the thought of the repercussions.

There would be a head-hunt. Security would be tightened. New troops would be ferried in from the African mainland. Suspicion would burn through the islands with all the ferocity of a runaway fire. Every move would be suspect.

Top would have to postpone their planned counter-coup for months. He himself would be stuck on the islands for another year. The inactivity would drive him crazy. He yearned to return to Rhodesia.

The war will be over before I get back if these idiots go ahead with their ridiculous coup, he thought. Damn you. They need me over in Africa. The young whites are emigrating in droves. They need more black battalions and men like me to lead them.

'My friends, you are brave and I'm proud to be your brother,' said Bart as the senior officer explained their plans. 'I'm a soldier and your secret dies with me.' Tears gleamed in his friend's eyes as he lifted his beer and saluted Bart. 'I have heard nothing. I know nothing. I will be on Praslin.' He grinned and lifted the brandy bottle again. 'Once I am away, the presidential guard will of course relax. I drink to your certain success.'

The men cheered and slapped one another on the back as Bart tilted back his head. He cupped his hands round the bottle and no one noticed that the level remained the same.

'Another bottle,' mumbled the senior officer, trying to hold his trousers up over his belly. 'And send for the girl,' he demanded. He scrabbled in the cabinet for brandy. 'She's young and willing. I give her to you, my brothers.' He fiddled with the projector. 'I'm too drunk to use her. Maybe later.' A smile lifted his jowls as he settled back to watch the panting figures on the screen once more.

The girl walked into the smoke-filled room, wrapping her gaily coloured pareo tightly over her bikini. She tried to appear unconcerned, but her lower lip trembled as she saw what the men were watching.

'Come here,' said the senior officer. The girl walked across to him hesitantly. 'Take it off.'

Her fingers tightened on her pareo. He reached up, thrust his fingers into the cleft between her breasts and tore away the fabric. The top of her bikini fell away with the pareo and she tried to fold her arms over her body.

'No,' he roared. 'Show my friends. Let them see what I'm giving them.' The men roared their approval as he pinioned her slim arms behind her back. 'Who's first?'

A deep-throated roar answered him, and the men lurched to their feet.

'Comrades,' called Bart. 'Seniority counts in the army.' He grinned at them lewdly. 'I hold a special position so I'm first.' Ignoring their jeers and catcalls, he spun the girl into his arms and his hands closed over her breasts. 'Don't worry, my friends, I'll leave some for you,' he said.

He pushed aside a curtain concealing the doorway into the bedroom and stumbled as he dragged the girl behind him. She shrank away from him as he pulled the torn pareo out of her hands.

'Come here,' he said roughly.

He wound and tied the thin material round her body. He swung her into his arms and carried her over to the window. She clawed at his back as he thrust her through the opening.

'Stop it,' he snarled. 'What do you want? A quiet afternoon with me or a free-for-all with those guys?'

She stopped struggling. She looked up into eyes that were cream and yellow and as deadly as the stone fish.

'Go to the boat. I'll be with you in a few minutes.' As she dropped from the window he caught her wrist, swinging her body into the wooden wall with a dull thump. 'Don't try to be clever. Wait for me.'

The girl nodded and limped away, rubbing her wrist.

Bart gave her a few minutes then swaggered out of the bedroom.

'Too much for you Englishmen,' his friend mocked. 'Our island girls spit you out like hairy mango pips.'

The officers guffawed. Adjusting his red costume, Bart's friend staggered to his feet. 'Me next, and I won't be back in a few minutes,' he boasted.

Bart pushed him back into the chair. 'Change of plan,' he grinned. 'That chilli is too hot for you. I'm taking her home with me.' There was uproar and he held out his hands as if in benediction, waiting for it to subside. 'Her friend will be up here in ten minutes. She'll quieten you lot. You'll crawl out of here, believe me.'

Mollified by the promise of a substitute, the shouting died to a low rumble.

'Never trust the English,' his friend mumbled. 'Never did anything for us in the seventy years they ruled the islands.'

Bart did not rise to the jibe. He knew that most of the islanders still felt closer to France than they did to England.

'Perfidious Albion,' he taunted as he walked across the room. 'That's me and I'm off to commit a perfidious act.' He paused as he reached the door, drew himself up smartly and snapped into a salute. 'Men, soldiers. I salute you.'

Groggily the officers lurched upright and returned Bart's salute.

'Brothers, I honour you,' said Bart and he wheeled out of the house.

The heat hit him with all the force of a blast furnace and he reeled beneath the blows. He had left his dark glasses in the house and his pale eyes watered in the glare.

'Get another girl for . . .' Bart whispered the senior officer's name to the barman, 'and make it quick.' He picked up a handful of paper napkins from the bar and mopped his face as he walked down to the beach.

The barman watched him with narrowed eyes but was silent. He knew that the Englishman held a secret appointment. There were many rumours over radyo banmbo, but Bart's actual position was a mystery. The islanders had learnt not to pry into army matters. They knew that the Englishman was close to the president, and they asked no questions.

Bart wove his way down the beach. He fell into the boat and flung his arm drunkenly round the girl's shoulders. That should fool them, he thought as he looked back at the crowded tables. A drunk soldier taking a girl off for a siesta. Innocent enough. He hung on to the girl as they walked to his car, and he felt her fear as he fumbled with the key to start the engine.

He deliberately swung the car wildly round the corners as they climbed up to the tea plantations, high in the mist forest. The car swept from one side of the road to the other, barely missing the deep stormwater drains lining the sides. The girl's knuckles were white as she clung to the door handle and her eyes were wide and dark with fear. Bart drew into the parking lot opposite the plantation tearoom and pulled the girl to him. 'My lovely,' he drawled, 'we'll have a good time together.' He covered her mouth and sucked at her lips and his hands groped under her pareo.

He waited until he felt her tense up. He knew she was ready to open the door and run.

Suddenly he broke away from her and slumped over the steering-wheel. 'Drunk,' he burbled. 'Too drunk. Have to take you home.'

She caught his hand before he could turn the key in the ignition. 'No, wait,' she said. 'I have friends here. They can take me home.'

Bart shook his head. 'Not possible. I must take my friend's girl home. Mustn't make him cross.'

'Please,' the girl pleaded. 'I won't tell him. Please leave me here.'

Bart pretended to study her blearily. Finally he nodded. She fled across the road. From the safety of the teashop she watched the beige car slither down the road to Victoria.

Bart waited until the teashop was out of sight, then he straightened up and spun the car over to the correct side of the road. Glancing at his watch, he depressed the accelerator and concentrated on the twisting road. The soaring forest trees and sheets of white water tumbling down the granite rocks passed by unheeded.

'I must be at the Yacht Club before five,' he muttered. 'They only give me ten minutes' grace for my contact call.' He swore as he swung across to pass a scarlet Mini-Moke filled with tourists. 'Curse of the islands,' he grunted. 'Drive at ten miles an hour. Think everyone's on holiday like themselves.'

He shook his fist as he passed the Moke. The tourists greeted his ill-humour with waves and piercing whistles. They had an island girl with them. Her long legs were stretched out on the running-board and her black hair blew in the wind like a pirate ship's banner.

258

Bart fumed. It was because of a red Moke and a slim island girl that he had spent hours up at Les Cannelles.

He raced through the quiet streets of Victoria and pulled up at the wire fence outside the Yacht Club. A branch of bougainvillaea heavy with papery white flowers danced above his head as he stepped out of the car. He swept it away irritably and jumped when a two-inch thorn ripped deep into his palm. Sucking his hand, he threaded his way through the white chairs and tables crowding the open verandah. He pulled a handful of rupees from his pocket and waited to hear them fall into the coin-box before dialling.

'Yes.'

'It's beautiful weather today at the Yacht Club,' said Bart, emphasizing the words 'Yacht Club'. 'I think it'll remain fine until six this evening.'

'It will.'

Bart replaced the receiver and sat down on the cement parapet enclosing the verandah. He leaned his head back against the pillar and closed his eyes. The breeze from the sea was warm, but it felt cool as it eased through his shirt. His two contacts would be at the Yacht Club before six o'clock. He would have to have his facts ready to present.

He opened his eyes at the squeak of wooden boards on the gangway to the jetty. A group of yachties, tog bags slung over their shoulders, were laughing and joking as they made their way to a tender. The youngest girl, burned brown as a coconut husk, bent down to draw the dinghy closer to the jetty. Her frayed denim shorts stretched tight, exposing the plump cheeks of her buttocks; they were startlingly white against her dark tan. As she stood up, holding the painter tightly to her side, she swept her blonde hair away from her face, and Bart was instantly reminded of Laura.

He was surprised at how empty and lonely the last few weekends had been. He sat up straight and watched as the girl climbed into the dinghy with her friends, and he turned away only when she boarded the yacht. Laura was constantly in his thoughts and it made him uneasy. Women had been necessary

259

to him but never important. *She* was becoming important. It's a case of wanting what you can't have, he consoled himself as he closed his eyes. Get her to Praslin for the weekend, scratch the itch and you can stop mooning about. Pull yourself together, Faulconer, he commanded silently.

'Come an' join us,' the raucous rendering of a drinking song startled Bart; two figures, dressed in cotton shirts splashed with vivid red-and-yellow hibiscus, green-and-orange shorts and black baseball caps, staggered on to the verandah. As they came closer, he grinned. His two sober safari-suited contacts, Job and King, were almost unrecognizable. Waving bottles of Seybrew, they stumbled over chairs and tables and collapsed in each other's arms on the cement parapet.

The crew cleaning down a game-fishing boat on the slipway of the marine charter looked across at the Yacht Club and laughed. The two drunks were pestering the yellow-haired soldier. He was waving them away but they ignored his rebuffs.

'That will stop him chasing the girls,' said the one deckhand. The men watched for a few minutes then returned to work, losing interest in the tableau.

'You're drunk!' hissed Job, keeping his mouth open in a wide smile. They wrinkled their noses at the rich smell of brandy.

'No,' Bart denied.

'We're leaving. Phone us when you're sober.'

'I'm sober enough to know that you will listen to what I have to say. If you don't contact Top tonight, you'll be queueing for the dole in London before New Year.'

'Talk,' said King, looking at Bart's red-rimmed eyes suspiciously.

The two men continued to sing and slap each other on the back, but their faces paled as they listened. 'The new government will have to be alerted.'

'No,' said Bart.

Job bristled at being contradicted by a soldier. 'It's hardly your place to decide—'

'Listen to me and listen well, desk-jockey,' said Bart, glaring at him. 'You can't tell the government. Knowledge of a possible coup will make them tense and edgy. They'll be seeing spies under every bed. We don't want a nervous government when Top gives the go-ahead for the counter-coup. No, they can't be told.' He pretended to push away a proffered beer. 'Let me talk to my army officer friends. They trust me. I can say there's been a leak, the government have heard rumours of a military coup.'

Bart looked at the men's closed expressions and sighed. Why can civilians not think like soldiers? he thought.

'The officers will accept the story. The islands thrive on rumours. Every time a dove calls on Mahé, the other islands are convinced there has been a takeover.'

The men smiled but only with their mouths, and Bart gave up any further attempts at humour.

'If I can convince the officers to postpone their proposed military takeover for at least six months, we won't have to change our plans.' He studied Job and King carefully, hoping that they would agree.

'Don't think Top will go for it. Puts too much responsibility on this one's shoulders.' Job nodded at Bart.

'I agree. He's as reliable as an alcoholic in a liquor store.'

Bart fumed but kept silent as the two men discussed him. The time would come when they would wish they had never met Bart Faulconer; but he needed them now. They had to convince Top to do things his way. He had to leave the islands and get back to a proper war.

Finally the men turned to go, having ordered him to sober up and contact them at ten the following morning.

Bart's eyes paled and his lips were as white as cuttlefish while he watched the two stagger across the gravel drive to their car.

Like sea birds selecting roosts for the night, the harbour suddenly filled with sails and the low putter of engines as boats and yachts came in to berth.

Bart stood up. He was in no mood to be sociable.

The frayed tips of the latanier palm fronds fluttered in the wind like grey soiled banners. It was a sullen day. The clouds had closed ranks and now glowered down on the island of Praslin.

Laura ducked beneath the thatched shelter at the entrance to the primeval Vallée de Mai and snapped open the back of her camera. She clicked in a fresh spool of film and ran her fingers across the celluloid strips, checking that the perforated edges fitted over the sprockets. Satisfied, she closed the camera and read the digital diplay. She looked up at the sky, judging the light, and frowned. She turned the adjustment ring from automatic to manual.

Restlessly she walked to the entrance of the sun-shelter. She gazed across at the car park, scooped from the thickly forested hillside. Only two cars occupied the red gravel lot, the battered blue car she had borrowed from her friend and a jeep which had brought a tour guide and three Italian tourists to the valley: the cathedral of the islands.

'I hope that Bart flew over from Mahé last night,' she muttered as she fiddled impatiently with the strap of the camera.

On the way to the valley she had seen the clouds hanging like unwashed bed sheets over the sea. She knew that, once they were tucked into the waves, the flights from the mainland would stop.

A flash of brilliant lime green distracted her from her scrutiny of the empty road and the parking lot. She squeezed the cap off her camera lens and stalked the endemic Praslin gecko clinging to the trunk of a young coco-de-mer palm. As she adjusted the ring to bring his hard fixed stare into focus, he spun away and ran along the large, curved, brown male inflorescence of the tree.

'Got you,' she crowed as she snapped him, twisting back to look at her. His green coat was starred with golden pollen and his tail rested lightly on the small flowers.

As Laura quickly adjusted the speed and aperture a flurry of

262

black and grey appeared in her lens and the gecko vanished. She lowered the camera in time to see an Indian mynah swoop down and pick up the bright-green tail which the lizard had dropped.

'Go away,' she shouted and, bending down, she picked up a dried stick and hurled it at the bird. 'Stop terrifying the geckos.'

'I thought this was a nature reserve and that everything was protected,' said a deep voice behind her.

Laura spun around and Bart caught her in his arms. He kissed her lightly on her mouth, lingering slightly over the fullness of her bottom lip. He held her away from him and whistled. Laura blushed and, embarrassed at her inability to control her feelings, she hung her head.

Bart had forgotten how beautiful Laura was. She stood before him, bronzed to the golden brown of polished tortoise-shell. Her hair hung down her back in a thick ash plait and the blue-and-white-striped shorts uncovered legs long and lean as a dancer's.

'I didn't hear your car,' said Laura to cover her confusion.

'That's because I didn't bring one,' laughed Bart. 'A friend dropped me off at his home down the road and I walked here.'

Laura looked puzzled. 'But how are you going—'

'To get home,' supplied Bart. 'I was hoping that a young lady would take pity on me and give me a lift.'

Laura smiled. 'Of course I will, with pleasure.'

Bart congratulated himself silently. It had worked: plan one is in operation; she'll come to the house. And spend the rest of the weekend there, he promised himself as the wind glued her thin shirt to her body.

'I have tickets,' said Laura, suddenly conscious of, and strangely excited by, his scrutiny. 'Let's go.'

She led the way into the valley. 'It's not a very nice day for your first visit to the Vallée de Mai,' she gabbled. 'The wind is strong today. It's usually so quiet here. As a little girl I used to think that this is where the world went to sleep.'

Bart nodded. Anxious to entertain him, she kept on chattering. 'My aunt Emma says that this is what the earth was like millions of years ago.' Bart grinned and shrugged his shoulders.

263

'She may be right,' Laura said defensively. 'The granite rocks here are over six hundred million years old. Emma says that it was the birthplace of Pan and Diana, the goddess of the moon.'

'Is she one of the star-crazy people?' he asked, dragging his thoughts away from the forthcoming weekend and concentrating on what Laura was saying.

'Oh no,' laughed Laura. 'She's a . . . well, she's interested in folklore and things like that,' she ended lamely.

'Ah,' replied Bart.

'She says that when one stands in the heavy silence at the bottom of the valley, one can feel the power of the gods.'

'Do you feel it?' asked Bart.

'No, but it feels holy. Like being in church . . . an enormous, quiet church.'

Bart glanced up at the soaring trees. Their leaves and fronds interlaced into a canopy so thick that only needle points of light filtered through. 'Quiet,' he said quizzically.

The wind raced across the valley and the coco-de-mer palm fronds clashed together with the discordant clang of cymbals. The dry fronds, large enough to shelter a dozen people, clattered and slammed against one another like loose wooden shutters.

'This place has all the sound effects of a science fiction movie.'

'It's usually still. My mother said that one found the silence of the dead in this valley.' Seeing the look on Bart's face, she hastened to add, 'She loved the Vallée de Mai. This and Aldabra were her favourite places in the islands. It can be so hot here sometimes that you feel you're choking. You want to run away, screaming for air.'

'I know the feeling.'

As they walked into the valley, the wind sliced away the humidity and it was pleasantly cool.

Bart let Laura describe the endemic trees and plants. He had little interest in ecology but enjoyed listening to her talk. He ran his tongue round the wet inside of his lips, tasting the softness he knew would be Laura.

A light-pitched whistle broke into Laura's monologue. 'The black parrot,' she said, her voice rising in excitement. 'Can

264

you see it, Bart? I must get a photograph. One sees them so rarely.'

Bart was studying the treetops when a movement in a small berry-laden tree caught his attention. 'There,' he whispered.

The camera clicked just as the dull-brown-and-grey parrot squawked and flew away deep into the forest. 'Wonderful,' said Laura, flinging her arms round Bart's neck in excitement. 'I've never managed to photograph one. Thank you.' She walked across to a wooden bench and sat down. 'I'll be a moment. Just want to pack my camera away.'

As Bart sat beside her and took off his moccasin to knock out the sand, the tour guide panted up the slope. Her drooping tourists trailed away behind her like the tail of a tropical bird. One of the tourists sat on a stump beside the path and held her head in her hands.

'You have watched the coco-de-mer trees mate in the moonlight,' called the guide. The tourist looked pale and puzzled. 'It is said that if you feel ill in the valley, it is because you are cursed. You have seen what is forbidden: the mating of the trees.'

The tourist smiled weakly and joined the group. 'No, no. It is the humidity.'

The guide leaned up against a granite boulder and picked up a coco-de-mer nut which was lying on the rock.

'Now we are going to hear a lecture on the love nut,' mocked Bart.

'Gordon of Khartoum thought it was the forbidden fruit. He was convinced that this valley was the biblical Garden of Eden,' said Laura.

'Bit tough on Eve's teeth,' Bart quipped, replacing his shoe and leaning back on the bench. 'That husk's about four inches thick.'

Laura giggled. 'Gordon said that it was the fruit of desire because, outside, the coco-de-mer looks like a heart and inside the nut is shaped like a woman's thighs and stomach.'

And other interesting parts, Bart added silently. The double coconut with its feminine curves and wiry pubic hair was the subject of many coarse jokes and stories in the officers' mess.

The tour guide's voice carried clearly on the wind. Bart let his hand rest on Laura's shoulder as they listened. His fingers played idly with the blonde tendrils curling in her neck. She sat motionless, afraid to move in case he took his hand away. They listened to the tour guide impress the tourists with the story of the famous coco-de-mer nut. They nodded wisely as she told them that the tree had the longest leaves in the world and the largest seed. The tourists grinned and nudged each other when she pointed out that not only did the nut resemble the child-bearing parts of a woman but, before the meat of the coconut was ripe, there was a white jelly in the top which was good to eat when fresh. A few days after the nut has been picked the jelly turns bitter and it looks and smells like human semen.

'Didn't know that,' said Bart. 'Perhaps old Pasha Gordon was right. This valley may have been the Garden of Eden.'

Cries of exclamation broke out among the tourists when the guide explained that the meat of the coconut was ready to eat only in the ninth month. She held up her hand for silence. 'After that, it becomes a very hard kernel. The seed emerges from this kernel.' The guide stuck her finger through the coarse hair between the cleft of the double nut.

'Ah,' giggled one of the women, 'a pipi.'

The guide nodded. 'When it is about six inches long it looks just like a male "pipi" and the two halves of the nut are the testicles.'

Laura felt herself flushing and she stood up quickly. 'We've been lazy. Let's go on down to the stream,' she said. The deep-pink stain spread from her neck to her cheeks. 'They say the biggest trees are down there.'

'Let's find them,' he agreed.

'Today you are lucky,' the guide called out as they walked past, 'you have the valley to yourselves. We have seen no one else.'

'*Comme Adam et Eva,*' said a young Italian tourist.

Bart winked at them as he followed Laura, and they clapped and whistled until the two blond heads disappeared from sight.

266

'Cheerful crowd, those Italians,' said Bart. 'They really enjoy life.'

'They're my favourite tourists,' said Laura, relieved to move away from the subject of double coconuts. 'They're always laughing and singing.'

Bart had a good voice and as they walked down the winding path to the floor of the valley he sang snatches of popular Italian songs. Laura joined in the refrain, and arm in arm they arrived at the stream which cooled the feet of the trees.

Laura took off her sandals and dabbled her toes in the water. She watched Bart trample in and out of the undergrowth, as erratic as a foxhound casting for scent. Suddenly he vanished. She sat quietly watching the camarins and freshwater crabs moving through the crystal shallows.

'Laura.' Bart's voice echoed across the water, but she could not see him. 'Come and see what I've found.'

She wriggled her wet feet into her sandals and crunched her way through the dense foliage.

'Here,' he called.

She started. His voice was close by but he had vanished. 'Where?'

Bart appeared from behind a set of giant coco-de-mer fronds which swept the ground like the rustling taffeta skirts of a ballgown. He was dwarfed by the immense beige-and-yellow fronds.

Laura picked her way carefully over the piles of leaves. 'It's like being in a yacht on a stormy sea,' she said, looking up at the palms that soared sixty feet above them.

The top-heavy female trees, burdened under almost four hundred pounds of nuts, swayed as ponderously as pregnant women in the wind. Their pointed fronds crashed together with the staccato crack of gunfire and the nuts fell with the dull heavy thud of cannonballs.

Laura stared up at the reeling canopy and it seemed as if the ground was swaying beneath her. She edged closer to Bart. He parted the fronds and let her squeeze through. The leaves closed behind her, muting the noise. A pale light slid between the stems of the fronds swinging from the trunk; it glimmered over a freshly broken green frond which had been placed over the bed of dried leaves. They were hidden in a tent of foliage, deep in the heart of the mystical valley.

Laura held her breath, praying that Bart wouldn't hear the thumping of her heart. Her eyes were wide with uncertainty as he took her in his arms. She felt gauche and awkward. She was certain that he would sense her inexperience and lose interest in her. She so desperately wanted to be worldly and to impress him. She closed her eyes tightly as his tongue pried her lips open and she gasped for air as his arms tightened round her.

'Kiss me back,' he murmured.

Tentatively she obeyed. It was easier than she thought.

Holding Laura in a tight embrace, Bart swayed as his feet sank into the carpet of dried leaves. Still holding her in one arm, he struggled out of his shirt and threw it on the fresh frond. 'Let's sit down,' he said softly, 'before I topple over like one of those coco-de-mers.'

He gently eased her down on his spread shirt. Seeing the look of apprehension which trembled her lips as he knelt over her, he pulled away.

'You're very lovely, Laura.'

She smiled tremulously and bit the inside of her lip to stop it shaking. Stop it, she commanded; he'll think you're just a kid.

'You're the loveliest woman I've ever met.' He ran his fingers lightly over her lips, letting them trail down her neck and rest on her breast. Laura shivered, and he smiled as he felt her tremble. 'You have the full lips of a passionate woman.'

Laura looked up at Bart. His well-trimmed beard tickled her chin and in his pale-amber eyes she saw only love and tenderness. She held her breath. He was a wonderful man and she was so lucky that he found her attractive.

He ran his eyes down her body, checking the whereabouts of the buttons on her shirt and the zip on her shorts. As he lowered his mouth to hers he gently rubbed the palm of his hand over her nipples. She stiffened as he forced her mouth open. He felt her nipples begin to harden under the thin cotton.

Laura fought for breath as his nose pressed against hers. The world swirled in grey circles behind her closed lids and she

268

became light-headed. She panicked. She would have to push him away. He would then know that she wasn't used to being kissed.

He moved his mouth to the nape of her neck and she gratefully breathed in great lungfuls of air. She knew that she should remove his fingers from her nipples. But as he skilfully massaged her breasts his mouth ran over her face and lips and his breathing was warm and heavy in her ears. Her body denied her mind.

She had been irresistibly attracted to Bart from the first day they met at Les Cannelles. It was a captivation which overrode caution and common sense. She lay, as malleable as mud in the stream, and Bart shaped her to his needs.

Laura clung to him as slivers of wind sneaked between the chinks in the leafy curtain and caressed her naked body.

The primeval forest excited Bart. His senses were attuned to the forces of nature. His blood raced to the thunder of the crashing fronds.

She gasped as she felt Bart's weight on her. Clenching her teeth, she stared up at the deeply channelled leaves. She knew that she should do or say something. In the films the women always knew when to gasp or claw the man's back. She felt so stupid, so unworthy of him. 'I love you, Bart Harden,' she whispered as he took her innocence.

'And I love you,' said Bart automatically. He had learned the rules of the game early and well. Love was a four-letter word which stilled all the pangs of conscience in women. He used it without compunction.

Laura smiled and tightened her arms round him. Everything was all right; Bart loved her. She would now be able to persuade him to come to La Retraite to meet Ashley and Pierre. She was certain that, once Pierre knew Bart, he'd like him. That silliness on Silhouette had been forgotten. Pierre was once again her friend and brother. She knew that her family would welcome Bart. They would love him as much as she did. She would have to ask Bart about his family. She knew nothing about his background. They had never discussed their families or their private lives. Bart always said that their time together was too precious to spend talking about other people. But now that they loved each other that would all change.

Bart gave an explosive grunt, shuddered and his head dropped on to her shoulder. Laura was surprised; it was over: she was a woman. Tentatively she stroked his tightly rippled hair. She felt a sudden and overwhelming tenderness towards him. He was now hers. They were one.

Bart lifted his head away from her fingers. Why can't women relax? They're all the same. Make love to them and they treat you like a pet cat. Pats or baby-talk.

He wriggled his hand under Laura's firm buttocks and, holding her close to him, he rolled over, swinging her on top. Laura felt very naked and vulnerable, spreadeagled over him. As she tried to move, he tightened his grip and his hands guided her into new movements of love.

The hours passed. The sky had darkened. Lazily Laura lifted her arm. There was barely enough light to read the dial on her watch.

She gasped. 'It's late. I have to be back in time for dinner.'

Bart kissed her lightly on her ear. 'Have dinner with me. Spend the weekend with me. The house is isolated. No one will see us.'

Laura hesitated. Ashley was down at Aldabra. He couldn't contact her. Giles and Emma were spending the weekend on Silhouette. Emma had found a bonnefemme du bois and, on the pretext of consulting her, was gathering information on magic and the properties of plants. They would return to La Retraite only on Monday evening. Pierre was at home; he could phone her friends on Praslin. He usually checked to see that she was all right. Then she remembered that he was worried about the rumour that a single-party state was going to be gazetted within the next eight weeks. He would probably be too busy to phone.

'Please,' said Bart, kissing her on the neck, 'stay with me. I love you.'

Laura nodded. Pierre would almost certainly be attending a meeting on Mahé. He wouldn't even be thinking about her. 'I'll have to make an excuse to my friends and collect my clothes.'

'You won't need clothes,' said Bart. 'You're my coco-de-

270

mer.' He ran his hands over her body. 'You're too beautiful to be covered.'

Laura was thankful that the gloom disguised her flush.

His fingers caressed her buttocks. 'Here's your lovely coco bum and your long, lovely coco thighs.' His fingers slipped between her legs. 'And this is where the magic of the coco-de-mer hides.' As his fingers moved, Bart saw Laura's eyes soften and her mouth open. This could be a good weekend, he crowed inwardly. The virgin stage is almost over. The girl learns fast.

The ridges in the palm frond were pressing deep into Laura's back but she lay still, her head resting on Bart's arm. She wanted to remember this afternoon for ever. She wished that she could preserve their loving in amber so that it remained precious and unspoilt. She listened idly to the story Bart was telling her.

'I should be able to get more weekends off,' said Bart. 'My friends in the army are so grateful to me for warning them of the leak in their plans that I'll be given whatever I ask for.' Bart, basking in Laura's admiration, was boasting to impress her.

'But why didn't you warn the government and let *them* punish the officers?' asked Laura.

Bart paused; he would have to be careful. 'Because they are really good men. They're my brothers-in-arms. They would die for me.'

Laura pressed closer to him at the mention of war and death.

'I owe them loyalty. They're only misguided. Some are afraid that a single-party state means communism.'

Laura nodded, satisfied with his explanation. 'I understand,' she said. 'I don't want a dictatorship either. It scares me. Governments should be re-elected every four years. Then they remain answerable to the people.'

'Yes,' said Bart, delighted that his explanation had been so readily accepted. 'It was a difficult time for me.'

'It must have been dreadful and very dangerous,' said Laura. 'You were very clever to have stopped the coup and saved your friends.'

271

Bart glowed as his pride was massaged. 'It's a case of thinking quickly and remaining calm,' he explained. 'Just like that incident when they tried to run me in for murder.'

'*What?*' said Laura, her voice high with shock and indignation.

'Fools,' Bart boasted. 'I stood up in court and showed them what idiots they were.' He ran his fingernails lightly across Laura's stomach.

She stroked his hand. 'Tell me about it.'

'This stupid island woman parked her Moke right in the middle of the road and then climbed in without waiting to see if any cars were coming.'

Laura stiffened.

'I had to swerve out for a parked delivery van and almost collided with a bus.' He laughed. 'If I wasn't such a good driver I'd have been killed.'

Bart waited for Laura's exclamation of outrage at the mention of his possible death, but she was silent.

'I missed the bus. It was the woman's unlucky day.'

'No!' Laura screamed silently. No, it has to be some other accident. It was not my love. It wasn't Bart.

'That fool in court tried to prove that it was my fault, but it takes more than some island hick to catch Bartholomew Faulconer,' he gloated.

'Faulconer?' whispered Laura. 'Bartholomew?'

Bart bit his lip and damned his lack of caution. 'That's what I was christened,' he explained quickly. 'But I use my second name, Harden, in the army. My father is of the old school and doesn't like his family name being dragged into the dirt of war.'

His words smashed into her like the fronds of the wildly swinging trees overhead. They resounded in her skull as heavily as nuts thudding into the soft earth. Laura felt the forest closing in on her. A cold sweat broke out on her forehead and she wanted to vomit. Her body felt clammy and dirty. She swept up the pile of clothes beside her and reached for her sandals.

'Laura!' shouted Bart, alarmed.

She turned to face him as she scrambled to her feet. Her eyebrows, dark as the wings of avenging angels, drew down

272

over eyes that were dead and cold with shock. She opened her mouth to speak but was mute.

Bart grabbed at her leg, wanting to hold her, to calm her. She shuddered at his touch and kicked out blindly. Her foot swung forward with all the force of a superbly fit young body behind it. As it connected high between his legs, Bart doubled over, gagging.

Laura fought to find a way through the hard screen of dry fronds. Unable to tear the twenty-foot-wide leaves apart, she crawled under the tip of one on her hands and knees. She dragged on her shirt and shorts as she stumbled over the rocks and plunged, knee deep, into the dry undergrowth. She sobbed with relief as she reached the path. She was still holding a bundle under her arm; she recognized Bart's slacks and flung them away from her. Frantically she rubbed her hands down her shorts, trying to clean them, to scrub away any connection with Bart.

She raced up the narrow path, stubbing her toes on stones and stumbling over roots. Disgusted and tormented, she fled headlong into the twilight. She did not see the black parrots hopping from branch to branch in the bilimbi tree, pecking at the cucumber-shaped fruit. She was intent only on finding her car and leaving the Vallée de Mai.

'Damned girl's neurotic,' Bart muttered as he straightened up and began to search for his pants. 'Taking off like that just because I mentioned a little accident.' He slung Laura's camera round his neck and pulled on his brightly patterned shirt. Gingerly he eased himself into his underpants.

He searched the leaf litter as he walked and soon picked up a patch of white gleaming in the dusk. He slung the slacks over his shoulder and winced as he forced himself to break into a run: he had to catch up with Laura; he must calm her.

'Wonder if she knew that woman,' he mused. 'Could have been a friend. She certainly wasn't a Challoner.' He searched his memory for Nicole's name. 'Daumier,' he grunted. 'Not even an English name. I wonder what connection she had with the Challoners.'

His ears strained for the sound of footsteps and his eyes

pierced the gloom, searching for a figure in blue-and-white-striped shorts.

He made it a habit never to enquire about his lovers' families; it kept the relationship impersonal and made it easy to leave them. But now he wished that he knew more about Laura's background.

'Fool,' he chided himself, 'you've ruined this weekend.' As he attempted to shrug off the incident, a small voice he hadn't listened to in years told him that he had lost something which could have been very special. Laura's ashen face wouldn't fade away.

He was beginning to breathe heavily and there was still no sign of Laura. He cursed as his leg brushed against a latanier and the spines protecting the base broke off, piercing his skin with the fiery sting of army ants. As he bent down to rub his ankle, the roar of a car's engine and the crashing of gears told him that he was too late to stop her. He sprinted the last hundred or so yards to the car park, just in time to see the red tail-lights vanish round the corner. The acrid smell of burning rubber swirled in the wind. Bart shrugged, shook out his white slacks and stepped into them. 'Silly girl,' he said as he set off for his friend's house.

Laura parked beneath the huge mango tree in front of her friend's house. The wind had strengthened and ripe mangoes bounced on the car roof with a hollow boom.

Laura sat slumped over the wheel. She had betrayed the memory of her *belle-mère*. She had loved the man who had killed Nicole. Her guilt was too deep for tears; her eyes stayed dry as she relived the horror of Nicole's death and the shock of Bart's revelation.

She stared at the house in front of her. She was too scared to close her eyes. She knew that she would see Nicole's thickly lashed blue eyes smiling at her.

Ashley. She gulped as she remembered her father. Her fingers gripped the steering-wheel tightly until they ached. He had trusted her; she had betrayed his faith in her.

Pierre. She could never face Pierre. She had lied to him and rejected him.

She climbed quietly out of the car and walked round to the back of the house. She slipped indoors and entered the bathroom; the slatted door closed behind her. There was no bolt on the wooden frame so she drew the curtain across the doorway. She stared at the red and yellow daisies patterned on the blue cotton then turned to the basin.

It was a stranger's face reflected in the speckled mirror. She turned away from it and focused her attention on the plastic-covered table standing beside the basin. She moved aside the coiled dark-green mosquito ring. She shook the box of matches beside it then pushed it under the coil. She stirred the toothbrushes around in the mug and sorted through the jars of cream.

She failed to find what she was looking for and her movements became more uncontrolled: she knocked over bottles and jars in her haste.

She spun away from the table, pulled aside the shower curtain and stepped down into the large sunken shower basin. Lying beside a cake of coconut oil soap was a man's razor. She fiddled with the top then broke the plastic case in exasperation. Now the blade was free. She ran it across the soap and it opened a deep gash as the soap peeled away from the steel edge. Holding the blade with the edge of the towel, she carefully wiped it clean. Satisfied that the silver sheen was unblemished, she sat down on the floor with her feet in the shower basin.

She pressed her hand back, extending her fingers, and the blue veins in her wrist leapt into prominence.

Laura studied the delicate skin curiously. It was paler than the back of her hand, and the veins seemed much thinner. She pressed down on a blue vein which ran from the base of her thumb towards her elbow. She traced the end of the blade lightly along it until the vein disappeared.

With a small sigh she drew the blade sharply across her wrist; it stung, as if a hot coal had been pressed into her skin. She bit her lip to keep from crying out. She leaned her head against the wall and watched the blood tattoo patterns across her arm. The shapes fascinated her. There were fairy terns writing with sharks . . . crabs with disjointed legs turned into fat turtles. Her arm was a crimson fantasia.

'Laura,' her friend called as she walked into the guest bedroom, jangling a set of car keys in her hand. 'Where are you? I found your keys in the car.'

The slatted door opened. 'I'm busy,' Laura called.

'I'll bet. You've been away all day, then you sneak in without telling me you're back.' She swung back the curtain. 'Come on, friends share things. Where have you—' She froze and stared at Laura. 'Oh!' she screamed. 'Oh!'

Laura heard her screaming for her mother as she ran from the room. She bent down to pick up the razor blade from the floor of the shower, but it was slippery with blood and slid away from her.

Suddenly she was being swung up into a pair of strong arms and was carried into the bedroom. She dropped her head wearily on the pillow and closed her eyes.

She didn't want to die, but she didn't know how to live with her shame.

'It's not too deep. We can tape the edges together,' said a male voice. 'She'll be all right.'

Laura sighed and the first tears rolled from between her closed lids.

━━━━●|❀|❀|❀| III |❀|❀|❀|●━━━━

The wood-and-iron house crackled and groaned as the wind raced round it. Fine mosquito gauze covered the windows, and gusts forced their way between the mesh as if squeezed through a mincer. The eddies swirled round the bedroom, carrying the pungent smoke of a smouldering mosquito coil across to the bed.

Giles wrinkled his nose. He threw off the thin sheet and leaned over the bed, studying the glowing tip of the green ring.

'Thing should be ashes by now,' he grunted. 'We don't need

it tonight. Mosquitoes aren't supposed to fly in the wind.' He was restless and irritable. 'Wish Emma didn't insist on having a stinking ring lit every night. These mosquitoes don't even carry malaria.'

He glanced at Emma, who had just flopped over on to her side with her back to him. He eased out of bed and tiptoed across to the dressing table, pausing every time a floorboard creaked. Carefully he swung the portable fan around to face the mosquito coil. He held his breath as he started it whirling with a sharp click.

Emma grunted and burrowed into her pillow but did not wake up. She hated a fan blowing cold air across her while she slept; she was convinced that it caused colds and arthritis.

Guiltily Giles climbed back into bed and folded his arms behind his head. The fan was blowing the smoke away from them. Perhaps now he'd be able to sleep. He closed his eyes, and pictures of Lyewood flooded in. Mentally he walked the fields and counted the stock. It's time we went home, he decided. This island life is addictive. We don't have to wait for Laura. She can come over in time for the start of term at college. Happy with his decision, he turned to face Emma, resolving to tell her in the morning.

Emma groaned and flung herself on her back. Her arm hit him across the throat and he choked.

'Bad dreams, my little witch,' he said as he placed her arm gently on her stomach.

'No! No!' Emma screamed, hitting out at him wildly.

Giles jumped up and tried to pinion her flailing arms.

'Emma, quiet! You'll wake everyone up,' he warned as he held her to him.

'No. Let her go,' she screamed as she struggled to free herself.

'Emma, wake up. You're dreaming.' Giles shook her hard and Emma opened her eyes. She stopped screaming once she had focused on his familiar face, but shudders continued to ripple through her body.

She bent over as if bearing down in childbirth. 'It's too late, Giles. Too late. It's all my fault. I've been enjoying myself.'

277

'Ssh,' Giles soothed, wiping her springy hair away from her face. 'Ssh. It's all right.'

'No. No, it's not,' she sobbed. 'I didn't bother to scry. I didn't protect Laura.'

'Our little wrestler is fine. You saw her two days ago. I've never seen her look happier.'

'Happy,' wailed Emma. 'Of course she was happy. She was in love. She was in love and I didn't see it. It's too late. I saw him, the blond with eyes of a cat. Laura gave herself to him. Her blue-and-white shorts were lying on palm fronds.' Giles tightened his grip on Emma. 'The noise. Oh, the noise.' Emma shook her head as if to clear it of the clatter of palm fronds. 'Blood, there was blood and death in the background.'

Giles was alarmed. Emma would not straighten. Her body remain curled as if in contractions. She was mumbling as he bent his head to hear.

'Hecate. I need your blackness. Hec . . .'

Giles threw Emma from him and her head snapped back. Her slanted eyes were black with shock as she stared at him. 'You are a priestess,' he hissed. 'You practise Wicca, the old and true religion. Black witchcraft has no place in Wicca.' His strong face, honest and true as that of an Old Testament prophet, loomed over her. 'Those who deal in black magic are taken by the forces of darkness. They die.' He held her by the shoulders. His hands twisted her around to face him. 'Tell me, Emma. Tell me the truth. Have you ever called on the powers of darkness? Have you used Hecate's minions?'

Her lips quivered and her eyes filled with tears.

'Don't lie to me,' he warned.

'No, Giles,' Emma lied. 'I'm true to our religion.'

Giles held her for long moments then let his hands fall.

Emma rubbed her shoulders. 'I wasn't thinking,' she said in a small voice. 'I didn't know what I was saying, Giles. It's Laura. I love her so much and I know she's in danger.'

Emma was frantic to allay his doubts. She was certain that he would bar her from the coven and probably divorce her if he ever discovered her secret. Giles was committed to Wicca and took his embodiment as the great god Pan very seriously. He

278

expected perfection and no hint of impropriety from the woman who was the earthly representative of the goddess Diana.

Emma was in torment. She worshipped her goddess of the moon. When she recited the Charge and celebrated with the coven, she felt pure and puissant. She knew the mystery and the full beauty of the Old Religion. But she had tasted the forbidden drug of power. She knew the potency of black magic. She believed that she was strong enough to keep the two forces separate.

'Giles,' she whispered, 'I love you.'

Her words swept away any suspicions Giles might have had. 'My little witch,' he said, sliding back on the bed and pulling her down beside him. 'We'll see Laura tomorrow at La Retraite. If there was anything wrong, Pierre would have phoned us,' he added to reassure her.

Emma stiffened.

'Or Cook,' said Giles, remembering that Emma still resented Pierre's friendship with Laura. 'You've been jumpy ever since Laura bought those blue-and-white shorts. Subconsciously it's worried you and you've had a nightmare.' He ran his hands under her cotton top. 'Come here and let me chase away those demons.'

Emma gave herself to him, but she knew that the demons were real. Something had happened to Laura.

IV

Cook stood at the top of the granite steps with her hands on her hips. Her pink bathrobe barely closed over her stomach and her plastic curlers bobbed as she shook her head at Pierre. 'Where have you been?' she shouted in Creole. 'Why didn't you tell me where you were going?'

'Cook,' Pierre teased her, swinging his legs out of the Moke, 'I'm a big boy now. You don't have to wait up for me.' He loped up the steps. 'It's Laura you should be worrying about. Not me.'

'Laura,' said Cook, anxiety hardening her voice. 'Where were you when she needed you? I phoned everywhere. You were at none of those stupid meetings. You—'

'Laura?' Pierre shook Cook's arm to stop her tirade. 'What's wrong with Laura?'

'She tried to kill herself.'

Pierre drew in his breath sharply. He counted the hairs on Cook's chin, refusing to accept what he had heard.

'She cut her wrists.'

Pierre's head swung with pendulum strokes of denial. 'No! I put her on the plane to Praslin. I've never seen her so happy.'

'She looked like a bride on her wedding day when she left here.' Cook agreed. 'But if her friend had not found her in the shower, we would be arranging her funeral.'

'I must go to her,' said Pierre, trying to push past Cook, but she stepped back and blocked the doorway as firmly as a vacuum seal on a preserving jar.

'*Ecoute*,' she said, holding up her hand. 'Listen to the wind. It is not a night for small boats to be on the water.'

'Cook, I can be in Praslin in two hours. Laura needs me.'

'Laura is asleep. They have drugged her. There is nothing you can do.'

'I have to be there. Don't you understand?' Pierre tried to pull Cook away from the door, but she was immovable.

'There is no fuel. The garages are closed.'

'The tanks are full. I filled them yesterday.'

'That', said Cook, 'was yesterday. Tonight they are empty.'

'Oh, Cook,' Pierre said brokenly. 'What have you done? I must be with her.'

'It was a night like this when your parents drowned. Also on a boat between Praslin and Mahé. Have you forgotten, Pierre?' Her voice softened. 'You will be with Laura. There's a seat on the morning plane for you.' Cook scrutinized Pierre's face in the dim light. 'You poor boy,' she said and drew him into her arms. 'You love her.'

He rested his head on her shoulder.

'Laura is not for you, Pierre,' she said softly, stroking his hair. 'She'll marry some rich Englishman. Emma says that the

280

farm, Lyewood, will be Laura's one day. She'll be a wealthy woman.' Pierre stiffened and pulled away from Cook. 'Don't cry for the stars, Pierre, or you'll become crazy like a dog howling at the moon. You must "*marche marche*". Live with some good island girls. Then settle down.'

'I can't, Cook. I can't.'

Cook patted his shoulder with all the sympathy one gives to an animal which is about to be put down. 'Come into the kitchen. A pot of coffee will help.'

'Ashley?' said Pierre, following the billowing pink folds of terry-towelling into the house.

'There's a yacht near Aldabra. The boys up at the wireless station have promised to get a radio message to it in the morning. Ashley should know by tomorrow night.' Cook held up a finger to forestall Pierre's question. 'They know only that Laura has had an accident. They will tell him it's not serious and that she is well.'

'Good,' Pierre said. 'He'll be back within ten days. Hopefully we'll have this all sorted out by then.' He winced as the coffee scalded his mouth. 'Aldabra is a cursed island for this family.'

'Emma says it's blessed. She says that Virginia's air crash saved both her and the family all the trauma of a long-drawn-out death. She also says that it gave Ashley an interest and kept him sane after Nicole's death.'

Pierre grunted and stirred more sugar into his coffee. 'Why?' he whispered as he watched the grains dissolve in the teaspoon. 'Why would Laura do this?'

'She's done something and can't face the consequences,' said Cook, folding her arms across her belly. 'That child has been led into something dreadful.'

'Laura may be young, but she's sensible, Cook. She'd never do anything bad enough to make her want to commit suicide.'

'But she did,' said Cook triumphantly. 'Perhaps she didn't know what she was getting into until it was too late.'

Pierre stirred his coffee listlessly. 'Laura's always open and honest.'

'Love changes things.'

Pierre dropped the teaspoon and hot coffee splashed over his hand.

'There's a man behind this. I know it,' said Cook with finality. She leaned over the table and helped herself to a slice of coconut cake.

Pierre did not argue. Cook was an expert on liaisons. She was a great believer in the practice of '*vivre en ménage*'. She had three children and each had a father '*en passant*'. Marriage was not considered a necessary corollary to relationships on the islands. Listening to Cook, Pierre was certain that these casual affairs gave her and the Seychellois women the keen observation of clinical psychologists.

'A man.' Pierre fled from considering the words as if from a shark attack. He knew and loved Laura. There could be no other man.

Long hours passed as Pierre rejected the idea of a lover in Laura's life, and he and Cook sought for clues to explain Laura's suicide attempt.

The moon slipped into the sea and Pierre's head slumped on to his folded arms. Cook moved his coffee cup away and settled back into a chair. In repose Pierre looked like the young boy who had come to La Retraite with Nicole. Cook sighed heavily. Pierre and Laura would make a perfect couple. They had been inseparable since children and as young adults were close confidants.

She started unrolling the curlers in her hair; she winced as grey strands caught in the plastic prongs. 'Tomorrow I will send out a message,' she muttered, pulling out a purple curler festooned with her hair. Cook had implicit faith in radyo banmbo. 'If there is a man with Laura, someone will know of him. I want his name.' She tugged at the curlers angrily as if tearing at the man who, she was convinced, had hurt Laura.

Pierre stirred uneasily as Cook finally hoisted herself to her feet and threw open the shutters. The great hump of Silhouette was etched in dark pen-strokes against the soft buttercup of dawn.

She plugged in the kettle and dropped four rashers of bacon into the pan. She dunked two slices of bread deep into a plate

282

of beaten egg then walked across to the kitchen table and gently shook Pierre. 'Breakfast is almost ready. I've made a good English one for you today. You have time for a quick shower.'

The events of the night awakened with Pierre. He felt nauseous as he sat up and massaged his neck.

'Cook,' he said as he pushed his chair away from the table, 'thank you.'

'*Allez,*' she said, waving a wooden spoon at him. 'Go, go and bring Laura back.' Her face folded into its habitual scowl. She tightened the belt of her gown and turned back to the stove.

Pierre shrugged. Her usual ill-humour had returned.

V

Pierre watched the luggage trolley being trundled across the tarmac. The porters glanced anxiously up at the sky, dark with tumbling cumulus clouds, as they splashed quickly through the rainwater puddles. They reached the safety of the small domestic terminal just as the first drops splashed wet rosettes on the canvas tog bags and suitcases.

Pierre pushed past the passengers waiting for their luggage from the Praslin flight and swung Laura's fuchsia-pink bag over his shoulder. He shouldered his way past tourists sheltering in the narrow passageway and dropped the bag at Laura's feet.

She was leaning against a verandah pole, staring up at the craggy mountains towering over the airport. She held her bandaged wrist behind her back.

'Stay here. I'll fetch the Moke,' Pierre instructed her.

Laura nodded and watched him run across to the parking lot. The fine leaves of the flamboyant and acacia trees provided little protection from the rain as he battled to unzip the canvas sides. His trousers bandaged themselves wetly around his legs and his shoes squelched as he threw the Moke into a tight circle.

He stretched his mouth into a wide smile as he pulled up in front of Laura, but he was worried. She had been subdued and silent when he fetched her from Praslin. She hung her head like

283

a whipped dog and refused to look at him when he thanked her friends for looking after her.

On the flight back to Mahé she huddled into her cramped seat on the Islander, her eyes masked by dark sun-glasses. She twisted the end of her plait ceaselessly, and when Pierre put his hand over hers to stop her fiddling she flinched as if he had punched her.

A young tourist ran to help Laura into the Moke. He held up the dripping canvas-and-plastic side door and handed her the tog bag. Laura stared at him. Pierre was embarrassed and over-effusive in his thanks. The young man stepped back on to the verandah and out of the rain, looking puzzled.

As the Moke toiled up the Le Niol road, Pierre chatted lightly about the meeting he had attended. He explained how divided feelings were over the implementation of a single-party state. To excite her interest, he hinted that he was no longer happy with the concept of an all-powerful single party. But Laura kept her head turned away from him and stared through the rain-streaked plastic side window.

Pierre glanced up at the old pink-and-turquoise plantation home guarding the first sharp bend on Le Niol. As he looked back at the road, a lorry swaying under its load of bricks came careering round the corner. Pierre swung the Moke violently to the left and Laura grabbed for the side strut, cracking her head on the roll-bar.

'Are you all right?' Pierre shouted, spinning the wheel to keep the Moke on the road and out of the deep storm-water ditches.

Laura nodded and rubbed her forehead.

'Dammit, Laura,' Pierre shouted, adrenalin pumping through his body and putting a quaver into his voice, 'answer me. You're not dumb.'

Laura dropped her head into her hands and her shoulders shook with mute sobs.

'I'm sorry,' said Pierre, immediately contrite. He took one hand from the steering-wheel, held it over her shoulder then let it drop. 'I shouldn't have shouted at you.' He searched for a place to pull off the road, but there were few suitable parking spots.

He put his foot down on the accelerator. He needed to talk to Laura, to apologize. He swung to the right, where the Beau Vallon police station split the road in two, and roared down to the beach. He drew the Moke up beneath the dripping branches of their favourite takamaka tree and switched off the ignition.

Two diving boats bobbed at anchor off the beach. A handful of people were swimming and enjoying the warm rain, but the long sweep of sand leading to Whale Rock was deserted.

'Come,' said Pierre, unzipping the Moke's side-door. 'Let's walk.' Laura shook her head. 'You have a choice, Laura: either you come with me or I carry you.'

'I can't,' she said in a tiny voice as he made to swing his legs over the side. 'Don't you see, Pierre? I can't.'

Pierre turned her face away from the side window and removed her glasses. She glanced up at him quickly then dropped her eyes. Pierre felt helpless. All the sorrow of mankind was mirrored in her eyes.

'Laura,' he whispered. 'Talk to me, please.' Her fingers played an erratic tune on her bandaged wrist. 'Laura,' he tried again. 'You could never do anything bad enough to make me stop loving you.'

Her fingers were still.

Pierre had had no psychological training, but Nicole had taught him that things were always easier to face if you could talk about them. As a child he had the natural reticence and insecurity of those born under the Crab sign. Nicole had broken his moodiness and secretiveness by making it easy for him to talk. Now he was trying to do the same for the girl he loved. 'Trust me. I'm your friend. You know that I'd never do anything to hurt you.' His voice was warm and filled with tenderness. 'Tell me about it. Is it someone you met?'

Laura shuddered and studied her fingers. Nervously she frayed the edge of her bandage.

'Someone you trusted, and they've hurt you?'

Laura's pale face answered him. Cook was right, he thought.

Anger boiled up in him and burned away at his self-control, so that he had to fight to keep calm.

'And you loved him?'

Laura nodded slowly. Then she shook her head and her plait whipped across her face. 'No. Not now.'

Rain streamed down the windows.

Who could this man be? he agonized. Names of friends rolled like a checklist through his mind. He discarded them all. It has to be someone we don't see very often, he thought. He started running through the list of their acquaintances and stopped again when he reached Redvers. Redvers . . . the name sickened him. He had used his profession to gain first Laura's trust, then her love.

Pierre's breathing tightened, but he sat silent, terrified that if he spoke now he would upset Laura and she would stop talking.

'I'm so bad,' she said quietly, wiping her wet nose on the back of her hand. 'Daddy will hate me.'

'No, Laura, you're wrong. No one'll hate you.'

'You see. You see, Pierre,' she murmured. 'You don't understand.' The pain in her voice broke Pierre's self-control and he put his arms round her to comfort her. 'No!' she screamed, pushing him away violently. 'No!' She flailed at him with her fists, breaking out of the circle of his arms.

'Laura,' he cried, horrified by her reaction. 'Falling in love with someone isn't bad. It doesn't make you a bad person.'

She cradled her bandaged wrist and rocked over it in agony.

'You must tell me what has happened. Let me help.'

'You can't,' she shouted. 'It's Nicole! Nicole! Nicole!'

Pierre looked at her, aghast. Her mind had snapped. She had gone back to Nicole's death. Perhaps he should not have questioned her. Who could he turn to for help?

Dr Redvers had saved her sanity when Nicole died – but he was the cause of this relapse.

Emma, he thought. She may be able to help. Laura loves and trusts her. They'll be back from Silhouette soon. He switched on the ignition and reversed on to the road.

286

'Laura,' he said gently, as they drove away from Beau Vallon, 'remember that we all love you and will stand by you.'

He spoke to the silent figure at his side, comforting and reassuring her, but he wasn't certain whether she had heard or understood anything he said.

<hr>

VI

Emma, Giles and Pierre slumped into wicker chairs on the verandah at La Retraite. The tropical storm had ended and the garden sparkled as the sun mopped up all traces of the rain. Giles ran his fingers through his silver-grey hair and dragged it back from his forehead. 'If we can't use Redvers, it looks as if Laura will have to come back to St Francis.'

'What do you mean, "if"?' Pierre snapped. 'He's the one who caused her relapse.'

'I know, I know,' said Giles, 'but I still find it very hard to accept. He seemed to be a man of such high integrity.'

'It's not him,' said Emma, 'I know it.'

'Then who is it?' Pierre asked, barely concealing his scepticism.

Giles flashed a look of warning at Emma; he did not want Pierre to know of Emma's scrying and witchcraft.

Emma held up her hands. 'I don't know his name, but I know him.'

Pierre snorted, and Emma flushed. Giles was about to intervene but let it pass. He liked Pierre and realized that the young man was suffering.

The low throb of a motor alerted them.

'Ashley?' Emma said, sitting up.

'No, he won't be back until tomorrow or the day after,' said Pierre, getting up and leaning over the verandah railing. 'Why do these things always happen when Ashley is down at Aldabra?' He spun around to face Giles and Emma, tense as a snake about to strike. 'It's him,' he hissed.

287

'Hello, there,' Dr Redvers called as he ran lightly up the steps. 'I'm in luck today. The whole family is at home!'

'Except Ashley,' said Emma.

Redvers kept his attention on the steps and only looked up at the sombre trio when he stepped on to the verandah. 'Have I come to the wrong address?' he said, smiling at them.

'You could say that,' answered Pierre, clenching his fists.

'Pierre,' Giles snapped.

'Sit down, Doctor Redvers,' said Emma.

The doctor lowered himself into one of the deep cane chairs and felt for his pipe and tin of tobacco. Pierre studied Redvers closely as Emma and Giles told him of Laura's suicide attempt. He began to feel a little uncertain as Redvers tamped tobacco down into his pipe and sucked loudly to get it to draw. He could discern no guilt in him at all: the doctor's manner was brisk and professional.

Redvers questioned Giles and Emma closely, then, satisfied that they had no more to tell him, he turned to Pierre. 'Pierre,' he said. 'You brought Laura back from Praslin. I'd like you to tell me exactly what she said and did from the moment you saw her: her expressions, her gestures – they are all important.'

Pierre ignored him and remained slouched on the verandah railing, staring out to sea. Redvers sucked at his pipe thoughtfully, not breaking the silence, content to wait.

'Pierre,' said Emma, 'try to think of Laura. She needs all the help she can get. Silence won't—'

Redvers held up his hand to quieten Emma.

'Where were you?' Pierre said suddenly, turning to face Redvers. 'Where did you spend the weekend?'

Redvers struck a match and held it over the bowl of the pipe, inhaling deeply. Flicking out the match, he dropped it into the clam shell resting on the table.

Giles fidgeted, wanting to break the tension but afraid to intrude.

'I was invited to Bird Island,' Redvers replied finally, 'where I spent a most enjoyable weekend.' He stretched out his legs.

288

'It's remarkably quiet at this time of the year and peaceful. You don't share the island with a million breeding sooty terns,' he said, turning back to Giles.

Pierre and Giles exchanged glances.

'I'm sorry,' Pierre apologized, pulling back a chair. 'I've been rude.' He sat down facing the doctor.

Redvers merely nodded and waited for Pierre to answer his original question.

'So you see,' said Pierre, 'I think she is feeling betrayed. But . . .' he faltered. 'I don't understand why she screamed Nicole's name.'

Redvers tapped his pipe on the edge of the shell, and tobacco peppered the pearl interior. Replacing the empty pipe between his lips, he gestured towards the front door. 'I'd like to see Laura now,' he said.

Emma jumped up. 'I'll take you.'

The front door banged and Cook sailed on to the verandah. 'Will the doctor be staying for lunch?' she asked.

Giles and Emma looked at each other and shook their heads.

'Set a place for him,' said Pierre in Creole.

Cook nodded. 'Is Laura speaking to him?' Pierre shrugged. 'She must,' said Cook, 'or he'll take her back to that hospital in England. This house is too quiet with only you and me in it.' She flung open the front door, still talking to Pierre. 'The doctor likes Creole cooking. I'll make chilli sauce for the snapper.'

'Not now, Cook,' said Redvers, stepping through the open doorway. 'But if there's any over I'd love some tonight. I'll be back to see Laura after work.'

Cook nodded and walked into the house. She stopped, put her ear to the slatted door and listened.

'Did Laura speak to you?' asked Pierre. 'Do you know what happened?'

Redvers picked up his tobacco tin and put it in his shirt

289

pocket. Emma damned the reticence of the medical profession. They would never commit themselves. Please tell us, she pleaded silently.

Redvers looked at the three anguished faces. 'No,' he said as if reading Emma's thoughts. 'But she seems to feel that she has betrayed the family.' He walked towards the steps. 'I'll pick up some medication at Les Cannelles. See you later.'

'Doctor,' said Emma, running up and holding on to his arm. 'Is it as bad as last time?'

Giles and Pierre flanked him, waiting for his answer, and behind the door Cook held her breath.

'It's early and difficult to say,' he replied. 'But I think we can calm her and get her over this experience, without having to resort to hospitalization.'

Emma squeezed his arm. 'Thank you,' she said, 'thank you.'

'If only we knew exactly what happened, we could rationalize it and help Laura accept it,' Redvers said as he walked slowly down the steps. 'Stay with her. Don't leave her alone,' he warned.

'We won't,' they chorused. 'One of us will always be with her,' Emma promised.

Cook left her listening-post when she heard the car start up. Doctor Redvers was going to cure Laura. She would make the best chilli sauce in the islands for him.

She glared at the black telephone on the kitchen counter. 'Sonnez,' she commanded. 'Ring and give me the name of the man who has done this. The doctor needs the help of radyo banmbo.' She slammed the kitchen door behind her as she marched into the garden to collect the fiery red chillis for her sauce.

CHAPTER EIGHT

The Seychelles and Sussex
1979

 I

The avenue of sandragon trees towered up high into the clear tropical sky. Their rippled trunks flowed into the ground and the raised roots swirled across the sandy path. A lacy mantilla of leaves shaded a group of men hunched over a ring of large silver *boules*.

Bart moved silently along the path but the men, engrossed in their game, were unaware of his presence. They're good, he thought, looking at the two agents arguing the lie of the balls with his army friends.

Within a few weeks of his warning they had infiltrated the group of rebel officers. They were always ready to pay for a round of drinks or hire a boat to go fishing. They were now accepted as two good-natured bumbling Englishmen looking for property on the islands.

The tranquillity was shattered by an explosion of colourful expletives as the players picked up their *boules*.

'Gentlemen,' Bart shouted. 'Such language! Remember, it's only a game.'

They spun around to face him.

'A game,' spluttered the fat officer. '*Boule* is not a game. It's a . . . It's a . . .'

'Culture,' suggested Job, wiping the dusty metal ball on the seat of his shorts and handing it back to the officer.

'Exactly, culture. Tradition,' he said exultantly. 'French tradition.'

'French?' teased King. 'The Egyptians were playing *boule* five thousand years before the birth of Christ.'

'*Merde!*' the fat officer swore. 'You always have these long stories.'

'It's called education,' laughed King.

The group roared with laughter and walked back to take up their positions.

'Do you want to play, Bart?' one of the officers asked, holding out two silver balls.

'Not yet. I'll watch you experts for a while,' said Bart. He settled himself down on one of the tree roots and leaned back against the trunk.

'She was too much for you?' one of his friends shouted. 'You are getting too old for these girls.'

Bart grinned but it was a thin and mirthless grimace. He had been unable to find pleasure in any of the island girls recently. None of their bodies had been able to erase memories of Laura; he tasted her on their lips and saw her love and trust shadowed in their eyes. She had ruined his insatiable appetite for sex.

He had slipped her camera into Redvers' office, hoping that she would come to collect it. But the day he went to get his release from doing community service at Les Cannelles, it was still lying on the desk. He had phoned La Retraite several times and had replaced the receiver when Laura didn't answer. Everything he did seemed to remind him of her. Memories of Laura lay buried deep in his psyche and he ached to see her. His weakness angered and humiliated him.

'Tell me,' he shouted across at the men. 'Do any of you know a Challoner?'

'Why?'

'He's some Pommie we're investigating.'

'Challoner?' said the fat officer. 'He's the blue-eyed boy here. Helped to save Aldabra. You're wasting your time with him.' He curled his thick fingers round the *boule* and with a quick upward movement launched it towards the jack.

'But you wouldn't be wasting time with his daughter,' said another officer coarsely.

292

Bart stifled the desire to smash the man's nose and wipe it across his grinning face.

'You should know the family, Bart,' he continued. 'That woman you wiped out was going to marry Challoner.' The officer roared with delight as the ball hit the sand with a thud and rolled forward a few feet, to nestle beside the jack.

With the clarity of the blind granted sight, Bart suddenly understood everything. The revelation sickened him: Laura was lost to him.

'Phew,' Job wheezed, throwing his *boules* down on the sand, 'I'm taking a break. You guys are indefatigable.'

'Big words again,' grumbled the fat army official.

'Play,' shouted the group. 'It's your turn.'

The coco-de-mer printed across his tee-shirt expanded as he swung his arm back to pitch the ball. Bart fixed his eyes on the coconut and his ears filled with the crashing of gigantic palm fronds and he heard a young voice whisper, 'I love you.'

Job nudged Bart. 'Did you hear me?'

Bart forced himself to concentrate on Job. 'Yes,' he replied automatically.

The agent frowned; he was concerned. Bart's behaviour had changed over the last few weeks. He knew all about the arrogant, soulless killer, but this new Bart was withdrawn and moody. Behavioural changes were dangerous. But the date for the coup had been set. It was now too late to replace or terminate Bartholomew Harden Faulconer.

'On the twenty-sixth of March, the Seychelles will officially become a one-party state. The nineteen seventy-six constitution will be replaced.'

Bart looked at Job blankly. 'Why care what it becomes?' he said.

'The twenty-sixth of March is the date,' said Job. Bart gave no outward sign of the adrenalin rush through his body. 'Don't hit the jack. Stop beside it,' Job yelled.

'The boat with the arms?'

'It came in two days ago. The crew are pleading fish-poisoning and are keeping very quiet on board.'

'Name?'

'*Le Vengeur*. The Avenger. Your password for the boat is the number twenty-six.'

'Hardly original.'

'No, but easy to remember.' Job turned away from Bart and cupped his hands over his mouth. 'Up the English,' he shouted. 'Show these Frenchmen how to play *boule*.' He turned back to Bart. 'Remember,' he said, 'keep away from the Yacht Club. Don't be seen near *Le Vengeur*. That place is out of bounds.' He glared at Bart. 'Top's orders.'

'Our soldiers,' said Bart, ignoring the implied threat.

'They're already here. They've been filtering in with the tourists over the last few weeks. The top men have also arrived. They're posing as a religious group.' Bart raised his eyebrows. 'They're having an open-air Bible meeting on Anse aux Pins on the twenty-fourth. It'll go on most of the night with a beach barbecue and hymns. No drinking. The sect is teetotal.'

Bart nodded.

'Your car will break down on the road near Anse aux Pins. You'll go to them for help and they'll invite you to join them. And try to be sober.'

Job shuddered slightly as Bart's eyes, yellow and implacable, rested on him. He would recommend his termination, once the coup was over. The man was unstable and dangerous.

'There has been no change in the plans. The men are all well drilled and will be in their positions by six a.m.'

'That should give us the island by about ten-thirty,' said Bart. 'At last we'll have some action in this dump.'

'Remember, as little killing as possible. Top plans a blood-less coup.' Like hell, thought Bart. 'People do not like govern-ments which sweep into power on a river of blood.'

'I'm a soldier,' said Bart, 'not a politician. I'll do what has to be done.'

'Remember when you go into action that you will have to face Top when it's all over.'

'Don't worry,' said Bart, standing up and dusting off his pants. 'The island will be ours on the twenty-sixth,' he boasted quietly to Job. 'Let me show you marble players how to play a man's game,' he shouted.

Job picked up his metal *boules* and followed Bart. He was worried. Bart's role in the coup was vital. He had to send the presidential security guard into an ambush and he had to secure the president.

The agent shook himself as he rejoined the players. He wished he could throw off the sense of impending disaster which enveloped him every time he spoke to Bart. Mustn't allow my personal dislike of the chap to cloud my judgement, he thought.

'Come on, Bart,' he called. 'Let's show them how Drake played bowls.'

'Drake?' the fat officer queried.

'One of our great sea-captains,' explained Job. 'He finished playing his game of bowls then cleaned up the Spanish fleet.'

'He set a damn fine example,' said Bart, 'which we're about to follow.'

King glared at him, and Bart grinned. He crouched and swung back his arm. The ball flew high and true and landed in a small puff of dust a few inches from the jack. He turned to King. 'Perfect,' he gloated. 'Victory to the Brits.'

The two agents went on playing *boule* with the army officers and Bart until the sun was directly overhead. Then, pleading an appointment to view some beach-front properties, they ambled away, arguing amiably about the sandragon trees.

'Blood of the dragon,' Job said, looking up at the soaring trees. 'Probably refers to the colour of the wood.'

'No. The colour of the sap,' King answered. 'Looks like blood when the tree is cut.'

The officers grinned as the agents' voices faded. 'I was hoping they'd join us for lunch,' said Bart's friend.

'You mean, you were hoping they'd pay for lunch,' quipped Bart.

'It helps,' the other answered, levering the cap off a bottle of beer. 'Army pay isn't that good.'

'It'll be better,' said the fat officer, stretching out his hand for a bottle. 'Just wait until we take over.'

Bart leaned up against one of the trees. The beers and the midday heat had a soporific effect on him. He felt a deep sympathy for the officers; these were men he understood. They knew the adrenalin flush of the chase and the thrill of the kill. They were his brothers-in-arms. They were his family.

'What if an "outside" coup took place?' he asked.

The suggestion was greeted with a roar of outrage. 'What do you know? What have you heard?' snapped his friend as the shouting abated.

'It was just a thought,' said Bart. 'But if a body committed to a multi-party system and sympathetic to us staged a take-over, we'd benefit and the islanders would see us as innocent.'

'To hell with what the islanders think,' snapped the fat officer, wedging his empty beer bottle between the roots of the tree. 'This is our island. We'll run it. We don't need any outside force.'

Most of the officers nodded.

'I'm a soldier,' said Bart's friend, 'not a paper-pusher. Desks bore me. They are for wimps and weaklings. I wouldn't complain too much if someone else did the desk work, as long as my pay-cheque increased.'

'You've got it,' said Bart. 'They do the dirty work. If they succeed, you benefit. If not, you keep your position and you still have "clean" hands.'

The men looked thoughtful.

'What would *you* do?' the fat officer queried, looking at Bart sharply.

'I flow with the tide,' laughed Bart. 'I'm a soldier. I fight for whoever signs my pay-cheque. But,' he added, 'if I was a Seychellois like you guys, I'd sit on the sideline and then side with the winner. I certainly wouldn't get myself killed for a regime I wanted to replace.'

The fat officer grunted and tossed the heavy metal *boule* from one hand to the other.

'I wouldn't get involved with all the boring details of running a country,' Bart continued, pleased with the effect his words were having. 'You sit in an office all day and half the night.' He winked at them lewdly. 'You know what you'd have to give up.' He smiled as they whistled and cat-called. 'If you're in government, you can never please everyone. There's always someone bitching at you.' He shook his head and took a long swallow of beer. 'No, thanks. I'm a plain soldier and the life suits me.'

A large number of the officers were nodding.

'Come, brothers,' said Bart, standing up. 'Let's have another game. The loser pays for lunch at the Yacht Club.'

II

Three surfboards were drawn up high on the tiny beach flanking the granite jetty on Round Island. The wind crept under the sails and they flopped on the sand, bright as butterflies' wings. The heavily wooded island, set in the middle of the St Anne Marine Reserve, used to be a leper colony but was now a popular venue for lunches. There were usually surfboards lying on the strip of sand, since it took less than half an hour for the island boys to sail across from the yacht harbour on Mahé.

Pierre and his two friends paid their lunch bill at the bar set up in what had originally been a prison cell. They paused outside the small arched building. Pierre looked up into the spreading branches of the flamboyant; it had lost its spectacular canopy of crimson flowers and the oblong leaflets danced in the breeze. 'Let's hope the wind picks up,' he said, watching the leaves, 'or it'll take forever to sail our boards back to Mahé.'

He had promised Ashley and Dr Redvers that he would be back before five o'clock. They were going to tempt Laura to go fishing with them. Dr Redvers still visited her every day. The medication had not cured her but it seemed to have stopped her depression becoming worse.

Pierre was scared that he had lost the Laura he knew and loved. He did not know how to handle the pale withdrawn girl who had replaced her. The last time he had lunched on this old leper island, Laura had been with him. She wove sprigs of crimson flamboyant flowers into her hair and skipped across the thick carpet of blossoms under the flame tree, pretending

297

she was royalty. Looking up at the thin shade canopy, Pierre could hear her laughter and feel the warmth of her smile – but, like the flowers, that girl was gone.

Pierre turned to his friends. 'Last one to have his board in the water pays for the beers when we reach the Yacht Club.'

The three men bounded down the steep steps leading to the beach. The light wind carried their laughter up to the diners lingering over their coffee in the thatched open-air building which used to be the chapel on the island.

The young men skirted Round Island, then clipped their harnesses to the booms as they prepared to leave the sheltered waters of the Marine Reserve and cross the deepwater Cerf Passage separating the harbour at Mahé from the islands in the Reserve.

Pierre leaned back to counteract the tug of the sail and listened to the water whisper beneath his board. He stared down into the turquoise depths as he skimmed over the coral heads. The exotic reef fish burned brightly in the translucent waters as they skittered away from the predator gliding above them.

The board sailors sped away from the protection of the islands and the deep water turned an inky blue. Pierre raised the daggerboard and sheeted out the red-and-yellow sail. The board quickly picked up speed on the broad reach and he raced past his friend who was gybing to avoid a floating palm trunk. 'See you at the club,' he teased. 'And watch out for flying fish!' The young man raised a thumb in reply. A board sailor had been hospitalized two weeks earlier when a flying fish smashed into his back, and the young men were now wary of the winged creatures.

Pierre sailed on with a smile. As his board cut through the waves he felt the power of the ocean beneath his feet and the force of the wind in his face. He was at one with the elements and for a short while Laura was washed from his mind.

Pierre glanced at his watch as he sailed into the inner harbour. 'Still time for a beer,' he grinned, 'and I won't be paying.'

He glanced back over his shoulder, looking for his friends.

A pair of iridescent purple-and-green sails were just entering the calm waters of the harbour. Pierre kicked down the dagger-board and sheeted in the sail as he manoeuvred round the tiny island of Houdol. As he drifted into shallow water at the slipway of the Yacht Club, a burst of laughter from the verandah attracted his attention.

The light died in his eyes. They were dead and dark when he looked up at the man with tightly waved blond hair. He recognized two of the officers sitting with Bartholomew Faulconer. They were part of a group that was rumoured in some circles to be renegade; furtive whispers suggested that they were running drugs through the island for distribution in Africa.

Pierre automatically stripped down the sailboard. His thoughts were centred on Bart. He had seen Faulconer only once since the court case, and he found that his anger and dislike of the man had not abated.

Tucking the board under his arm, he picked up the furled sail and boom and ran lightly to the Moke. He screwed the luggage holders on to the roll bars and tightened the straps round the board and mast. Satisfied that the board was secure, he walked back to where his friends were dragging their boards out of the water. 'See you in the club,' he called. 'I'm dying of thirst.'

'We'll have a Seybrew,' they called. 'Remember: winner pays.'

Pierre shook his head. Settling his dark glasses firmly on his nose, he walked round the building to the verandah. One of the officers glanced up at him blankly then turned his attention back to Bart.

Pierre chose a table close to the officers and sat down with his back to them. He wanted to hear their conversation but did not want to have to look at Nicole's murderer.

'You're getting old, Bart,' mocked the fat officer. 'They tell me that the cook on *Le Vengeur* will melt your teeth.'

'She's British and blonde,' added his friend. His hands traced curves in the air as he tried to cajole Bart into boarding the yacht.

'And sick,' said Bart. 'They're all down with food poisoning.'

'That was three days ago. They are probably ready for a little company,' said the fat officer. 'You owe us one, Bart. We took you on the French catamaran. Remember the captain's wife?'

Bart groaned. He had been drinking heavily, secretly celebrating the date set for the coup.

Pierre was disappointed. The men were drunk and talking nonsense.

'If you don't come with us and persuade the Brits to invite us on board, then we'll go on our own,' the officer threatened. 'They're sure to have some sweet grass.'

'What!' said Bart's friend. 'A motorized yacht that size! They'll have snow and the big H. There's money in that boat. They won't waste their time with cheap drugs.'

'Then let's go,' said the fat officer, bouncing back his chair.

'No, wait,' Bart slurred, 'one more drink.'

'On *Le Vengeur*,' the officers insisted as they scraped back their chairs.

Bart drained his glass and licked his lips. He combed his short beard with his fingers and tried to marshal his thoughts. Alcohol had fuddled his thinking and he could find no solution to the problem. 'Wait,' he called as the officers stepped over the cement balustrade on to the jetty. 'I'll be with you in a few minutes.' He lurched towards the toilet. He needed to soak his head in a basin of cold water before warning Job and King.

Pierre watched Bart leave the group, and he followed him. Bart was bending over the basin, holding his breath, and his yellow hair rippled under the water. Pierre felt an almost overwhelming desire to press his hands against the back of Bart's neck and force his head down in the basin until he drowned.

He slipped into the toilet unnoticed and closed the door. Bart raised his head, snorting and grunting. Pierre waited until the tinkling sound in the urinal had stopped then cautiously peered out. The men's room was empty. Pierre walked towards

300

the door, chiding himself for being so childish. Stalking the man! I'm like a kid playing games, he fumed.

Suddenly he froze. Bart was leaning against the wall, staring out across the verandah down to the jetty, where the officers were clambering into one of the dinghies belonging to the Marine Reserve. Water dripped from his hair on to the telephone receiver which was pressed tightly to his ear.

Bart stiffened as he listened to Job's recorded message. Damn, the one time I need them and they're out. 'I'm at the Yacht Club with our friends,' he said quickly, anxious to have the message recorded before the officers became impatient and sent someone to look for him. 'They're about to visit Le Vengeur. Coke and heroin are the attraction. Come and join us. It's now twenty-six minutes past five. Twenty-six.' Bart replaced the receiver quietly.

Pierre shot back into the toilet, fumbling with his zip. Bart glanced at the empty corridor behind him, shrugged and walked away.

No footsteps broke the silence and Pierre tucked his tee-shirt into his cotton shorts. He would have to hurry if he wanted to join Ashley and Redvers on the fishing trip. He glanced at his watch. It was not yet five o'clock – but Bart had emphasized that it was twenty-six minutes past the hour.

Pierre frowned and bit his lip. The army officers and Bart were involved in something strange. Perhaps they were not merely going to Le Vengeur on the off-chance that they could scrounge a handful of drugs. Perhaps they were dealing in drugs and the yacht had brought in supplies.

Pierre smiled as he fumbled in his wallet for coins. He dropped them carefully into the slot on the pay phone and dialled. He lowered his voice as he spoke. The man he was contacting had been one of his father's closest friends and now held a high position in the new government. That should take the smile off your face, Bartholomew Faulconer, he thought as he walked down the corridor to the verandah. Let's see you grin when the police and special army unit raid the yacht, looking for drugs.

301

'Hey,' he called to his two friends as they concentrated on carrying glasses and bottles to a table overlooking the jetty. 'Let's have something to eat. I'm hungry.'

'You've just had lunch, and anyway the deal was beers, not sandwiches.'

Pierre laughed. 'I'll pay for the food.'

'Good, then we'll order.'

Pierre picked up the pieces of chicken which had spilled from his toasted sandwich and chewed them thoughtfully. The harbour was quiet and tranquil. The sun polished the sea to a high gloss and the boats seemed to preen over their mirrored reflections.

The Marine Reserve dinghy purloined by Bart and the officers floated off the stern of *Le Vengeur*. The yacht itself seemed to be deserted.

Pierre watched with interest as a thick-set man with ginger hair appeared and refused to allow the group on board. Finally he permitted Bart to board his boat and, after a lengthy conversation, the officers were also invited on deck. Bart stood, staring at the Yacht Club for a long while, before following his friends below. It seemed to Pierre as if these cold eyes were staring straight at him.

'Well,' said Pierre, rubbing his hands on a paper napkin and squeezing it into a tight ball. 'That was good. I must go. I have a fishing—'

He broke off as he saw with satisfaction a group of uniformed soldiers and Seychellois policemen stride on to the wooden gangway that led to the jetty; their boots clumped dully on the boards. They ignored the stares and murmurs of surprise from the patrons of the Club as they marched past.

Sunlight filled the hatchway, flaming the captain's hair. He sat on the steps, sipping his coffee and studying the officers seated at the table with Bart. He was disturbed by the break in security and hoped that his yellow-haired contact would soon leave the yacht. He did not like extending hospitality to men he might have to kill.

The fat officer had wedged himself up close to the cook. Bart was impressed with the effortless way she kept the man at bay, fending off his clumsy advances with the indifference and experience of a brothel-keeper. She had placed steaming mugs of coffee in front of the men, explaining that it was a 'dry' ship.

'Dry ships sink,' exploded the officer. 'A man needs a drink. All ships are wet. All men drink.'

'Not this ship, mate, and not these men,' said the captain, dropping sugar lumps into his mug.

The officer rolled his eyes at Bart. If *Le Vengeur* had no drink on board, they were unlikely to have any coke or heroin. He inclined his head towards the hatch, a mute appeal to leave the boat.

Bart ignored him; his eyes were fixed on the girl. He sipped his scalding coffee and stared at her through the steam. Her blonde hair was plaited and he longed to dig his fingers into the thick coils; he wanted to see it cover her shoulders in yellow silk as Laura's did. He needed to pretend that she was Laura. The steam softened the girl's alert eyes and they changed to the dreaminess of Laura's. He gulped. The coffee scalded his lips and tongue and he whistled in shock.

The young woman looked across at him. His ears knew that she was offering him a glass of water, but his heart heard the soft words of a girl in love. Laura's words: 'I love you.'

Bart shook his head. He could not love Laura. Love was a crutch for fools. There was no room for love in a soldier's life. But as he studied the girl and accepted her offer of water he knew that he would find a way to contact Laura. He would apologize to her. For the first time in his life he was going to

303

plead for forgiveness. He was still too afraid and too arrogant to admit to himself that he loved Laura, but he knew that he needed her.

The light pouring into the main cabin suddenly faded. The captain swung around and stared up at the hatch. A pair of highly polished black shoes hung over the edge and the blue uniforms of the Seychelles police force blotted out the sky. The captain glanced at Bart. 'More of your friends, I presume?' he said coldly. He handed his coffee mug to the cook and scrambled up the ladder.

A babble of voices speaking in French broke out round the table. Then they were silent, listening to the murmured sounds on deck. Bart strained to hear, but the voices were low and unintelligible. Fend them off, he pleaded. Don't let them stay on board. He listened to the clump of heavy boots overhead. He counted silently and paled; it was a strong force, not just a few curious policemen. The murmur of voices deepened into an angry hum. He heard the captain shout.

'*Il a des ennuis*,' grunted the fat officer to his friends. 'I don't need trouble on my day off,' he said to Bart. 'Let's get out of here.'

Before he could ease himself across the wooden seat, the captain came down the ladder backwards, closely followed by the police and army team.

'What's wrong?' Bart asked, not recognizing any of the men.

'Some do-gooder overheard your friends say that they were coming aboard *Le Vengeur* for drugs. Drugs!' he snorted. 'I've never touched the filth.' He knocked over his coffee as he backed into the table in order to allow the last of the police officers into the cabin. The dark liquid trickled over the edge of the table and soaked into the blue carpet. The young cook shuddered. The spreading stain looked like a bleeding heart.

'No one is to leave the yacht until our search is over,' the police officer announced, ushering his men through to the galley and cabins. He ignored the threats and abuse heaped on him by Bart's friends.

'Damn police,' murmured the fat officer. 'Can't even do one

a favour. Refuse to bend the rules. It's all that training in England. They come back here thinking they're better than us.'

The policeman glared at him and placed one soldier at the foot of the hatchway and another at the door leading to the engine-room.

The captain watched the men fan out over his yacht, then he stared at Bart and answered his unspoken question. 'They have some sort of paper giving them the authority to search the boat.'

Bart blanched but kept his face expressionless. He had hoped that they could have the search put off until the next day; that would allow them to offload the guns during the night.

'This crowd,' the captain continued, gesticulating to the two soldiers guarding the doors,' are some sort of SWAT team seconded to the police when carrying out drug raids.' He moved closer to Bart. The soldiers immediately rested their fingers on the triggers of their assault rifles. The captain's eyes were long and flat as he looked at Bart. 'No celebration on the twenty-sixth, and all because you and your friends need to blow your minds on pot. I hope you fry in hell,' he whispered.

Bart did not try to defend himself. He listened to the thumps and bangs as the team tore the boat apart.

The kettle whistled on the stove and the girl squeezed herself out from between the curved seat and the table. The soldier gesticulated sharply with his rifle, and she sat down again on the edge of the bench. The shrill screech boiled in Bart's head and he gritted his teeth. 'Let her switch the damn thing off,' shouted the fat officer, annoyed at being treated like a common criminal. 'It's driving us mad.'

The soldier responded to the voice of authority and allowed the cook into the galley. The captain wiped his hands on the seat of his trousers. This was not going to be a cursory search; they were taking too long.

The girl came back and leaned against the table near Bart and the captain. She slid her fingers nonchalantly under the tabletop but withdrew her hand at an imperceptible shake of the captain's head.

A torrent of Creole rang out from one of the cabins, and Bart's friends stiffened as if smashed in the ribs with rifle butts. The soldier guarding the door leading to the cabins ran and stood in front of the captain, his rifle at the ready.

'So,' said the senior police officer, swinging through the door. 'So, you are smuggling drugs?' He laughed mirthlessly. 'Your drugs are the arms of revolution.' He tore the greased paper from an AK-47 assault rifle and threw it on the table. 'You think you were very clever to have double false bottoms in the bunks?' He dropped a RPD light machine gun on top of the rifle. 'You forget that we build boats in the islands. My men know boats. Look at this,' he said, holding out his hands to the soldier who had followed him into the main cabin. 'The RPG-7 rocket launcher.' Belts of ammunition and boxes of cartridges tumbled from the soldier's arms and lay in a heap on the floor. 'Revolution. Is that what you are bringing to our islands?' spat the policeman.

The fat officer looked at Bart's face and the beers churned uneasily in his belly. 'You knew,' he whispered. 'You knew.' He realized that, as Bart's friends, they would all be painted with the same brush of betrayal.

The soldier disappeared into the cabin and came back with a handful of egg-shaped grenades and a box of fuses.

'You wish to bring death to our islands?' queried the policeman, studying the Cyrillic letters stencilled on the wooden box. 'And you have traitors in our army to help you.'

Bart opened his mouth to speak, to explain that his friends were innocent, but the police officer swung out his arm imperiously. 'Take him,' he said, pointing to the captain.

'No,' screamed the young cook.

Bart froze. The voice he heard was Laura's as she ran from him in the Vallée de Mai. The blue eyes were hers, filled with realization and terror.

'No, leave him,' the girl screamed again.

She scrabbled under the table top and brought out a heavy Heckler & Koch 9mm parabellum. She had squeezed in the handgrip, releasing the safety mechanism, and her finger was on the trigger. Seconds stretched into eternity as Bart saw the soldier at the foot of the steps lift his rifle.

'Stop,' he shouted, throwing himself in front of the girl and chopping the pistol out of her hand. 'Don't shoot.'

The crack of the AK-47 reverberated in the cabin, cutting off his words.

Bart slammed into the girl as if clubbed by a giant iron mace. The bullet tore through his shoulder, shredding the veins and arteries. It ripped the top off his lungs and the hydrostatic shock jellied the surrounding tissue. It sped on through the young girl's throat, severing her carotid artery, and lodged in the stomach of the soldier who was still guarding the door to the engine-room.

'You swine,' whispered the captain as he pushed past the policeman and dragged the girl's limp body away from under Bart. Her eyes stared up at him blindly. Clear pink blood gushed up high from her throat then cascaded on to the carpet, absorbing the dark coffee stain.

The soldier's screams filled the cabin as he doubled over. His fingers were stained bright red when he dug his hands into his stomach.

Bart lay on the carpet, his head resting in the girl's blood. The strong acrid smell was familiar: it was the smell of war, a smell he loved.

His erstwhile friends looked on helplessly; two armed soldiers kept them pinned in their seats. The policeman barked out an order and his men ran to obey.

Bart felt detached and light-headed as two soldiers bent down to lift him. Pink bubbles, delicate as dewdrops, beaded his lips when he tried to smile at his friends. The fat officer stared at the rosy froth bubbling from Bart's mouth and wiped his hand across his eyes. '*Poumon*,' he said gently. 'He has been hit in the lung.'

Bart's friend shook his head. The officer had pronounced a death sentence. Bartholomew Faulconer, his friend and deceiver, would die.

Bart closed his eyes against the piercing blue of the sky as they hurried with him across the deck to the tender. He heard the raucous cries of gulls wheeling above the tender, but he was too tired to look at them. Red and gold circles danced across his eyes as the sun burned down on his closed lids. He tried to lift his arm to shield his face but it lay at his side, heavy as an iron ingot.

He heard excited shouts and cries when the tender bumped against the jetty and he smelt the surge of people. He wondered why they were celebrating, then he remembered: Top was arranging a counter-coup. It must have been successful.

He forced his eyes open. He was a hero. He wanted to see the joy on their faces. He frowned as a dark-haired young man pushed forward and bent over him. The face was familiar and he focused on the man's crooked front teeth. 'Remember Nicole,' the man whispered, putting his mouth to Bart's ear. 'Remember Nicole Daumier.' Pierre drew back as the soldiers pushed past. A thin red moustache was traced on his upper lip, stamped there by Bart's blood-soaked hair.

Long sprays of white and cerise bougainvillaea hung from the side of the Yacht Club and the soldier grunted as the thorns clawed at his arm.

Pierre followed the winding red path laid by Bart's blood and watched the soldiers ease Bart into the back of the police car.

Red and green pennants, colours of the People's Party, fluttered against the azure sky. Bart's eyelids drooped and the blood from his nose ran into the pink foam in his mouth. As his head dropped loosely to the side, he stared at the blue sky. He clutched tightly to the colour. It was the blue of Laura's eyes. They were luminous with love and warmed him. He smiled.

The soldier sitting in the back spat out of the window. 'He is dead,' he said. 'And the traitor smiles.'

Pierre pulled away from the window. He hated the man who had killed Nicole; but he had not meant to be cause of his death. As he watched Bart die he felt a sense of deep pity and sadness for the man.

He stood on the gravel square, watching the police car until it was out of sight. He waved to his friends and walked slowly out of the Club grounds to the Moke.

════════◗|◈|◈|◈| IV |◈|◈|◈|◖════════

Cook sailed across the lawn at La Retraite carrying a tray of tea and fresh lime juice. Ashley stood up to help her, but she waved him away. She dusted leaves and twiglets off the table, set in the shade of the old bois de rose, and thumped down the tray. She flicked her tea towel at a yellow wasp hovering over the picnic basket.

'Careful – those things have a dreadful sting,' Dr Redvers cautioned as the angry wasp buzzed past his face.

Ashley ducked as it circled his head. 'Let it have a taste of the cake, Cook,' he pleaded, 'then perhaps it'll leave *us* alone.'

Cook tucked the tea towel firmly round the basket. 'I won't have wasps or flies on my food.' Ashley lifted his eyebrows at Redvers, who shrugged in sympathy. 'And where is Pierre?' she grumbled. 'It'll soon be too late to go out fishing, and my good food will be wasted.'

She placed a glass of juice in front of Laura, who sat staring at the sea, taking no part in the conversation.

'Drink it up,' said Cook, standing in front of Laura with her hands on her hips. 'It'll bring back the roses to your cheeks.' Laura obeyed, dutiful as a child. 'Ah, here he comes.' She poured an extra cup of tea and placed it at the end of the table for Pierre.

'Sorry,' he shouted as he bounded down the steps. 'I was held up at the Club.'

'Beers or blondes?' Redvers teased, sipping his tea.

'A blond,' Pierre answered, pulling back a chair. 'A male blond.' He bumped the table as he sat down.

'What!' exclaimed Ashley.

Pierre carefully emptied the tea in his saucer on to the lawn before replying. 'There was trouble down at the Yacht Club. The police raided *Le Vengeur*.'

309

Ashley looked puzzled. 'That's the new sixty-footer that arrived a few days ago.'

Redvers nodded. 'I saw her yesterday. She has lovely lines. But why would they raid her?'

'They were looking for drugs and apparently uncovered boxes of ammunition, rifles and grenades.'

'How do you know?' Ashley asked, his raised cup still held half-way to his mouth.

'Three people were shot on the yacht. The soldiers taking the wounded one to hospital told us.'

'Was he badly wounded? Who is he?' asked Redvers.

'Who *was* he,' Pierre corrected him. 'He died as they left the club.' He studied Laura and Ashley before he went on. He did not wish to cause Ashley more pain by talking about Nicole's murderer. Since his return from Aldabra, the day after Laura's suicide attempt, Ashley had hardly left Laura's side; he seemed a broken old man. 'He was Bartholomew Faulconer.'

Ashley replaced his cup in the saucer very gently. 'Doctor Faulconer's son,' he said, his head bowed over his cup. 'The man who killed Nicole.'

Redvers straightened in his chair and fumbled for his pipe as the connection between Bartholomew Faulconer and Nicole Daumier became clear to him. He had noticed the name 'Ms Daumier' when he glanced through Bart's file at Les Cannelles, but he had not connected her with the Challoners. They had not mentioned Nicole's surname when they brought Laura to him at St Francis.

'The Fates punish those who escape man's justice,' quoted Ashley and he put his hand over Laura's.

He was rewarded with a vice-like pressure from her fingers. He looked at her in surprise. She was listening to the conversation avidly.

'So that is the end of Bart Harden,' said Redvers, sucking hard on his empty pipe.

Ashley winced as Laura's nails dug into his hand. Her lip trembled as she stared at Redvers. 'Bart Harden,' she whispered. 'Is he really dead?'

Pierre nodded.

Cook was stunned by the transformation in Laura. Her voice was firm and the vacant stare had vanished. Cook wrung the tea towel in her hands. It's true, she thought. What they say at Les Cannelles is true: she loved this man Bart. What I refused to believe is true. The towel twisted into tight coils as she turned it the way she would have liked to twist Bart's neck.

'Harden?' queried Ashley.

'Harden . . . Faulconer . . . all the same man,' said Redvers, turning to Ashley. 'The court sentenced Faulconer to do community work at the hospital. He persuaded the resident doctor to let him use his second name because of the stigma attached to the case.'

Laura ignored his explanation. She was free. Now she would not have to forfeit Ashley's love and pride. He need never know that she had loved Bart Harden.

She pushed back her chair, and the three men stared at her in surprise as she put her arm round Cook's waist.

'It's too late to go fishing, Daddy,' she said, 'but would you mind if Pierre and I took the boat out for a while?'

Ashley nodded, astonished at the transformation in his daughter.

'We promise to eat the picnic food,' she said, releasing the delighted woman from her embrace and picking up the basket.

Pierre cracked his shin on the table in his haste to join Laura.

'Clumsy,' she said with a soft smile. 'Let's go.'

'Don't be too late,' called Ashley. 'Remember, Emma will be phoning.'

Laura paused and thrust the picnic basket into Pierre's hands. 'I'll meet you down at the boat. I'll only be a few minutes,' she said as she spun round and raced into the house. 'Have to talk to Aunt Emma now.' Her voice floated across to them as the front door banged shut behind her.

Ashley watched Pierre walk down to the jetty and he shook his head. 'Explanation, Doctor, please.'

Redvers sighed. 'It's all so obvious now. Laura met Bart at Les Cannelles. He was very attractive to women – and persuasive. I can understand how Laura was fascinated by him. And

311

she would have known him only as Harden when she fell in love with him.'

'Love!' said Ashley. 'Love! Why didn't you warn her that he was Faulconer?'

Redvers smiled his thanks while Cook poured him another cup of tea. She flicked at the wasp sitting on Laura's glass of lime then turned away from the table. She didn't need to hear the doctor's explanation. She knew what that man Harden had done to Laura and she was happy that he was dead.

'I wasn't on duty at the weekends. That's when she met him. She asked to help out over the weekends.'

Ashley ran his fingers through his hair. 'Of course,' he said.

The men sat in silence for a while, mulling over the implications of Laura's liaison with Bart Harden.

Ashley started as Redvers cracked his pipe on the edge of the table. 'I've got it,' he said. 'The weekend she spent on Praslin.' Ashley waited for him to continue. 'It was the same weekend that Harden stayed away from Les Cannelles due to some mythical illness. He met Laura on Praslin. Probably prearranged.'

'Laura would never lie,' Ashley protested. 'She was spending the weekend with a friend.'

'When young hormones spin, lying becomes easy,' said Redvers. 'And intense sexual attraction is often confused with love.'

A fody hopped on to the table, looking for crumbs. Ashley studied it as he came to terms with his daughter's womanhood.

'Yes,' mused Redvers. 'She believed that she loved him and then discovered that he was Faulconer.'

'The shock would have been sufficient for her to try suicide,' said Ashley.

'Probably not.' Ashley was about to protest when Redvers continued. 'I think he was her lover. I think Laura had committed herself to him completely.'

Ashley did not want to hear what Redvers was saying. Laura was his lovely daughter. She would never have an affair. Especially a clandestine affair.

'Love is very important to Laura,' Redvers continued. 'Once

312

she had given herself to Bart, she would have been unable to accept his betrayal. That's where the razor blade came in.'

Ashley was silent. He respected Redvers but found it difficult to accept his explanation of Laura's behaviour. 'She has always confided in me,' he said quietly, crumbling up a biscuit for the fody.

'As a young girl,' agreed Redvers. 'But now she is a woman. There will be secret dreams and thoughts which she will never share.'

'Do you mean she won't ever tell me of this affair? This love which almost killed her?' asked Ashley.

Redvers answered compassionately. He knew how difficult it was for fathers to accept their daughters' sexuality. 'Laura will probably tell you about it someday, but don't try to force her confidence.'

Ashley sprinkled crumbs into his palm and held his hand out to the fody. He didn't answer Redvers.

'Try to understand. Laura hasn't deliberately deceived you. She is just behaving like a woman.'

'Thank you,' said Ashley gravely. He leaned heavily on the table as he stood up. The fody chirped and flew away in a flutter of crimson feathers. 'The sun is dropping over Silhouette. It's time for a whisky.'

Redvers glanced at the humpbacked mountain, now blending into the grey twilight, and nodded. 'Sounds good.'

'Let's have the drinks down at the jetty. I'll fetch them,' said Ashley, walking quickly towards the house. 'I'll see if Laura has spoken to Emma. I'll send her down to the boat. Those two can talk for hours.'

Redvers smiled. He knew that Ashley was impatient to have Laura back at his side. He needed to be reassured that her depression was truly over.

CHAPTER NINE

Epilogue

 I |⊛|⊛|⊛|◅━━━━

The old brindled cat's eyes were slit in ecstasy and its claws dug into the thick folds of Emma's cloak. She tickled the cat behind its ear and listened as it purred out a song of love and devotion.

'You shameless slut,' she said, 'I saw you flicking your tail around the woods. Don't you know that you're too old to attract toms?'

The cat rubbed its head against her arm and thin strings of saliva hung from its mouth.

'At least you've had kittens,' she said, moving her fingers under its chin. The cat's eyes closed and its neck stretched out in ecstasy.

'You're a lucky hussy. I've always had to share someone else's baby. I've only had Laura.'

At the thought of Laura, she stopped tickling the cat and leaned across the table. Her fingers closed round the crystal ball and she flicked off the dark velvet cloth.

The cat straightened and its whiskers brushed the cup of mugwort tea which Emma brought to her lips. Emma lowered the cup to the level of the cat's face and smiled as it shied away from the strong aromatic smell. 'You can see the spirits without the help of herbs,' she said. The cat paid no further attention to her but concentrated on cleaning the steam from its whiskers.

Emma ran her hand lightly over the crystal ball, sensing the other hands which had caressed the cold orb over the centuries.

She leaned over the crystal. The ball clouded and swirled as if with rising marsh mists. The cat paused in her grooming and her citrine eyes widened.

A head of short yellow hair waved across the crystal. Emma stiffened and then gasped as blood matted the man's hair to the bitter red of a Seville orange. Her eyes watered as she strained to see his face. It had to be the blond man.

Suddenly a pair of dark-brown eyes peered at her through the bloodied hair. They stared at her mercilessly. They knew her secret. 'Brown eyes?' she whispered. 'The blond man has yellow eyes!' As she spoke, a smiling mouth with crooked teeth matched the dark eyes. 'Pierre,' she breathed. 'Pierre has killed the blond!'

The figures swirled and melted like hot wax. She held her breath, willing the crystal to reveal more. Laura's face filled the ball. Not the silent girl she had left at La Retraite, nor the vibrant laughing Laura she knew. This was a woman, beautiful and composed. A new Laura . . . a stranger. She held up her face to be kissed. Her eyes were closed. Her lips were soft and willing. The lips of a woman meeting her lover.

'No!' Emma screamed as a mouth covered Laura's. 'No!' she shrieked as Laura's fingers ran through Pierre's cropped hair and held him close.

Emma dug her long fingernails into the cat's stomach; it hissed and lashed out at her. Red gashes opened from her wrist to her elbow. The blood trickled on to her black cloak unheeded. She felt nauseous with shock. Her fingers were patched with white as she tightened her hold on the ball.

'No,' she whispered. 'Not a wedding. I won't have it.'

The crystal ball swirled with the colourful skirts of sega dancers. Laura twirled with them, holding her long white veil over her arm. Pierre faced her and, as he lifted his arms, Emma saw the gold of a wedding band on his finger. 'You lie,' she shouted, shaking the ball.

The wedding celebration faded and the islands of the Seychelles appeared. They lay on a satin bed of the deepest turquoise, displayed like brooches and pendants crafted in emeralds and encircled with pearls.

'They will marry and live in the Seychelles. I will never be able to initiate Laura into the wonder of Wicca. She will never know the deep joy of being a witch.'

Emma bowed her head over the crystal as it cleared and she did not hear the secret door to her witch's room being flung open. The cat fled past Giles; its ears were pasted flat and its tail beat angrily against his legs as it ran into the study.

'Telephone for you, Emma,' he said. 'The daily has been searching the house for you. Luckily I came home to collect these notes for the meeting this evening or Ashley's phone bill would be astronomical.'

Emma struggled to compose herself before facing Giles. He expected her to observe her duties during the day. He disliked her scrying or using her secret room when strangers were in the house.

'I've put the call through to your study. It's Laura.'

'Tanith?' said Emma, smoothing down her frizzed hair.

'Yes. She sounds wonderful.'

Emma bent low as she stepped through the door and Giles patted her rounded bottom lovingly. She smiled at him tremulously and ran to the phone. She looked small and fragile, enveloped in the flowing cloak. 'I'm a lucky man to have her,' he decided as he watched her expression brighten when she heard Laura's voice.

It had been a battle to persuade Emma to leave Laura in the Seychelles and return to Lyewood. She now considered herself to be Laura's mother and she wanted to nurse and protect her. Ashley had to promise to phone every day with an account of Laura's health befeore Emma would consent to leave the islands.

'Laura, my love, please don't apologize,' said Emma, holding the receiver tightly. 'We love you so much. Giles and I were only worried about you. No one was upset or angry.'

Emma beckoned to Giles and he walked across to her desk. She held his hand to her cheek and kissed it as she listened to Laura. 'She's well,' she whispered. Emma was tense with excitement and her face was radiant as she looked up at Giles. 'Tanith's well. It's all over.'

'I told you that our little wrestler would defeat this one,' he answered. He moved behind her and, wrapping his arms round her slim waist, he pressed her to his body.

She rubbed her head against his chest, nodding as she listened to Laura. 'That's wonderful news,' she said, her voice high with exhilaration. 'The very best.' She put her hand over the receiver and spoke to Giles. 'She will be here by the end of the month to start her course at art school,' she announced. Then she returned to the telephone. 'I do understand that Ashley can stay for only a few weeks. Of course you won't be any trouble. We've always wanted a daughter in the house. I'm so happy, Laura.'

Giles felt Emma tense. She pulled away from his embrace.

'A son? How would I also like a son in the house?' Emma listened in silence. She picked up a pencil and scratched viciously on the note pad lying on her desk. She kept her eyes on the paper, not trusting herself to look at Giles. 'Tanith, your friends are always welcome at Lyewood, you know that.' Her tongue worried at the gap in her teeth. 'Yes, Laura, Ashley did tell Giles that Pierre was coming to London for two years to do an advanced business course.' She ran her fingers through her crimped grey hair and it stood out like a paper fan. 'Of course he can spend the weekends at Lyewood. Though I'm sure the temptations of London will attract him more.'

She tugged at the crinkled ends of her hair while she listened to Laura. Giles pressed his face close to hers with his ear above the receiver, but Laura's voice was only a mumble. He straightened up and studied Emma anxiously. There was a false brightness in her voice and she had twisted the sleeve of her cloak into a tight ball.

'Yes. I do remember telling you that one day, when the time was right, you would find a man to love. A man like Ashley.'

Emma paled and the pencil snapped in her fingers.

'Pierre?' she croaked, then she coughed. 'Pierre Payet?' She picked up the broken pencil and jabbed it back into the paper. 'Tanith, you are still very young and you'll meet . . .'

She gnawed at her lip as Laura interrupted her.

'Yes, I do remember when we all searched for the first

primrose of spring. Yes, I do still believe that a wish made on the first primrose will come true. But what has that got to do with Pierre? We haven't done that since Virginia . . .' Emma broke off. 'Of course I will keep a secret. I swear.'

Giles saw Emma's expression and he grabbed the phone. 'Wrestler. It's Giles. Emma has just run to free the cat. She's locked out and is yowling dreadfully. She'll be back in a minute. What's this I hear about you coming to live with us?'

Giles listened for a moment, holding Emma to his side.

'Wonderful news. I'll make a horsewoman of you yet. And Pierre? We'll make a rider of him as well. A big kiss, I must go. Here's Emma.' He handed the phone back to Emma with a warning glance.

She looked up at Giles and the desolation in her gaze tore at him, but he kept his expression stern.

'Your primrose wish is to marry Pierre,' Emma echoed hollowly. 'And you're going to make that wish on a star tonight as there are no primroses in the Seychelles.' Giles loomed over her and she kept her voice calm and even. 'We will welcome whoever you love, Tanith. Giles and I want you to be happy.'

'And Pierre is a fine young man,' said Giles, putting his mouth to the receiver. He heard Laura's clear laughter ring out as he pulled away to let Emma talk.

'He comes from a line of murderers and thieves,' she hissed, holding her hand over the mouthpiece. 'He is not going to have my Tanith.'

Giles shook his head. Emma's obsession with Laura had increased with age. He knew that he should stay and talk to her; he should make her accept Pierre. He worried when she became irrational about Laura. But he was late and she showed no sign of ending her conversation with Laura. He bent down and buried his mouth in her hair. 'I must go now. I'll be home late, don't wait up for me.'

Emma nodded. He turned to look at her when he reached the door. She smiled at him, a tight unhappy smile.

He pursed his lips into a kiss. 'Love you, my little witch,' he mouthed and closed the door quietly behind him.

Emma finally replaced the receiver. 'I will not let this

318

happen,' she muttered. Her shoulders shook and she sat doubled over in the chair, as if nursing stomach cramps. 'You're too old,' she told herself. 'You no longer have the strength to command and compel the dark ones.'

The oak chair creaked as she rocked in an agony of indecision.

'You're afraid, and fear attracts death when dealing with the black forces,' she whispered.

Her thoughts were disturbed only by the brindled cat's adenoidal snores as it lay, curled up on the window seat. Emma's elongated eyes were flat as she looked at the old feline.

A small voice nagged at her. Listen to Giles. Laura is a woman. She will fall in love and marry. She cannot remain a child. Accept it.

Emma closed her eyes. She saw Pierre bend over Laura. Saw him slide down the zip on Laura's wedding dress.

'Never,' she said. 'You'll never have my Tanith.'

Her cloak swirled round her ankles as she ran to the door of her study. She glanced up and down the corridor. She slammed the heavy door shut and pocketed the key.

Easy, warned the little voice. You cannot rush into an evocation. Success depends on preparation and strength. You're upset and weak. The black ones will know it.

Emma buried the small voice of reason in her madness and jealousy.

She stood on tiptoe and slid the vase of peacock feathers off the mantelpiece. The vibrant blue-and-green peacock eyes brushed her face as she delved into the jar to find the key to the hidden drawer in her desk.

The drawer slid open easily and Emma took out her Italian copy of *Grimorium Verum*. Her hands trembled as she stroked the cover. She quickly flipped through the pages in the first part of the grimoire.

'Drowning,' she decided. 'Pierre is always diving or fishing. Death at sea is what I need.'

She skimmed through the pages. The air hissed sharply between her teeth as she caught her breath.

'Glasyalabolas, the winged dog? Seere? Vepar, the mermaid

who creates death at sea and disaster? Maybe the demon Focalor is the one I'll evoke.'

She continued to turn the pages, and she frowned. 'A kid. I don't have time to fetch a kid or a lamb.'

The brindled cat grunted in its sleep. Emma's eyes gleamed, green and cold. She slid the book back into the drawer and walked to the window seat. The cat grumbled and stiffened as she scooped it up into her arms. She automatically fondled the scarred ears. The cat relaxed and purred softly as it recognized her. A pink tongue rasped the back of her hand when she carried it into her witch's room and rheumy eyes looked up at her face in adoration.

The hours passed quickly as Emma prepared herself to face and instruct the demons. Her hands trembled and shivers kicked through her body like the spasms of a dying animal.

The daily help knocked on the study door. She put her ear to the keyhole, but all was hushed. She walked back to the kitchen, shrugged into her navy-blue coat and tied a scarf over her head. The kitchen door banged behind her when she left and the home lay, as silent as fear, in the late-afternoon sun.

━━◆◈◆◈◆◈◆| II |◈◆◈◆◈◆━━

Giles kicked off his muddy shoes at the door and padded into the dark kitchen in his socks. His stomach rumbled as he ran his hand along the wall, looking for the light switch. He sniffed but could detect only lingering traces of polish and soap.

'Emma,' he yelled as he pressed down the switch and yellow light flooded the kitchen. He frowned and moved across to the stove. He bent down and pulled out the warming drawer; it was empty, and there were no pots on the stove.

The passageway was grey and the tiles were cold beneath his feet as he walked to the front of the house. He paused at the arched door to Emma's study. 'Emma,' he called again. He turned the iron ring, but the door remained closed. 'She'll be in bed,' he decided. 'She probably went to lie down after her talk to Laura, and fell asleep. Poor Emma. Her life centres round Tanith.'

He fumbled in his pocket and brought out a bunch of keys. Sorting through them, he selected a long black key. It slid easily into the keyhole and he pushed the door open. He felt his way across to her desk and turned on the desk lamp. The study was neat and tidy.

He was about to leave when he noticed the wooden acorn hanging loosely from the frieze above the fireplace. He grinned. He would be able to tease Emma about her age and increasing forgetfulness. He fitted the acorn into place and turned it, locking the secret door. He paused: something was wrong. His skin tickled and itched as if sensitive to wool. He twisted the acorn again and the door swung open.

Doubling up his large frame, he stepped into the room. The stench of congealing blood and the icy sense of evil hit him with the brutal force of a heavyweight's punch. He recoiled and shook his head, refusing to believe the horror of the room. The air pulsed with malevolence and he shivered. He held on to the frame of the secret panel. He did not want to walk into the room. Then he saw Emma.

He drew himself up to his full height and strode across to the triangle drawn outside the magic circle. Emma lay on her back. Her eyes were wide and staring. All the horrors of the damned were imprinted on her green pupils.

Giles knelt down quickly and pressed his fingers deep into the delicate skin under her jaw. No soft flutter answered the pressure. He pressed down harder, frantic to feel her life beat. He pressed his face to her nose willing himself to feel her warm breath on his cheek. For long seconds he waited. Slowly his hands fell away.

He gathered her naked body into his arms and carried her into the protection of the magic circle. There he knelt over her and his broad thumbs gently closed the delicately veined lids over her eyes. He could no longer bear the terror in her gaze. He wanted to comfort and love her. He bowed his head and his mane of silver hair swept over Emma's face. 'My little witch,' he sobbed, 'what have you done? Where have you gone?'

He kissed her lightly on the eyes and mouth, but her skin was cold to his lips. He held his face to hers as if to warm her, and his tears cooled on her dead flesh. He ran his lips over the deep scratches on her arm, and he rested his mouth on the palm of her hand. 'Oh, my Emma. Emma,' he cried. 'How could you leave me?'

He cradled his wife in his arms, caressing and talking to her until the farmyard rooster crowed sleepily. Wearily Giles dressed Emma and carried her into her study. 'I could not protect you in life but I will protect you in death,' he whispered. He settled her in the chair with her head resting on the leather top of her desk.

'A heart attack,' he whispered. 'That's what doctors say when the cause of death is uncertain.'

He returned to the witch's room and spread her cloak on the floor. Quickly he tumbled the accoutrements of black magic on to the wool. He picked up the bloodied knife and cursed the powers of evil as he threw it on the pile.

Tenderly he lifted the old brindled cat from the altar. Its head flopped against his thigh. Its pink tongue was impaled on its teeth and blood had dripped from its torn ears and stained its fur. 'Poor old girl,' he whispered as he put the cat on the cloak. 'Emma didn't mean it. She just—' he choked. 'She just couldn't help herself.'

Giles knotted the cloak into a bundle and hurried outside. He hid it under some empty fertilizer bags in the back of his Land Rover and locked the doors.

The men were going to burn hedgerow clippings in Briar Meadow this morning. He would do the burn himself as soon as he had phoned the doctor. Emma's secret would blow across the farm in smoke and ashes. His little witch would be safe.

He collected a pail of water and some cloths from the kitchen and disappeared into the secret room.

'Forgive her, great and merciful Mother Diana,' he breathed as he looked round the room, now clean and stripped bare.

'Great Pan, be kind to the one who loved you truly,' he added as he swung the pail of reddened water up from the floor. 'Her mad actions were those of a woman who cried for a child of her own. I should have seen the signs and shielded her.'

He closed the door and twisted the acorn out of the carved wood. Placing the pail of bloodied water in the passage, he wedged the acorn into the jamb of the iron-bound door. His muscles, hardened by farm work, bulged as he closed the door. The acorn shattered for ever, sealing the entrance to the secret room. He gathered up the fragments and dropped them into the pail. As the water closed over the pieces, he wiped his arm across his red-rimmed and haunted eyes.

His voice was ragged as he continued to intercede with his gods. 'It was not the woman wise in the ways of Wicca who turned away from you and traded with Hecate and her minions.

'Oh Queen of Heaven. Queen of Hell. Queen of all witches.' He closed his deepset eyes as if blotting out the horror. 'Forgive your child.'

He sat on the arm of the chair and stroked Emma's hair. It sprang up beneath his fingers as if charged with electricity.

He lifted the telephone. His broad hand shook as he listened to it ring.

Tears channelled down his carved face.

'Forgive her,' he whispered.

III

Ashley and Redvers sat in companionable silence on the sun-warmed planks of the jetty. The splatter of wavelets against the pylons soothed Ashley. He sipped his whisky slowly, savouring its smoky warmth.

The faint putter of an engine alerted him. As he searched the darkness, the sound faded. He looked at Redvers. The doctor had his head thrown back and was studying the sky, absorbed in the immensity and majesty of the heavens. Ashley shook himself. He was imagining things. There was no boat. It was too soon to expect Laura and Pierre back.

The boat had rounded the headland and Laura knew they would reach the jetty in a few minutes. She took a deep breath.

'Pierre, could we stop here?'

Pierre glanced at Laura sharply. Her face was indistinct but her voice was calm and firm. 'Sure,' he answered, spinning the wheel. 'But a little further offshore. We don't want to end up on the rocks. It'll be a long swim home.'

He cut the engine and the boat wallowed on the dark water. Laura was silent and he waited.

'Pierre, I want to apologize. I must apologize. I'm very ashamed of my behaviour and the worry I've caused you and the family.'

'Laura,' said Pierre, patting the seat behind the wheel. 'Come here.' Laura sat down on the hard white seat and waited for the lecture. 'You're a very special person, and we all love you. No one is perfect,' he said, tucking her hair behind her ears. 'Families are there to turn to when you're hurt or in trouble. You don't have to apologize.'

Laura caught and held his hand. 'Pierre, you don't understand. I did something terrible.'

'It would have been terrible if you'd succeeded,' Pierre agreed.

'No, not my cut wrists.' Laura gulped. She squared her shoulders and lifted her chin.

Pierre recognized the childhood gesture of hers: she was about to make a confession.

'Do you remember the night we watched the turtle?' Laura felt Pierre's fingers stiffen, but she held on to his hand tightly. 'I lied to you, Pierre. There was someone else: Bartholomew Faulconer.' The words dropped with the dreadful finality of a guillotine blade.

Pierre turned his head away and stared into the darkness.

Laura's voice broke. She was both the victim and the

executioner. 'I knew him as Bart Harden. He never used the name Faulconer. I loved him.' She talked to Pierre's back. She was determined to be honest with her closest friend and the man who loved her. 'I know that you must despise me. I deserve it.' The silence lengthened and Laura felt suffocated. She gasped for air as if a pillow was being held over her face. 'Please try to forgive me, Pierre. Not now, but one day,' she whispered. The only sound was the murmur of the waves as they slapped against the boat. 'You once said that I could never do anything bad enough to make you stop loving me. I have. And I'm so, so sorry.'

Pierre turned back to face her, and she cried out silently at the naked pain in his eyes. 'We've always shared secrets, Laura. Why did you hide this?'

She hesitated before she answered. She suddenly realized that she was facing a much greater loss than that of her pride and self-respect: she was going to lose Pierre.

'I was afraid that, if you knew, you would tell Daddy. I didn't think he would like Bart. After all, he was much older than I. I was afraid that Daddy would stop me going up to the hospital.' Her voice dropped to a whisper. 'After the moutia, I couldn't tell you because—'

'Because you knew I loved you.'

'Yes.'

'I still do, Laura. Love doesn't die with deceit, it just becomes unbearably painful.'

'Oh, Pierre,' she said, her voice broken and tiny. 'I've always loved you as my friend and my brother. I know now that I love—'

Pierre put his finger over her lips. 'Don't, Laura. I couldn't live with another mistake. Don't use me.' Laura shook her head vehemently, but Pierre kept his finger on her mouth. 'You've had a traumatic experience. Give the scars time to vanish. I'll always be here.' He took his finger away from her lips. 'Do you understand?'

'Yes,' she whispered and her heart sang with hope. 'Pierre, could this be our secret? Please?'

Pierre hesitated. 'I think Ashley should be told, Laura. It's not healthy to keep this sort of secret. He loves you and will understand.'

'Please.'

'*I* won't tell him but—'

'I will. I promise,' said Laura, 'but not yet.' She fumbled with the chain round her neck. Pierre held her hair to one side so that she could free the delicate gold links. The ankh swung, heavy as a pendulum, between them.

'Will you wear this, Pierre? It's the key of life.'

Pierre studied her solemn face and understood that this was her way of making a commitment.

He took the chain from her. 'Life? Our life?' he said softly.

'Please,' she answered. Her eyes were wet with unshed tears as she slipped the chain over his head.

He patted her hand lightly and turned the key in the ignition. Laura looked up at the stars as the boat sped back to La Retraite. They were scattered across the sky like the first primroses in the fields at Lyewood. Laura smiled nostalgically. As a child she remembered her excitement on finding the first yellow flower nestling in its circlet of green leaves. She had told Emma that she was going to make a primrose wish.

She looked at the first star she had seen and screwed up her eyes. 'Let Pierre trust me again. Let him never stop loving me,' she whispered.

She opened her eyes to find Pierre peering at her quizzically.

'I'm wishing on primroses,' she explained, 'because primrose wishes always come true.'

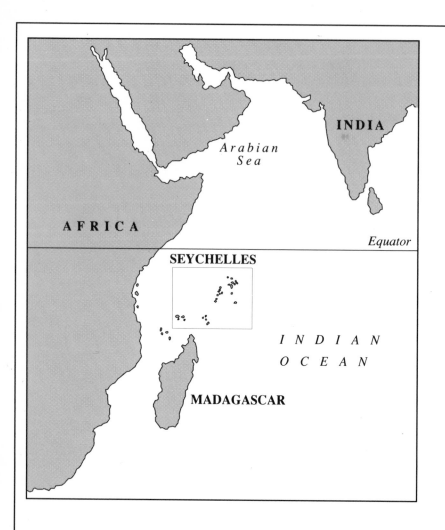

INDIA

*Arabian
Sea*

AFRICA

Equator

SEYCHELLES

*I N D I A N
O C E A N*

MADAGASCAR

S   E   Y   C   H

Aldabra

ALDABRA GROUP

Cosmoledo

FARQUHAR
GROUP